This signed edition

has been specially bound by the publisher.

Jill Shalvis ☺

To my favorite Target shoppers!

It seems like just last summer, I was writing to tell you all about *Rainy Day Friends*. And now this summer, I'm just as proud and excited to bring you *The Lemon Sisters*—also set in beautiful Wildstone, but with a whole new set of characters—inspired by the relationship between my daughters.

We start with two sisters who just might be lemons in life and love . . . Whether that's true or not, they know one thing: you can't run far enough to outpace your demons. And when long-dead secrets surface, they'll have to overcome their differences and learn that sometimes the one person who can help you the most is the one you never thought to ask.

And because this is a Jill Shalvis book, there's also plenty of romance. It's complicated, of course, as these things always are. ☺ And both heartbreaking and heartwarming. But sometimes the best thing in life is finding that one person who knows all your mistakes and weaknesses and still thinks you're completely amazing, right? So dig in! I promise lots of emotion and adventure and humor to go along with the romance. And, as life tends to do, it all comes down to letting it go or living it.

I hope you enjoy *The Lemon Sisters*.

XOXO and happy reading!
Jill

Praise for Jill Shalvis

"Sisterhood takes center stage in this utterly absorbing novel. Jill Shalvis balances her trademark sunny optimism and humor with unforgettable real-life drama. A book to savor—and share."

—Susan Wiggs, *New York Times* bestselling author, on *The Lemon Sisters*

"Jill Shalvis's books are funny, warm, charming, and unforgettable."

—RaeAnne Thayne, *New York Times* bestselling author

"With a fast pace and a lovely mix of romance and self-discovery, Shalvis's novel is chock-full of magnetic characters and seamless storytelling, rich with emotions, and impossible to put down."

—*Publishers Weekly* (starred review) on *Rainy Day Friends*

"The love story you need to read this summer isn't what you expect: it's about the love between sisters. Jill Shalvis has written something totally different for your beach read this year—and you're going to love it."

—*Bustle* on *Lost and Found Sisters*

"Shalvis has crafted a wonderful summer read that will fit right in with beach blankets, flip-flops, and maybe a little moonshine."

—*Library Journal* (starred review) on *Lost and Found Sisters*

The
LEMON
SISTERS

ALSO BY JILL SHALVIS

WOMEN'S FICTION NOVELS
Rainy Day Friends
The Good Luck Sister
Lost and Found Sisters

HEARTBREAKER BAY NOVELS
Playing for Keeps
Hot Winter Nights
About That Kiss
Chasing Christmas Eve
Accidentally on Purpose
The Trouble with Mistletoe
Sweet Little Lies

LUCKY HARBOR NOVELS
One in a Million
He's So Fine
It's in His Kiss
Once in a Lifetime
Always on My Mind
It Had to Be You
Forever and a Day
At Last
Lucky in Love
Head Over Heels
The Sweetest Thing
Simply Irresistible

ANIMAL MAGNETISM NOVELS
All I Want
Still the One
Then Came You
Rumor Has It
Rescue My Heart
Animal Attraction
Animal Magnetism

The
LEMON
SISTERS

A Novel

JILL
SHALVIS

wm

WILLIAM MORROW

An Imprint of HarperCollinsPublishers

P.S.™ is a trademark of HarperCollins Publishers.

THE LEMON SISTERS. Copyright © 2019 by Jill Shalvis. Excerpt from WRAPPED UP IN YOU © 2019 by Jill Shalvis. All rights reserved. Printed in the United States of America. No part of this book may be used or reproduced in any manner whatsoever without written permission except in the case of brief quotations embodied in critical articles and reviews. For information address HarperCollins Publishers, 195 Broadway, New York, NY 10007.

HarperCollins books may be purchased for educational, business, or sales promotional use. For information please email the Special Markets Department at SPsales@harpercollins.com.

FIRST EDITION

Designed by Diahann Sturge
Title page and chapter opener art © Janna Mudrak / Shutterstock, Inc.

Library of Congress Cataloging-in-Publication Data has been applied for.

ISBN 978-0-06-274192-9 (paperback)
ISBN 978-0-06-274191-2 (hardcover library edition)

19 20 21 22 23   LSC   10 9 8 7 6 5 4 3 2 1

I always wanted a sister. It never happened for me,
but it makes my heart full to have raised four girls,
knowing they'll always have one another. Over the years,
they've been like a pack of kittens sometimes—
can't stand to be together, can't stand to be apart.
But at the end of the day, they love each other fiercely,
and it makes me so proud. So to all the sisters,
of blood or heart, this one's for you.

CHAPTER 1

"I get that life sucks right now, but that's
never a reason to wear granny panties."

Without warning, the helicopter dipped sharply, and
Brooke Lemon's stomach went along with it. Her view
of a pretty sky shifted, and suddenly they were sideways and
she was staring out at a craggy mountain peak, seemingly close
enough to touch.

Compounding the terror, the previously benign sky had
given way to a sudden cloud pack, dark and turbulent, and
her heart pounded in tune to the *thump, thump, thump* of the
rotors. The chopper shuddered, straining to right itself. Her
palms went slick and nausea welled, making her regret that
extra sleeve of cookies she'd inhaled at lunch, which now
seemed a lifetime ago.

Struggling through vertigo, she swallowed hard at the sight

of the jagged cliffs, shooting up thousands of feet into the air, vanishing in the clouds.

There was nowhere to land.

"Brooke."

"*Shh.*" Afraid to so much as blink, she leaned forward, unable to tear her gaze away.

"You're green, Brooke. Close your eyes. Take a deep breath. In fact, you've been at this for ten straight hours. Take a nap."

"I can't nap! I have to stay awake for the crash!"

"There's no crash this time, I promise."

Pulling off her headphones, Brooke leaned back in her chair and gulped in a deep breath. The video paused, the lights came up, and a few words rolled across the screen.

Brooke Lemon, producer extraordinaire . . .

"Funny," she managed, fighting her way back from the flashback.

"And true." Cole stood and studied her for a long beat. "You okay?"

"You promised not to ask me that anymore."

"You miss being out there," he said. "Being the one shooting the footage instead of putting it all together."

"No." She still hadn't taken her eyes off the screen, and the word *producer* was mocking her. Sure, it was safer on this side of the camera, but hell yeah, she missed it. She missed the old days like she'd miss air.

Not that she was about to admit that to her boss. Not only would Cole pity her, he'd want to talk about it.

And she never talked about it. What was the point? The only way to fix this was to face her past. Her mistakes. And she couldn't do that. She didn't know how. Avoiding Cole's attentive eyes, she rose and grabbed her backpack just as Tommy poked his head into the editing room. "Hey, sweetness, how about some dinner?" His smile faded at whatever he saw on her face, and he exchanged a long look with Cole, who gave a slight head shake.

Tommy held out a hand to Brooke. "Come on, *chica*, I'll buy."

She knew when she was being managed. The three of them worked on a Travel Network show called *Around the World*, which followed adventure seekers, documentary-style, as they took on different goals such as climbing "unclimbable" mountains, rafting "unraftable" rivers . . . basically anything high-danger and high-adrenaline.

Once upon a time, Brooke had been the principal photographer, but these days she worked solely from the studio, editing the footage and writing up the scripts for the so-called reality show, living a very different life from the one she'd always imagined herself living. But it worked for her. It was all good.

Or so she told herself.

Cole was *Around the World*'s showrunner and director. He was also a friend and, when it suited them both, Brooke's occasional lover. It'd been a month since the last time it'd suited them. The show's funding had been cut, leaving them on a tight budget and an even tighter deadline, which meant they'd been at each other's throats much more than at each other's bodies. Lust tended to take a back seat to murderous urges, at least for Brooke. Men didn't seem to have a problem separating the two.

Tommy was the show's makeup artist and hairstylist, and Brooke's BFF. They'd never been lovers. Mostly because Tommy preferred relationships with more than one person at a time, and she wasn't wired that way.

Since both guys knew her way too well, she avoided eye contact by going through her backpack to make sure she had her keys and wallet. Which she already knew she did, because she was a teeny-tiny bit compulsive about such things. Still, she touched each briefly and then zipped her pack. And then, because she liked things in even numbers, she unzipped and rezipped it a second time.

Tommy turned to Cole accusingly. "Why is she upset? Did that new publicist cancel on her for that concert last night?"

"You actually went out with that guy?" Cole asked Brooke. "I told you I'd take you."

"I canceled the date." She shrugged. "He wears too much cologne."

"I don't," Cole said.

Tommy still had his eyes narrowed at Brooke. "And the guy before him. Didn't you say he had a crazy mother?"

"He did." But that hadn't been the only problem. Before the waiter had even brought them drink menus, he'd told her he wanted to get married that year. Preferably in the fall, as that was his mother's favorite season, and also, his mother wanted a big wedding with all the trimmings.

The thought of being the center of attention like that had nearly given her hives, and at the memory, she ran the pads of her thumbs over the tips of her fingers, back and forth, back and forth. It was an old habit, a self-soothing mechanism. "Why are we even talking about this?"

Tommy caught the movement of her hands before she could stop herself and he frowned. "Because you're upset about something."

She shoved her hands in her pockets. "I'm fine."

"She had a flashback," Cole said. "She always gets especially testy after one of those." He met Brooke's gaze, his own warm and full of concern. "Come home with me tonight. I'll make you feel better."

Though she knew he could do just that, she hadn't shaved in a few days. "I said I'm fine." She slung her backpack over her shoulder. To keep either of them from following her, she went up on her tiptoes and brushed a kiss first on Tommy's scruffy jaw and then on Cole's shaved one. "I'm *fine*," she repeated. "I'm also out. Saving you some overtime."

"You're on salary."

"Yeah, which reminds me, I'm due for a raise." She shut the door before he could respond and exited the studio into the LA heat.

It was seven p.m. in Los Angeles, and ninety-eight degrees in late May. The humidity was high enough to turn her ponytail into something resembling a squirrel's tail. Not that it mattered. She had no one to impress, nor the will to change that. Twenty-eight years old, and she was completely burned out on men.

And possibly on life.

She drove home, which was a rented bottom-floor condo in North Hollywood only eight miles from the studio—thirty minutes in gridlock traffic, like tonight. So she added LA to the list of things she was burned out on. She missed wide-open spaces. She missed fresh air and being outdoors. She missed thrill and adventure.

She parked in her one-car garage and headed through the interior door into her kitchen, mindlessly counting her steps, doing a little shuffle at the end to make sure she ended on an even number. Another self-soothing gesture. Some days required more of that than others.

Inside, she took a deep breath and tried to let go of the ball of stress in her gut. The flashback had been the first she'd had in a long time, and she'd nearly forgotten the taste of bone-deep terror, a sensation most people would never experience.

She looked around. Her place was clean, her plants were alive—well, semi-alive, anyway. Everything was great.

She was working on believing that when a knock came at her door. And actually, it was more of a pounding, loud and startling in the calm silence of her living room. Not Tommy—he would've knocked while yelling her name. Cole would've texted her before getting out of his car.

No stranger to danger, Brooke grabbed her trusty baseball bat on the way to the door. She hadn't traveled the planet over and back more times than she could count without learning how to protect herself. Just as she leaned in to look out the peephole, there came another round of pounding.

"Brooke!" called out a female voice. "Oh God, what if you're not home? Please be home!"

Brooke went still as stone. She knew that voice, though it'd been a while. A long while. It belonged to her older sister, Mindy. Mindy had her shit together. She wore a body armor of calm like other women wore earrings, didn't have to count in her head, and had never lost her way or screwed up her entire life.

The frantic knocking continued, now accompanied by something that sounded suspiciously like sobs.

Brooke yanked open the front door, and Mindy fell into her arms. They hadn't seen each other in over a year, hadn't spoken in months, and the last time they had, they'd hung up on each other.

"What the hell?" Brooke asked.

They weren't a demonstrative family. Hugs were saved for weddings and funerals, or the very occasional family gathering where there was alcohol, copious amounts of it. Emotions were kept tight to the vest. But Mindy was demonstrating boatloads of emotion at high volume, clinging like Saran Wrap while crying and talking at the same time in a pitch not meant for humans.

"Min, you gotta slow down," Brooke said. "Only dogs can hear you right now."

Mindy sucked in a breath and lifted her head. Her mascara was smudged so badly that it was possibly yesterday's mascara that just hadn't been removed. She wore no other makeup. She was at least fifteen pounds heavier than Brooke had ever seen her. Her clothes were wrinkled and there was a suspicious-looking dark stain on her T-shirt, which was odd because Mindy didn't wear tees. Her shoulder-length hair was the same honey color as Brooke's, but Mindy's hair always behaved. Not today. It was outdoing Brooke's in the squirrel-tail impersonation and looked like it was a week past needing a shampoo. Mindy hiccuped, but thankfully stopped sobbing.

Brooke nodded gratefully, but braced herself. She had a very bad feeling. "Okay. Now who's dead?"

Mindy choked on a low laugh and swiped beneath her eyes, succeeding only in making things worse. "No one's dead. Unless you count my personal life."

This made no sense. Mindy had been born with a plan in hand. At any given moment of any day, she could flip open her fancy binder and tell you exactly where she was in that plan. "You've got a little something in your hair," Brooke said, and gingerly picked it out. It was a Cheerio.

"It's Maddox's. He was chucking them in the car." Mindy's eyes were misting again. "You don't know how lucky you are that you don't have kids!"

It used to be that a sentence like that would send a hot poker of fire through Brooke's chest, but now it was more like a dull ache. Mostly. "Why are you falling apart? You never fall apart."

Mindy shook her head. "Meet the new me. Remember when we were little and poor because Dad had put all his money into the first POP Smoothie Shop, and everyone called us the *Lemon* sisters?"

"We *are* the Lemon sisters," Brooke said.

"Yes, but they made it a play on words, like we were *lemons.* As in, *bad* lemons. As in, worthless. Well, I'm a bad Lemon!"

"First of all, *you* were the one who told me to ignore it back then because we weren't worthless," Brooke said, "so I'll tell you now—we're still not. And second, you've got a great life, a life you've planned out in great detail, I might add. You married a doctor. You now run and manage the Wildstone POP Smoothie Shop. You bake like no other. People flock to the shop on the days you bring in your fresh stuff to sell alongside the smoothies. You've got three kids. You live in a house with a real white picket fence, for God's sake."

Mindy sniffed. "I know! And I get that on paper it looks like I'm the together sister, but I'm not!"

That shouldn't have hurt, but it did. Mindy didn't have the first clue about Brooke's life these days. Which was another problem entirely. "Min, what's really going on here? We don't do this. We're not . . . close."

"Well, whose fault is that?" Mindy's eyes filled. "I burned the school cupcakes and the firefighters had to come, and now the whole block knows I'm losing my shit. Dad wants to sell off some of the POP Smoothie Shops, including the Wildstone one, so he can 'retire'"—she put "retire" in air quotes, probably because their dad was already pretty much hands-off with the business—"which puts me out of work. Linc says I should buy it, and I love that store, you know how much I love working that store, but I can't so much as potty train Maddox, even though he's thirty-two-point-five months old." She drew in a shuddery breath. "And I think Linc's having an affair with Brittney, our nanny."

Whoa. Brooke stopped trying to do the math to figure out how old 32.5 months was in years and stared at her sister. "What?"

"Look, I know you hate me, but when it all started to fall apart in the car on the way home from Mom and Dad's in Palm Springs, I looked you up. Google Maps said you were right on the way home to Wildstone."

Wildstone. Their hometown on the central coast of California,

tucked among wineries and ranches and gorgeous rolling hills
dotted with oaks. Just the thought of it conjured up a sense of
longing so painful it almost buckled her knees. "I don't hate you,"
she murmured. She shook her head. "And do you really think
your husband, the guy you've been in love with since the second
grade and who worships the ground you walk on, is having an
affair with the nanny? And since when do you have a nanny?"

"Since I went back to work at the shop right after Maddox
was born." Mindy sighed. "She's only part-time, but yes, I really
think he's cheating on me. Which means I'm going to be single
soon." She clutched Brooke's arm, the whites of her eyes showing. "I can't go back to being single, Brooke. I mean, how do you
know which way to swipe, left or right?"

"Okay, first off . . . breathe." Brooke waited until Mindy had
gulped in some air. "Good. Second, why do you think Linc's
having an affair?"

"Because *Cosmo* says that married couples our age are supposed to have sex two to three times a week, and we don't. I'm
not sure we managed to have sex once this whole month!" She
tossed up her hands. "It used to be every day. Every day, Brooke,
and we used to role-play, too, like sexy bad cop and sassy perp,
or naughty nurse and—"

"Oh my God." Brooke covered her ears. "Please stop talking."

"We have a chest full of costumes and props that we never
even use anymore."

"Seriously," Brooke said, with a heartfelt grimace. "I can still
hear you."

"I miss it. I mean, I *really* miss it. I need a man-made orgasm
or I'm going to have to buy more batteries."

"Okay, I get it, you miss sex! Jeez! Let's move on! So you've got the problems with Linc, the nanny, and your, uh, lack of new batteries . . . but instead of fixing any of these problems, you, what, ran away from Wildstone six hours south to Mom and Dad's in Palm Springs?"

"I don't know what I was thinking," Mindy said. "It was a rough visit. Mom thinks Millie needs therapy because she'll only answer to 'Princess Millie' and that Maddox should be talking more than barking. And Dad says Mason shouldn't wear pink shirts, but it was salmon, not pink, and he picks out his own clothes and dresses himself. I don't want to squash that. Also, Dad thinks that my ass is getting fat."

"Dad did *not* say that," Brooke said. The man was a quiet, thoughtful introvert. He might think it, but he'd never say it.

"Okay, no, he didn't," Mindy admitted. "But it's true and *that's* probably why Linc won't sleep with me!" She started crying again.

"Momma."

At the little-kid voice, Brooke and Mindy both froze and turned. In the doorway stood Mindy's Mini-Me, eight-year-old Millie, outfitted in a yellow dress with black elephants and giraffes on it. Her hair was held off her face by a headband that matched the dress. But it was her eyes that got to Brooke. They were the same jade green as Mindy's. And as her own, she supposed. "Millie," Brooke said. "Wow, you're all grown up."

"Hi, Aunt Brooke," Millie said politely before turning back to her mom. "Momma, Mad Dog peed on Mason again." She held up her hands like a surgeon waiting to have her gloves put on. She ran the pads of her thumbs across the tips of her fingers four times in a row. "I've got to wash my hands. Can I wash my hands?"

"Down the hall," Brooke said, heart tugging for the kid. "First door on the right's the bathroom."

Millie ran down the hall. They heard the bathroom door shut and then the lock clicked into place. And out of place. And back into place. Four times.

So maybe Millie was more Brooke's Mini-Me than Mindy's . . . Brooke didn't know much about kids, and she was certainly in no position to tell her sister how to live her life, but things did seem out of control—something Mindy had never been a day in her life. Her car was parked in Brooke's short driveway, the doors open. Two little boys were rolling around on the grass. One was naked.

"Yours, I presume," Brooke said.

Mindy was staring at them like one might stare at an impending train wreck. "Yeah. Want one?"

She ignored the way her stomach clenched. "Tell me more about Linc."

Mindy sighed. "I keep up the house, work at the shop thirty hours a week, and handle all the kid and life stuff. I'm the heavy. The bad cop. And I get that Linc and his brother, Ethan, had to take over their dad's medical practice when he had a stroke, but that wasn't in our life plan. And now Ethan's having some sort of midlife crisis and taking a lot of time off, which leaves Linc working seventy hours a week. When he finally walks in after a long day, I'm invisible. And the kids, they *love* the good cop. *I* want to be the good cop."

"So be the good cop," Brooke said.

"I *can't* be the good cop. I've tried. I'm too anal." Mindy lowered her voice to a whisper. "I want to be you, Brooke. You get to bounce all over the planet, living out wild adventure after wild adventure, and you get paid to do it. No wonder you never come home."

It wasn't adventure that kept her away from Wildstone. Shame, maybe. Okay, definitely. And regrets. Lots of regrets. She'd been haunted by them for seven years, throughout which she'd stayed away from her childhood town, only four hours north of here.

But sometimes in the deep dark of the night, she dreamed about going back.

Pushing those thoughts aside, she stared into her sister's red-rimmed, despairing eyes. She knew despair. She knew it to the depths of her soul, and some of the pent-up resentment she'd been holding for Mindy and her very perfect life shifted slightly. It didn't fade away, not exactly; more like it just moved over to make room for a teeny-tiny amount of compassion and empathy. "Why don't you head into the kitchen and pour yourself a glass of wine," she said. "I've got the kids for now."

"You do?" Mindy asked with clear disbelief.

"Yeah." If there was one thing Brooke had down, it was the ability to bullshit her way through any situation. She'd summited Mount Kilimanjaro, the roof of Africa. She'd been one of the few to get to and photograph the limestone formations of the Stone Forest in China. She'd gone swimming with giants—migrating humpback whales—along the waters of Ningaloo Reef in Australia. Certainly she could handle her sister and her kids. She waited until Mindy had vanished inside before calling out to the boys wrestling in the grass. "Hey."

Neither of them looked at her.

She put two fingers in her mouth and whistled. Loudly. All destruction and mayhem stopped on a dime and two sets of eyeballs turned her way. "Inside," she said. "Everyone to the couch."

The boys met up with the freshly washed-up Millie in the living room, and they all sat, even the naked one. Brooke winced, but let it go. She opened her laptop and scrolled her way to a menu of Disney flicks to stream. They were rated by viewer age, which was helpful. "Okay, so you're almost three," she said, pointing to the nudie-patootie, Maddox. "And almost four, right?" she asked the one *with* clothes, which meant he was Mason. He nodded, and she turned to the oldest. "Millie?"

Millie didn't answer.

Brooke looked at Mason.

"She's almost eight," he said.

Brooke looked at Millie. "Is this movie okay?"

Millie didn't answer this question, either.

"You have to call her *Princess* Millie," Mason said. His knee was bloody. "She only answers to Princess Millie."

"Right." Brooke sent a glance toward the kitchen, but heard nothing from Mindy. Either she'd made a run for it through the garage, or she was hiding out, drinking her wine in peace. Brooke went to her backpack, pulled out the first-aid kit she always carried with her, and grabbed the antiseptic.

Mason covered his knee. "Only need a Band-Aid."

While she could appreciate the sentiment more than he knew, the cut was dirty. She doctored him up and looked at Millie. "Back to the movie. *The Lion King* or no?"

Millie shook her head. "The dad dies and it makes Mad Dog cry."

"Yeah, me, too," Brooke said, and scrolled to *Toy Story 3*.

"That one makes *all* of us cry," Millie said. "And you can't play *Frozen*, either. Mason will sing it for three straight days until Momma says she needs a pill."

They finally settled on *Cars 3*. Brooke brought Maddox his clothes.

"Don't forget a diaper!" Millie said. "Or we'll all be sorry."

Right. A diaper. Brooke helped the kid into everything. She then tented a big soft blanket over the back of the couch to the coffee table, pinning it in place with several heavy books, one of which was filled with her own photography. From the old days, back when she was actually having the adventures Mindy thought she was still having.

"Yay, a fort!" Mason yelled enthusiastically.

Maddox barked with equal enthusiasm, flashing a smile and a devastatingly adorable dimple while he was at it.

"Aunt Brooke is the *best*," Brooke heard Millie whisper to her brothers.

She smiled with pride, and felt a sense of warmth and affection that had been all too rare in her world lately. But along with the goodness came something else. A sense of dread. Because blood or not, family or not, this couldn't happen. She couldn't fall for Mindy's kids, no matter how much she wanted to.

"Mad Dog!" Millie suddenly cried out, voice muffled like maybe she was holding her hand over her mouth. "You pooped!"

This was followed by a giggle. Mad Dog, presumably. Thank God for diapers.

"You're supposed to do that in the bathroom!" Millie yelled. "Mom said!" And then she yanked the blanket down around them to dramatically gasp in some fresh air.

Mason and Maddox were rolling with helpless laughter.

"Boys are disgusting," Millie announced.

Brooke shrugged. "You might think differently in a few years."

"No way." She jabbed a finger at Maddox. "He needs changing. If you don't do it right away, he gets a rash and screams bloody murder."

Brooke slid another look toward the kitchen. Still nothing from Mindy. So she scooped up Maddox and then nearly staggered back from the stench coming off the sweet little boy.

At the look on her face, Maddox giggled again and drooled down her front.

"You know what would be even funnier?" she asked, walking him out to Mindy's car to find his diaper bag and then changing him outside on her porch lounge so that she didn't have to hazmat her place afterward. "If you used the toilet like a big boy and showed your siblings what you're capable of."

He stared up at her, not committing to anything, but clearly considering it.

When she was done, she brought him inside, sprayed some Febreze, and re-created the blanket fort. Then she walked into the kitchen.

No Mindy.

Troublesome. Brooke filled a bowl with cut-up apples and a pile of almond butter for dipping, and thrust it into the fort.

It was immediately accepted with squeals of delight.

Proud of her aunting skills, Brooke went in search of her sister. It was with great relief that she found Mindy in her bedroom, sprawled out on the bed with a bottle of wine.

No glass.

"You're drinking in my bed," Brooke said, trying not to hyperventilate.

"Do you mind?"

Her OCD sure did. "Um—"

"Mom called," Mindy murmured, staring off into space. "She told me that my husband and children are perfect." She took a swig of wine. Clearly not her first. Or tenth. "Which means it's me."

Brooke took the bottle and set it on the nightstand.

Mindy flopped to her back on the mattress. "Oh my God, Brooke. This bed. It's heaven." She rolled around. "Your sheets are clean. You've got plants that haven't been eaten. There's no poop anywhere. It smells delicious."

"Okay, seriously." Brooke sat on the edge of the bed. "You're scaring me. Who are you and what did you do to my sister?"

From the bathroom in the hallway, Mason called out, "I finished!"

Mindy sighed. "He doesn't wipe efficiently and needs to be checked. As for what happened to me, I had babies."

Brooke didn't flinch. Progress. "You still haven't told me about Linc, other than that he's working long hours and is the good cop."

"I never see him. A few days ago, he left for a conference in Florida with some colleagues and suggested I take the kids to Mom and Dad's while he's gone. So I asked Brittney if she wanted to come with me, but she said she couldn't. Then later that same day on her Instagram, she was on a beach."

"Okay," Brooke said. "So . . . ?"

"So what if she's on a beach in Florida with my husband?"

"*Is someone going to come check me?*" Mason yelled.

Brooke stuck her head out the bedroom door. "Listen, kid, you're going to need to hang on a second, or handle the paperwork yourself." She turned to Mindy. "Have you actually talked to Linc?"

"No. He's too busy. We've got a rule—when he's traveling, we only check in via text once a day unless there's an emergency. It's because he's so busy, and when he doesn't call me all the time, I tend to get murderous and want to kill him. Hence the rule."

Brooke loved Linc, and she got it. Mindy could be incredibly . . . needy, but she thought the rule was pretty shitty. "Maybe you're wrong about all of this. And anyway, what does this Brittney chick have that you don't?"

"Uh, boobs that haven't been ravaged by three babies. And a waist. And I bet she doesn't pee a little when she sneezes."

Brooke grimaced. "Okay, let's stay on topic. You're the goal-orientated one here. What's your goal?"

Mindy stared at her blankly.

"What do you *need*?" Brooke prompted.

"Linc to say he can't live without me. In lieu of that, I could use a day or two away from the merry-go-round before I fall off and can't get up."

"You need to tell Linc this, all of it."

"But I want him to just *know*." Mindy reached for the wine and took another swig before squeezing out a few more tears.

Brooke sighed. If there was one thing you could say about the Lemon sisters, it was that they were night and day. Oil and water. Apples and oranges. But here was the thing—night and day melded together twice every twenty-four hours, oil and water could be forced to work together with a good shake, and apples and oranges were still both fruit. "What if I take the kids away for a few days?" she heard herself say. "You could stay here and relax."

"Where would you go? To Wildstone?"

The thought brought a burst of hope and an equal burst of gut-wrenching anxiety. To go to Wildstone, she'd not only have to face her past, but the *consequences* of that past. "I was thinking maybe Disneyland. I've got some free passes. Perks of the trade."

Mindy looked so hopeful it hurt. "You'd do that for me?"

Damn, she'd really been a crappy sister. "Yes. Now go to sleep. We can make plans in the morning," she said, hoping this whole meltdown thing wasn't contagious. Once again, she wrestled the wine away from Mindy's hot hands and set the bottle on the dresser. Then she pulled off her sister's sneakers and eyed the rest of her clothes. "How comfortable are those yoga pants?"

"They're my skinny-weight ones. But since I'm not at my skinny weight, they're not comfortable at all." Mindy paused. "I'm not even at my medium weight. I'm the heavyweight champ right now, but I threw away all my heavyweight clothes."

"Why?"

"Because my skinny-weight self is a complete selfish bitch who thought I had more control than I do," Mindy wailed.

"You're not fat, you're just . . . easier to see." Brooke tugged off Mindy's leggings and set her hands on her hips. "I get that life sucks right now, but that's never a reason to wear granny panties. Like, ever."

"My skinny panties give me wedgies." With a sigh, Mindy turned on her side and curled up in just her T-shirt and granny panties.

Brooke spread a blanket over her.

"But the kids," her sister said, eyes already closed. "I've gotta make sure the kids brush and floss and clean up . . ."

Mindy infamously micromanaged everything and everyone around her because she hated surprises. Brooke was the opposite. If you asked anyone who knew her, they'd say she was the free bird, the wanderlust spirit, the . . . well, the crazy one.

They had the crazy part right, especially given what she was about to say. "I got them. Just sleep." *And please God, wake up like your usual calm, unruffled bitch self . . .*

"Thanks," Mindy murmured. "I owe you one."

"*Wiiiiiiipe meeeeeeee!*" Mason bellowed.

With a sigh, Brooke headed down the hall to save the kid, thinking she was going to have no problem *not* falling for these kids after all.

CHAPTER 2

"The cats have been fed, do not listen to their bullshit."

The next morning, Brooke had the boys in the car and was just waiting on Millie to make her way from the front door. They'd all said good-bye to Mindy. Millie had gone last and was skipping toward the car and counting her steps. "One, two, three, four, one, two, three, four, one, two, three, four . . ."

Brooke's heart squeezed, but she smiled at the girl. "Hop in."

"Do you have hand sanitizer?"

"Always," Brooke assured her. "In my backpack. Help yourself."

Millie smiled gratefully and went to climb into the car, shuffling her feet at the last minute because she was only on "three" and needed one more step to get to "four."

The kids had no idea what their destination was. All they

knew was that they were going to get to spend two days with Auntie Brooke—yay! Mindy had said it was best to surprise them to keep expectations low. Brooke was pretty sure that was a statement on her ability to "aunt," but she got it. She had things to prove, to the both of them. She hoped to surprise the kids and herself.

Up ahead was a freeway transition. If she stayed where she was, they'd go south. South would take them to Disneyland. If she changed lanes to go north, it'd take them up the coast of California. They could go to Santa Barbara. San Francisco.

Or Wildstone.

She bit her lip, thoughts racing. Disneyland would be a huge hit. But anyone could survive a trip to Disneyland. She didn't want to just survive. Been there, done that . . . barely. And then there was the real problem. Thoughts of Wildstone wouldn't leave her alone. She'd left there without looking back under less than ideal circumstances of her own making. She'd hurt people, people who hadn't deserved it.

So maybe she could go do something constructive for a change, something to right some wrongs. At the thought, she channeled her inner Mindy and organized herself, formulating a plan for how to fix not just her sister's problems, but her own as well. Her mental list was:

1. Face Wildstone again.
2. Kick Linc's ass.
3. Face her own regrettable past actions, the worst of which had affected a certain six-foot-tall blast from her past whom she'd not faced since.

The only problem with this plan was it was an odd number of things. So she added one more:

4. Return to LA a new Brooke. Or, better yet, the old *old* Brooke, so she could get her life back, including the principal photography job she missed.

A quarter of a mile left to make her decision. Sucking in a deep breath, she changed lanes. They were going north. To Wildstone. She was going to be unselfish, she was going to fix things, because that's what grown-ups did, and she was supposedly one of those now.

"You're going sixty," Millie noted very seriously.

Brooke nodded. "It's the speed limit."

"Earlier you went to sixty-four."

"Yes. I was passing someone."

Millie met her gaze in the rearview mirror. "You like even numbers like I do."

The solemn expression on the little girl's face cracked Brooke's heart wide-open, making her more honest than she might've been. "I do."

Millie thought about that for a beat and nodded, a very small smile crossing her mouth. "I've never met anyone like us."

Brooke's heart pinched again, and when her phone buzzed, she had to swallow the lump in her throat to answer.

"Am I on speaker?" Mindy asked. "And the correct answer is yes."

"Of course you're on speaker," Brooke said, and, grimacing, put Mindy on speaker.

"Now make sure Millie's got her headphones on and isn't listening."

Brooke eyed Millie, whose head was now bopping to some kid tunes. "Done."

"She's got some things you'll need to work around," Mindy said.

"Things?"

Mindy sighed. "She needs to have her hands clean at all times. She can't touch stuff if she thinks it's dirty. She counts in fours, often out loud. Things have to be even. Even steps. Even miles per hour for your speed in the car. The thermostat. Everything, it all has to be even."

"So?" Brooke asked carefully.

"So it's who she is. Her pediatrician says the OCD isn't a problem right now, and we're watching it, but people don't always understand her quirks, and that upsets her."

From a young age, Brooke had done the same things as Millie, but knowing she was different, she'd hidden her "quirks," even from Mindy. That Millie *didn't* hide them made Brooke's neglected heart ache with pride for the kid. "I told you I've got this, and I do. I'll take care of her." *Great job on not getting attached* . . . "Of all of them."

Mindy was quiet a moment, and when she spoke, her voice was soft and grateful. "Thanks. You're a good sister."

She wasn't, not even close. But she was going to fix that, too. "And I changed my mind on the vacay at you-know-where. We're going to Wildstone, so take your time to rest up and stuff, and then you can meet us there."

"Oh my God, really?" Mindy asked, voice now filled with

excitement. "You're going home? That's amazing! Thank you! Are you sure?"

"One hundred percent." Okay, maybe ten, but that could be her own little secret. "Gotta go, Min. Don't drink all my wine, and don't drink it in my bed."

The drive up the California coast was stunning—rolling green hills on the right, the shiny blue Pacific Ocean on the left—but the kids weren't impressed. It took all of ten minutes for them to get restless. Mason was thirsty, Millie wanted to switch seats, and Maddox kept barking. "What do you all want to be when you grow up?" Brooke finally asked out of desperation.

"A space cowboy," Mason yelled with glee.

"He means astronaut," Millie said. "He just can't say it."

"Can so. *Ass-not.*"

Millie lifted a palm, like, *See?*

Brooke eyed Mason in the rearview mirror. "To be an astronaut, you have to study hard, go to college, and learn a lot of science."

Mason shrugged, unconcerned. "So? That's just three things."

Brooke had to laugh at the brilliant simplicity of that statement. "Maybe you should become a motivational speaker."

"Do they get as much candy as they want?" Mason asked.

"*I'm* going to be a *real* princess," Millie interrupted. "And I'm not going to have to marry a prince first, either."

"Arf!" Maddox said.

"He's going to be a dog," Millie translated.

And so the drive went. At one point, Maddox dropped his favorite stuffed puppy into Millie's lap.

"Finders keepers," Millie said.

Maddox started wailing.

"Millie," Brooke said. "Can you hand that back to him, please?"

Millie was playing on Brooke's iPad and didn't respond.

"Millie."

Nothing.

Brooke sighed. "*Princess* Millie, give your brother back his puppy before I stop this car and take away the iPad."

Millie shoved the puppy back into Maddox's arms. He instantly stopped the crocodile tears and flashed a cute, dimpled smile at Brooke via the rearview mirror.

Thirty-two-point-five months old, and already a lady killer.

They were past Santa Barbara and into the home stretch when they stopped for gas. Brooke was out of the car for maybe a total of four minutes, but when she got back in, Mason's lip was bleeding. Neither of his siblings could tell her what had happened.

At least they knew the first rule of Fight Club. "Let's fix that up, kiddo," Brooke said.

He covered it with his hands. "No. A Band-Aid will do it . . ."

That seemed to be his life motto. The kid was a genius.

"He doesn't like being doctored up," Millie said.

"Well, who does," Brooke murmured, understanding Mason on a base level.

Four hours outside LA, they finally pulled into Wildstone, a mid-California coastal town of rolling green hills and pristine beaches. Back in the late 1800s, it'd been a gold-mining town, complete with clapboard sidewalks and a commercial row made up of saloons and whorehouses. Luckily the town fathers had changed with the times, and 150 years later, Wildstone was thriving. But it wasn't thanks to saloons and whorehouses. That honor went to wineries and ranching.

Commercial Row had put on some new lipstick since Brooke had last driven through. The buildings were freshly renovated, but the place still said "Wild Wild West"—part of its charm, she supposed. She passed the redbrick firehouse where she and her family used to go for the annual pancake breakfast on July 4. The county library where in the very back corner they shelved the historical romances that had given her the best sex ed a girl could get. Then Caro's Café, which had the best maple bacon on the planet as far as Brooke was concerned.

Then, on the far side of town, she drove by the state park where she'd broken her arm falling out of a huge oak tree, which still stood there. She'd received her first kiss leaning up against that thick trunk. She'd been playing tag with their neighbor Garrett Montgomery—number three on her new life plan. Back then, he'd been fourteen to her twelve, but his life experiences had made him seem years older than her.

She'd loved every second of that kiss and had spent the rest of her youth chasing silly dreams and fantasies. But her love life had not gone in the comfortable, safe, cozy direction that Mindy and Linc's had. She and Garrett had not found their happily ever after.

She was still thinking of that as she pulled into the driveway of her childhood home. Garrett might've been her first crush, but she'd always been far too flawed for more. She was still too flawed.

"Home!" Mason yelled jubilantly.

Home . . . Mindy and Linc had bought the house from her parents, and it sat between a horse ranch and a homestead. Still sitting behind the wheel, Brooke was bombarded with memories. Scaling the side of the house at age thirteen to sit on the roof, much to her parents' horror. Running over the mailbox at sixteen. Leaving at eighteen to find adventures.

Shoving that all aside, she helped the kids out of the car and eyed the front lawn. There was a complicated trail of yellow plastic that looked like some sort of obstacle course running up and over an upside-down wheelbarrow, around a tree, and down the porch stairs, with a sharp curve that ended in a kiddie pool. "What the—"

"Daddy and Uncle Garrett built us a homemade Slip 'N Slide," Millie said. "We're only allowed to use it when Momma's outside with us cuz she thinks it's dangerous."

"Nuh-huh," Mason said. "She said 'stupid.'"

Brooke had to agree with her sister. "So your daddy and . . ." She paused on the name. "Uncle Garrett are close?"

"They're best friends," Millie said. "They do everything together."

Oh boy. She'd known Garrett was still in town because she followed Mindy on Instagram and had seen the occasional pic of him. She hadn't realized he and Linc had stayed close. Her stomach churned as she stared up at the house where she and Mindy had grown up playing, fighting, laughing, fighting some more . . . A lot of that with Garrett.

As a rule, she didn't spend much time dwelling on the past. She liked to think she had a good head on her shoulders, but she did tend to bypass her brain and lead with her gut instead of thinking things through. She loved her parents, but they'd often acted without thinking, too. They'd fallen in love young and had gone on to marry and divorce, then marry and divorce again, after which they hadn't spoken for years.

Now they were "dating" again, and kept saying, "We'll just see what happens . . ."

Brooke knew what that meant. They'd run off somewhere to stand in front of a judge and say their vows. Again. And then they'd fight over the business. Again. Or where to go on vacation. Or their very different definitions of the word *monogamy* . . .

It was a crazy way to live. An even crazier way to raise kids, but hey, who was she to judge? Still, she'd learned a few things. She didn't want a relationship like that. And though she loved what Linc and Mindy had—assuming Linc wasn't sleeping with the nanny—she didn't want that, either. For a long time, she thought what she wanted was adventure.

But the helo crash had changed everything she thought she knew about herself, and now, even seven years later, she still didn't know who she was.

She unlocked the front door with Maddox in one arm and Mason in the other, meanwhile nudging Millie along with a knee—seriously, why did people have three kids when they had only two hands?

In the foyer, one wall was lined with tools and a stack of tarps. Linc and Mindy appeared to be in the midst of a remodel, which turned out to be a blessing. With everything looking so completely different, she didn't drown in memories. A bonus. Boosted by that, she got everyone inside, and Mindy was right—it *did* stink in here. "What's that?"

"Smells like one of Mad Dog's diapers," Millie said, wrinkling her nose.

Sure enough, the trash hadn't been taken out. Brooke handled that pronto and then gathered everyone in the kitchen.

"I'm hungry," Princess Millie announced.

"Me, too," Mason said.

"You only said that because I said it," Millie said. "You're a copycat."

"But I *am* hungry," Mason said.

Maddox barked, whether to say he was hungry or in agreement that Mason was a copycat, Brooke had no idea. She went through the kitchen and knew she'd have to go to the store first thing in the morning. If she'd been home, she'd just order groceries online and have them delivered same day. But when she brought up a food delivery app, she discovered Wildstone hadn't joined the digital age. There was no same-day delivery. There was no delivery service at all. In the freezer, she found some gluten-free, dairy-free mac and cheese that sounded . . . *not* promising. But there were also chicken hot dogs. So she panfried those, nuked the mac and cheese, chopped up some broccoli, and tossed it all together.

"Momma says the mac and cheese is for emergencies only," Millie said. "Our plates are supposed to have at least three colors. Mostly we have to eat stuff that comes from the ground."

"Tonight's orange and brown!" Mason said cheerfully, and licked his plate clean.

"And green," Brooke said. "That's three."

Millie held up her hands and walked to the sink to wash

them for the hundredth time that day. She carefully dried off, then stared at them. "My skin's ir-cated."

"Irritated. And maybe you could try and skip a few washings."

"Can't."

Brooke nodded. She got it. She pulled a hand lotion from her backpack and set it on the counter. "Use this after you wash. It'll help."

She then unpacked the kids and ran laundry with everyone underfoot, making her realize she hadn't had a second alone to herself, not even to pee. Apparently privacy went the way of the dodo bird when you were a mom. She texted Mindy to check in and then ignored her sister's million subsequent texts attempting to micromanage from LA.

She was really starting to understand Linc's single-check-in-text-a-day rule.

At some point, Maddox had stripped and was running around with his biscuits hanging out. Mason was trying on Millie's clean clothes, and since this didn't seem to upset Millie in the least, Brooke let him be. When she got down to the socks in the clean laundry basket, she whistled for everyone to gather round. "We're going to play the sock game. Whoever matches the most pairs wins and gets to pick tonight's movie."

"Don't let Millie win," Mason whined, wearing a sunshine-yellow sundress and black tube socks. "She'll pick a princess movie!"

"The princess movies are all broken," Brooke said, and was surprised when everyone accepted this as gospel. *Hey,* she thought, *maybe this isn't so hard . . .*

BUT BY BEDTIME, Brooke was stick-a-fork-in-her done. She got the kids into their beds and watched Maddox fall asleep on his back, arms and legs flung out, blissfully peaceful.

"Don't grow up," she whispered, and stroked his hair from his face. "It's a trap."

She wandered the house. Her childhood bedroom was now Millie's. The master bedroom suite was available, but that didn't feel right. So instead of going to sleep, she got herself a big, fat bowl of the ice cream she'd found in the freezer and stepped out onto the back porch.

The silence was the first thing to strike her. She'd forgotten the quiet of Wildstone. No highway noise, no trucks, no temper-driven honking from drivers stuck in traffic, no city lights . . . nothing but the sound of the night breeze in the oak trees, the singing crickets, the faraway sound of a coyote howl, and . . . a meow.

She straightened and strained to hear it again. When it came, she left the porch and followed the sound across the yard, passing the homemade Slip 'N Slide, to the house next door. For her entire childhood, the neighboring property had belonged to a wonderful woman she'd known only as Ann, who'd been a foster parent to so many kids over the years that Brooke had lost count.

She ended up on Ann's back deck, where she was pretty sure the soft, hungry, sad-sounding *meow* had come from. "Hello?" she called softly. "Are you hurt?"

"*Meow.*" The cat that came out from beneath the porch was black as night, except for four white paws, and massive. With a welcoming *chirp,* she trotted toward Brooke, belly swinging to and fro with every step.

"Aw." She bent down as the cat wrapped around her ankles. "Are you scared? Have you been abandoned? Are you hungry?"

"No, yes, and yes," came an almost unbearably familiar male voice.

Garrett Montgomery rose out of a porch chair she hadn't even noticed and gestured to a small wooden sign that read:

THE CATS HAVE BEEN FED, DO NOT LISTEN TO THEIR BULLSHIT.

Brooke had stilled at the sound of Garrett's voice, but now she choked out a laugh. "Yours?" she asked, nodding to the cat.

He gave a single, barely there nod.

She had so many questions. How had he been, what was he doing here in this house he'd grown up in, did he hate her . . . In the end, she asked the only question she could. "What's her name?" she managed.

"Princess Jasmine. She was abandoned a few years ago by a neighbor who moved on without her. Not that he deserved her, anyway. And yes, she thinks she's hungry. She's always hungry. I can't quite convince her she needs a diet."

Brooke was having a hard time getting air into her lungs. Not in the same way as she did in her nightmares; nothing as simple as that. This felt like a ball of nostalgia, yearning, and need all mixed together and stuck dead center in her throat. Garrett had been one of Ann's foster kids. He'd also been Brooke's first crush. Her first heartbreak. Her first everything.

And they hadn't spoken in . . . well, years.

All her doing.

The air crackled with awkwardness and regrets. So much regret. And while she was shocked to the core to see him, she could tell he wasn't surprised in the least to see her. She let out a shaky breath and met his gaze for the first time in seven years. His eyes were amused but distant—which she 100 percent deserved. "You adopted her," she guessed. "And let Millie name her."

"Actually, she adopted me, and yes."

The ball of emotion in her throat swelled. It might've been seven years, but she knew this man, knew that he knew a little something about abandonment and had lived his life accordingly. "Sucker," she said lightly, and scooped up the cat, who lifted her face to rub against Brooke's. "You'd adopt a coyote if it came knocking at your door in need."

He lifted a shoulder in a guilty-as-charged gesture.

They stared at each other some more, and something heavy slid through her. More regret, and the sense of a future lost. Swallowing hard, she handed him his cat. "How've you been?"

He gave one short, mirthless laugh. "You're kidding, right?"

Yeah, he was right. Turned out you really couldn't go home again. She'd actually thought she could. She'd told herself he deserved the closure, and if he hated her, she'd just have to take it. And in the meantime, she'd get to know her niece and nephews before heading back to LA. But she'd been stupid to think she could handle any of it. "I'm sorry," she whispered.

One sardonic eyebrow raised. "For?"

She was short of air again. Dammit. "You know what? It's

late. Good night." And acting like the coward she'd been for the past seven years, she walked away. Actually, she ran, her sneakers making squeaky noises on the grass as she counted her steps. Because maybe the old Brooke had been fearless and brave, but the new Brooke was nothing but a big, fat scaredy-cat, and she'd just proven it.

CHAPTER 3

"You going to make mashed potatoes with
that thing, or hit me over the head?"

Back at the house, Brooke collapsed in exhaustion on the couch in the living room. "That's *definitely* enough today-ing for today . . ." she murmured, and closed her eyes.

She was awoken an hour later by an unfortunately familiar sound.

Someone was throwing up. And that someone was throwing up while padding down the hall toward her.

Maddox.

He was crying, nose running, puke-faced, and she was torn between wanting to cuddle him close or run in the other direction. Her sense of auntie obligation won, so she scooped him up. She had to hold her breath, but she got him cleaned, changed, and tucked back into bed.

That's when Princess Millie appeared and also threw up.

And where there were two, there were always three. Not ten minutes after she'd soothed Maddox and Millie, then Mason was also getting sick.

And then the cycle began all over again.

She'd stepped into her own horror flick.

HOURS LATER, UP to her elbows in poop and puke and exhausted to the bone, Brooke laid Maddox back into his little toddler bed and stroked his hair from his face as he clung to her hand.

"You're going to be okay," she whispered softly.

He sent her a sweet, sleepy smile and flashed that dimple, and her damn heart snagged in her chest. Seriously, how was she supposed to resist? He had huge green eyes and drooled when he smiled at her, and he hugged her with his grimy, disgusting hands and loved her with his sweet, undamaged heart. *Gah.*

Since dawn was making an appearance, she didn't bother to attempt sleep. Instead, she obsessively scrubbed the sick germs from every nook and cranny of the entire house, including under the couch. She was demolishing all the dust bunnies when she found a tortoise.

A live tortoise.

She texted a pic of it to Mindy with a "WTF" and got a response that Ketchup the Tortoise was Mason's; he was shy and considerate. He had an aquarium on the floor in the laundry room, complete with a heat lamp and drinking water, but it was left open so he could have the freedom of the place. He went to the bathroom next to his aquarium on a bed of paper towels and he ate out of a pie tin that Brooke should put lettuce and strawberries in once a day—which was all in the instructions Mindy had emailed, and why wasn't Brooke reading her emails?

"I can't even," Brooke said to the room, and then proceeded to lose her phone while using it as a flashlight to stare at Ketchup. She frantically slapped her pockets for an embarrassingly long moment before realizing she was an idiot. She moved to the kitchen and stared out the window, wishing for . . . what? A nap? Caffeine?

A one-way ticket to Mars?

She heard the front door open and close, then footsteps heading her way—light, unhurried footsteps, like maybe her home invader/thief/possible murderer was in no rush. Well, that made one of them. Whirling around, she grabbed the first thing she came to. A potato masher.

Garrett stood in the doorway. "You going to make mashed potatoes with that thing, or hit me over the head?"

She considered hitting him over the head, but wait a minute. He was holding . . . a bag from McDonald's. Be still her heart. Setting the masher down, she turned to wash her hands. Twice.

"You okay?" Garrett asked.

She might've taken comfort in the question, but his voice held that same cool, distant tone as it had last night. He had not forgiven her. She told herself she understood that. "I'm great. I mean, I did just spend a full minute looking for my phone while using it as a flashlight, but everyone does that, right?"

His smile was polite, the kind he'd always reserved for

teachers and adults in general, and if she'd had any heart left, it would've cracked. She chalked that up to being awake all night, and she was pretty sure she still smelled like puke. Garrett, on the other hand, looked better than anyone had a right to this early in the morning. "So what are you doing here?" she asked. "And why do I feel like I'm the only one of us surprised to see each other?"

"Mindy called me yesterday. Said you were coming home with the kids."

Her pulse was thundering so hard she was certain he could hear it. "Mindy called you?" she repeated inanely.

"Yeah." He handed her the coffee, opened the bag, and held out an Egg McMuffin. "And again this morning. She wanted me to tell you that it's possible the kids got food poisoning from your mom's egg sandwiches the morning they showed up at your place. She said she feels really bad about it, but didn't know until she got a text from your mom late last night—"

He stopped talking and went brows up when Brooke took a long, deep pull of the coffee like her life depended on it. Because it did. "So you're still tight with Mindy," she said when the caffeine hit her bloodstream. "And . . . you live next door."

"Yes. I bought Ann's house a while back."

She'd first met Garrett the day he'd shown up as the new kid on the school bus. When a stupid boy several years older than all of them had started to pick on Mindy, Brooke had gotten up to sock him in the nose, but Garrett beat her to it.

Neither Mindy nor Brooke had ever had to take a stand again, although Brooke had still done so, unable to stop herself from being what the school liked to call *difficult*.

She'd made that a lifelong thing. From a young age, all she'd ever wanted was adventure. She'd been the only one in her family with the "wanderlust," as her mom called it, becoming absorbed early on in photography and rock climbing. The minute Brooke had turned eighteen, she'd left home to work for an adventure guide company, working her way up from scrub to guide for a few years before landing a job at the Travel Network. Her parents hadn't been thrilled, but they'd let her go. She'd used Wildstone as her home base, but she'd been gone more often than not, which had suited her because there'd been no future for her in Wildstone beyond working for her dad at POP Smoothies. And while she loved a good smoothie, she needed more.

She'd gotten it, along with a whole bunch of things she hadn't counted on.

Garrett was lounging against the granite countertop, calmly studying her. She had no such ability to be calm. Not with her very messy, god-awful past and her equally messy, murky present colliding. *Which was why you came here,* she reminded herself. To make amends. To apologize, so that maybe she could also forgive herself and then move on. She could go back to LA and be the Brooke of old again.

But she didn't have the words for all that, mostly because she couldn't stop staring at Garrett. He was tall and broad, with messy, sun-kissed brown hair that she'd bet hadn't been brushed by more than a casual flick of his fingers. He'd never given a single fig about his appearance, and why would he, when he looked like he did? His T-shirt advertised a Wildstone surf shop and fit his toned body just right, as did his jeans.

He wore battered hiking boots and a soft, worn leather jacket against the chill of the morning, but that wasn't what held her captive. It was his light hazel eyes, set beneath black lashes and the dark lines of his eyebrows. His hair was longer than he used to keep it, and the lines of his face more defined by the intervening years, but the way he looked at her—like he could see everything, including all her messy faults—hadn't changed.

But *she'd* changed plenty, and she turned away to go back to staring out the window. "Thanks for breakfast, but Mindy shouldn't have bothered you to come check on me."

"I didn't come for you."

She closed her eyes against the memories that low, husky voice of his brought up. "No?"

"I'm a general contractor, among other things. Your sister and Linc hired me to renovate this house. I'm working on the master bathroom this week. I came a little early to check on the kids. As you probably know, Linc's out of town, and Mindy's . . . not herself right now."

Well, that was one way to put it. And what did he mean, "among other things"? She was startled out of her thoughts by a metallic banging.

Pushing off the counter, Garrett opened the fridge, grabbed some lettuce and a few strawberries, and vanished into the pantry. When he came back out, his hands were empty. "Ketchup," he explained. "He bangs on the pie tin in the mornings to be fed. You won't have to worry about feeding him again until tomorrow morning." He turned to leave the kitchen, but then paused. "Also, Mindy seems . . . better. She said your bed's comfortable."

Brooke let out a rough laugh. "Well, as long as she's comfortable."

From upstairs came an angry bellow and then a *thump*. Brooke set down her food and coffee and went running. Garrett beat her to the boys' room.

Mason and Maddox were playing dodgeball, only instead of using a ball, they were chucking other things at each other. Shoes, boots, toys . . .

The place looked like a cyclone had hit it. "What the hell?" Brooke asked.

Mason stopped in the middle of throwing a pillow at his baby brother. "That's a bad word."

Maddox tipped his head back and howled like a coyote.

Millie wandered in. "You're both going to be in trouble," she informed her brothers loftily.

"Why are you all even awake?" Brooke asked, boggled at the level of destruction.

"Cuz it's morning," Mason said.

Barely. "But you were both sick last night."

"Not anymore."

She checked them all for fever. No one had one.

"They're resilient," Garrett said.

Yeah, like cockroaches. She pulled out her vibrating cell phone. Mindy had resorted to texting instructions now, since "apparently you're ignoring emails." Brooke sighed. "I'm supposed to get you all to camp."

"And I'm going to work," Garrett said.

Once he was gone, Brooke looked at the kids. "Okay, this is going to be a team effort. First up, everyone brush your teeth."

Five minutes later she went into the bathroom to see what was taking so long and found all three struggling for the power seat over the vent to keep their butts warm. She pointed at Millie first. "Go get dressed."

"What should I wear?"

"Whatever floats your boat." Brooke turned to Mason next. His wild-man-of-Borneo hair was doing its thing. He said, *"I can do it!"* and also took off. This left Maddox. His pj's were on inside out—her bad—and he had a now familiar odor about him. Damn. "Have you ever thought about losing the diaper?"

Maddox tilted his head to the side in a classic male *huh?*

"If you wear real undies," she said. "You're no longer a baby. You're practically a grown-up. Grown-ups get to do a lot of fun stuff that babies can't."

He smiled and barked, and after she changed him and set him free to find clothes, he showed up dressed in Hulk sweats. No diaper.

Progress.

Mason had pulled on Millie's dress from the day before. Brooke looked over at Millie.

"It's okay with me," Millie said. "I already wore it this week."

"Is camp going to be okay with it?" Brooke asked.

"Yes. They appreciate gender fluidity."

Brooke blinked. "Are you going on eight, or thirty?"

Millie shrugged and slowly washed her hands. For the fourth time in the past few minutes. She carefully applied lotion afterward and then showed Brooke. Way less red today.

"Nice," Brooke said. "Now tell me why you seem to be stalling about getting dressed."

"Because Charlotte's going to be at camp."

"Okay. And . . . we don't like her?"

"She copies me, everything I do. Riding bikes. Hopscotch. Basketball. She even pretends she has to wash her hands and count by fours. And she doesn't do any of those things as good as I do."

Brooke looked at her adorable, wonderfully confident but slightly too full of herself niece. "Have you ever heard the saying 'Be the girl who fixes another girl's crown without telling the world it was crooked'?"

"I don't have a crown anymore. Mommy took it away because she didn't like my bad 'tude."

"It's a metaphor," Brooke said. "Which means figure of speech. It's not a real crown. Do you understand what I'm saying?"

"Yes. I shouldn't tell her she's a copycat and that I don't like her."

"Exactly."

Millie sighed dramatically.

"All you can do is your best," Brooke said.

Mason had pulled a sweatshirt on over the dress and was struggling with the zipper. Kneeling before him, Brooke tried to take over, but he yelled, *"I can do it!"*

A theme, it seemed. She lifted her hands in surrender and he hunched over in concentration, tongue between his teeth, in a battle of wills with the zipper.

"Mas—"

"I can do it!"

Brooke backed off, but watching him was painful, especially because he hadn't yet managed to line up the teeth on the zipper, which meant this was going to happen approximately never. "How about I just get it started, and—"

"*I CAN DO IT!*"

Okay, then. She called the camp. "Listen, my nephew's going to be a few minutes late because apparently he can zip his jacket all by himself."

Millie came back into the room wearing black tights with strawberries on them and a strawberry-red dress. She pointed to the pockets. "I've just got to fill my snack holes and I'll be ready to go."

Brooke thought this was brilliant. "Every outfit should have snack holes."

Millie nodded sagely.

Five minutes later, they were in the kitchen working on breakfast when Garrett reappeared. He eyed Maddox, facedown on the floor crying. "Problem?" he asked over the din.

"Whyever would you think that?" Brooke asked.

This got her the slightest of lip twitches.

Mason and Millie just kept eating their granola with chopped-up bananas. After she got to the store later and bought fresh stuff, she'd be able to get more than two colors in their bowl.

Garrett glanced at the still facedown-on-the-floor Maddox. "What's wrong with this one?"

"He's upset that his sweatpants match his sweatshirt, even though he dressed himself."

Garrett nodded like this made perfect sense. He crouched low, balanced on the balls of his feet, and murmured something softly for Maddox's ear only, rubbing the toddler's back with an easy, warm affection.

After a minute, Maddox got to his feet and hitched up his sweatpants, like, *Okay, I'm good.*

Garrett held out a closed fist, and to Brooke's surprise, Maddox bumped his baby fist to it.

"How did you do that?" she demanded.

Garrett shrugged. "I run the soccer program at the rec center and do a lot of the coaching. Maddox loves soccer."

She was more than a little boggled by this grown-up, easygoing, and—dammit—sexy-as-hell Garrett as he headed to the stairs. "I'll be working if you need anything else," he said, and then was gone.

"I can do it," she said to the room. "I've got this."

Note to self: She didn't have this. Not even close.

Mindy's texts had included a whole lot of rules, including the correct way to load her dishwasher (complete with a diagram), how to manage the overwhelming amount of laundry three kids generated, and also what could and couldn't be in their lunch. "Damn," Brooke muttered, reading through the texts. "You're not supposed to have anything white."

Millie, hands raised like a freshly scrubbed surgeon, pointed at the last of the McMuffin Brooke was eating. "You're going to be in trouble."

Brooke started to blow that off, but suddenly remembered how much it had frustrated her when her parents had given her some arbitrary rule and then blithely ignored the rule themselves. So even though she wanted these kids to grow up and be self-sufficient in a way Mindy wasn't really great at, Brooke wouldn't take away her sister's authority. "You're right," she said, and set the rest of her sandwich aside.

She'd eat it later, when they were at camp, like a responsible adult.

By some miracle, they eventually got out the door and on their way to camp—which was easier said than done, since all three programs started at the same time, but at completely different spots in Wildstone.

She was starting to appreciate Mindy's problem.

Millie got dropped off first. "Remember, be kind to everyone," Brooke told her. "Including Charlotte."

Millie shrugged. "All I can do is try my best."

"A-plus for using my words against me," Brooke said dryly.

Millie smiled cheerfully.

By the time Brooke got everyone where they needed to be, hit up the grocery store to buy more "colors," put the groceries away, and got all the blankets and towels and bedding washed and dried after last night's puke-mageddon, it was nearly time to start picking up the kids. Leaning against the dryer in exhaustion as she waited for the last load to finish, she worked her way through a packet of SweeTarts that she'd found in Millie's bedroom.

Garrett appeared. He'd shed his leather jacket and added a tool belt, slung low on his lean hips. He seemed far more delectable than the SweeTarts, and that was saying something. Then she remembered her list, her reason for being there. She opened her mouth to start what was sure to be a very awkward conversation, when she realized he was looking her over, a small smile on his lips. This prompted her to turn and glance at her reflection in the laundry room window. Her hair looked like she'd come out the wrong end of an explosion. Her face was pale, and she realized she hadn't managed a shower or change of clothing yet. She looked as insane as Mindy had when she'd shown up at Brooke's door . . . Had that been just two days ago? It felt like years.

Garrett reached out to take a SweeTart, and she clutched the packet to her chest. She needed those SweeTarts. She *deserved* those SweeTarts. Before she could tell him so, there came a buzzing sound. She really hoped it was an oncoming brain embolism, but it turned out to be Garrett's phone. He looked at the screen, then answered with a soft "Hey." He paused and listened. "Sure. See you then." He disconnected and slid the phone away again.

She waited for him to explain.

He didn't.

"Hot date?" she asked with what she hoped sounded like casual interest and not nosiness.

He gave her a one-shouldered shrug. Right. None of her business. She was racking her brain on how to start the difficult conversation she needed to have and came up with nothing.

"Don't you have to get the kids?" he asked into the awkward silence.

Crap! "Yes! Gotta run!" Ignoring his low laugh, she raced out of there.

Forty-five minutes later, they were back, and there was no sign of Garrett. She didn't know if she was relieved or . . . not relieved. She'd barely set her backpack down when Millie came to her, face worried. "I can't find my candy."

Uh-oh. "I'm thinking your mom probably doesn't even allow candy in this house," Brooke said.

"But my camp boyfriend gave me a bag of SweeTarts. They were under my pillow."

Yep, that's right where Brooke had found them when changing the sheets. Just before she'd eaten them. "You have a camp boyfriend?"

"Yes."

"You're eight."

"He's eight, too."

"Does your mom know?"

"She told me I couldn't have a boyfriend."

"I'm here to second that," Brooke said firmly.

"And Daddy said I couldn't have a boyfriend until he was old or dead, whichever came second."

Brooke nodded. "I second that, too."

"But he's not *really* my boyfriend."

"Good," Brooke said. "So why did you call him that?"

"So he'd give me his candy."

Oh boy. "Honey, that's not cool."

"I know. But I told him the truth, that I only liked him cuz of his candy, and he gave it to me anyway. Do you think a bad guy came in and stole it?"

No, not a bad guy. A bad aunt.

"Will you help me look?" Millie asked.

"Sure," Brooke said, just as she caught sight of Garrett coming through to refill his water bottle, a mocking—and annoying— smirk on his face. He waited until Millie was head deep into the clothes hamper, searching, before he mouthed a single word to Brooke.

Monster.

Then he walked out of the room. She did her best to shrug it off as she and Millie "searched" the house for the "stolen" candy. They were in the hallway, Millie melting down and Brooke close to doing the same—how the hell did Mindy do all this and work the smoothie shop thirty hours a week?—when Garrett reappeared and tossed a packet of candy to Millie.

SweeTarts.

He'd replaced them. His gaze met Brooke's. He was still smiling, but as whenever he looked at her, the smile didn't quite reach his eyes.

Monster . . .

He'd been joking, but she'd taken the word to heart because she knew that it was actually true.

CHAPTER 4

"Sometimes you just need to lie in bed
and rest for a couple of years."

Mindy's plan had been to sleep in Brooke's condo for three days straight. She managed two days, not leaving the bed except for the important things, like when the remote fell off the nightstand, or to answer the door for Tommy, who'd marathoned *Law & Order: SVU* with her, and then dragged her out to eat at the most amazing places. She'd told herself that whatever calories she consumed while on brain vacay didn't count. And for the first time in her life, she'd been grateful for Linc's one-text-a-day rule. It meant she hadn't yet had to admit she'd sent the kids off with the sister she hadn't seen in a year.

As for work, the only thing she'd had the energy to do had been to call into the shop. Though she had a wonderful assistant manager, Xena, a longtime coworker whom she trusted, she knew Xena hadn't counted on being in charge for an extra couple of days. Keeping the scheduling, deliveries, and book-keeping in order was more than a full-time job, and it was a lot to ask of someone. For a while now, it'd been too much for Mindy. Running the shop had gone from something she loved to something that took too much of her time and effort and completely drained her. The only thing she'd missed about work in the last two days was the baking she did to sell out of the shop's front display, because baking fueled her soul.

"No problem!" Xena had said easily when Mindy got a hold of her. "My horoscope said there'd be a new opportunity for me this week because Jupiter and Earth are aligned. You do you, sweetness, you've been high-strung for a while now."

Mindy winced. "I'm sorry."

"Don't be. Burn some sage, cleanse your aura. Just worry about yourself. I've got this."

Mindy hung up, feeling better about that one area of her life, at least. She'd spent most of her life trying to be perfect, which had finally sucked the soul out of her and left her feeling like she was free-falling into an abyss.

She didn't know how to do it anymore.

She was lying in Brooke's amazing bed, smelling delicious from all Brooke's products, going through Instagram, when she came upon a post of Linc's. His account was private, and usu-ally his pics were of her and the kids. But today there was a pic of him at his conference. He was looking extremely handsome in a suit, sitting at a table surrounded by his colleagues, all male except the woman at his right. Linc had thoughtfully typed in everyone's names: Dr. Gerry Lepenksky, Dr. Carlos Ramirez, Dr. Scott Wells, and Dr. Sam Whitney, all of whom she'd heard him mention many times. What had not been mentioned was that Sam was a woman. A tall, beautiful, auburn-haired woman who was smiling at Mindy's husband like maybe he was lunch and dinner and dessert all in one.

A long minute—or a year—went by. When Mindy could breathe again, she called Brooke.

It'd been a long time since they'd been each other's go-to person, but suddenly she needed her sister more than she needed her next breath. Only problem, she'd called home so many times that Brooke was now answering the phone with "Hot Mess Hotline, how can I help you?" which was making Mindy feel even more guilty. She disconnected before the call could go through.

And then called Garrett.

He answered with a sigh, reminding her that she'd also called him a bunch of times, wanting details on how Brooke and her kids were doing. He was a close friend and often her voice of reason—and okay, throughout the years she'd also had a periodic crush on him, so sue her. "How's it going?" she asked.

"Fine."

"The kids?"

"Also fine."

It was her turn to sigh. "Can we pretend the word 'fine' doesn't exist and try again?"

She could practically hear him roll his eyes. "The kids did get food poisoning."

Which she knew from all her calls and texts to Brooke. But her sister spoke less than the men in Mindy's life. She knew the kids were okay, but were they *okay* okay?

"Brooke seemed to handle it just fine—" He broke off when she hissed at his word choice. "She handled it *well*. Relax, Mindy. Breathe."

She gulped in air and relief, and disconnected. Everything was okay, meaning she could take this last day and head home tomorrow morning.

But the very thought made her stop breathing again. She was still panicking when Tommy let himself in, carrying a pizza box.

She'd discovered that Tommy was an amazing friend. She wouldn't want him for a lover, since he was utterly disinterested in keeping anyone for more than one night. But as a friend, he was damn near perfect. He was funny and smart, and he loved food as much as she did. And being tall, dark, and gorgeous, he also gave her something to look at. But it was the pizza catching her gaze now. "You know I try not to eat gluten. Or too many carbs."

"Duh," he said. "That's how you stay a MILF." He set the box down on the bed. "It's a cauliflower crust, topped with chopped veggies like kale, spinach, and peppers. No gluten. Low carbs."

Mindy sat up and reached for a piece. She took a bite and moaned. "Oh my God, I love you. Can I steal you away from Brooke?"

"Not a chance. And if you tell her I let you eat in her bed, you're dead to me."

The twinge of jealousy wasn't attractive, she knew this. But

Brooke had everything: an exciting job, great friends, sexy lovers . . . She'd met Cole last night when Tommy had brought him along for dinner, and *wow*. The guy was smoking hot and clearly had a thing for her sister. Even more impressive, Brooke had managed to get herself this fab life away from Wildstone and their parents' expectations. Her sister's life was infinitely more exciting than hers. And easier.

Tommy sat his very fine ass on the corner of the bed.

"Why are you being so nice to me?" Mindy asked.

"Brooke asked me to." He smiled to soften the words. "Also, you've got edges. I like edges. You call him yet?"

They'd talked about this over the past couple of days. Tommy wanted her to fly out to Florida and meet up with Linc. Since she refused to do that, he thought she should call and actually talk to him—like, *really* talk.

"I don't know where to start," she'd said. "We've lost our way. We're in a rut, everything is rote, 'hi, bye, love you' . . . They're all just phrases we throw around without meaning. Has that ever happened to you?"

Tommy smiled. "Honey, the most common phrase in any of my relationships is usually '*You* sleep in the wet spot.' Now stop stalling and call your man."

She actually wanted to. She yearned to hear Linc's voice and longed for the comfort that usually came with it. But she was feeling so raw and emotional, she knew she couldn't. Not yet. She needed to be able to have a conversation without bursting into tears the second she heard him. "I'm working my way up to it."

Tommy pulled a bottle of wine from a bag. "Liquid courage."

It was a Capriotti red, one of her favorite wines in the whole world, made at a local winery in Wildstone. She felt her eyes fill at Tommy's kindness.

Tommy accepted her tears the way he accepted everything else about her, without blinking an eye. He handed her a box of tissues and opened the wine.

Half an hour later, the pizza was decimated and she was pleasantly buzzed from two full glasses. "Best diet food ever."

"I said it was gluten-free. I didn't say it was diet food."

Mindy glanced at the empty pizza box. "Nutritional labels should really include a 'what if I eat the whole damn thing' section."

"You're stalling." Tommy nudged her phone toward her.

She picked it up. "Maybe I should check on the kids again first."

"Remember what Brooke said."

Mindy blew out a breath. Earlier Brooke had said she'd text Mindy hourly updates *if* Mindy promised not to call and micromanage her anymore. If she couldn't control herself, the deal was off, and Brooke would take off.

Not for a minute did Mindy believe this. Mindy might be the older of the two, and maybe she was also the one who, on the surface, looked to be the most responsible and accountable, but it actually wasn't true. Mindy was the perennial people-pleaser, and she cared what people thought.

Brooke wasn't and didn't. And she didn't break promises. Ever. Nope. She just walked away without looking back . . .

"Still stalling," Tommy said.

"This is stressful."

"You're stressing when you don't even know if there's stress to stress about."

"It's a way of life." But she hit Linc's number. He'd texted earlier, a quick "miss and love you," and she hadn't responded yet. She did miss and love him. She also missed *not* being lonely.

He picked up on the third ring, right before she got sent to voice mail, and immediately Mindy's back went up. "Did I catch you in the middle of something?" she asked.

"Nothing as important as this. Good to hear your voice, babe."

The old Mindy, the want-to-be-the-perfect-wife Mindy, melted at that. But she shoved it aside because she was a new-and-improved Mindy. A cool-as-cucumber Mindy. "How's it going there at the beach?"

"I wish I knew. Haven't been out of the hotel. I just finished up a panel on analyzing and early detection of nondifferential diseases," he said. "It's fascinating."

"I'm so glad. How are the people?" she asked, trying to steer to one "people" in particular—Dr. Sam. "You enjoying them, too?"

"Been too busy. How're the kids? How're you?"

"Tired."

"Me, too," he said. "Exhausted, actually. But the takeaways are so amazing." He began to tell her about some new stitching technique and material, something to do with bone grafting, and she realized that this phone call was everything that was wrong with her marriage. They lived entirely separate lives. They got up early, went their own ways, and weren't alone together again until late at night. And then they had only about five minutes of catching up while they were brushing their teeth before crashing into bed, claimed by exhaustion.

And she got it. Linc was brilliant, and he worked so hard. But so did she, and guilt and fear of losing him had kept her from telling him how she really felt.

Talk to him, Tommy mouthed.

"Linc . . ." She closed her eyes. "When I say I'm tired, I mean I'm *really* tired. As in, need-a-break tired."

"From the kids?" he asked sympathetically. "They're going to grow up, Min. It'll get better, I promise."

The thought of the kids growing up and leaving her brought a sharp pang of regret. She didn't want to just survive these years. She wanted to *live* them.

"In the meantime," he said, "take whatever time you need. You've got Brittney."

Do I? Or do you have Brittney? she thought. *And maybe also Dr. Sam . . .* "I guess you probably need to get back to things."

"I'd like to get to things with you," he said playfully, and her eyes drifted shut as they always did when he spoke to her in that voice, the one that said he knew her like no one else did, the one that made her lose track of the bones in her knees. But she opened her eyes and locked her legs, because she owed him the truth. "I'm in LA, Linc. The kids are in Wildstone with Brooke."

Linc didn't say anything. All she could hear was static.

"Linc?"

"Mindy? Dammit, I think I lost her," he said to someone. "The connection's bad."

"I'm here!" Mindy yelled. "Can you hear me? Did you hear what I said? I'm in LA and the kids are—"

"Babe, it's a really bad connection. I'll call you back as soon as I can, okay? Screw the rule."

She nodded like he could see her. "Yes, please," she said, buoyed by Tommy's insistent nod. "Because I think I'm burned out, Linc. Between keeping the smoothie shop going and the kids and the house . . . I mean, I know it was my idea to run the shop, and I'm the one who wanted to stay home and take care of our babies. I get it. I planned for all of it, carefully and purposefully, and maybe that's why it's so hard to admit that I'm sinking." She drew in a deep breath. "But the truth is, it's not at all what I thought it would be. I haven't been all I wanted to be." She shook her head. "And I've pushed people away. I lost track of you. And us. I mean, I don't even know who I am anymore. It all feels like a facade, and I'm messing it up." She hesitated. "I'm scared," she admitted softly. "I've always played my role—daughter, sister, caretaker, mother. But the only thing I've never really done is be me."

There.

She'd said it.

She'd laid it all out. She let out a breath and waited for a response.

Which didn't come.

"Linc?" She looked at her phone.

Call failed.

Tommy took the phone from her limp fingers and pulled her up. "He'll call you back. In the morning. Come on. We've got things to do."

"Like jump off a cliff?"

"Are you kidding? You want to throw that fab body of yours away? What if reincarnation is real and in your next life you come back as a dog? Or a cat? Or worse, a man? You'll have wasted it."

She shrugged. "I'd be a good cat. I'm bitchy and I don't like anyone."

"Okay, there's no pity parties on our agenda today," he said firmly. "We've got too much to do for that." He made a few phone calls and then drove her to some secret location that turned out to be a studio, where he had to flash a badge to the night watchman.

"Where are we?" she asked.

He glanced over at her as they walked inside a huge hangar where she could see everything from sets to set dressings to cameras, and more equipment than she had names for. "This is where your sister works," he said.

Mindy stopped walking. "Brooke works outside—on adventure reality shows. On mountaintops and crazy raging rivers and hard-to-reach remote landscapes."

Tommy stopped, too, and turned back to her, head cocked. "Baby doll, how long has it been since you asked your sister about her job?"

She blinked. "Uh . . . I don't know? But I do know she's a great photographer, and daring and adventurous as hell. I see her pics on Instagram sometimes."

Tommy's smile faded, and he looked like he felt sorry for her. "You shouldn't rely on Instagram to get news on your sister.

Social media's nothing but smoke and mirrors. You see only what the people posting want you to see."

She felt a ball of anxiety low in her gut, followed by a defensiveness she hated. "I know that. It's just that I've been pretty busy, and—"

"I know." He took her hand again, but he wasn't smiling as easily as he had been before as he led her through a maze of hallways and sets and doors.

Mindy was chewing her lip, worrying. "But Brooke's still an action photographer for your show, right?" she asked his back. God. What if Brooke had lost her job and had been too ashamed to tell anyone? What if Brooke's life was in as much turmoil as her own? And what had she done? She'd let Brooke take on her crazy, chaotic life, without a single thought to what was going on with her sister.

Shame had her quiet as Tommy stopped and opened a door to two women, who introduced themselves as Tommy's staffers. One was a masseuse and the other a nail stylist. They'd re-created a day spa room, complete with soft music and snacks and more wine. Mindy got a massage, a mani-pedi, and some 411 on Brooke, including the fact that her current job was apparently nothing like Mindy had imagined, info she had to save to think about later or she'd fall apart even more.

Tommy did her hair. They changed her hair color and cut off her long braid. It felt so drastic, but when Tommy turned her to face the mirror a couple of hours later, she stared at herself in awe. Her hair had been long. Too long. Hanging nearly down to her elbows and usually pulled up on top of her head or braided.

He'd cut it to her shoulders and given her some long layers in front that gave her face a frame. And the color. He'd given her both high- and lowlights, so her hair was now the color of a fawn in the sun, which was to say it was a million different colors, giving it depth and shine.

She hardly recognized herself.

Her phone buzzed in her hand. *Linc.* She answered, breathless.

"Mindy," he said with clear relief. "I finally got reception. I'm sorry."

"It's okay."

"It's not," he said. "I tried to get out of here a few days early, but couldn't since Ethan had to get home to work some things out."

Of course he did . . .

"But I'll be home in a few days, okay? Is there anything I can do from here to help?"

Her heart warmed a little bit. "You just did. Just by asking."

"What were you trying to tell me before?" he asked.

"Nothing," she lied, not wanting to repeat it all in front of her audience. Or ever . . .

"Text me later?" he asked.

"Yes."

"Love you, Min."

"Love you, too," she said, but felt a lot less warm without him on the line.

Tommy distracted her by taking her to craft services. There was a juice bar set up, and suddenly, she was in her element. She created unique juices for her entire squad based on what she'd learned of them over the past hours, and they all squealed in excitement, gushing over her skills.

From there, they went to a bar, and then a late dinner, and then a club.

She had the time of her life. Or so she told herself.

"You okay?" Tommy asked her.

"Sure, I'm great."

"Is that why you kept sneaking into the bathroom to check your phone?"

She sighed. "Mom guilt." And wife hope. But nothing more from Linc.

Tommy reached for her hand. "You love your family. You miss them. That's the hard part. The good part is that you're taking a little well-deserved time to put yourself back together after cracking."

She looked at him. "You think I've cracked?"

"Like Humpty Dumpty, sweetness."

She thought about that as she crawled into Brooke's comfy, clean bed, luxuriating in the fact that she didn't have to share it with a husband and at least one kid. Tommy was right. She *had* cracked. She just hoped she could put all the pieces back together again, and quickly, since Brooke was expecting her home tomorrow. But even as she thought it, she knew she wasn't ready. She needed more time, a few more days.

Or months . . .

She was awakened the next morning by the banging in her head. *Damn wine,* she thought, and started to fall back asleep.

But then Tommy was standing at the bedside, looking disgusting healthy and not hungover in the slightest. He held out his phone. "For you," he said.

"'Lo?" she managed, holding her head onto her shoulders.

Damn. Thirty years old was too old to drink until two in the morning.

"When you're not dead," Brooke said in her ear with false politeness, "you return a damn phone call."

Mindy gasped, sitting straight up. "The kids, is everyone—"

"They're good. They're great, actually. But jeez, Min, tell me you're not still sleeping while I'm over here working on no sleep at all."

Mindy let out a breath of relief. "Not still sleeping, at least not anymore. And hey, sometimes you just need to lie in bed and rest for a couple of years, ya know?"

"I hate you."

Mindy could hear Maddox crying in the background. "What's wrong with my baby?"

"Lots of things," Brooke said. "But at the moment it's the fact that I won't let him get into the oven with my sweet lemon bread."

Mindy snorted, but only because she totally understood. There was no reasoning with Maddox on the best of days. "You're making my kids your sweet lemon bread?"

"Yeah. Figured it was more acceptable than a pitcher of frozen margaritas. So it's been the agreed-upon two days, Min. What time are you coming home today?"

"Yeah, about that . . ." Mindy bit her lower lip, torn between momma guilt and the need to clear her muddled head. "I'm not."

CHAPTER 5

When life gives you lemons . . .

B rooke stood in the kitchen staring out the window, running the pads of her thumbs over the tips of her fingers, back and forth, back and forth.

The calming gesture wasn't working today. It'd been an hour since Mindy had told her she wasn't coming home, and Brooke was still trying not to freak out.

Mindy wanted the rest of the week.

Brooke had taken personal time off from work for these past few days, and that hadn't been a problem. Calling out for the rest of the week would be. Cole had a lot of good qualities. Patience wasn't one of them. He'd most definitely bitch about it.

Or he'd show up here in some misguided attempt to take her back. Sweet, but she didn't need him here. She had this.

Restless, she stepped out back to sit in the only shady spot on the deck. She had a glass of homemade lemonade—because when life gives you lemons, and all that—but wished it was something stronger.

A lot stronger.

She turned the glass around in her hands. Exactly twice. Then twice more. Rolling her eyes at herself, she drew in a deep breath of fresh air. Late May in Wildstone was just about perfect. Seventy-five degrees, with a light breeze that was scented with oak trees, sea air, and . . . more than a hint of lost hopes and dreams.

She didn't miss LA. That was the shocker. She didn't miss her current job, either. That wasn't a shock at all. No, the things she missed, like the weight of her camera around her neck and the ability to go adventuring, hadn't been within her reach in a long time. They were within her reach now. Or so she told herself. After all, she had her plan: Help Mindy and kick Linc's ass. Apologize to Garrett. But that was proving harder than she'd thought it would be, and she'd thought it'd be *really* hard. He'd been right in front of her, and instead of apologizing for what she'd done, she'd . . . She shook her head. She'd ended up tongue-tied and unable to bring it up at all. She had no idea what was wrong with her, but all her feelings for him from that time in her life seemed stuck in her throat. Fact was, she was crushing on him all over again, and that couldn't happen. She needed to handle this chapter of her life and move on. Go back to LA, talk to Cole about getting her old job back or one like it, and live life again.

She couldn't wait. She'd absolutely *loved* traveling the planet on someone else's dime, going home between gigs, keeping both worlds in motion. Loved the freedom that had allowed her to wander to her heart's content, but also have a place to call home.

That's what she missed.

With the kids still at camp for another few hours, she set her head back and closed her eyes, which was when she heard it, an odd *thunk, thunk, thunk*. Rising, she followed the sound to the side yard, passing the Slip 'N Slide, which appeared to have gotten bigger and longer than the last time she'd seen it.

The fencing was open rail. The neighbors to the back and right of the house were both horse ranchers. Garrett was to the left. He had enough land to ranch, but at the moment, it was just the house, the barn, and empty pasture.

Following the rhythmic noise, she made her way through a break in the fence, finding herself insatiably curious in a way she hadn't been when she'd grown up here. The barn door was open. Three cats sat in the doorway, one of them Princess Jasmine, all watching someone inside with intense interest. Brooke moved closer and solved one mystery.

Garrett stood in the center of the barn wielding an ax in the same way he'd handled his hard-knock life—with effortless ease. But that wasn't what stopped her in her tracks and had her heating up from the inside out. No, that honor went to the fact that he'd stripped off his shirt, leaving him in nothing but low-slung jeans and work boots as he attacked a mountain of wood rounds.

Once upon a time, he'd been tall and skinny to the point of gauntness. But Ann had nurtured him to good health with her home cooking and abundant and overflowing love, just as she had for every single kid she'd ever taken in.

Garrett had spent his teenhood as the third musketeer to Brooke and Mindy. At first, Mindy had crushed on him, privately lamenting his cluelessness to Brooke. Given how many girls Garrett had gone through during his Dumbass Boy years and how smart he'd been, Brooke had always known he'd never been clueless. But she'd played the game with Mindy so her sister hadn't been forced to face her first real rejection.

Then Linc had stepped up and claimed Mindy's heart, and that had been that. Mindy's friendship with Garrett had adapted, and become much more real. It wasn't until one night during the summer after Brooke had graduated from high school that *her* friendship with Garrett had adapted and taken on a whole new level.

They'd both agreed it was a one-time thing.

Especially since she'd been gone for long stretches of time for work, which was anything but work in her mind. Photographing the wild adventures of thrill seekers, she'd been sent on assignments with little more than a camera around her neck. It'd been heaven on earth.

And okay, yes, when she'd come home between gigs, she and Garrett had had another "one-time" thing. And then another. And so on, until it became a joke between them. But it had allowed them to keep their emotions in check. Until it didn't. By the time she was twenty-one, she'd realized Garrett was one of the few real things in her life, that he actually grounded her in the very best of ways, and she'd started to wonder . . . could they ever make it work for real?

Turned out that the question was moot, because she'd gone on to screw up and destroy everything.

Clearly *not* bogged down by the same memories, Garrett continued to wield the ax without so much as glancing at her or slowing down, which was actually an incredibly difficult thing to do. His sleek muscles bunched and released fluidly with every movement. The boy had turned into a man, and she wasn't above taking the time to appreciate that and his current rangy, cut look. He hadn't gotten that way in a gym, either. Nope, that body was born of years of manual labor and the heavy lifting required to build and renovate homes with your own two hands.

The cats were riveted, and so was she. He'd had some ink done. Bold black roman numerals across one pec, just above his heart. There was more script around his right biceps, and then just above that was the outline of rolling hills dotted with oaks. It signified Wildstone, she realized, betting that the numbers were the longitude and latitude of the town.

The afternoon sun slanted in through the barn's windows and the doorway in which she stood, giving the air a golden halo-y effect. Dust and wood particles floated around Garrett, landing on his shoulders, chest, and arms. This didn't appear to bother him in the least as he moved, seemingly oblivious to anything around him.

But she knew that wasn't true. He was never oblivious to anything. He knew she was there. It used to be that she could tell whenever he was near as well. She'd feel a shift in her force field in the form of goose bumps and an undeniable longing running through her veins.

He knew she was watching. He either didn't care or couldn't be bothered to acknowledge her.

She knew she should walk away, but she didn't. She continued to watch, and even from the distance she could see the roughness of his hands as he raised the ax high above his head and slammed it down powerfully, easily splitting a log. The sound reverberated off the barn walls and rang loudly in her ears.

"You should move back," he finally said, picking up another log and dropping it on the block. "This stuff flies everywhere."

"I've gotten dirty before."

He looked up from his task, the intensity of those hazel eyes still as piercing as ever, his expression unreadable. His body wasn't the only thing hard about this man. His heart was hardened, at least to her.

When she didn't move back as suggested, he merely shrugged and swung the ax again. Wood shards flew everywhere, hitting him in the chest and shoulders, but he carried on without a flinch. His skin shone with sweat from the exertion, and she bit her lower lip, remembering with sudden clarity what that skin tasted like under her tongue.

Suddenly, he tossed the ax aside. When he moved toward her, the air backed up in her lungs, even as unexpected hunger for him pooled inside her. Would he put those strong hands of his on her and pull her into him?

And what would she do? She had no idea.

No, that was a big, fat lie. She knew *exactly* what she'd do. She'd climb him like a tree.

With every step he took, her pulse kicked harder. Her heart was pounding in her ears. She looked at his mouth, knowing from experience that it would be both soft and hard, and suddenly she needed it on hers so badly she trembled. Once upon a time, her world hadn't worked without him in it. But she'd learned to be okay without him. In fact, she was really good at being alone. But what she wouldn't give for even an hour in his arms, knowing that he could make her forget all her problems. Hell, he could make her forget her name when he set his mind to it.

He stopped an inch from her, chest glistening. She could feel the heat pouring off his body and into her own chilled one.

"The kids?" he asked.

Her entire body tightened in anticipation of what that question meant. Was he asking if they were alone? "Still at camp," she said breathlessly, and slowly lifted her eyes to his.

She knew what was probably in her gaze. Lust. Longing. Need. And now she also knew what was in his.

Nothing.

Face carefully blank, he nodded. Then he gave a jerk of his chin to the cats and the three of them strode into the barn like royalty. Garrett waited for them and then . . . slowly slid the barn door closed, leaving him on one side of the wood and Brooke on the other.

AN HOUR LATER, she was in Mindy's kitchen slicing her fresh-out-of-the-oven sweet lemon bread, concentrating on making an even number of slices. When in doubt, she baked. And she did a damn good job of it, if she said so herself. Not up to her sister's standards, but *no one* was up to her sister's standards. Mindy could give Martha Stewart a run for her money in the baking department.

But Brooke had needed the distraction, desperately. Every

time her mind rewound to the barn, she flashed hot with mortification. "Not thinking about it," she reminded herself. She was going to find a way to say what she'd come to say and do what she needed to do to make sure Mindy was okay. Then she was out of here, and she wouldn't think about Garrett again.

Ever.

Her phone sat on the counter, judging her. "Stop looking at me like that," she said, still counting slices—*three, four* . . .

Her phone didn't respond, but the silence was filled with 'tude. She had a whole slew of texts and messages from Mindy, who, in spite of her chosen absence, still felt the need to direct from two hundred miles south in Los Angeles. There were also four missed calls from Cole, and a text that read, *Tell me you're home and are coming to work tomorrow.*

Dammit. She called Cole on speaker and kept slicing.

Cole answered with "Why do I have a bad feeling about this call?"

She made a big show of sounding sick, because telling him she was still in Wildstone would worry him enough to maybe actually drive up, and she didn't need him in protective mode. "Caught something from the kiddos," she said. "I need the rest of the week." She sniffled for good measure.

"You need more phlegm on that lie," Garrett said from behind her.

She went to cut piece number seven but slashed herself with the knife—proof that odd numbers were evil. The cut wasn't deep, just enough to completely annoy her.

"Shit," Garrett said, and grabbed the paper towels.

"It's nothing. Just a nick. A Band-Aid will do it," she said, having adopted Mason's motto. When you had a cut, a Band-Aid will do it. When your world fell apart, a Band-Aid will do it . . .

Garrett took her hand to inspect the injury. He'd put his shirt back on, which was definitely for the best. She could think much better when he had his shirt on. She pulled free.

"What's going on?" Cole asked tightly from the phone.

"Nothing," she said, glaring at Garrett. "My brain just has too many tabs open." She jabbed a finger at the door, an obvious demand for Garrett to get the hell out.

"Why don't you sound sick anymore?" Cole asked.

"It's . . . complicated," she said, and grimaced. "And hard to explain."

"Uh-huh. Maybe you'll try over dinner tonight. I've got veggie tofu stir-fry leftovers."

Garrett, who hadn't budged in spite of her repeated and dramatic gesturing in the direction of the door, made a face, probably at the tofu. Cole was a vegetarian. Garrett was most definitely not. The sexy jerk took up his favorite position leaning against the counter, looking better than the sweet lemon bread, damn him, as he casually reached out and stole slice number six.

Which left an odd number of slices. Clueless to her turmoil, he added a slab of butter to his piece and dug in.

"Brooke?" Cole asked.

She turned her back on the sight of Garrett inhaling her bread. "I'm still in Wildstone." There. The truth.

Silence from the phone.

"Cole?" she asked. "You okay?"

"Are you going to come back?"

"*Yes,*" she said definitively.

"Then I'm okay. What's going on, sweetness?"

Incredibly aware of Garrett in the room, she drew a deep breath. Cole cared, deeply, and that caring was in his tone and in everything he *wasn't* saying. He was a good enough guy to assume she was a grown-up and would tell him if she needed help.

So maybe he didn't know her quite as well as she thought. "What's going on is that I've got some things to take care of up here. I need more time. That's all."

"Do you need me?"

She closed her eyes against the onslaught of guilt. He would take her as is, right now, if she wanted that. She'd told him she wasn't meant for a deep relationship, and he'd taken her at her word. She could love him for that alone. "I'm okay."

He paused, then simply said, "Call if you need me," and disconnected.

A beat of silence reigned in the kitchen. Then Garrett spoke. "You're still good at that."

She turned to face him. He'd indeed taken a second piece.

"To leave an even number of slices," he said quietly.

She lifted a startled gaze to his. *He knew.*

"I've always known," he said.

She'd have to dwell on that later, how her own family had never figured it out, but he had. "Good at what?" she asked instead, ignoring the quiver in her belly.

"Keeping people who care about you at a distance."

"Cole's my boss."

Garrett licked some crumbs and butter from his thumb and shrugged, like it was no concern of his what Cole was or wasn't to her. "You still make amazing sweet lemon bread."

Her phone rang again and she glanced at the screen. "It's Mindy."

"So answer it," he said.

"I can't—she wants to know if I made Millie floss this morning and I didn't."

Something about his amused snort made her hit answer on speaker. "Hey," she said, in a false upbeat tone.

This had Garrett's small smile spreading, the ass.

"Hey back," Mindy said. "Why are you talking with your fake happy voice?"

"I don't have a fake happy voice."

"You *so* have a fake happy voice."

Garrett nodded in agreement.

She flipped him the bird. "What's up?" she asked her sister. "I'm super busy keeping your children alive."

"I'd freak about that," Mindy said, "but when I talked to Millie, she said you were the best and that I could take my time coming home."

"Millie doesn't know shit. You should most definitely *not* take your time coming home."

"You're not swearing in front of my kids."

"You know what?" Brooke said. "I am. I'm swearing in front of your kids. Come home and kick me out."

Garrett laughed.

"Who's that?" Mindy asked.

"Your annoying-as-shit neighbor," Brooke said, glaring at him.

"Oh good, you're there, too," Mindy said with obvious relief. "Listen, I was going to send Rafe over with food for the next few days. He's the chef and owner of the new Mexican place in town. Be nice to him, Brooke, okay? He's single and I'm going to set you two up. Don't you think they'd be great together, Garrett?"

Garrett shrugged. "Sure, if she likes assholes."

"Oh crap, really?" Mindy asked. "He's an asshole? I guess that makes sense. He's way too hot. Okay, no worries. How about Dennis? Remember him from high school? He runs his own landscaping company. He'd be perfect for her, right?"

"Right," Garrett said. "And I'm sure his fiancée wouldn't mind at all."

"*Seriously?*" Mindy asked. "How did I miss the fiancée part? Damn. I thought if I fixed Brooke up, she'd stick."

"Standing right here," Brooke said.

"Don't worry, I'll think of someone. Garrett, you think, too, okay? You must know a guy suited for her."

Garrett, who hadn't taken his eyes off Brooke, kept mum.

Brooke rolled her eyes. "I'm here to help you," she told her ungrateful sister. "So get your shit together, woman." She disconnected and put her hands on her hips. "And you're here why?" she asked Garrett, baffled. Irritated. *Embarrassed.*

"It's my job."

Right. Unlike her presence in his barn, his presence here in this house had nothing to do with her. "I thought general contractors ran their companies from behind a desk, not getting their own hands dirty building homes," she said.

"Being behind a desk isn't my thing."

Something she knew firsthand from all those long, hot summers they'd spent climbing every mountain and rafting every river within a couple of hundred miles of here.

"I don't build homes, I renovate them," he said. "I like to do the work myself, with my own hands. Fixing something old is far more satisfying to me than building new." His phone rang and he pulled it from his pocket, eyed the screen, and blew out a breath.

"Hey," he answered, his voice soft and . . . *sweet*? "Yeah, I planned to be there, just like I promised you the other day. Sure. Tonight, then." Disconnecting, he shoved the phone back in his pocket.

And because she couldn't help herself, she asked, "Wife? Girlfriend?"

"Neither."

"Liar."

"Nope," he said. "That's *your* specialty."

She let him walk away because it was true. She *was* lying. Or at least omitting. Because even though he believed he knew everything that had happened to her, he was wrong. Not that she intended to tell him—or anyone—anything different.

CHAPTER 6

He was screwed, upside down and backward, screwed
in every way but the way he wanted to be.

I t's not you, it's me."

This wasn't the first time Garrett had heard the line, but
usually *he* was the one saying it. He looked across the high-
top table at Lisa Weston. Over the past month or so, they'd
been out three times. On night one, before their drinks had
even been delivered, she'd told him this wasn't a friends-with-
benefits situation because they weren't friends, just benefits.

Not exactly a hardship for him, since she was sexy and fun.

On night two, she'd reminded him of their deal. In fact, her
exact quote had been "You give good benefits, so let's leave it
at that."

Again, fine with him.

On night three, there'd been no talking at all. Even better.

Tonight was night four. They were in the Whiskey River Bar and Grill in downtown Wildstone—the word *downtown* being a bit of a deception as the main strip was two streets wide and two blocks long. And because Whiskey River was the only bar in town, it was packed. But Lisa wasn't seated with him. She stood tableside wearing an apron, the pockets stuffed with tips and an order pad. She worked as a waitress in the restaurant part of the bar and was on a break.

From everything, apparently, including him.

"Actually," she said. "I take that back. It *is* you."

"Me?"

"Yes, Man of Mystery and Very Few Words." She shook her head, sighed, and put her hand over his. "Look, you're great, okay? And better yet, you're not only employed, you're successful, and your work's hugely sought-after. And you look sexy as hell in a tool belt."

"I'll add that to my résumé," he said dryly. "But if I'm all that, what's the problem?"

Her smile was just a little sad as she sat and looked at him. "We go out, we sleep together, and after, you get up and go home and I don't hear from you for days or even a week, unless I contact you."

All true, although when she said it out loud like that, it made him sound like an asshole. "You made it clear you didn't want to get serious," he said.

She met his gaze. "I lied."

He hadn't expected that. She'd told him they weren't going

to be a thing, and he'd taken her at her word without putting much thought into it. But he could see by her expression that he'd hurt her. Not what he'd intended.

"I want love," she said.

Hell. Okay, yeah, they had a problem. He wanted a family—actually, he wanted that quite badly. But to get there, he had to fall in love. Love hadn't exactly worked out for him. In fact, love had led to a whole lot of loss. His mom. Ann. And then there were the people who'd *chosen* to walk away from him, like his dad. And Brooke. And in a way, being walked away from had been even worse, and Brooke being back in town had stirred all that up inside him again. "Lisa—"

"Don't panic," she said. "I get that this is my fault. I wanted you, and I thought I could sneak my way into your heart." She paused, clearly waiting for a response.

He didn't have one, at least not one she'd like. His heart was guarded. The last person he'd let "sneak" in was Brooke. He could admit he'd been half in love with her from the day he met her. Her adventurous spirit had drawn him in, but what had held him spellbound was her innate sweetness, proving quite the contrast to her bravado. Up until that point, he hadn't had much sweetness in his life, and no one had asked so little of him and rewarded him so much for what he'd given.

Lisa shook her head. "It was a mistake—my mistake, because you, Garrett Montgomery, are emotionally deficient."

He thought about that on the drive home. He opened up to people when it suited him. Didn't he? He strained to remember the last time he'd done so, but couldn't.

Huh.

He pulled into Ann's driveway. No, *his* driveway, he corrected himself. Ann had been struggling financially, unable to keep up with her mortgage, not to mention the house itself and all the land that came with it. At the time, the market had been shit. She'd been upsidedown on a loan.

It'd taken some doing, but he'd bought the place just before she lost it. For most of his life, everything he'd owned could fit into a backpack, which he'd taken with him from foster home to foster home.

Until Ann.

He was twelve when he'd landed on her doorstep after a run of really bad homes. She'd kept him. Given him his first taste of home cooking, his first affection from an authority figure, and his first real home.

No way could he have let her place go to the bank.

So he'd bought it for more than what it was worth at the time, which had allowed her to stay in her home in her old age as she wanted. Not living far from her in a rental in town, he'd been able to help her out as needed after work and in between jobs. She'd wanted to renovate, and he'd just gotten started two years ago, when she died. That's when he'd moved in.

Shrugging off the memories, he entered through the front door and was greeted by three pissy old ladies who tried to tell him he'd starved them half to death. He sighed and crouched low, petting each in turn.

He didn't turn on the lights. He didn't need to, and also, the electricity in the entryway was faulty. He needed to get on the renovations, but he hadn't. Hadn't wanted to. He'd kept the house with the idea of someday filling it up with his own family. Except that hadn't happened. Probably because apparently he was "emotionally deficient."

Feeling twice his thirty years, he stripped and stepped into the shower. He stood there, head bent, letting the water hit his shoulders and back until it cooled. As he stepped out, he heard a knock at his back door. Wrapping a towel around his hips, he strode through the house and into the kitchen, stopping short at the sight of Brooke looking at him through the square glass window.

The woman who'd indelibly changed his life every bit as much as Ann had.

Growing up next door to the Lemon sisters had been both the best and worst thing to ever happen to him. He'd thought they were both a little crazy, but in a good way. Their closeness had been magic to him, a kid who'd had no family to call his own.

He'd been their neighbor, their ride-the-bus buddy and eager cohort in crime. As they'd all hit their teens, he'd known Mindy had sometimes crushed on him, but she'd been a little too tightly wound for him. Brooke, the easygoing, fun-loving one, had definitely been more his style, but she'd been too young. So they'd all just been friends.

Mostly.

Okay, he and Mindy had been just friends. He and Brooke . . . well, he'd lived through it and even he couldn't put exact words to what they'd been to each other.

From the other side of the door, Brooke was watching him watch her. Her wavy honey-blond hair had been wrestled into a messy bun on top of her head, but more than a few silky strands had tumbled loose, framing her face and giving her a tousled, just-out-of-bed look. She was wearing an oversized scoop-neck heather-gray tee that had fallen off one shoulder and a pair of knock-'em-dead denim short-shorts—emphasis on *short*. Her body was slim, athletic, and mouthwatering. The entire package screamed "sweet girl next door," but Brooke had too much of an edge to be the girl next door.

As he well knew. Something else he knew: He didn't trust himself to keep his emotions in check when it came to her.

When he didn't make a move, she raised an empty measuring cup. "Got milk?" she asked through the glass, with not a little irony in her voice.

He let out a long breath. Her face was freshly scrubbed and makeup-free. She looked the same as she had when he'd fallen head over heels for her, but he'd hardened himself to her. She'd destroyed him once, and he had no intention of letting her get another shot. With a good amount of annoyance at the both of them, he opened the door.

"Hey," she said softly, her small smile giving him a chest pain.

He shook his head, because this was the problem, his problem. He had a hard time resisting her, always had. "Don't do that."

"Do what?"

"Act like we're still friends."

Her smile faded. "Okay."

Feeling like a complete dick, he took the measuring cup and filled it up from the gallon of milk he'd bought the day before. He made sure to pour an even eight ounces before turning to hand it back, where he caught her staring at him.

She had the good grace to look guilty. "I'm sorry. But you still have the best butt in Wildstone—which is annoying as hell, by the way."

"I think we both know that's not even my best body part."

She snorted, defusing his tension with that one little sound. He shook his head. "You were staring at my ass like you wanted to bite it." He paused and sent her a knowing look. "*Again.*"

"Hey, *one* time! And it was a very long time ago!"

He couldn't help it—he grinned at the memory, one of his few memories of her that didn't give him a pang. "You nibbled on lots of things back then."

She blushed—which was fascinating—and stared at the milk he'd poured for her, running her finger over the eight-ounce mark. "We're not like that anymore," she said softly.

"No kidding."

Something crossed her face at that, something he didn't expect—sadness and regret—and seeing it wiped the amusement out from beneath him. Her eyes were the same deep, lose-yourself-in-them green with gold specks floating around. She had a slight sunburn across her cheeks and nose—probably from walking the beach with the kids, which he'd heard about from Mindy when she'd called to ask him to spy on Brooke. He'd refused.

"I didn't expect that you'd still be in Wildstone," she said quietly. "I sort of assumed you'd be long gone."

"Why?"

"I don't know. I shouldn't have assumed that at all given how much you always did love it here." She gestured around her. "I'm glad you're in this house. It makes sense, and it suits you. You're renovating."

"No."

She took in the tarps, the ladder, the tools scattered about, and gave him a questioning look.

"The project's on hold," he said.

"Why?"

He was saved from explaining something he didn't understand himself by Princess Jasmine, the only one of the three cats interested in a newcomer past bedtime. She rubbed herself around Brooke's ankles, demanding love.

Brooke dropped to her knees and gave it freely. "What a sweet thing you are." She looked up at Garrett. "Never pegged you as a cat guy. How did that happen?"

"You ask a lot of questions."

"And you called me a monster," she said lightly, though he had the feeling she felt anything but light.

"You were helping your niece look for the candy you'd just eaten," he said. "And you know I was kidding."

"Do I?"

They stared at each other, but he wasn't going to touch that one. No way. Brooke had left him without a word and hadn't looked back. Like he'd been nothing to her. Less than nothing. But hell if he'd give her the satisfaction of explaining herself now, all these years later.

They stared at each other some more, and when he felt himself wanting to ask her questions, too—like, was Cole really just her boss?—he forced himself to turn away. Moving to the laundry room off the kitchen, he pulled a fresh pair of jeans from the dryer. Dropping his towel, he pulled them on.

The choked sound from behind him meant Brooke had

gotten a good look. He turned back to find her gaze unabashedly still on him.

She didn't have a false sense of modesty in her, never had. She'd always been very comfortable in her own skin, something he'd found extremely attractive. He loved a woman who owned her sexuality. In fact, the two of them had discovered their sexuality together, and she'd rocked his world and changed his life. He used to think she'd changed it for the better, but now he wasn't so sure.

"How's Ann?" she asked.

He stilled, surprised she didn't know.

Taking in his expression, her eyes widened. "Oh no," she murmured softly. "When?"

"Two years ago."

"I'm sorry, Garrett. I know what she meant to you."

"I've lost people I love before."

She looked away for a beat and then turned back to him, eyes shadowed. "I was hoping we could talk about that."

He shook his head.

"But—"

"Leave it alone, Brooke. It's best that way."

Her eyes were guarded now, mouth grim. She was, what, twenty-eight? Almost twenty-nine? And yet she still looked the same as when she'd been twenty-one, the last time he'd seen her.

She was running her finger along the outside of the measuring cup, right at the eight-ounce mark, back and forth, back and forth. He hadn't been sure if she still needed things in even numbers. Not that she'd ever told him about her OCD. As far as he knew, she'd never told anyone. Brooke just did as she did—accepted that she was different, and kept to herself about it.

"Thanks for the milk," she said.

He nodded. "So you'll be sticking around a little bit longer."

"Until Mindy's back. As you heard, she needs a few more days."

And she'd given them to her. "That's . . . kind of you," he said. "And selfless."

"Well, we all knew I had to grow up sometime, right?" She looked away. "And anyway, I don't really mind. The kids . . ." She glanced down at the kid monitor hooked on her belt. "They're pretty amazing."

He nodded, something warming for her deep inside without his permission.

"Anyway, thanks again," she said, toasting him with the milk. "Maddox won't eat his cereal without it in the morning, or at least that's what I *think* he was telling me with all the barking." She turned to go, and he let his gaze run hungrily down the body he'd once known as well as his own, feeling a soul-deep yearning to reach for her and remind them both of what they'd been missing.

"Now who's looking at whose ass?" she asked as she walked off into the night.

He heard his own rough laugh, because that's exactly what he'd been doing as she left him alone with his thoughts. Staring at her and trying to land on how he felt. He knew how he'd felt about her in the past.

He just had no idea how he felt about her in the here and now.

THE NEXT DAY, Garrett was outside Mindy and Linc's kitchen, cutting tiles for the master bathroom. During a lull from the loud tile cutter, he heard an angry voice coming through the open kitchen window.

Brooke.

"Don't you judge my nephew on my past behaviors," she was saying, clearly on the phone. "So *I* was a handful, I get it. But Mason's not, he's an angel—" There was a pause. "Okay, yes, I get it, he's wearing his sister's dress. But if it's okay with her, then I don't see what business it is of yours— No, you can't take this up with his mom. I'm in charge right now, so you get to deal with me, and I say the kid gets to wear what the kid wants to wear—" She paused. "Oh," she said, much softer and without attitude. Almost . . . apologetic. "No, I didn't realize today was horseback riding. Yes, I can see why a dress probably wasn't the best choice. Sure. I'll send him better equipped tomorrow."

Garrett had to laugh as he started to go back to his work, but the total and complete silence coming out that kitchen window was filled with a strained sadness he couldn't ignore.

Don't do it, man. Be smart. Just go back to work.

He didn't go back to work. He entered the kitchen, which was empty. He couldn't have said why, but he went in search of the prickly, frustrating, irritating woman who could still drive him crazy, and found the living room glass slider open. Stepping out onto the deck, he surveyed the large yard. Mindy and Linc hadn't done much with the land, although he and Linc had sure managed to make the most of it, creating the huge Slip 'N Slide for the kids. It was an ongoing project, getting bigger weekly.

Past that, the place was lined in the back with huge overgrown oak trees. The previous generation of Lemons had added lemon trees as well, and then there was a hill that led down to a valley of wineries and vineyards stretching as far as the eye could see.

At the base of one of the lemon trees sat Brooke, knees up, arms hugging her legs as she stared out at the view. He was about twenty feet from her when she spoke without looking at him. "Go away."

Yeah. He really, *really* wanted to do that. Instead he moved closer still and crouched down at her side, balanced on the balls of his feet.

"You never listen." Her voice was low and, dammit, quavering. She had dark circles under her eyes. She looked exhausted.

A pissed-off Brooke he knew how to handle. But a sad Brooke . . . he didn't have a clue. "I *always* listen," he said. "I just don't always agree. Do I need to go beat someone up at Mason's camp?"

Her response was a low, mirthless laugh. "No. Turns out that was my bad."

He shrugged. "Mistakes happen."

"Not to Mindy."

He laughed, and utterly unable to help himself, reached out and stroke a wayward strand of hair from her face, tucking it behind her ear.

Brooke stilled at the touch, then lifted her gaze to his, her eyes suspiciously shiny, and so green it almost hurt to hold her gaze.

And yet he didn't look away. "Mindy would be the first to tell you that's not true," he said quietly. "She makes mistakes. We all do."

"You don't."

"I do," he said.

"When?"

"You're not sleeping," he said instead of answering.

She shrugged.

"Why?"

"I don't know. Maybe because I'm a monster."

"Brooke, I was kidding. You're not a monster."

"I am. I lost our baby."

He let out a slow, careful breath. He was in no way prepared for this walk down Painful Memories Road, but neither could he turn away from it.

Or her.

They'd never talked about it—not for lack of trying on his part. She'd been twenty-one and had been back in Wildstone a whole week that time. They'd made the most of each and every night while still pretending it was just a "one-time thing."

But deep down, he'd known he'd wanted more—a lot more. He'd never known what she'd wanted. She'd kept her own counsel.

Two months later, she'd shown up again, pale and sick and practically vibrating with tension. When she told him she was pregnant and that he was the only one she'd been with in the past year, he'd somehow been both terrified and elated at the same time. But not wanting to pressure her, he'd let her take the lead on what she wanted to do. Her body, her decision. When she'd put her hands over her belly in a protective gesture, he'd offered to marry her.

She couldn't have committed to a dentist appointment back then. Hell, neither could he, for that matter, but he'd been willing to try.

And, shocking him, so had she.

That same day, she'd been called back to work. Having not had time to process any of it, they'd decided to keep the pregnancy to themselves for the time being, much like their so-called relationship. Brooke told her bosses she had to give up the climbing and dangerous jobs and keep her feet firmly on the ground, and they'd promised her it wasn't going to be a problem.

And indeed, the job she'd gone on, taking photos from the safety of a helicopter over Machu Picchu for a crossover special between the Travel Network and Nat Geo, should have been a piece of cake. But there'd been a surprise storm and the helicopter had been forced to try to land at high altitude. Gale-force winds had taken them out. They'd crash-landed, and the survivors had been stranded on a steep precipice for twenty-four hours before being rescued.

The conditions had been brutal. Brooke's injuries had been more so. Concussion, cracked ribs, pierced lung, broken leg, and internal trauma that had damaged her spleen beyond repair, pierced a piece of her liver, and some other things that had culminated in her losing the baby and nearly her life.

And none of it had been her fault.

Garrett, along with her family, had flown to the hospital in Peru, terrified she'd die. But by the time they got there, she was out of her first of two surgeries and aware enough to make sure no one would mention the baby she'd lost to her family. Only he and the doctors had known.

As far as he was aware, she'd never told another soul, not even Mindy.

When she was finally liberated from the hospital and had come home to recover, she'd brushed off everyone's concerns, saying she was fine.

With hindsight being twenty-twenty, along with seven years of questionable personal growth and maturity, Garrett had come to realize that Brooke had been too young to deal, so she'd carefully buried it deep and convinced everyone that all was good.

One of her best lies.

She'd left as soon as she could, and because she was a master at evasion when she wanted to be, she'd managed to successfully avoid him every time she'd been in town since.

Which had been few and far between.

"You didn't lose the baby on purpose," he said carefully. "Tell me you're not blaming yourself."

She didn't answer.

Shit.

"Brooke," he said softly.

She covered her face. "Don't be nice to me about it—I'll fall apart. You're mad at me, and you should be."

"Stop." He pulled her hands from her face and held on to them, squeezing gently. "How could you think I'd be mad at you for losing the baby? My God, Bee, is that what you think of me? I'm *that* guy, that selfish bastard who'd blame you for what happened?"

She stared at him, her eyes luminescent—whether at the use of his old nickname for her or his question, he had no idea. "Then why are you mad?" she whispered.

"Brooke . . ." He shook his head. "There's no reason to go there."

"But there is." She drew in an unsteady breath, like she was fortifying herself. "You're part of the reason I'm here."

"What are you talking about?"

"I promised Mindy I'd take the kids for a few days to give her a break. I was thinking Disneyland, but while I was driving, I started to think about my sister, and how hard she always tries. If Mindy the control freak can ask for help, then I could man up, too."

"About what?"

Her gaze met his and she let out another long, purposeful breath. "For a long time now, I've known I need to make some changes. My life . . . it's not what I thought it would be. So I formulated a plan and changed lanes, and came north."

He was fascinated in spite of himself. "What was the plan?"

She held up a finger. "One, to face Wildstone again." Then a second finger. "Two, help Mindy by kicking Linc's ass."

He choked out a laugh.

She held up a third finger. "And three . . . apologize to you."

He didn't know what to make of that. "That's only three things," he said. "There's no way you made a list with an odd number of things on it."

She looked surprised at how well he knew her, which he could admit rankled. "You're right," she said. "Four, I want to return to LA and get my old job—and my life—back. The life I've been missing."

He wasn't sure how to feel about that. "What's the apology for?"

She drew a deep breath. "For what happened after the helicopter crash. Not just for how I left, or that I stayed gone. But how I ruined you and me." She swallowed hard. "And that I never acknowledged that you'd been hurt by the crash, too, and the loss of our baby, every bit as much as I was."

He hadn't realized until that very moment how much he'd needed to hear that from her, but she was breathing roughly, the air hitching in and out of her lungs, and her eyes were shiny, so shiny he could have drowned in them. He pulled her in and tried to soothe her with his body heat. "Losing the baby wasn't your fault. You're hearing me, right?" He'd say it as many times as she needed him to.

When she didn't look at him, he gently wrapped his fist up in her hair and gently tugged her face to his. "Listen to me, okay? Listen and really hear me—the crash wasn't your fault. The injuries, all you went through . . . losing the baby," he said carefully. "None of it was your doing."

She closed her eyes. "We both know how I felt about getting pregnant."

He did know. She'd been clear on that. When she found out, she'd been upset, in shock, and not at all sure she wanted to be a mom. At the time he'd had zero idea of how *he* felt about it, but in the end, it hadn't mattered.

In the years since, he'd had plenty of time to dwell, and he'd come to a realization. He wanted to be a father someday. He wanted that quite badly. But when it was the right time, with the right woman. "You were young—"

"Twenty-one," she said. "Old enough to conceive that baby, and old enough to face the consequences. And what did I do? The day I found out, I—" She squeezed her eyes shut and tears leaked out, pouring down her cheeks. With a frustrated sound, she covered her face, trembling from head to toe with suppressed emotion. "I wished our baby away."

Heart aching, he pressed his forehead to hers. "It doesn't work like that, Brooke. None of what happened was your fault. Please tell me you know that."

"But what happened after was. I walked away from Wildstone, from my family. From you."

And he'd never understood why. He'd assumed she'd simply decided to put it behind her. All of it, including him. Her gaze was shattered and haunted, and his breath caught at the pain she'd kept hidden. "I really didn't want to come back here and face this," she said. "You have no idea how close I was to going to Disneyland."

"But you came here."

She shrugged off what he actually considered to have been an incredible gesture on her part. "When I got here, I felt . . ." She shook her head. "*Everything*. It all came back, what I lost by walking away. I destroyed my relationship with Mindy. And I did the same thing to us. I'm sorry, Garrett. I know I should've said all this a long time ago, that it's way too late, but—"

He set a finger over her lips. "There's nothing to forgive," he said truthfully. "Your body, your life, your choice, Brooke. Always."

"No, you can't say that," she murmured. "You don't know."

There were tears in her voice again, and through the mixed feelings that her presence caused, he ached for her. "What don't I know, Bee?" he asked softly. "You can tell me. You can tell me anything."

"Can I?"

How could she not know?

Because you've been a dick. Aloof. Distant. You made it clear that we weren't going to be anything to each other, not ever again. He took her hand and pressed it to his chest. "Yes, you can. Tell me why you stayed away so long. Tell me why you wouldn't let me back in."

"I can't get pregnant again. I can't have another baby."

The words ran through his brain for several long seconds before they penetrated, and even then, he was stunned into silence. "I . . . didn't know," he finally said.

"I know." Her eyes drifted shut. "I didn't want you to. I didn't want anyone to know. I didn't want pity when I didn't even fully understand how it would affect me."

He stared at her, wishing she'd open her eyes and look at him. "You should have told me. Or at the very least, told your family. You shouldn't have gone through that alone."

"I wanted to be alone," she said, and finally met his gaze. "I have no regrets about that, Garrett. And if I had to do it all over again, I'd do the same thing. Actually, if I could go back and change anything, it would be to not tell you about the pregnancy to begin with, so that you didn't have to suffer the loss, too."

He was surprised by how much she could still shock him. Hurt him. Rising, he turned away. He'd thought he no longer cared, that he'd moved on, but seeing her again and hearing what she'd gone through all alone had proved him wrong. A fact that, in turn, scared the hell out of him. Her walking away from him had left its indelible mark, had changed him, made him more protective of his heart. The heart that at one point had beat in his chest for *her*.

And it was beating for her right now, too, but in frustration—something that he didn't know what to do with. "That's not how relationships work, Brooke. You share the good *and* the bad. Especially the bad. You lean on each other and get through shit because of it. You don't do it all alone—you've got to understand that by now. Hell," he said with a rough laugh, "who am I kidding? Clearly, you still don't know that at all." He scrubbed a hand down his face. "I wanted to help you through it. I wanted to be there for you."

Her face crumpled. "I know, and I'm so sorry—"

"No. Stop." He took a deep breath. "I get it. And thank you for the apology, but I don't need it." He rose to his full height, but she grabbed his hand and tugged until he looked at her again.

"I was trying to protect you," she said. "We were young and stupid and got pregnant. People would have talked."

"I never cared about that. I only cared about you."

She stood up, too. "That would never have held up, considering what you now know."

He stared at her. "Are you suggesting that I would've wanted out because you lost the ability to physically bear a child?"

"Yes."

"Jesus." He shoved his hands through his hair, not even sure what to say. "What did I do so wrong that you could think that of me?"

She shook her head. "Don't forget—I saw you, Garrett, I saw your face when I told you. You were way more excited about the pregnancy than I was."

He let out a sound of stunned disbelief. "That doesn't mean I wouldn't have wanted you if you couldn't have babies, Brooke.

I wouldn't have cared about that. I didn't care about anything other than making sure you were okay."

She gave a slow head shake. She didn't believe him. And if there was one thing he knew about Brooke, it was that you couldn't change her mind unless she wanted to change it. He looked at her, *really* looked, and felt something clench inside him, something that lessened his frustration. Her dark circles had dark circles. She wore no makeup. Her eyes were red from crying, but it was more than that. She looked beyond exhausted. "Okay, seriously," he said, "when was the last time you slept?"

She shrugged. "What day is it?"

Not willing to play, he shook his head and took her into Mindy and Linc's house. "Which bedroom are you using?" he asked.

She didn't answer.

"Brooke."

"The living room couch."

His brow furrowed. "Why?"

"I didn't want to dislodge any of the kids. And I didn't want to sleep in my mom and dad's old room, which I realize is Mindy and Linc's now, but still. The couch is fine."

"The couch isn't fine," he said. His personal feelings aside, it bothered him that she had so thoroughly ignored her own needs as if she felt she didn't deserve to have them. "It's uncomfortable as hell and has been since the day Mindy brought it home from some sale warehouse." Still holding on to her, he strode back out the kitchen door and across the side yard to his own kitchen door.

Where they were immediately bombarded by a trio of *meows*.

"They love you," Brooke said.

"No, they stalk me. Ali McClaw and Chairwoman Miao were Ann's. I'd like to rehome them, but I'm pretty sure they'll refuse to go anywhere."

"You would never abandon them. Or anyone or anything that needed a place to call home."

Uncomfortable with the realization that she knew him every bit as well as he knew her, he shook his head in automatic denial. "Don't kid yourself. I'd dump them in a hot minute for a dog."

The cats ignored this for the bullshit it was. So did Brooke. She hadn't taken the time to look around last night. He knew because he'd been watching her so closely. But she looked now, and he knew what she was seeing. Just like Mindy and Linc's house, this one had changed since she'd seen it last. The flowery wallpaper was gone, as was the beat-up old furniture. This version was much more masculine, the furniture big and comfy, all in deep colors. Shelves were lined with books and mementos, along with photographs, and he wondered if she was surprised to see herself in several of them. He took her upstairs to his bedroom.

"Someone's a little sure of himself," she said, remaining in the doorway.

"Trust me, we're not going there. You need some sleep before you fall over."

Ali McClaw jumped onto the bed with an *oof* and sat on his pillow.

"Ignore her," Garrett told Brooke. "Although I wouldn't try to dislodge her."

She looked amused. "Are you afraid of your own cat?"

"*Ann's* cat," he corrected. "And hell yes, I'm afraid of her. She sits on my head, shoves her butt in my face, bites my feet, stretches out across my chest whenever she feels like it, puts her entire face in my dinner, and if I so much as touch one single little toe bean, she bitch slaps my hand, like, how dare I not respect her personal space?" He came to the doorway to get her, towing her to the bed. "*Sleep,*" he said. "I'll wake you in time to get the kids." Then he turned to go.

"You're leaving?"

"Yes."

She climbed onto the bed. He had to look away because he was going to walk away, even if it killed him. She'd been through hell, and he ached for her to the depths of his soul. But that didn't mean he trusted her with his heart. Because he didn't. Couldn't. Not ever again.

He was just shutting the door behind him when he heard it, a tiny little telltale sniff that she'd clearly tried to smother, but couldn't.

Not your problem. But he couldn't seem to get his feet to take him away, no matter that she'd done that exact thing to him. Kicking off his boots, he lay down on the bed with her.

She was trembling with the force of holding herself together. "Hey," he said quietly, rubbing his hand up and down her back. "The past is the past. It's done and gone. Life moves on, and it's okay for you to move on as well. You're not a monster, Brooke. I never should have said that."

This caused another sniff.

With a rough sigh, he pulled her to him, her back against his chest, spooning her as he wrapped an arm around her and held her tight. "Let it go," he murmured, running a hand down her arm. "Just let it all go."

She exhaled the breath she'd been holding and shuddered as the storm broke free, leaving her sobbing as if her heart were breaking. His certainly was.

"I'm sorry I didn't tell you all of it," she hiccuped out, clutching him. "But I couldn't tell anyone. I was just . . ."

"What?"

"Ashamed."

Ah hell, she was killing him. "Never be ashamed of who you are," he murmured into her hair. "That's your parents' job."

She choked out a laugh and craned her neck to look at him with those beautiful, drenched eyes, and in that moment he knew. He was screwed, upside down and backward, screwed in every way but the way he wanted to be.

CHAPTER 7

"Worried about shrinkage?"

Brooke jerked awake and practically had to peel herself off the ceiling. *Garrett's* ceiling. *What the . . .*

Three sets of narrowed cat eyes glared at her for daring to disrupt their beauty sleep. Brooke shook her head, confused and befuddled from the first deep sleep she'd had in more days than she could count. She eyed the time. It'd been three hours.

The kids!

She leapt out of bed and realized she had a sticky note on the center of her chest, stuck to her upside down so she could read it: *I got the kids, and Brittney's back. She's with them and I'm working.*

She let out a shaky breath as she looked around her. There was no evidence that Garrett had taken a nap with her, but she knew he had. She'd dreamed about that sinewy hard body holding her close, keeping her warm, his calm infusing her with the same. That calm fled in a single heartbeat when she remembered the brush of his mouth against the nape of her neck.

She rubbed her hand to the spot and realized she had goose bumps. The very best kind of goose bumps. But clearly the kiss had just been part of the dream, because though Garrett might've held her while she slept and kept life at bay for a little while, the mental mileage between them couldn't be bridged. Not after how she'd walked away. Yes, she'd apologized, and he'd seemingly accepted it with a grace she wasn't sure she deserved.

But too much time had gone by, not to mention that she wasn't the same person anymore. But sometimes, like now, when she was fuzzy with sleep and especially vulnerable, she ached for all she'd lost. Her sense of home. Garrett. Her sister . . .

Her mom said she and Mindy had been like a pack of kittens: They couldn't stand to be together, but they couldn't stand to be apart, either. They'd been quite the set, the two of them against the world.

She missed that relationship deeply. And it was hard, so hard, to be with her sister's beautiful, wonderful babies, because every second of every day she spent here, they wormed their way into her heart, and she was reminded on a visceral level that she'd never have her own.

It was a terrible thing to feel, and she knew it, but it didn't stop the emotions. Instead it cut to the deep insecurities she hid, the little whisper inside her that cruelly taunted her—
you're not whole.

One of the things Brooke had always prided herself on was how capable she was. She could do anything she set her mind to. But that was no longer true. She'd lost a major option in the crash, and now it was gone forever, leaving a void, an empty place inside her.

Garrett had been every bit as important in her life as Mindy, not that she'd ever told him so, and walking away from him had been more painful than her injuries. Far more. To survive, she'd learned to bury her feelings deep.

It wasn't smart to let those feelings surface now. But knowing that and keeping herself distant were two very different things.

Leaving Garrett's house, she walked across the yard and entered Mindy's kitchen.

Brittney was at the table with Maddox in her lap and Mason at her side. Princess Millie was seated across from them, and they were all playing cards while Ketchup the Tortoise ate from his tin. The twentyish-year-old at the table was everything Mindy had said she was: fit, cute, and perky.

"Go fish!" Millie yelled cheerfully. She was wearing dishwashing gloves, for which Brooke needed no explanation—clearly the cards had germs.

"Hey," Brooke said, and the kids rushed to greet her with hugs and, in Maddox's case, with two extremely sticky hands. It took everything she had not to go wash up, but Millie was watching her very carefully for just that urge, so Brooke had to mentally shake off the invisible germs.

"I'm so glad you're back in town," she said to Brittney after introducing herself. "Mindy told me you go to your college classes in the morning and then you come here. I'll be so grateful for your help until she gets back."

Brittney rose to her feet. Her smile was nervous now, and anxious, too, it seemed. "I love the kids. And I need this job, but"—she lowered her voice to a barely there whisper—"I'm giving my notice."

Brooke's heart stopped. "What? Why?" She bent to pick up Maddox, who'd been very busy trying to climb her leg like a little monkey.

"I was hoping you wouldn't ask that," Brittney said.

Oh, shit. She gave the kids slices of sweet lemon bread and pulled Brittney aside. "Did . . . someone step over the line with you?" she asked the nanny carefully, thinking she'd have to kill Linc dead if that were the case. And that would be very sad, because she loved her brother-in-law, and not just because he made cute babies. He cared about Brooke and had always been there for her when she'd needed him, and even once or twice when she *hadn't* wanted him to be there, just like a true brother.

Brittney shifted on her feet and looked away. "Um . . ."

"What did he do?" she asked.

"He?" Brittney looked confused. "No, it's Mrs. Tennant."

"Mindy?"

"Yes," Brittney said, looking pained. "She . . . doesn't like me. I can tell. And she's always so stressed-out and tense, and it makes the babies stressed-out and tense, and it's hard because I always think I'm doing something wrong, and—"

"Mindy," Brooke repeated. "It's Mindy, not Linc?"

Brittney nodded. "Mr. Tennant's very patient and kind."

Brooke let out a breath of relief and also a laugh. "Something I'm guessing you can't say about Mindy?"

Brittney gave a small grimace. "I always seem to mess up her plans."

"I grew up with her as an older sister, so I know what you mean, but I can promise you she doesn't mean to be . . . um—"

"Bossy? Stern?"

"Well, those are nice ways to put it, I suppose. But really she has no idea she's those things. She's got a plan and a schedule, you see, and she's pretty single-minded when it comes to both."

Brittney went to one of the drawers and pulled a huge three-ring binder from it. "I've got the plan and schedule." The binder was filled to bursting, including dividers and folders. "I'm supposed to follow this to the letter."

"Oh, so *that's* where she keeps it," Brooke said.

Brittney gasped in horror. "You haven't been following the schedule according to the master plan?"

Brooke shrugged. "I never found the binder." She left out the part where she hadn't looked very hard.

"Maybe you should quit, too, before she fires you."

Brooke smiled. "She can't fire me. We're blood. So . . . how about we put the binder back where it came from and forget about it? We'll take care of the kids together, and if I can't get Mindy to chill once she gets home, then I'll tell her you've given notice if you still want to go."

Brittney scooped up Maddox, who laid his cute little head on her shoulder with sweet trust. She brushed her hand over his wild hair and, after a moment of hesitation, nodded.

"Thank you," Brooke said with huge relief.

Maddox suddenly barked loudly and wriggled frantically to be freed.

Brittney set him down and he went running down the hall. He slammed open the bathroom door, and a few seconds later, they heard him peeing in his special little portable potty. Then he came running back into the room.

Brooke pointed in the direction he'd come. "What did you forget?"

Maddox looked down at himself.

"I didn't hear the lid go down. I know for a fact that your mom has a firm no-lids-up policy. Also, you forgot to wash your hands."

With a nod, he went running back down the hall.

"With soap!" Brooke called after him.

"Wow, you're potty training him," Brittney said with admiration. "None of us have been able to talk him into it. What did you do?"

Maddox came back into the kitchen and held out his hand, palm up.

Brooke slapped a piece of candy into it. "Bribed him," she said to Brittney.

Brittney grinned. "Nice."

"So you'll stay?"

She nodded.

Brooke felt hugely relieved. "Thanks. I'll make dinner."

"And I'll do the bedtime thing," Brittney said.

Since bedtime was utter chaos—"I need water," "I need another story," "He's looking at me!"—this was a good deal for her.

After dinner, Brooke happily made her way out to the porch for a few minutes of quiet. There she went through some work emails while having three separate text convos with Mindy, Tommy, and Cole.

Mindy told her that no, she still hadn't actually talked to Linc. They'd been texting, though, and he was due to come home tomorrow night at some point.

Perfect. Brooke looked forward to some answers. Or ass-kicking. Whichever was required.

Her text conversation with Tommy was about Mindy. She was apparently doing great, but Tommy missed Brooke. Good to know. He wanted to know if she needed him. She told him not to come up because one, there were no strip clubs, and two, she was coming back the *second* Mindy got her ass home, and that if he wanted to aid the cause, he'd stop doing her sister's hair and taking her out at night for all the fun.

Cole also wanted to know if she was okay and when she was coming back. She told him she was fine, that she needed to do this for Mindy, and that she'd see him soon.

Tucking her phone into her pocket, she stared out at the view. It was that time of year when the days were getting as long as the shadows and the sun stayed warm until it set. At the moment, it was nearly gone behind the horizon. The temps would drop fast now, along with the daylight. She watched the last of it work its magic on the land, casting the sea of vineyards and rolling green hills beneath a glow of gold.

The beauty took her breath.

Or maybe that was the man about twenty feet away, crouched low in front of the hose spigot, cleaning off what looked like drywall tools. As the day turned to night, she watched, transfixed by his efficient movements. He almost didn't even seem real to her. He was a past crush, and there was too much bad history. She kept telling herself this, but it didn't stop her from wanting him.

Good thing lust was different from love.

From the other side of the fence, the one that belonged to the neighbor to the right of Mindy and Linc, a horse stretched her neck and used her big head to give Garrett a shove between his shoulder blades.

He turned his head and smiled at the horse. "Hey, Moose. Feeling neglected?"

Moose snorted.

Garrett laughed, the sound low and sexy and dangerously contagious. Knowing damn well that he knew she was on the porch watching him, Brooke said, "Didn't anyone ever tell you it's dangerous to talk to strangers?"

"She's not a stranger. She's a neighbor." He sent Moose a long look. "A grumpy, stubborn one."

"Is she aware that *you're* also grumpy and stubborn?"

He didn't try to deny this, and when the horse gave Garrett another shove, he rose to his feet. "Fine. You win." And he held out the hose.

Moose took a long drink and then tossed her head, spraying Garrett with water. He was in jeans, a gray henley, and battered hiking boots, all of which were now splattered with drops of water.

"Not cute," he said, and wiped his face.

From over the fence, the horse set her big head on Garrett's shoulder.

"So *all* the females fall all over themselves to please you," Brooke said.

"Not all."

Their gazes met, and Brooke's stupid heart gave a hard kick.

Clearly not liking the competition, Moose gave Brooke the side-eye and pressed her big face to Garrett's. He simply took Moose's affection as his due, reaching up to stroke the horse's jaw. When Moose had finally had her fill, she turned and walked away.

Garrett looked at Brooke. "You thirsty?" He held out the hose as he had for Moose.

It was practically a dare. So she took the hose and twisted it, letting the water hit him in the chest. "Oops. My bad," she said, waving the hose around a little, making sure to get him wet everywhere before carefully bringing the water back toward herself to drink. She got one good swallow in before he snaked an arm around her, clamping her tight to his chest.

She braced for him to take control of the hose and douse her, but he didn't. He liberated it from her hand and dropped it to the ground before wrapping his other arm around her as well, making her realize he didn't have to nail her with the hose. Nope, his torture was far more subtle as he pressed his entire body into the back of hers. Since she'd drenched him, he was able to get her just as wet without trying, and she gasped at the chilly water suctioning her to him. She fought for a moment to get free, in case anyone in the house was looking out the windows, then realized it was already dark. No one could see them. "I suppose you think this is funny."

"It's payback."

"For squirting you, or . . . ?" She broke off, unable to bring herself to say it. *The past.*

Without answering, he turned off the hose and then looked her over, not above clearly enjoying his handiwork as his eyes went from amused to . . . something else, something that heated her up. "You're cold."

Sure. Let him think that. It was safer than the truth.

With a shake of his head, he took her hand and led her across the yards to his back deck. He lifted the lid of his hot tub, his soaked shirt sticking to the muscles of his shoulders and back as he moved. He hit the jets and the steamy water began to gently swirl.

Then he crooked a finger at her.

The water looked amazing, but her inner *BAD IDEA* alarm was blaring.

"The temp's set at one hundred," he said. "Not ninety-nine. Not one hundred and one. One hundred."

She bit her lower lip. The man certainly knew how to speak her language.

"We've done this before," he pointed out.

True, but at her parents' house. They'd hot-tubbed several times, in fact, all of them late, late at night—and without any clothes. "Is this a come-on?" she asked.

He laughed.

Okay, fine, it wasn't. Suddenly irritated down to her frozen little toes, she yanked off her shirt, shoved down her jeans, and then checked the jets, turning the knob off and then back on. And then again. Finally satisfied, she climbed into the hot tub in her extremely plain white sports bra and matching bikini panties. *Yeah, great way to make an impression.* And yes, she'd have liked to make an impression. She wanted him to take one look at her and die of wanting. But then she glanced at him and nearly swallowed her tongue.

He stood still as stone, eyes hot and locked on her.

Feeling vindicated, she gestured at his clothes.

He pulled his shirt off, leaving him in just low-slung jeans that had slipped so low on his lean hips, they were a few inches past decent. *Sweet mother of God.* The unexpected urge to nibble every inch of him as if he were an all-you-can-eat fried chicken special nearly overcame her. But—as of right this very minute—she no longer gave in to her questionable impulses, so she carefully rolled her tongue back into her mouth and played it cool, cocking her head. "Problem?" she asked. "Worried about shrinkage from the water?"

"We both know I have nothing to worry about."

She snorted as he shucked the jeans, and then she was hit with déjà vu, flashing back to a long ago time when she'd been in her parents' hot tub. She'd had the place to herself that night and had made margaritas. She'd been soaking in the tub, drinking the margaritas right out of the pitcher and listening to music loud enough to affect her heart rate. Or she'd thought it was the music, but in hindsight, it was undoubtedly the sight of Garrett coming upon her and joining her party of one, executing a playful striptease for her.

He'd thrown his clothing over his shoulder one piece at a time as he'd stripped. Which had made it a lot of fun when her parents came home early and Garrett had been forced to run around like a wild man to collect his clothes and shove them back onto his wet—and hard—body.

In the here and now, he slid that body into the water and sat across from her, eyes dark and filled with things she could no longer read.

"Your dad nearly kicked my ass that night," he mused with a small smile, apparently having no trouble reading *her* thoughts.

"He's a foot shorter than you and probably a good hundred pounds heavier," she said dryly. "I think you could've taken him."

He didn't say anything. Didn't have to. They both knew he'd never lay a finger on anyone in anger, especially her father, who'd been incredibly kind to him while Garrett was growing up.

Speaking of her parents, the phone she'd set on the edge of the tub rang. Sliding Garrett—and his wet, broad shoulders and chest and tousled hair—a long look, she slid a finger across the screen and answered on speaker. "Hey, Mom."

"You're home in Wildstone?"

"Yep. Helping out Mindy for a few days." *Or a damn week . . .*

"That's so sweet of you. When she was here in Palm Springs, I suggested she do yoga during the day and wine at night, but I imagine having her sister in Wildstone is better than all of that. She's missed you, Brooke. We all have."

She squirmed a little and stared at the phone rather than the man watching her. "Thanks, Mom."

"I mean it, honey. I hope you know how important you are to all of us. I know you've pulled back, and I'm sure you have your reasons for that, but I'm glad you're there. I just wish we weren't six hours away."

Uncomfortable with the emotions in her throat, she shrugged, but of course her mom couldn't see the gesture.

"Brooke?"

Avoiding Garrett's gaze, she said softly, "I'm here."

"We'd love to come see you."

"'We'?"

"Your dad and me. We're . . . working things out again, and it's going well."

Because of their smoothie shops, her parents were local celebrities of a sort, and if they came to town, it'd be a nightmare for poor Mindy. "That's nice, but don't worry about making the trip," she said. "I'll come to you when I leave here."

"Promise?"

She crossed her fingers. "Yep!"

"So . . . catch me up. Are you seeing anyone?"

Brooke looked across the lazily rising steam at Garrett, who'd leaned his head back and closed his eyes, his arms spread on either side of him, resting out of the water on the edge of the hot tub. He looked . . . lickable. But at her mom's question, he lifted his head and met her gaze.

"Gee, Mom," she said. "We've got a bad connection—"

"Fine, you don't want to talk about it. I'll take that to mean you're single. Are you ever going to settle down and have a family of your own?"

Brooke pinched the bridge of her nose. "I should've started this conversation with the fact that I've recently updated my privacy policy. From now on, no one's allowed to ask me about my future plans."

"I'm your mother."

"The rules apply to everyone." Standing up, she turned her back on Garrett. "Oh, and would you look at that? One of the kids needs me, gotta go!"

"Brooke—"

She'd intended to hit disconnect, but two arms came around her. One braced on the edge of the tile at her hip. The other reached toward her phone and a single finger disconnected the call.

"If you told her the truth, she wouldn't bring it up like that," he said quietly. "And you wouldn't keep getting hurt." His other hand came down on the tile as well, effectively closing her in.

"Lying saves her from the pain."

She could feel him shake his head in disapproval, but all he murmured was "Such a hot little liar," his mouth nearly at her ear.

Her stomach quivered. Correction: The parts *south* of her stomach quivered. She worked really hard at not tilting her head to give him better access to the spot on her neck he used to kiss, lick, and nibble, the one that never failed to drive her wild. "Is that *temperature* hot, or—"

"Hotheaded," came the low rumble of his voice. "Hot in your wet skivvies. Hot in a way that is very bad for me."

She'd started to melt at the feel of his mouth teasing her skin, but at the "bad for me" part, her spine stiffened and she elbowed him in the gut.

Laughing deep in his throat, he backed off and sat back down, seemingly unaffected.

Not her. She glanced at herself to make sure he hadn't magically melted off her bra and panties, because yes, he was just that good.

"The scar," he said quietly. "That's from—"

Her hands went to the spot low on her belly where the impact of the crash had done the most damage. The doctors had had to remove her spleen, part of her liver, and some intestine, and had also done their best to repair the damage done to her reproductive organs. "Yes."

"It's almost faded completely away."

"Not enough, if you can see it," she managed.

"I've got X-ray vision."

She rolled her eyes. "And what about this . . ." She ran a finger along his wet, hard pec and the tat with the bold roman numerals that she wanted to nibble. "What's this?"

He looked at her for a long moment. "A date," he finally said.

"I figured." She struggled to remember what she'd learned about roman numerals way back in high school. "What's the significance?"

Another long pause, and she lifted her gaze to his. The emotion she saw there had her swallowing hard. "The date of the helicopter crash," she whispered.

"The date I lost you," he said. "And our baby."

She couldn't speak. Hell, she could hardly breathe. But she managed to shift a little closer, her fingers still on his smooth skin, the skin he'd marked for the loss of their baby.

"I hate that you went through that," he said quietly.

She shook her head, having to swallow hard to speak. "I'm okay."

"Yeah, you are."

That hung in the air a moment while her heart went a little squishy in her chest. But going down that road wasn't going to happen. Ever. One, he deserved a *whole* woman, one who could let him in and love him without baggage and hang-ups, *and* give him the kids she knew he wanted. And two . . . she couldn't handle the pain of losing him a second time. She wouldn't survive it.

Which meant she had to remove herself from the temptation. "I think it's time for me to go to bed."

"You mean time to run from me. But you don't have to, you know. There's no reason for there to be anything but honesty between us. We're in a different place now, so there aren't any expectations between us."

A minute ago, she'd had to fight back tears. Now, suddenly, she was fighting the urge to strangle him. But that was all pride. Maybe he no longer wanted her, but she . . . damn. She still wanted him. "Don't worry. I'm not feeling you, either."

He did another of those annoying "yeah, right" brow raises, which made her even madder. "Hey," she said, and poked a finger into his pec. His hard, ungiving, sexy pec. "If I was feeling it, you'd know."

"How?" he challenged.

"I'd be . . ." She had to think about this. "Flirty. I certainly wouldn't be thinking of all of your many, *many* faults."

His mouth quirked. "And what are these so-called faults?"

"Well, for starters," she said, "you're wearing black knit boxers with bananas on them."

This made him laugh outright. "Someone sent me a sub-scription box," he said. "They come once a month. Last month's pair had cocks all over them."

"Like chickens, or . . . ?"

"If you're curious, I'd be happy to wear them tomorrow and give you a peek."

"Whatever," she said. "But the fact that some woman sent you a subscription to undies is another reason I'm not feeling it. I bet you've stayed friends with every single person you've ever met."

"And that's a fault?"

She shrugged. Of course it wasn't a fault. It was the opposite of a fault. "Well, except for me, of course."

"Because you don't answer phone calls, texts, emails . . ."

Oh. Right.

He tilted his head. "Tell me something."

Oh boy. "What?"

"What's that Cole guy to you?"

"I told you, he's my boss."

"But you're sleeping together," he said, his hazel eyes holding hers prisoner. "Or you were."

"How do you know that?"

"You just told me."

Dammit. She crossed her arms over her chest. "We're not to-gether, if that's what you're asking."

"Why?"

"Because I don't like him like that."

"Because you're just *not feeling it*?" he asked mockingly.

"Funny." She paused, painfully aware that he'd been far more open with her than she'd been with him. "As you may have noticed, I'm not good with letting people in." She paused. "I seem to have a problem being emotionally vulnerable."

Any residual humor faded from his eyes. "I know," he said very quietly, no longer teasing. "Look, you waited seven years to tell me how you felt about the accident and the aftermath. I hate thinking of you facing what you did all by yourself."

"It was a long time ago."

"To you," he said. "It was a long time ago to you. But I just found out, and I'm . . . reeling."

"I'm sorry," she whispered. "I don't know how to say that and make you believe it, but I am. I'm so sorry."

"I know," he said. "And I don't want you to feel like you have to say it again. I just don't know what to do with the"—he shook his head, like he couldn't find the words—"the hot mess of emotions inside me."

She gave a sad smile. "Join my club. I'm still messed up."

"You seem pretty together to me."

"Hello, did you see how many times I had to turn the knob on the jets? I'm a walking wreck."

He shook his head. "I don't think you're as messed up as you think you are. I've seen you with the kids. You're holding both your life and Mindy's together."

She thought he was giving her more credit than she deserved. "I hide behind my fears. But here's me facing one of them. You asked me about Cole. And now I want to ask you about your girlfriend, the one you said you don't have. The one who called you the other day for a hookup."

"It wasn't for a hookup," he said. "She dumped me."

This gave her an unexpected laugh. "Right. You expect me to believe a guy who looks like you do and is funny and smart like you are got dumped?"

"Yeah, I do." He shifted close until they were knee to knee. "Because I've never lied to you, Brooke. Never will."

She stared up at him, caught between memories and reality as somehow the gap between them closed. She felt a little dizzy from all they'd revealed to each other, but that didn't stop her hands from going to his shoulders as his slid beneath the water to her hips, guiding her tightly into him so there was no space between them, not even for the water.

The air shimmered with steam and mist and a whole lot of memories that left her tense with longing and desire. Garrett leaned in and brushed a kiss to her lips, soft, sweet, before pulling back a fraction, pausing as they shared a breath. He lifted his gaze to hers for a questioning look before coming back for more.

Not soft this time, not sweet.

With a low moan, she gave herself up. He was at once familiar and entirely new to her and she breathed him in, touching everything she could reach, his chest and shoulders, the contours of his back, over and over again, forgetting to count in her head, forgetting to make it all even numbers. And he seemed to feel the same, creating trails of shivering heat from the inside out with his knowing hands.

His mouth was at her ear, his breathing ragged when he

whispered his old nickname for her, the one he'd first called her in high school when she'd disturbed a beehive while climbing trees for fun.

"Bee."

That was it—all he said, or rather growled out in a rough groan that spoke of reluctance and regret along with all the heat as he pulled back. "Okay, so, obviously the attraction between us is still there."

Attraction. Combustion. Explosive combustion . . .

"The difference is that this time, we're grown-ups," he said. "Our eyes are open. This is a colossally bad idea for so many reasons, not the least of which is that you're going back to LA any second, and then hoping to go back to your photography job, which will take you even farther away for who knows how long, correct?"

She managed to nod in agreement. Correct.

He nodded, too, then let out a rough breath before rising from the hot tub in one easy, graceful movement. "I think the best thing to do here is to say good night." And then he walked away, no towel, water pooling in his footsteps.

Brooke let out a careful breath before getting out herself, wrapping herself in both of the towels hanging off hooks on the deck before heading across the yard to Mindy's house.

Brittney was on the living room couch watching TV. She did a double take at Brooke dripping water all over the floor, but just said, "The kids are asleep."

"Thanks. I've got it from here."

Brittney handed her the kid monitor and left. And even though not a soul was stirring, not even a mouse, Brooke quickly stripped out of her wet things and put on sweats, and then went to check on the kids anyway.

She found Maddox awake in his bed, studying the ceiling. He looked over at her and smiled, and her heart melted. She stroked the hair from his forehead and whispered confidentially, "The next time I open up to someone will be at my autopsy."

He softly barked his agreement.

CHAPTER 8

Dr. Linc wakes up.

B rooke woke to small, warm hands patting her cheeks. If the slightly sticky feel to them didn't fill her in on her visitor's identity, the sweet baby breath in her face did. "Maddox, my little man," she murmured, and opened her eyes.

He grinned at her, and a line of drool slid out of his mouth and onto her arm. Poor guy was teething. "Your gums hurt?" she asked.

He climbed onto the couch with her and rubbed his jaw to hers. That's when she realized it was morning, and she sat straight up with gasp. She'd only just managed to fall asleep sometime around four. "Are we late for camp?"

Maddox shrugged.

She glanced at the time—okay, they were good—kissed Maddox, and set him down so she could get up. He waddled off into the kitchen, and she sucked in a deep breath and took stock. She had a kink in her neck and a cramp in her ass. She staggered to the bathroom and found Princess Millie sitting on the throne reading Dr. Seuss, her cute little Wonder Woman pajama bottoms around her swinging ankles.

"'One fish, two fish, red fish, blue fish,'" she read, and smiled up at Brooke. "This book counts in fours!"

"It's a great book."

Millie nodded. "Adam at school says I'm a weirdo cuz I count in my head. And because when it's my turn to turn off the lights, I like to do it four times."

"You're not a weirdo," Brooke said fiercely, wanting to go have a little chat with this punk Adam. "Different is *not* weird."

"I know that, Auntie Brooke."

"Oh." Some of Brooke's ruffled feathers smoothed out at her niece's easy acceptance of herself. "Okay, then. So why aren't you using your bathroom upstairs?"

"Because Mason left the lid up and didn't flush, and now the bathroom's stinky. Why are boys so stinky?"

"One of life's little mysteries."

"If Mom was here, he'd be in trouble for the lid-up thing. She doesn't like it when she has to go in the middle of the night and she falls in."

"No one does." Brooke looked in the mirror and grimaced at her pale, exhausted reflection. "You know what? How about we skip camp today and take a field trip instead?"

"Yay, a field trip!" Millie paused. "What's a field trip?"

Thirty minutes later, Brooke had managed to shower and

round up the kids in the kitchen. Brittney had shown up and was at the stove, calmly making breakfast. Millie was watching, dressed in jeans and her favorite Wonder Woman tee. Mason was on the floor in the laundry room, going through the basket of clean clothes that Brooke hadn't folded yet. He was doing that with one hand, his other shoved into a box of Cheerios. He found his favorite pj's—a one-piece pink T-rex number—and began to tug it on. Having learned to pick her battles, Brooke let it happen. Plus, she had bigger problems.

Maddox was naked and zooming around, barking like a crazy Chihuahua. He accidentally kicked over Mason's box of cereal, which of course scattered the Cheerios from here to China. She reached for the hand vacuum attached to the pantry wall, turning it on just as Brittney said, "Watch out, Mason's terrified of that thing."

And sure enough, Mason leapt to his feet. Gaze glued to the vacuum, the whites of his eyes showing, he squeezed in between Brooke and the vacuum in a protective stance against the beast, every limb trembling as he held off the evil monster.

Heart. Melted. "Oh, baby." Brooke picked Mason up and hugged him. "You're my hero."

Brittney pulled out a broom to sweep up the Cheerios.

"Best nanny on the planet," Brooke said to Mason.

"Oh, I know," Brittney said, not at all flustered by the chaos. "I'm pretty great."

"Brittney's girlfriend loves Brittney, too," Millie said.

Brittney smiled in agreement at the little girl. "She does."

Brooke kissed Mason and set him back down. She looked for

peanut butter to spread on the pancakes Brittney had made. "I hope your girlfriend knows how lucky she is to have you," she said, struggling to get the jar open.

The nanny blushed, but took the peanut butter and used a vinyl potholder to open it. "My mom once tried to talk me out of being gay by telling me I'd have to go through life without having someone to open jars for me. In hindsight, I kind of love that the only use for a man she could think of was opening jars."

Brooke nearly snorted her coffee out her nose.

"My daddy can do more than open a pickle jar," Millie said in defense of men. "He and Uncle Garrett make a really great Slip 'N Slide."

"That's cuz he's one of the good ones," Brooke told her. "So about our field trip. It's not really warm enough today for the beach—"

Garrett appeared in the kitchen doorway, looking disturbingly yummy in faded jeans, hiking boots, a hoodie, and black mirrored sunglasses. He flashed a smile at everyone except Brooke, whom he looked at last, holding her gaze the longest. Then he pushed the glasses to the top of his head and revealed those see-all hazel eyes, filled with equal parts heat and irritation.

Felt about right. Every time she thought about their hot-tub kiss, heat rushed through her, leaving her aching and hungry for him. That's when she remembered *he'd* backed off, and the irritation kicked in.

"We're going on a field trip!" Millie told Garrett at high decibels.

"Beach!" Mason yelled.

Maddox tipped his head back and howled in what Brooke assumed was delight.

"Not the beach," Brooke said. "It's too cold—"

Her phone rang. Of course it was her mom again. "It's Grandma," she told the kids, and made the mistake of answering on speaker. "Hi, Mom—"

"Honey, listen, I know you don't want to discuss this, but after I talked to you last night, I called my dear friend Nancy Garrison, who still lives in Wildstone. Her son's single, too, and we think you'd be perfect for each other."

Oh, for God's sake. "Did Mindy put you up to this?"

"No, of course not. She just mentioned that if we found someone for you, you might stay longer . . ."

Brooke groaned and then remembered she had an avid audience. "Look, I was just trying to keep it to myself, but . . . I *am* seeing someone."

"So you *do* have a boyfriend! I had a feeling! Is he tall? What does he do for a living?"

Her mom's two measurements of a good man: height and employment. "Yes, he's tall. And he's a . . ." Her gaze caught on Garrett and her mind went completely blank. "Um . . ."

"How can you have a boyfriend and not know what he does?" her mom asked, distressed. "Oh God. He's unemployed, isn't he? Honey, if he can't hold down a job, he's not the one."

"He renovates homes," her mouth said.

Garrett's brows went so high they vanished beneath his hair.

Shit! "Gotta go now, Mom." She slid her phone in her pocket and refused to look up at Garrett ever again. "Obviously, that was just to get her off my back," she said, to the kids' collective confusion. "Never mind, it's a grown-up thing."

"What's it like to be a grown-up?" Mason wanted to know.

"Well . . ." Brooke tried to think of something positive. "You get to eat ice cream whenever and wherever you want."

His face lit up.

"But you have to buy it yourself."

He went from delighted to devastated. Aaaaannnnnd her work here was done.

Garrett just gave her a long, amused look.

She gave him a don't-mess-with-me glance. He didn't seem bothered by it in the least.

"Field trip time!" Mason called out. "Hey," he said, and tugged on Garrett's hand. "Will you come, too?"

Garrett looked at Brooke.

"Yay!" Millie said. "We're all going to the beach!"

It was like the worst game of telephone Brooke had ever played. "No," she said. "There's no 'we' here."

"Momma says we're *always* a 'we'!" Millie said exuberantly.

"How about we hike the bluffs?" Garrett said, apparently on board with the "we."

"No," she said. Hell no. "That's too high for them." This actually wasn't true, but she hadn't done anything other than sit in front of a computer screen in a very long time, and just the thought of doing more made her start to sweat.

Garrett studied her for a moment. "The trail's wide," he said. "They'll be safe." He paused meaningfully and held her gaze with steady purpose. "We'll *all* be safe."

Okay, she got that *he* had no fears, but she was not in the mood for this. Not today. And maybe not any day soon, either.

"We could bundle them up and walk the beach?" Garrett said. "That's safe enough, right?"

Blowing out a breath, she caved, and went about packing a picnic while trying to wrestle her growing anxiety. When she pulled out celery to go with the peanut butter, everyone moaned and groaned.

"We don't like green food," Millie said.

"It's not green food," Brooke said, swiftly knifing peanut butter onto the celery and then topping each piece with four raisins. "It's ants on a log."

"I love ants on a log!" Mason declared.

Maddox barked.

"So does Mad Dog," Mason translated.

Even Princess Millie gave it a go, while Brooke hunted for more food to bring. She found carrots and the last of the fresh broccoli. "Trees," she told the kids when they groaned. Tofu became "rocks."

"Crafty," Garrett said.

"That's me," she said. "Master of craftiness. Everyone to the car."

Garrett put his hand on Brooke's lower back to get her attention. "Want me to drive?"

"Uncle Garrett, you can't touch a girl unless you ask first," Millie said. "My teacher says."

"You're absolutely correct," Garrett said, and turned to Brooke, a small twitch on his lips, his tone benign enough, but she heard the sarcasm. "Is it okay if I touch you?"

"Sure. If it's okay that I touch you back," she said, because the next time she touched him, it would be to sock him one.

He smiled knowingly.

"I'll drive," she said. "I've got the car seats."

They hadn't even gotten out of the driveway before Mason had to make a pit stop. When he was finished and buckled back in, they actually made it to the end of the street before Maddox had to go.

"You, too, Millie," Brooke said, as she freed Mason from his seat belt.

Nothing from Millie.

Brooke sighed. "*Princess* Millie. You, too."

"But I don't have to go."

"But by my count, you'll have to go in about two minutes," Brooke said, and that's when she looked up.

Maddox was in the middle of the grass on the front lawn, wearing absolutely nothing, peeing on a tree.

Brooke just leaned forward and banged her head on the dashboard. And then again to make it an even number.

Garrett laughed. "Come on, you'd do it if you could."

Probably true.

WHEN THEY FINALLY got on the road, they drove through town and made a pit stop at POP Smoothies. It was a twofold mission. One, the kids were bouncing in their seats with excitement over the idea of each getting a kid-sized smoothie of their choice. And two, Mindy had texted Brooke to ask her to spy and make sure the shop looked like it was being managed properly.

Brooke had no idea what "properly" was. She'd worked here

with Mindy from age sixteen to eighteen, and during those years, their boss had been their dad. He'd been a tough taskmaster. They'd had to keep the place immaculately clean to suit him.

Shortly after Brooke left Wildstone, her dad had begun opening more shops all over the state. He was no longer active in the day-to-day operations. He'd hired smart managers, like Mindy, who'd taken on the Wildstone shop, hoping to eventually buy it.

That had never been Brooke's dream. She needed more variety. And freedom. But as she walked into the quaint, welcoming, and admittedly adorable shop, the bright colors and delicious scents immediately bombarded Brooke with good memories.

The walls were a cheery yellow. The oak tables with sunshine-yellow stools were clean, and pretty strings of lights and fun music invited one to stay awhile. At the counter were displays of the fresh fruits and veggies available for smoothies, as well as an entire area dedicated to Baked Goods by Mindy. At the moment, that area was empty, but everything else was full and bustling and looking pretty amazing.

Behind the counter sat a thirtysomething woman: tall, dark, and beautiful, her midnight-black hair piled on top of her head, her equally dark eyes smiling. "Brooke Lemon," she said. "You look just like your sister."

And she looked like a real-life Warrior Princess. "You must be Xena."

"I am." She came around from behind the counter and hugged the kids, each of whom seemed to adore her. They shouted out their smoothie orders.

Xena wasn't at all flustered; she simply got to work. When she'd finished with the kids' smoothies, she winked at Garrett. "The usual, I presume, handsome?"

"You know it," Garrett said with a warm smile, like they knew each other pretty well. "Thanks."

"A Pumpkin Smash, coming right up."

Brooke looked at Garrett.

"Pumpkin and cinnamon," he explained. "It's like a pumpkin pie."

"It's seasonal, but we make it special for Garrett," Xena said.

Of course they did. Brooke ordered the mystery special of the day and watched Xena create the smoothies and then effortlessly clean up afterward. She had to admit, the woman was a better employee than she'd ever been. And when she took a sip of her mystery special, she nearly moaned. "Delicious."

"Strawberry, banana, and oats." Xena waved off Garrett's money. "I don't charge the boss or her kids," she said. "Give Mindy my love."

Brooke glanced up, surprised.

"She sent you, right?" Xena asked. "I love and adore her, but we both know she's a control nut."

"If it helps, I plan to tell her you're amazing," Brooke said.

Xena smiled. "Oh, honey, she already knows that."

Garrett tucked some bills into the tip jar, and they left. Fifteen minutes later, they pulled into the beach parking lot. A food truck was just setting up at the base of the bluffs, sitting back about a hundred yards from the shoreline. Other than that, their only company was a handful of surfers. The tide was coming in, shrinking the beach.

"Bad timing for a walk on the sand," Garrett said. Then he turned and eyed the stairs to the top of the bluffs, where the hiking trails Brooke had once upon a time known better than her own hand seemed to mock her.

"Yeah!" Millie shouted. "Let's go up there."

"Up there" was a problem. "Up" anything was a problem, and had been since the crash. Brooke got vertigo like no other now. She wouldn't call it a phobia. It wasn't a phobia. She refused to have it be a phobia. After all, she was going to leave here soon and go back to having wild adventures, where there would be lots of "up."

Garrett leaned in close. "I can put Maddox in his backpack on my shoulders and hold on to Mason's and Millie's hands. We could head east so the sun isn't slanting into our faces."

She was still staring at the stairs, her heart pounding in her ears. "I hate it when someone says something like 'head east.' Who am I, Lewis and Clark? Do we turn right or left from the food truck in the parking lot?"

Garrett smiled. "I forgot that you could locate any food source without direction, but other than that, you get lost finding your way out of a paper bag."

Annoyingly true.

"I don't need my hand held," Millie announced. "I don't like to hold hands. *You* hold Auntie Brooke's hand, Garrett, okay?"

"I'll have to ask first," Garrett said very seriously, and when Millie nodded in approval with all her eight-year-old feminist heart, Garrett turned to Brooke. "May I hold your hand?"

Brooke couldn't seem to take her gaze off the stairs. From the corner of her eye, she could see Garrett's proffered hand.

Truth be told, normally she wasn't a fan of hand-holding any more than Millie was, but at that moment, his hand felt like a life-saving flotation device, and she grasped it like she was going down for the count.

"Are you two going to get married?" Millie asked. "Because Grandpa holds Grandma's hand and they might get married again. And Daddy holds Momma's hand and they're married."

Brooke volleyed that one to Garrett by looking at him. *Let's see you handle this one, Ace . . .*

"Holding hands can also be a just-friends thing," he said, very calmly.

Show-off.

"And usually people fall in love before they get married," Garrett added.

Unimpressed, Millie wrinkled her nose. "Love seems kinda dumb."

"You don't plan to fall in love someday?" Garrett asked her.

Millie shrugged. "Maybe. If the person can make pancakes as good as Brittney's."

Garrett nodded. "Wise. Always hold out for what you want." He met Brooke's eyes, his own filled with something, but hell if she knew what.

A couple of seagulls landed near them with a *squawk* and began to stalk them.

Maddox pointed at them. "Bad dog!" he yelled.

Everyone stared at him.

"You can talk?" Brooke finally asked.

"Well, sure he can," Millie said. "He's almost three, you know."

"But I've only ever heard him bark."

Millie shrugged. "He likes to bark."

Okay, then.

Two women and a gaggle of kids got out of their cars. One of the women stopped and smiled at Mason's pink dinosaur pj's. "Cute. Is that a boy or girl?"

"It's a T-rex," Brooke said.

The group moved on, and Garrett looped an arm around her neck and tugged her into him. He smelled heart-stoppingly amazing, damn him, as he brushed a warm kiss to her temple. "Like the way you operate," he murmured.

Millie pointed at them. "You just kissed. See? You *do* like each other."

Brooke decided to play deaf on that one. She was too busy facing the trail with all the enthusiasm of someone walking to the guillotine.

"You okay?" Garrett asked softly.

"Of course. This is nothing." She looked at him, daring him to say otherwise.

He merely gestured for her to go first.

So she did. Three steps in, she made the mistake of looking back, because in doing so she could see what felt like miles and miles of blue Pacific, outlined by an unending line of bluffs. She gulped and began to count to herself. *One, two, three, four. One, two, three, four—*

"Brooke?"

She waved off Garrett's low tone of concern. Hell no, would she give in now, not in front of an audience. *One, two, three, four.* "I'm good." And then she proved it to herself by walking the damn trail.

An hour later, she was shocked to admit to herself that it had gone well. Unlike any other mountain adventure in her life, this one had been extremely tame and very easy and . . . a lot of fun.

After, they sat on the low stone wall between the parking lot and beach, eating Brooke's snacks, de-dusting, and drinking water. A couple came down the trail behind them, carrying hiking sticks and wearing hydration packs and vests with a lot of pockets, all bulging with supplies.

"Glad to see you hydrating the kids," the woman said with a little bit of judgment in her voice, prompting Brooke to look over her motley crew.

Millie had walked the trail in Crocs. Mason was carrying his stuffed unicorn. Maddox was filthy from happily rolling in the dirt as often as possible. Not a single one of them had suffered in any way. In fact, they'd all enjoyed themselves and were still grinning, which meant the fun police needed a chill pill, though Brooke refrained from telling her so.

Garrett waited until the couple moved on before saying, "Admit it, you wanted to kill her."

"Only a little."

"Proud of you," he murmured.

She had no idea why, but the words warmed her to her toes.

A little bit later, they pulled back into Mindy's driveway. While the kids were running around on the lawn like wild things, Brooke turned to Garrett. In spite of the day they'd had and the "proud of you," he was now looking at her like maybe she was a puzzle he couldn't solve. Or didn't want to. "What?" she asked.

He shook his head. "It's irrelevant."

"I doubt that."

He stared at her for another beat. "It's irrelevant because I no longer give in to impulses that are going to mess me up."

She felt herself run the pads of her thumbs over her fingertips, back and forth. "And you think I'm going to mess you up."

"I know it," he said.

"Wow." She absorbed the blow of that. "Nice."

He shook his head. "I'm not trying to hurt you, Brooke. I'm trying to avoid getting hurt. Like I said, we're in a different place now, and I promised myself I wasn't going to go there with you again. Not ever."

"Says the man who had his tongue down my throat last night." Nodding like it all made perfect sense, and also to show that she was fine with it, she began to move toward the house. Because she was totally 100 percent fine, dammit.

"Brooke—"

"No, it's good to know, and I hear you. Loud and clear. Kids!" she called. "Let's go!"

Garrett scooped up Maddox and helped them all into the house, in spite of Brooke not wanting him to.

There they found a surprise in the kitchen.

Linc.

He'd removed his suit jacket, loosened his tie, and kicked off his shoes, and was drinking Brooke's lemonade right from the pitcher she'd had in the fridge.

"Daddy!" Millie cried, and flung herself at him. He set down the pitcher—and just in time, because Mason was right behind her, with Maddox closing up the parade. Linc caught Millie, hugged her, and slung her around his back so she was hanging from his neck. Mason went into one arm and Maddox into the other.

"Hey, big man," he said, giving each of his babies a squeeze and a kiss. He palmed Maddox's tush. "No more diapers?"

Maddox grinned.

Linc shifted Mason onto the same arm as Maddox so he and Garrett could bump fists and do one of those half man-hugs, aka slapping each other on the back.

"Daddy, Maddox doesn't understand the lid-up rule," Millie said. "I fell into the toilet last night!"

"We'll have to work on that if any of us wants to live," Linc said, but his attention was now on Brooke, his eyes full of questions. "Not that it's not great to see you, but where's Min?"

"Still in LA," Brooke said. "She didn't tell you?"

"No. Granted, I had terrible reception, so we only texted. What's wrong?"

"We need to talk."

"Hey, kids," Garrett said. "Let's go build a fort." Loading them up on him one by one, he then pretended to stagger to the door, making monster sounds. The kids were squealing in delight as they all left the kitchen.

"Is she okay?" Linc asked the minute they were alone.

"Physically, yes. Mentally? I don't think so. She lost her collective shit, Linc. And I'm about to lose mine on you."

"Okay," he said. "You're freaking me out. Talk faster."

She blew out a breath. "She had a meltdown of epic proportions on the way home from Palm Springs. She showed up on my doorstep and fell in love with my bed. She was sad, overwhelmed, and exhausted. Long story short, she stayed in LA, and I brought the kids home. She needed some time off."

Linc looked surprised. "From the kids?"

Brooke gave him a long look.

"From me, too?" He seemed stricken by this. "Why? And what do you mean, she's sad?" He pulled out his phone, but Brooke put her hand over his.

"Before you call her, I need you to tell me you're still in this marriage."

Linc met her gaze, his own not defensive or guilty, but utterly shocked. "Of course I'm in this marriage. What the hell's going on?"

His reaction was real. She knew him well enough to know it deep in her gut. "She feels alone."

He inhaled a deep, shaky breath and nodded, like he'd absorbed the situation and made an assessment. "Okay, I'm going to LA. I'll see if Garrett can watch the kids so you can leave—"

"No," she said. "I'm not leaving until she's home and okay."

He looked both hugely relieved and touched by this. It had always been incredibly difficult to be mad at Linc for anything. For one, he was fun and charismatic as hell and, though somewhat softer than Garrett given the differences in the physicality of their jobs, still very fit. And two, he'd been her friend for as long as she could remember, and there'd been some really good times before she'd screwed up her entire life and left everyone and everything behind in Wildstone.

"I don't think you should go after her," Brooke said. "She knows you planned on being here today. She'll come home when she's ready."

Linc shook his head. "But—"

"The best thing you can do for her right now is let her feel like she's in control, Linc."

He ran his hands over his face. "What do you know that I don't? Tell me all of it. Everything, Brooke."

"She said something about you and the cute, perfect Brittney. And then some hot doctor she thought was a guy, but is really a woman. And oh yeah, you don't 'see' her anymore. Or"—she grimaced—"do things to her anymore, including using the costumes from your secret sex chest. And I'm never going to forgive you for making me say that."

Linc let out a breath. "I see her. She's the only woman I've ever seen or wanted. And as for Brittney, she's gay. And a *child*," he added, sounding horrified at the accusation.

"And Dr. Sam?"

"She's a professional associate."

"With breasts," Brooke pointed out. "Perky ones."

Linc grimaced. "She's just a friend."

"Well, I'm sorry to be the one to tell you, Linc, but good-looking husbands, especially husbands married to my sister, don't get to have female friends with good breasts."

"You do realize that entire sentence is insulting."

"Good. Maybe it'll wake you the hell up."

"Look, I know I've been busy—"

"Nonexistent," Brooke corrected, "and not there for your children and your wife. And that's bullshit, Linc."

"I know it's been crazy. I've been working at getting new partners for the practice, which would allow me to cut my hours. I tried to sell the practice to the hospital—they've made several great offers over the past few years—but Ethan won't sell."

"Yeah, well, your brother's a dumbass. And I don't care about him. I care about Mindy and your kids."

Linc looked frustrated. "I know, but Ethan's family, too."

"Yeah. I get that." She waved her arm, gesturing to herself being in the kitchen. "People will do just about anything for family, dumbass or otherwise. But that isn't going to help me help Mindy. I need you to wake the hell up."

A balloon floated into the room, attached to Ketchup the Tortoise.

"What the hell?" Linc said.

"We kept losing him, so we tied a balloon around his shell."

Linc gave a slow blink. "Somehow that makes perfect sense."

"Of course it does," Brooke said. "You know what doesn't? The fact that you work fourteen hours a day and leave before the kids get up, and then get home when there's maybe half an hour before bedtime, and you think that's okay."

"I'm a doctor," he said. "You know my brother and I took over my dad's practice. And Ethan's marriage is falling apart, so I've been having to take up the slack."

She gave him a long look.

He paused and then grimaced. "Okay, yeah, I heard it as I said it. I'm putting my own marriage at risk. I need to spend more time at home."

She sighed and softened slightly, knowing he was a good man in a tough spot. "These are your kids, Linc. Half an hour a day isn't enough." She poked her head out into the living room.

Garrett's long legs stuck out from under a big blanket tented between the back of the couch and a recliner. From inside came a bunch of giggles. "Hey," she called out to the kids, "when's the last time Daddy took you to the park?"

They all stuck their heads out and blinked. Clearly no one could remember.

"Well, guess what?" she asked brightly. "Daddy's taking you to the park now. Aren't you, Daddy?"

"Daddy" looked a little nervous, but he smiled gamely. "Everyone load up!"

Garrett stood. "I'll be upstairs working on your tile."

"Or . . . ?" Linc asked meaningfully.

"Or . . ."

"Or you'll be with us."

"Or I'll be with you," Garrett said smoothly.

"Yay!" the kids yelled, and jumped up and down.

"I've got to coach a soccer game at six," Garrett warned.

"You come with us and then we'll go with you," Linc said.

The two men bumped fists and Brooke rolled her eyes. "That was cheating," she said to Linc. "But A-plus for effort and creativity."

Before they left, Linc stepped outside to call Mindy in private. Brooke pressed her ear to the window, but couldn't hear a thing. "Dammit."

"Maybe you could trust him to do the right thing."

At the sound of Garrett's voice in her ear, she jumped a mile in the air and sent him a baleful glance. "I'm not big on trust."

"No shit."

Linc came back in, and he and Garrett left for the park with the kids. Brooke left, too, and took herself on a drive around Wildstone, waiting for the urge to keep going on the highway heading south.

The urge didn't come, so she drove back to the beach, parked, and walked up the stairs. And then she forced herself to walk the bluffs again. This time she only flop-sweated half her body weight.

Progress.

She got home to a quiet house and took a long shower, thinking, damn, she was proud of herself.

Linc and the kids came home a bit later. No Garrett.

"He's taking his team home," Linc said. "He'll feed them first, since most of them are without any adult supervision or authority figures."

Brooke tried to not let that into her heart and failed. Of course Garrett would take care of kids who had no one. Because he'd once been that kid himself.

"It's bedtime," Linc said. "Right?"

"Right," Brooke said. "And you're up at bat."

He nodded. "Sure," he said, but didn't move.

"Are you kidding?" she asked. "You don't know what to do?"

He sighed. "Okay, I get it. I'm an asshole. But I know there's a binder around here somewhere. Maybe you could get me the notes."

"No," she said. "Pretend I'm not here. Consider it practice."

She stayed downstairs with a glass of wine—a big one. It wasn't quiet, but Linc did the job, running the kids through a bath assembly line, getting them into pj's with minimal meltdowns, supervising their teeth brushing, and tucking them into bed with somewhat decent efficiency. Which she knew because she tiptoed upstairs and snuck a peek. The house looked like a tornado had hit, but everyone was in their beds.

"Impressive," she said a few minutes later when she met him in the kitchen. He was looking like he'd been through a car wash. Without a car.

"I bribed them," he said. "With another trip to the park, God help me."

She laughed.

Not Linc. He stumbled into the laundry room, stripping off his shirt as he went. Balling it up, he lifted the washing machine lid and tossed it in. Then he stared at the digital display.

"Don't tell me you don't know how to use a washing machine," Brooke said.

"Okay, I won't tell you." He touched the display and it lit up like the Fourth of July. "Want to know the things a guy doesn't know he's bad at until he's married? Making the bed, laundry, being correct, and breathing."

"If you think I'm going to feel sorry for you—"

"No. I needed my ass kicked, especially if it's like this every night." He shuddered. "Holy shit."

"It's usually worse."

He looked sick. "I really fucked up."

"Yeah." She clapped him on the shoulder. "But you're going to fix it."

He slid her a look. "You think I can?"

"Let's put it this way—if you don't, I'm going to kill you, so it doesn't matter."

He nodded grimly. "And I'll deserve it."

Dammit, it was no fun to kick a man when he was down. "I'm sorry it was so horrible today," she said.

"It wasn't horrible. Not even close." He gave what looked like a reluctant smile, flashing a sexy dimple that told her Maddox was going to kill it in the charm department someday. "You were right. I've been missing a lot."

"Yes," she said. And because he was actually going to try, she pointed out the right settings on the washer.

"Thanks." They moved back to the living room. Linc headed straight to the couch and collapsed into it, looking a little shell-shocked. "So how did you potty train Maddox? We've been after him for a while now."

"'We'?" she asked.

"Fine. Mindy. *Mindy's* been trying to potty train him for a while."

She shrugged. "I mentioned a few times how going without a diaper would make him a little man instead of a baby. And then the other day, he did his thing right before camp and brought me a diaper to change him. I told him he was going to have to wait a few minutes because I was helping Mason build a fort, and that only potty-trained kiddos could get inside it."

Linc stared at her. "You're a little scary."

"And smart."

"And smart," he agreed. "Smarter than Mindy and I put together. And we've got three degrees between the two of us."

Feeling a little sorry for him—a very little—she poured him a glass of wine, handed it over, and laughed as he gulped it like it was her lemonade.

"Did you know that Maddox could talk?" he asked after a few moments of blessed silence.

"I just learned that today, in fact."

He shook his head. "I thought we were still in the barking stage."

"What did he say?"

"He told a lady in the park with two infant twins that she had nice puppies. Right after that, Millie kicked sand on a kid twice her size for making fun of Mason for wearing a girl's dinosaur costume. The kid's mother wanted me to make her apologize."

"Did you?"

"Hell no. I told her my kid would apologize right after hers did the same for being a little asshole."

Brooke grinned. "You've got really great kids, you know."

"I know." He sighed and closed his eyes, head back. "We went to McDonald's on the way home. Even though Millie told me that Maddox always throws up McDonald's. And guess what? Maddox threw up his McDonald's. In my Mercedes. Everywhere."

He rubbed his hands over his face. His hair was standing on end. He was pale, and now that he mentioned it, he did smell vaguely of vomit.

"I've got no idea how Mindy does this day in and day out," he said quietly, eyes closed. "No wonder she went nuts. She's lucky to have you. Do you think she's ever coming back?"

She'd better. "Maybe she just needs a few more naps and some carbs."

He laughed, but went serious again. "I want to help her through this."

"You tell her that?"

"Yes. I've been an idiot."

"Yes. Now tell me you've got this."

"I've got this."

Dr. Linc wakes up, she thought.

She just wished she could.

CHAPTER 9

"I love my kids. They're . . . amazing. But holy shit,
they're also the cutest little soul-suckers I've ever seen."

A few days later, Mindy Lemon-Tennant pulled into Wildstone with a whole bunch of mixed emotions. She'd waited
until dark to come home on purpose. She'd loved LA. She'd
loved Brooke's place, Tommy's company, and how clearheaded
she'd felt after catching up on her sleep. She'd also loved being
away from the responsibility of the POP Smoothie Shop she'd
once upon a time wanted to own with her whole heart.

But she also loved Wildstone, and felt her heart clutch as she
pulled into her driveway. And as much as she loved this house
she'd grown up in, she'd missed what was inside it even more.
Missing her kids and Linc was an actual physical ache in her
chest that no amount of food or wine or antacids had been able
to ease.

But . . . she had no idea how to come home again. Especially to the sister who'd saved her life this past week, the same sister who'd pulled back so much emotionally that they were strangers.

It was eight thirty, past the kids' bedtime. The house was quiet, but not dark. Someone was up. Brooke? Linc? On a normal workday, he never came home before nine, so she figured he was still at work. Taking a deep breath, she headed in, crossing through the dark living room to her favorite room in the house—her kitchen. She'd missed her kitchen. She'd missed her beloved appliances. She'd missed her oven. She'd missed baking . . .

Brooke was sitting on the countertop drinking out of Mindy's favorite mug. It was one of those mugs you could write your own slogan on. She'd always worked hard at finding just the right uplifting message to use every day. She'd written the last one on the morning she'd left, and it had read, *Find the Calm in the Chaos.*

It now read, *My sister went to LA and all I got was this lousy mug.* Fair.

"Hi, honey, I'm home," she quipped.

"Good. And I especially liked the way you timed your homecoming to miss bedtime," Brooke said.

Okay, not exactly a hug and kiss hello, but it was more than the usual silence she'd gotten from Brooke over the past few years. Mindy set her purse on the table. She wanted to see the kids more than anything, but she didn't know where she and Brooke stood, and she wanted to. She'd been in freak-out mode when she'd showed up on Brooke's LA doorstep, and though they'd texted multiple times a day since then, it had been all about the kids. "Everything okay?" she asked.

"Yep," Brooke said, popping the *P* sound. She refilled the mug from a nearly empty wine bottle behind her, answering the mystery of what she was drinking. "Although I've been worried sick, and here you are, looking like a million damn bucks in new clothes and new hair and . . . wait—*are those my shoes?*"

Mindy felt a warm glow that Brooke had been worried about her and looked down at the fabulous wedges she'd liberated from her sister's closet. "They felt neglected."

Brooke looked her over. "New hair, new clothes, you've lost two pounds, and you're wearing makeup. Tommy had the girls give you a makeover."

Mindy preened a little bit; she couldn't help it. It was a thrill to not look half dead. "I've been working out, too. Weights and treadmill."

"Okay, who are you and what have you done with my sister?" Brooke asked. "You hate running. You used to say that if you were ever found dead on a treadmill, we should know that you were murdered elsewhere and dumped there."

"I still hate it. But two pounds! You could tell?" she asked, pleased.

"Tommy told me," Brooke said. "He texts me a hundred times a day."

"Oh," Mindy said, feeling a little deflated.

"He's my best friend, Min. Of course he kept me updated on your well-being. I was worried sick about you. He said you were doing good, looking happy while living my life."

Brooke hadn't said that with a single drop of sarcasm, but

Mindy winced just the same. Because it was true. She'd just spent five days with Brooke's things in Brooke's world, which had been a kind of stolen intimacy she hadn't realized she'd missed so much. Being in LA, living Brooke's life with no Brooke, had made her ache for her sister more than she'd thought possible. "I appreciate what you did for me." She paused, understanding that they were in a different place than they used to be, but wishing they could go back to when they'd been BFFs. "I miss you. And if I did something to make you stay away all this time—"

"Stop." Brooke closed her eyes. "You didn't. Me staying away was about me, not you. And for what it's worth, I'm sorry for that."

Mindy felt the knot in her chest loosen slightly. But only very slightly, because she knew Brooke was clearly still holding back. "It's worth a whole lot, actually," she said quietly. "But I really need to go kiss my babies now." She turned to the door, but stopped at Brooke's words.

"Linc handled bedtime. He fell asleep in Maddox's bed with him."

"He's home from work?" Mindy asked in disbelief.

"Yep. He says he's going to try to get home by six every night."

That didn't compute. "Maddox's bed is a three-foot toddler bed. How in the world does my six-foot husband fit in there?"

"I don't know, Min," Brooke said with a shrug. "Love makes you do some pretty stupid shit. And he does love you, by the way. Oh, and he's not doing Dr. Hottie. He was laboring under the false impression that he could have female friends with perfect boobs. He's not doing Brittney, either, who, bee-tee-dub, is very happy with her girlfriend."

"Oh," Mindy said, feeling very small. "I didn't know."

"The kids knew."

Mindy heard something in Brooke's tone that put her back up. "She doesn't talk much to me."

"Because you intimidate her." Brooke topped off her mug with the last of the wine. "Remember when we were kids and we wondered why our parents were always in a bad mood? Now I'm like, okay, yes, it all makes perfect sense."

"You don't usually drink wine," Mindy said. Confusion was becoming her default emotion. "I'd have thought you'd have gotten into Mom's vodka, which is still in the freezer."

"It's two-thirds water, not vodka."

"Why would it be two-thirds water?" Mindy asked.

"Because in high school, I used to steal it and replace it with water."

Mindy let out a long, shaky breath. She was in overload mode. "Are we going to talk about why you hate me?"

"I don't hate you. I'm actually impressed at what you pull off here every single day. And I get why you lost your shit. Even with Brittney's help, it's . . . a lot. But I gotta say, it's also pretty damn great. If you slowed down a little and let up on that tight grip of the reins, you might like it more."

Mindy felt her eyes fill. Dammit. "I do like it. I love it. I've missed being here. I missed Linc and the kids. I missed every-thing, even the dirty footprints on my bed. I already miss your sheets, but at least today was sheet-washing day here. Page two, tab seven in my binder—" She broke off because Brooke had looked away. "And . . . you didn't wash the sheets today." Mindy nodded. "It's okay, you were probably swamped with everything. It takes a lot of practice to get it all under control."

"That's what I'm saying, Min. Things don't always have to be in perfect control. It's okay to forget to do laundry or go grocery shopping sometimes."

"Says the girl who's twenty-nine and still has four frozen pizzas in the freezer in case she's drunk and hungry."

"Hey," Brooke said. "Those pizzas are gluten-free, *and* the crusts are made out of cauliflower. That makes them a vegetable. And I don't turn twenty-nine until next month, so bite your tongue. Also . . . I'm glad you missed being here, but there're a few things you should know."

Mindy felt her stomach clench. "Like?"

"Like I gave Brittney a raise. And before you say a word, she deserves it."

"I know. The kids are—"

"Your kids aren't the problem. Your kids are wonderful. It's you. You're trying too hard. You're Mom, Min. And I mean that in the most loving way possible. You micromanage the shit out of everything and everyone, but you don't have to. Brittney's good, she knows what she's doing. And . . . there's one more thing."

Oh God. Mindy had to sit. "What?"

"I didn't use the binder."

Mindy stared at her. "What do you mean? But I told you—"

"I know. But it didn't work for me."

"That doesn't even make any sense. It's an organizational tool. Everyone needs a little organization."

"A little?" Brooke asked dryly. "That binder's got hundreds of pages of instructions on how to run your world."

"So?" Mindy was wishing she'd poured herself a mug of wine. "It's called real life, Brooke. You ought to try it sometime!"

"Wow."

"Wow, what?"

"I'm trying to remember if you were always so judgy," Brooke said.

"Yes, I've always been this way! And you've always been"— she gestured at Brooke—"that way."

"What way?"

She'd tried to hold back, tried to be kind, but she said it anyway. "Selfish."

Brooke's eyes narrowed. "Since that's actually true enough to be fair, you should know something else that's true—the kids *thrived* without the damn binder."

Mindy blinked. "But . . . how did you know all the things, like who goes to bed when, and who'll eat what?"

"We winged it. Oh, and newsflash, Mason will most definitely eat a sandwich with the crust still on it. He only makes you cut off the crusts because that gives him an extra minute of your time and a hug."

Mindy put her hand over her mouth and felt her eyes fill again, and Brooke's expression went from anger to wary. "What are you doing?" she asked.

Mindy sniffed. "Nothing!"

"Oh my God. You're crying."

"It's allergies!"

Brooke let out a rough breath, turned to the tissue box on the counter, and pulled out a tissue. And then another. And then another. And then a fourth . . .

This only made Mindy cry harder. "Oh my God, and now you're counting in even numbers like Millie. Did I do that to you both?"

"Min . . ." Brooke blew out a breath. "I've *always* been like Millie. I was Millie before there even was a Millie."

Mindy blew her nose. "How come I didn't know?"

"Look, you're good at what you do, and I'm good at what I do. Which is hiding. A lot."

Brooke shrugged, and Mindy felt like the worst sister on the planet. Seemed like she had a lot of things she needed to be better at. "You've been here almost a week and you don't look like you're falling apart or losing your mind. What's the secret? And how come you're better than me at everything?"

Brooke snorted. "Are you kidding me? The only thing I'm better at is pretending to be better. And I survived your life because I'm only here for a very short time. I'm the fun aunt—not the same as being Mom." She softened her voice. "Who's been essentially single parenting on her own. And just because no one starved or died this week doesn't mean they didn't miss you, Min. They did. The kids did. Linc did. Hell, even I did."

"You did?" Mindy whispered hopefully.

"Yes. Do you know how hard it is to read *Where the Wild Things Are* with the same high level of enthusiasm a thousand times in a row? And if you skip even one little word, Maddox makes you start over."

Mindy let out a shaky breath. Okay, so having Brooke actually miss her for real had been too much to hope for. "So you *did* read the binder!"

Brooke shrugged. "Maybe I flipped through it a time or two." She paused and gave a reluctant smile. "Or four hundred. You're a nut, you know that, right?"

"Yes." Oh, how she knew it. "Thanks for being here for me this week," she said softly. "I know it couldn't have been easy for you since you don't have kids of your own."

Brooke's smile faded. "Why do you always say it like that?"

"Say what like what?" Mindy asked.

"You throw it in my face that I don't have kids, like it makes me a lesser woman than you. You do realize that lots of people never have kids and can still take care of others just fine, right? You've got no idea what my life is or isn't. Maybe it's completely fulfilling just the way it is, did you ever think of that?"

Mindy was taken aback by her sister's vehemence. "I didn't mean anything by it," she said carefully. "But I did just live your life for a week."

"So?" Brooke asked a little testily.

"So . . ." Mindy knew enough to tread lightly. "It was . . . nice."

"Nice?" Still sitting on the counter, Brooke crossed her arms. "That doesn't sound like me at all."

"That's sort of my point," Mindy said unapologetically. "After a few days walking in your shoes—"

"Literally," Brooke interjected.

"Whatever, you have great shoes," Mindy said. "But your life . . . it's . . ."

"Exciting? Adrenaline-fueled? Adventurous?"

Mindy had no idea how to do this, how to tell Brooke she knew the truth about her job. "I was going to say lonely."

Instead of being insulted, Brooke rolled her eyes. "That's because you weren't working twenty-four-seven. You had no real responsibilities. Trust me, if you'd taken on my job instead of just my friends and my bed, you'd be exhausted."

Mindy hesitated, but decided to go for it. She went to the doorway and dragged in the duffel bag she'd packed for Brooke. "I brought your cameras home."

Brooke look shocked. "What?"

"Found them in your closet when I was packing some clothes for you."

"You mean stealing my shoes," she said, not bending down to take the duffel bag. In fact, she was eyeing it like it was a bomb.

It was all adding up to an equation Mindy didn't like—Brooke was also in crisis mode. But she was going through it all alone because she'd rather die than ask for help. "There was a lot of dust on your equipment, which surprised me," she said quietly. "Your cameras were always your babies."

Brooke's expression was carefully blank now. "It's pollen season," she said, more than a little defensively. "Dust gets everywhere. And I'm going home, so I didn't need more stuff."

"You don't have to rush off."

"Yes, I do," Brooke said. "I've got work to get back to."

Mindy warred with herself for a moment, but it was clear Brooke wasn't going to tell her the truth on her own. "I met Cole," she said. "Tommy introduced us."

"I know."

"We all had dinner a couple of times," Mindy said. "When I told him about how you haven't been home in forever and how much I needed you, he said you never took any personal time and that you had several weeks saved up that you could take if you needed."

Brooke shook her head. "No way. Cole wouldn't say that. He wants me back in LA."

"He said it."

Brooke narrowed her eyes, running the pads of her thumbs over her fingertips, back and forth the way Millie did, and that more than anything broke Mindy's heart. How had she not ever seen that before?

"What did you *really* tell him to make him say it?" Brooke asked.

Mindy bit her lower lip, feeling a little bit guilty about this part. "I might've mentioned that I thought you needed this get-away for yourself as well for me."

"Because?"

"Because maybe you needed me as much as I needed you."

"You used his emotions for me against him? That's some bullshit, Min, even for you." She hopped off the counter and turned to the sink, staring out into the dark night. "You're un-believable, you know that? And there's no way I'm staying in Wildstone."

Mindy's chest got tight. She was messing this all up. "I prom-ise I won't ask you to babysit another second, but please? Please stay? We haven't spent time together in so long."

"I can't just abandon my job, Min. I'm super busy. There's a lot of travel, and stuff to do—"

"There's no travel." Mindy drew a deep breath and met Brooke's gaze. "Tommy's staff told me."

Brooke completely closed up. "Told you what?"

Heart aching, Mindy said, "That you work behind the scenes now, producing, editing, and writing scripts. You're really great at what you do, but you're not out there risking life and limb anymore. Also that June is a very slow month in the studio, that's why Cole can give you the time."

Brooke looked away. "How long were you going to let me go on about how busy I am traveling?"

"Honestly? I was prepared to let you lie straight to my face for as long as you needed to, because though I don't know why you changed jobs, it was obviously important to you to keep it a secret from me." She paused. "Which, for the record, I hate."

Brooke remained silent, and Mindy knew she was losing her. "Please stay," she whispered again. "You can keep being annoyed at me if you want to—I just really need you here. I brought enough of your clothes to last until the zombie apocalypse. You'll be happy here."

Brooke craned her neck to meet Mindy's gaze, her expression speaking volumes on her doubt about that.

"We're barely even family anymore," Mindy said softly.

Brooke actually laughed genuinely at this. "You've just re-arranged my life so it works in with yours. The only one who would dare do that is my sister. That's about as family as family gets."

"So you'll stay?"

"You really still need me here?"

"*Yes,*" Mindy said with feeling.

Their gazes met and held, and Brooke sighed. "Then I'll stay. But once you're good, I'm out, okay? No more manipulations. I'm going back to get it together."

"Get what together?"

"My life." Brooke's smile was sad. "Because I think it's possible I'm as messed up as you are." With that, she left the kitchen.

Alone with her thoughts, Mindy stood for a long moment alone in her bright white kitchen, the one with the stainless steel appliances she'd hand-picked and the pretty see-through cabinets and wood floors Garrett had put in, all of her prized baking tools displayed on the countertops. It was just what she'd wanted.

And yet nothing felt right.

Brooke was as messed up as she was? Why hadn't Mindy noticed? Why hadn't she tried to help? Turning, she moved through the dark living room, startled to see her sister curled up on the couch pretending to already be fast asleep.

Mindy stilled. She hadn't given a single thought to the fact that there wasn't a bedroom for her sister, at least not unless Brooke had transplanted a kid or two, which she clearly hadn't. Feeling like a big, fat jerk, she swallowed hard, but the sudden lump in her throat didn't dissipate. She had to do better, for everyone in her life, she told herself as she grabbed a throw blanket and spread it over Brooke, who pulled the blanket over her head and rolled away.

"Tomorrow we'll move you to the guesthouse, okay?" Mindy whispered. "It's got a kitchenette and a really comfortable futon that I ordered from the shopping network. Ellen DeGeneres loved it."

No response from Brooke.

Telling herself Brooke understood, that she would fix it—she would fix everything—Mindy headed up the stairs. The night-light in Millie's room allowed her to see that the room was shockingly clean, with toys in the bin and all the clothes hung up. Her daughter was wrapped around a huge stuffed teddy bear, smiling in her sleep. Probably plotting her world takeover.

She tiptoed into the boys' room next. Mason was asleep in his bed, his feet on his pillow, his head under the covers. She gently turned him around, tucked him in, and brushed a kiss to his brow.

Maddox had his face smashed into his toddler bed, his butt in the air, fast asleep.

No diaper.

She was a little worried about that, but didn't want to wake him. So she concentrated on the man curled up in the tiny bed with him.

Dr. Linc Tennant, father of her children, keeper of her heart, which started pounding like crazy with nerves, anxiety . . .

Love.

His dark eyes opened, heavy-lidded as he worked to come awake, and as it had since they were little kids, her heart took a big, stupid leap at the sight of him: hair messy, eyes sleepy, a crease on his cheek from the pillow. He was in his old college sweats and a T-shirt that read TRUST ME, I'M A DOCTOR.

He blinked at her and slowly sat up, wincing, as he unfurled his long body and stood. Taking her hand, he held a finger to his lips and pulled her from the room into their master bed-room. There, he flipped on the light and turned to stare at her.

She knew what he was seeing. She was showered, dressed, and in makeup—all put together for the first time in . . . forever.

And he wasn't. He looked like how she'd looked every day since having kids—a wreck—and she couldn't help it . . . she smiled.

He smiled back and reached for her, but she put a hand to his chest to stop him.

Covering her hand with one of his, he gently squeezed as he ducked down to look into her eyes. "You look beautiful, and I want to hear about your week, but first, I know we've got some things to talk about. I know I've screwed up."

Oh God. So Brooke had been wrong about him not fooling around. She stilled and dropped her gaze to stare at his chest, wondering how long it might take to clean up the mess if she killed him right here and now. "Define 'screwed up,'" she said carefully.

With a finger under her chin, he brought her face back up to his. "It's not what you're thinking. It never will be. Brooke shocked me with what you believed about me. She was like a pit bull about it, too, but I convinced her—I hope I convinced her—and I plan to convince you, too."

Brooke had taken on Linc for her. Something to think about. "But—"

He put a finger over her lips. "What I mean is that I've screwed up my priorities. I get that you think I've forgotten our vows, but I haven't. I wouldn't. We'll circle back to that in a sec and discuss why you think I could ever, *would* ever, do that to you or the kids." He paused, and in the silence, she could hear her heart pounding in her ears. "Mindy," he said. "You need to know that you're not the only one not getting what you want or what you planned on."

Now her heart completely stopped.

"I've missed out on being with you and the kids," he said. "And the years are going by too fast. I'm trying to fix that."

The words were both a balm to her soul and a worry. "Do you mean it? Because I don't want to be the one who makes you do something you don't want to do, Linc. That will only cause more problems."

"No, it won't. I've let my life rule yours, and that's not fair. I want to be around more for you. Starting with Hawaii."

This caused a surge of excitement. A long time ago, they'd planned to honeymoon in Hawaii, but she'd been three months pregnant and sick as a dog when she'd walked down the aisle. They'd canceled the trip and had never been able to reschedule due to Linc's crazy work schedule. "Don't tease me."

"I'm not." He smiled. "I rescheduled it for two weeks from now. Your parents said they'd come stay at the house and watch the kids if we needed them to. Ethan's going to handle the practice while we're gone, and beyond that, he's going to have to step up to do his fair share."

The hope dwindled as fast as it'd come. She didn't want to talk bad about his dumbass brother, but, well, Ethan *was* a dumbass. "Linc—"

"He owes us."

"Yeah, he does," she said. "Because you've always been there for him, but he's never returned the favor, not once. You know damn well he's going to pull the poor-me routine and back out on us at the last minute."

"Not this time," Linc said firmly. "He promised. And I'm promising you." He took her hand in his and drew her in closer, pressing her palm to his chest. "I missed you, Min. I want this. I want to make you happy. I'm pretty sure I'm going to make mistakes. Hopefully not too many, but we both know I will. I'll try to learn from each of them, though. Is that enough for you?"

She drew in a deep breath, still raw from her talk with Brooke. She'd really thought she'd gotten herself together, but as it turned out, she was more screwed up than she'd thought. "I want it to be."

"Okay, we'll start there." He was watching her think, his gaze pensive. "Do you really think I'm having an affair?"

She looked away from his searing gaze. "I don't know what I think. You're always gone, working with cute nurses and doctors. We never see each other. Why wouldn't I wonder?"

"Because we're married and I love you." He shook his head. "Remember when my dad was dying, and Ethan and I agreed as his sons to take over his practice? We talked about that, you and me, about the long hours, about me being gone a lot, and you said it was okay with you, that I should step up and handle the practice rather than sell it."

"I did say that," she said. And at the time, she'd meant it. But that had been before Maddox had been mobile, plus a couple of crazy, sleep-deprived years during which she hadn't always felt human. "And I still think you did the right thing. I guess I just didn't realize how much you'd be working. I thought between the two of you, you'd actually be working less."

"It's been a busy season." His eyes never left hers. "And as for cute nurses and doctors . . . you're the only one I want."

She really wanted to believe that, but it was hard. "Do you remember the last time we made love?"

"Of course." He paused, clearly thinking, and then flashed a sexy smile. "Before I left, we got into the costume chest and played my favorite—the sexy flight attendant, whose job it is to cater to her only passenger's every whim. You gave me the best blow j—"

"That wasn't right before you left. That was over a month ago."

He blinked. "No."

"Yes. And I'm asking if you remember the last time we *both* had an orgasm."

Another slow blink. "It was that same night," he said.

She cocked her head. "Was it?"

He paused, staring at her. "Min," he finally said softly, pained, clearly upset at himself.

"*No*, it's okay. I can't remember the last time I had an orgasm, either, so it's not all on you. It's more because I never have enough energy to really concentrate."

This seemed to shake him even more. "You have to concentrate?"

She let out a breath and closed her eyes. "I haven't felt sexy. I've felt . . . overwhelmed and behind on everything, and I never have a second to myself. Before this past week, I can't even remember the last time I was in the bathroom alone. But it's even more than that."

"I know," he said. "You think I don't see you anymore." She felt his hands gently take hers and she opened her eyes to find that he'd stepped closer. Slowly, he raised their joined hands to his mouth, brushing a kiss across her knuckles. "Min, to me, you're still the *only* woman in the room. In any room. Tell me what you need."

"You," she whispered. "I need you."

His eyes darkened and he closed the gap, brushing his body to hers. "You've got me."

"That's not what I mean." She gave him a gentle nudge back because it was hard to think when he turned on the charm. "I'm not sorry that I'm a mom and a wife, but I can't be those things if I've lost myself. I think I need some more time."

He gave a slow nod. "I understand."

"Do you?"

"Yes. I took the kids to the park and then to dinner yesterday, and I needed a nap afterward."

She let out a low laugh. "So a few hours on your own with them and you were done in?"

"I love my kids," he said. "They're . . . amazing. But holy shit, they're also the cutest little soul-suckers I've ever seen." His smile faded. "Time to yourself. To find yourself. Done, Min. What else?"

"You know it's not going to be that easy."

"We'll make it easy," he said.

"I've asked Brooke to stay for a little while. I don't know if she will. We're . . . not in the best place."

"And you want to fix that, too."

"I want to fix everything," she said. "I need to, in order to find my happy."

His hands slid up her arms to cup her face. "We'll do it. We will. Just keep talking to me, okay? Keep telling me what you need."

She nodded.

He smiled and nudged her backward until the mattress hit the backs of her knees. As he urged her down, she opened her mouth to tell him that she didn't know if she was ready, but he gave her a gentle, tender kiss and then . . . covered her up with a blanket. "Sleep," he said. "Let's just start with sleep."

It was one of the sweetest things he'd ever done.

WHEN SHE WOKE up a solid eight hours later, she was alone. Linc appeared in the doorway. Maddox was snoozing on his shoulder. And drooling.

Her heart melted.

"He woke up a couple of hours ago," Linc whispered. "I'll get them ready for camp."

Wow, she thought. Maybe they had a shot after all . . .

CHAPTER 10

"I'm feeling a lot of things, Brooke.
But pity isn't one of them."

Brooke woke up on the floor. At some point in the middle of the night, she'd fallen off the couch and just stayed down. Now she had a kink in her neck and she felt like twenty-eight going on eighty-eight.

She eyed her phone for the time and found a group text from Cole and Tommy.

Cole: In the interesting news department, I managed to do my job and yours this week. Which means I'm not sure why I pay you, other than that your sweet and sunny disposition is such a joy.

Brooke: You miss me. Cute.

Cole: I'm not cute.

Tommy: True. He's been moping around all week.

Brooke: It's because my job isn't as easy as he thinks. And I'm still gone because you were both stupid enough to let Mindy work you over like a bunch of amateurs. So now it's going to be a bit longer.

Cole: How much longer? Tommy makes shitty coffee.

Brooke: Aw. That's almost romantic. And it's hard to say how much longer exactly, because in MY interesting news department, REALITY CONTINUES TO RUIN MY LIFE.

Tommy: Yeah, but are you getting any? I'm on a sex fast to cleanse my palate.

Brooke: On that note, I'm out.

Cole: You didn't answer the question. And let's be clear, the right answer is no, cuz you miss me too much.

Brooke: I've been taking care of three kids. Not only am I not getting any, I'm too exhausted to get any. But I do miss you. Both of you.

Cole: I could be there in four hours and fix all your problems.

Brooke: I know, and thank you, but I've got to do this alone.

Tommy: Alone isn't as much fun.

The convo quickly deteriorated into boy/sex humor. Brooke slipped her phone away, got up, and stretched. She found Linc in the kitchen feeding the kids. Or at least she thought maybe that was his intention, but there was a lot of commotion going on. The kids were running around like puppies, yelling and laughing and yelling some more.

Garrett came in the outside door and ignored the mayhem in the way only a man could, grabbing a big bowl, adding cereal. He and Linc reached for the nearly empty gallon of milk on the counter at the same time.

"Wrestle for it!" Mason exclaimed, and all the kids clapped their hands in glee.

Linc and Garrett grinned in unison and sat at the table, where they began to arm wrestle, staring deep into each other's eyes.

Rolling hers, Brooke stole Garrett's cereal bowl, added the last of the milk, grabbed a spoon, and leaned back against the counter to eat as she took in the show. "Are you two serious right now?"

"Very serious," Millie said. "This happens a lot."

"Who usually wins?" Brooke asked.

"Uncle Garrett."

"Thanks, baby," Linc grunted.

"You do good, Daddy. Uncle Garrett just does gooder."

Garrett smirked.

The men were pretty evenly matched; the only sign of struggle as they continued to arm wrestle was that both of their faces were flushed, their bodies tense with exertion.

Idiots. "You guys realize that no one's ready for camp yet, right?" she asked the room.

No reaction. Both men were starting to sweat now. Clearly this was going to take a while. She leaned in, keeping her voice down. "Maybe the two of you could play this game of Whose Dick Is Bigger later, when impressionable children aren't watching and learning how to become Neanderthals."

Neither responded. They probably didn't have any oxygen left in their pea brains. She let out a piercing whistle and everyone froze, including the guys. She pointed at Millie. "Go get dressed for camp." She pointed at Mason. "The same for you." She looked at Maddox. "How you doing, kid?"

He patted his bum through a pair of shorts. No diaper. She high-fived him. "You're my favorite."

"Hey!" Millie yelled from the other room. "I heard that!"

"Good," Brooke yelled back. "Help your brothers!" She looked at the guys. They'd stopped arm wrestling at least. Linc hadn't showered or combed his hair. He was in a dirty T-shirt and sweats, no shoes. "Wow," she said. "You look like shit. And not at all like a man who got his wife back last night."

He ran a hand through his hair. "I'm trying to regain her trust. Maddox had an accident at four a.m., so I had to get up and start laundry. But then Mason got up because he was thirsty, and he spilled OJ everywhere, so I've got another load to do and I haven't even managed to switch over the first one yet."

"Sometimes success is just getting the laundry into the dryer before the mildew sets in," she said.

Linc just shook his head.

"I have no idea how Mindy's kept her sanity this long."

"Uh, in case you haven't noticed, she hasn't."

"I'm such a dick."

"No arguments here," she said. "And also, my work here is done." She headed out the door.

"You're leaving?" he asked, sounding panicked.

"Don't worry. You can google how to work the dryer when you forget." She gave him a little smile. "But no, I'm not *leaving* leaving, at least not today. Figure you might need me to yell at you some more." And plus . . . she wasn't quite ready to go, which made no sense. She'd done what she'd come to do. Handle Linc. Have it out with Garrett . . . She accidentally looked over at him and found him watching her, giving nothing of his thoughts away. She turned from him, too, feeling unsettled and off and . . . sad, all at the same time, never a good combination for her.

She heard Garrett rise from the table. "That wasn't a tie," he said to Linc. "You forfeited."

"No way. Brooke stopped us."

"Yes, and she's *your* sister-in-law." The implication being that she was related by marriage to Linc, and nothing at all to Garrett.

But he'd kissed her. He'd touched her. He'd looked at her in a way that told her she was *more* than nothing to him. So she was confused, to say the least.

Then he came close and relieved her of the cereal bowl. Holding her gaze in his, he took a bite and then left the room.

With the cereal.

Ass.

"What's with you two?" Linc asked.

"Nothing."

"Want to try that again and make me believe it?"

"Nope."

Linc took that in stride in the way only a man who couldn't multitask would. "I know I can fumble my way through taking care of my kids," he said, "but I don't know what to do for Mindy. Help?"

"I think maybe you're already starting by just being here for her."

"That can't possibly be enough. If you were me, what else would you do?"

"I'd make her waffles."

"Is that because Garrett just stole back his breakfast and *you* want waffles?"

"Yes." She smiled. "But also because *Mindy* loves waffles and rarely lets herself have them. But you should also make pancakes because, well, you've met her. She needs choices."

"Good idea. And here." He handed her a key.

"What's this?"

"The key to the guesthouse. Now that I'm back, I'll take the kid watch. You don't need to be woken in the middle of the night. And you'll have more privacy."

She took the key because she was done with the living room floor. "It'll only be a few days," she repeated. "At the most. You're going to get it together and keep it together, yeah?"

"Yeah." He slung an arm around her neck and brushed a kiss

to her temple. "But you're welcome to stay as long as you want. We miss you. I hope you know that."

She'd gotten by for years now because she'd cut ties to her emotions. But those emotions were suddenly spreading through her like wildfire, going after her heartstrings.

Stupid heartstrings.

She lugged her backpack and the ridiculously huge duffel Mindy had packed for her out to the guesthouse and stood in the doorway. "Guesthouse" was a fancy way to say "pool house." And since it was filled with crap, it was really just a closet.

But it was all hers, all 250 square feet, including the tiny bathroom and kitchenette. She'd take it just to escape the insanity of the big house. Dropping her stuff, she moved to the far wall. It was all windows, and that's where she discovered an unexpected bonus.

A direct view into Garrett's kitchen.

And it was like Christmas and her birthday all in one, because he was currently shirtless and sweaty and doing pull-ups in the doorway. Her mouth went dry and her body tingled, both of which were majorly annoying. But damn, she missed intimacy. Or at least the illusion of it. She wanted a man's hands on her. She wanted to feel a warm, hard body against hers and have it take her outside herself, if only for just a little while.

The thought had her aching. Shaking her head, she pulled the shades down and stripped for a shower. Only problem: The water didn't get hot. Or even lukewarm. She waited a few more minutes to be sure, but nope. Just icy-cold water. She could handle a whole hell of a lot of things, and had, but a cold shower wasn't going to be one of them.

With a sigh, she wrapped herself in a towel. Going back to the big house to shower meant joining the circus, and she needed a few minutes to herself. Out the window, she saw Garrett crossing the yard. He'd dressed in jeans and a T-shirt, a tool belt strapped low on his hips, looking better than any man had a right to look. He went into Mindy's house.

Brooke took a good look at Garrett's place. She'd bet her last dollar *he* had hot water. And as a bonus, his house was empty . . . Grabbing her duffel bag, she slung it over her shoulder and stepped outside, looking right and then left to make sure the coast was clear before sprinting barefoot across the yard.

Garrett did indeed have hot water. In fact, his shower was *heavenly*. She used his soap, which turned out to be a mistake because now she smelled like him, meaning sexy as hell. Just pressing her nose to her own arm nearly gave her an orgasm. Dammit. She turned off the water and had to open the door to clear the steam. When she could see, she nearly swallowed her tongue.

Garrett was sprawled out on his bed, hands behind his head, boots crossed.

She held on to her towel and stared at him. "What the actual hell?"

"Right back at you, Goldilocks."

"I needed hot water." She grimaced. "I'm sorry. I should've asked."

He waved a hand, like, *Mi casa es su casa* . . .

So she could use his house, but not his body. Or his heart. Check. "What made you come back?"

"I was looking out Mindy and Linc's bathroom window when you did your cat burglar imitation."

So much for stealth. "Go back to work," she said. "I've got to get dressed, and then I'll get out of your space." She dropped her duffel bag on the bed, but he didn't move. She raised a brow.

"I won't look," he said, and closed his eyes.

She did some mental knuckle cracking. He'd seen it all before, of course, but she hadn't been mad at them both at the time. And she *was* mad at them both. She was mad at herself for caring and at him for making her care. But screw it. If he wasn't into her, it didn't matter, right? So she dropped the towel.

At a low, rough male sound, she glanced up and found Garrett's eyes open and on her. "Hey," she said, scrambling to wrap the towel around herself. "You said you wouldn't look!"

"I lied." His gaze wandered down her body and then slowly back to her eyes, his own dark with heat. "I learned from the best."

"Not funny."

"I wasn't going for funny." He rose from the bed with an effortless grace she couldn't have managed on her best day—which this clearly wasn't. Not sure what he was planning, she let out a squeak at his approach, and with as much dignity as she could, given that all she was wearing was a towel, she grabbed her duffel bag and ran.

Back in the guesthouse, she rushed to get dressed, half braced for Garrett to follow her.

He didn't.

Telling herself that's what she wanted, she went through the rest of the duffel bag, more from curiosity than anything else.

Her sister had thrown in plenty of clothes, and . . . indeed, her cameras. She pulled out her favorite, an older Nikon that had never failed her.

The minute she had it in her hands, the ache inside her deepened. Great. Now she needed sex *and* to get outside and take pictures. She put the strap around her neck and hopped into her car without saying a word to anyone. She went back to the bluffs and hit the stairs. At the top, she stood back so far from the edge of the bluffs that she couldn't see anything. But she needed forward progress on *something*, so, rolling her eyes at herself, she took two baby steps off the trail and gulped in air.

"You're being ridiculous," she said out loud.

No one cared, especially her feet, which refused to take her any farther. "Dammit." Slinging her camera from her front to her back, she dropped to her knees and then sort of shuffled another few inches toward the edge. *One, two, three, four . . .*

"You okay, ma'am?"

She nearly leapt out of her skin as she craned her neck to look behind her. A teenage kid had come down the trail. *Ma'am?* Was he kidding? Did she look old enough to be a damn ma'am? "I'm fine."

"You need help down?"

"No!" She took a deep breath and added a hopefully normal smile. "I'm okay, thanks."

He shrugged and ambled away, continuing down.

"Ma'am," she muttered. "I'm not a damn ma'am." She forced herself to shift another few feet toward the edge. She still had like twenty feet to go and was sweating in places that shouldn't be sweating as she moved inch by inch. *One, two, three, four.*

One, two, three, four . . . Her initial goal had been to hang her feet over the edge, but just the thought made her want to throw up.

Baby steps, the therapist she'd seen after the helicopter crash had told her.

Right. Baby steps. That worked, as long as they came in even numbers. She did eventually get there, but she did not hang her feet over. She sat and concentrated on breathing. When she no longer felt like she was an impending stroke victim, she spent an hour there taking pictures and almost forgetting she'd left that world behind.

Going down was very slightly easier, and afterward, she sat on the beach awhile, until the sound of the surf and the feel of it vibrating beneath her soothed her soul. She'd done what she'd come here to do. She'd set Linc straight. She'd helped Mindy. She'd talked to Garrett and made things as right as she could. That meant she could go.

But oddly enough, she wasn't quite ready to leave.

It was the end of the day before she walked in the back door to Mindy and Linc's, needing food and possibly alcohol.

Her sister was in the pantry, rearranging the shelves.

"I thought you were at the shop today," Brooke said, knowing Mindy had gotten up early to bake a bunch of goods for the front display and to cover for Xena, who'd taken the week off now that Mindy was back.

"Was at the shop," Mindy said. "Just got back."

"So you got up at the crack of dawn and baked for the shop, then you worked the shop, and now you're cleaning?" Brooke asked.

"It's a little thing called my life."

"I know," Brooke said. "But I bet Brittney would do some of it for you."

"I know, but . . . I like doing it." Mindy shook her head. "She's upstairs with the kids, who are home from camp. I apologized to her."

"For treating her like crap, you mean?"

Mindy winced. "Yes. She said not to worry about it. So she's playing with the kids and I'm cleaning."

"Proof positive that one of us was switched at birth."

Mindy smiled. "Garrett just said the same thing to me. It's so nice to have him next door again. He's happy there, though he's not home much. He works with the rec center and soccer league for at-risk kids, and he even does some emergency fostering when the need arises, but he's also been really in demand with work, so—"

"Why are we talking about Garrett?"

Mindy looked surprised. "I don't know. Because we were all close friends? And I guess I wanted you to know how great he's been to me. So great that . . ." She grimaced. "So this part's actually kind of embarrassing."

"You could just stop talking."

But apparently Mindy couldn't. "Once Linc and I went into our rut, I started crushing on any guy who smiled at me."

Brooke slid her a look. "Including Garrett?"

Mindy grimaced again. "You know what? Forget it."

Brooke wanted to, but it was a little late now. "You're married, Min. And he's your *neighbor*." *And he had his tongue down my throat, so . . .*

"Well, it's not like he's an old geezer with a spare tire and false teeth," Mindy said, clearly defensive now. "He's smart and funny and . . . well, hot. I mean, if you could see him in the mornings after his run—"

"Jeez, Min."

"What? Let's be honest, it's not like I'm the only Lemon sister who ever crushed on him. You had a big, fat crush on him in high school. You know you did."

That's when they both heard a noise behind them. Hoping it was Ketchup, but knowing her luck didn't run in that direction, Brooke turned to find, yep, both Linc and Garrett in the doorway. Awesome. Linc was in a suit, Garrett in battered jeans, battered boots, and a T-shirt that had some sawdust still sticking to it, both men clearly coming in from work.

Linc glanced at Garrett, then back to Mindy. "Tell me there's dinner."

Mindy blinked. "That's what you want to talk about?" she asked. "Not my crush on the sexy guy who lives right next door?"

"I skipped lunch," Linc said. "My stomach's eating my other organs."

Garrett raised his hand. "I want to talk about the fact that you think I'm sexy."

"I hope it's steak," Linc said, sticking his head in the fridge.

Mindy went hands on hips. "So you don't care about my crush?"

Linc shut the fridge. "Do you still have it?"

Mindy looked at Garrett.

Garrett raised a brow.

"Would you be jealous if I said yes?" Mindy asked Linc.

Linc eyed his wife, suddenly appearing to realize she was 100 percent serious. He paused. "You really have a crush on my best friend?"

Mindy sighed. "No, my *vagina* had a crush on him, not the rest of me. And he's also *my* best friend."

"Please never say 'vagina' again," Brooke said.

Linc looked at Garrett.

Garrett lifted his hands. "Hey, there's enough of me to go around."

Mindy smacked him. "Oh my God. Tell him nothing ever happened!"

"That's true," Garrett told Linc. "Mostly because she's a little . . ." He circled his finger at the side of his head, the universal sign for crazy.

Mindy smacked him again.

"Ow," he said. "And see?"

"Look," Mindy told her husband, "it was a temporary crush. Like I said, my—" She broke off and eyed Brooke. "—lady parts wanted him. But my heart wanted you, the end."

Brooke went to the freezer for the vodka.

"I thought you said that was seventy-five percent water," Mindy said.

"It's still twenty-five percent vodka." She poured a healthy glug into a cup and knocked it back.

"Is no one going to ask Brooke about *her* crush on Garrett?" Linc asked. "Maybe she's still got one."

Everyone looked at Brooke.

Brooke considered a second shot of vodka.

Mindy took that bottle away. "Do you still have a crush on him?"

"Gee, it's such a shock that I don't come home anymore," Brooke said. No way was she spilling the beans, not on their past, and not on whatever that had been in the hot tub. It wasn't that Mindy and Linc wouldn't understand. It was that she didn't know how to talk about her and Garrett from that time in her life, not without losing it. And there was no reason to do so anyway, since it wasn't like they were going to be a thing now.

Or ever.

"And I don't have a crush on him," she said without looking at Garrett. "If I ever did, and that's a big if, it was because I was young and stupid. *Very* stupid."

"How disappointing," Garrett said dryly.

Mindy laughed. "It's just like old times!" She looked at Brooke. "And see? You *can* have fun here, so you can't leave. And . . . I've got a surprise for you." She pointed to the camera still around Brooke's neck. "The county's going to pay you for your pics."

Brooke blinked. "What?"

"Wildstone's mayor stops by the shop every day for a smoothie. She says they're putting together a new tourism package that includes brochures and a website. They need content of everything from the beaches to the wineries to the ranches to downtown . . . *everything*. I got you the job."

Brooke shook her head. "I've got a job."

"This one's flexible. And it pays really well."

Brooke fingered her camera. "I'm out of practice. I might suck."

"You don't."

"What if I hate it?"

"Well, then you'll suck it up like the rest of us tax-paying citizens for the sake of eating."

Linc was flipping through Mindy's binder. "Oh shit, my bad, it's *my* turn for dinner." He smiled at Mindy. "I've got this, babe. Garrett, set the oven to 450 degrees—we're having pizza rolls."

Mindy looked a little panicked, and Brooke knew why. Pizza rolls were not on her list of approved foods. But as Linc was one, actually home, and two, trying to be in charge of dinner, she knew Mindy wouldn't take it from him.

As Garrett set the oven, Linc pointed to his jeans. "Did you know you have cat hair all over you?"

Everyone looked at Garrett, who was indeed wearing cat hair from the knees down. He shrugged. "They like me."

"They're not rubbing up against you because they like you," Linc said. "They're doing it to mark you as their bitch."

Garrett gave him a banal look. "I beat you in arm wrestling all the time. So who's whose bitch?" He shifted away from the oven, having to brush up against Brooke to do so.

The last time she'd seen him, she'd been bare-ass naked and he'd been fully dressed. It should've pissed her off, but it had done the opposite. It'd turned her on. "I'm up for pizza rolls," she said. "I'll be in the outside closet. Someone let me know when they're ready."

"It's a pool house," Mindy said. "And you've already had too much alone time. Wait with us for the artery clogging. Please?"

The "please" was progress, and Brooke let out a long breath. "Just so you know, my alone time is for your safety."

Mindy made a face and Linc laughed.

"Hey," Linc said when Mindy glared at him. "You're the one who needed her own alone time in LA."

"Marriage," Garrett said in the tone of an off-camera narrator. "When dating goes too far."

"Someone tell the old cat lady to stay out of this," Linc said.

Garrett told Linc he was number one with his middle finger.

THE OVEN DINGED and Brooke pushed past the guys, grabbed a hot mitt, and pulled out the perfectly browned, deliciously cheese-and-meat-stuffed pizza rolls. "Yum."

Garrett reached past Brooke to grab a pizza roll, which he popped into his mouth. "*Shit*. Hot . . ." He waved a hand in front of his mouth, which didn't stop him from taking another.

"I haven't had pizza rolls since I was a kid," Brooke said, watching Garrett eat. Did the guy have a hollow leg? Where did he put all the food he inhaled every day?

Catching her staring at him, he picked up another pizza roll and brought it to her lips.

Surprising herself, she opened her mouth and took it, barely resisting biting his fingers while she was at it. He must have seen the urge in her eyes because he laughed low in his throat.

Mindy had her hands on her hips, staring at them both. She turned to Garrett, eyes narrowed. "What was that?"

Clearly Mindy thought Garrett had just made some sort of move. Of course she had no way of knowing it was all old news.

Really old news.

"Can I talk to you a minute?" Mindy asked Garrett.

Oh boy, thought Brooke.

"Sure," Garrett said easily.

"No," Brooke said.

"I didn't ask you," Mindy said.

When Garrett didn't make a move to step out of the room with her, Mindy grabbed his arm.

He planted his feet, taking the time to grab a third pizza roll before letting her tow him out the back door by his biceps and across the yard, backing him up against his truck before getting in his face.

Which Brooke knew because she and Linc both moved to the window over the sink to watch. "Your wife is scary," she said.

"No offense, but all the Lemons are scary."

He had her there.

Outside, Garrett did the universal male hands-up not-my-fault gesture, and Mindy backed off an inch. Garrett calmly said something and Mindy listened with her head turned away, toward the street. Finally, she nodded.

Garrett straightened up and they hugged. Then, with a ruffle of her hair, he walked off.

He didn't look back. Fine. Whatever. He really didn't want her. There were plenty of other men who would.

Probably.

Maybe.

"I thought you were going to fix things between the two of you," she said to Linc.

"I'm working on it. In fact, I had an announcement to aid my cause, but then you ate a pizza roll out of Garrett's fingers like you two are a thing."

"We're not a thing! And anyway, what is this, high school? What's your announcement?"

"You'll see."

Mindy walked back into the house and Linc took her hand. "I've got a surprise for you," he said.

"You do?"

"Yeah." He proudly thrust a file folder into her hands.

Mindy opened the file and looked at the papers. Brooke watched her face go from curiosity to dread.

Clearly, Linc didn't read the mood change. "I bought you the shop," he said proudly.

Oh, dear God. Dead husband walking, and he didn't even know it.

Mindy lifted her head and stared at him. "Wait. Are you serious? You bought me the shop? Without talking to me about it?"

His smile faded some. "We did talk about it, lots of times. It's all you've ever wanted."

"Yes, years ago . . ." Mindy turned away and started for the door, but stopped and turned back. "But you know what we *just* talked about? The fact that you work nonstop and we never have any time together. We don't do date nights, nothing. You travel to do surgeries on weekends at clinics, and I . . . I run this life we planned together, all by myself." She shook her head. "I already don't have time to breathe, and you . . ." She stared at him. "I can't believe you did this, that you clearly talked to my parents and spent that kind of money before discussing it with me."

"Because I thought we were on the same page," Linc said carefully.

Mindy let out a long, shaky breath. "We're not even in the same book, Linc. I mean, yes, maybe before I had kids, this would have been my dream. But that was a long time ago. I haven't had time for that dream in forever." Her eyes welled. "I can't . . ." She shook her head. "I'm tired," she whispered. "Like, *all* the time. I already told you—"

"I know." He took a step toward her. "You've been swamped taking care of the kids, the house . . . me. All I wanted to do was to take care of you."

"I can take care of myself, Linc."

"I know that, I just thought this would make you happy."

She slapped the file against his chest. "You thought wrong."

Completely bewildered, he caught the file.

"Don't," she said. "Don't look at me like that. I've been trying to tell you that I can't manage what I have on my plate now, much less the responsibility of owning a business."

There was a horribly strained silence in the kitchen. Brooke didn't do horribly strained, so she made to leave.

"Don't you dare," Mindy said. "Did you encourage this? It has your name all over it."

"Sorry," Brooke said. "I'm not stupid enough to try to rearrange someone's life without talking it out first."

Linc had the good grace to grimace.

So did Mindy.

Brooke took a peek at Linc, who still appeared to be in shock that his plan hadn't been better received. She turned back to Mindy. "You do know that he was just trying to fix things, right?"

"He *bought me the store*."

"I know," she said. "And as I lived your life this week, I get it. But Linc is pretty new to this whole parenting thing—"

Linc winced again.

"—so you might need to give him a minute to catch up. I mean, he's good in an ER, but he's got a lot to learn, and you're a good teacher. Think of it this way, Min—he deserves you."

"Thanks, Brooke," Linc said.

"Stay out of this," Mindy said to Brooke. "You don't have a family, and that's your choice. But don't tell me how to run mine." She had started yelling, and her words echoed throughout the kitchen and inside Brooke's head.

You don't have a family, and that's your choice . . .

She swallowed the sudden lump in her throat, nodded once and headed to the door.

"Brooke," Mindy said with regret. "Wait."

Oh, hell no. She stormed to the "guesthouse," grabbed her ID and a credit card, and walked into town. It wasn't far, only half a mile or so, and she needed the fresh air to think. She felt like a bundle of raw nerves. She couldn't put thoughts together past the single fact bouncing around in her head. She didn't really belong anywhere—her own doing, of course. She'd pushed people away for so long that she didn't know how to stop. A problem because she needed . . . to be needed.

If only for a night.

The Whiskey River Bar and Grill was full and rowdy, and as she made her way through the joint to the bar, she was glad for that. A full house. Anonymity. At first glance, she saw a lot of men. Good. And she didn't recognize anyone. Better yet. She sat, ordered herself a vodka and lemonade, and took a longer look around. People were dancing, eating, laughing, talking, but what she didn't see was anyone else there on their own.

When had a simple, mindless hookup gotten so hard?

"What's wrong, dating apps not doing it for you?"

She sighed and met Garrett's eyes as he slid onto a barstool next to her. "I'm not on any dating apps," she said. "Tonight I thought I'd find a Tinder date the old-fashioned way." She finished her first drink and gestured to the bartender for a second. "At a bar."

"You're going to get drunk and sleep with a stranger?" he asked, his voice not revealing a single thing.

"Oh, I have no intention of sleeping," she said.

He stared at her. Then he stared down at his feet for a moment. Clearly not finding any answers in his beat-up old hiking boots, he shook his head. "This isn't you, Brooke."

"Actually, you don't know that. I've changed. And you've made it clear we're not friends or . . . anything, so go away, you're scaring off all my potentials."

But Garrett didn't go away. He joined her in her perusal of her choices at the bar. "The guy on the end might be good," he said conversationally. "His name's Judd Roberts. Of course, he's pushing eighty, and he just got a pacemaker put in. I'd take it easy on him if you don't want him toes up by morning." He gestured to another guy. "Now, Keith's more age-appropriate— late twenties—but he's a plumber, and rumor is that he's not a big hand-washer."

With a shudder, she tossed back her second drink and felt the burn go all the way down her throat to her gut. Look at that—she *could* feel something after all. She raised her hand for the bartender, but Garrett caught it in his, bringing their now entwined fingers down between them.

"Brooke," he said softly. "What are you really doing?"

That low, rough voice, she thought, closing her eyes. It got to her, every time. It said she was special in his life, that he cared. But that wasn't true. She'd blown that. "Well, I'm not sure how many drinks equals happiness, but so far it's not two." She pulled her hand free. "And anyway, the real question is, what are *you* doing?"

"Being your wingman." He stood, tossed down some cash, and gestured with a chin jerk toward the door.

"Are you kidding me? I'm not going anywhere with you. And you suck as a wingman."

"I know. And I lied about being your wingman. You're not sleeping with a stranger tonight, Brooke."

"Well, I'm sure as hell not sleeping with you."

"Why not?" His usually sharp eyes were softer now as they met hers and held. "I'm a sure thing, and you know I'm good."

Her lady bits tingled at the remembered truth of that statement, which annoyed her to no end. Her lady bits were *not* in charge here. "I'm not going to be your pity fuck."

That got her a smile. "I'm feeling a lot of things, Brooke. But pity isn't one of them." And then he tugged her out into the night.

CHAPTER 11

"Grilled cheese sandwiches are life."

I n the time since Brooke had arrived at Whiskey River, the
night had gone dark and windy. As Garrett walked her out,
a heavy gust knocked her right into him. "Oops, sorry," she
started, but the words backed up in her throat as he used her
momentum against her, his arms closing around her.

And damn, if he didn't smell amazing. She sucked some of it
in before she could catch herself.

In response, he blinked lazily and smiled, practically a sex
act all in itself, and she pointed at him. "Stop that."

"Stop what?" he asked innocently.

Uh-huh. "We're not like that, remember? And I have plans
for the night."

"You still do." Leaning in, he put his mouth to her ear. *"Me."*

She laughed. She might be halfway drunk—and at least two

inches shorter just from melting for him—but she hadn't lost her memory. "I don't think you understand exactly what my plans are."

"Actually, you made them quite clear."

She pushed him back a step and turned to walk across the parking lot, proud of herself for two things: resisting Garrett, and her ability to walk a straight line. Halfway across the asphalt, the sky let loose and started dumping.

She was drenched in seconds.

At her side, Garrett did his best to shield her with his body as he nudged her into the passenger seat of his truck. When the doors were shut, she sat there, dripping water everywhere, gasping at the shock of it. Garrett jogged around and slid behind the wheel.

"The entire night's out to get me," she said.

Garrett turned to face her, just as drenched. He stared at her for a long beat. "I've handled this all wrong from the start. I've handled you wrong."

"Please," she scoffed, looking away so he couldn't see the unmistakable thrill that zipped through her at the thought of being "handled" by him. "You couldn't handle me even if I came with instructions."

He gave a rough laugh and leaned in, tipping her face up before brushing his mouth to hers. Not a kiss, exactly. A pledge, with his intense dark eyes locked on hers, his voice serious. "You wanted something tonight."

"Yes. Mindless sex."

"I'm on board with that."

"Have you forgotten you don't want me, not ever again?"

"I've wanted you from day one, Brooke. What I don't want are the games."

She had no comeback for that. "So what *do* you want?"

"Same thing as you," he said quietly, stroking a finger along her temple, tucking a wet strand of hair from her face.

Mindless sex.

For the night.

It was what she'd told him, and the thought of being with him was admittedly a thrill, and also a comfort, because there was no doubt they were extremely compatible in bed. In fact, in bed was where they'd done their best work. The question was, once morning came, could she walk away from him again?

GARRETT HELD HIS breath on Brooke's response. She was in a pair of white shorts that were killing him, and in a gift from the gods, her cute little top, which had started out the night as pale peach, was now sheer, revealing a thin nude bra that might as well not exist at all.

He'd spent much of his high school years fantasizing about seeing Brooke Lemon naked, and then his wild early twenties making that a reality, and still, he never got tired of looking at her. Once upon a time he'd loved her so much it'd been painful. And now . . . now he had nothing in his heart for her. Or so he'd been telling himself. But the truth was, he'd merely bricked and mortared around the poor beleaguered organ. If she blasted her way through those walls he'd built in self-protection, he had no idea how he'd survive Hurricane Brooke II. It was a good thing, then, that he had zero delusions of her sticking around.

She still hadn't spoken, but when her gaze dropped from his

eyes to his mouth, he knew he had her. They reached for each other at the exact same moment. He lifted her over the center console, adjusting her so that she straddled him, and there in the dark, ambient lighting, they stared at each other as the storm went crazy outside. He had the feeling it was about to get just as crazy inside.

He wasn't sure who lunged first—all he knew was that suddenly, they were in the middle of a no-holds-barred, tongue-to-tonsils, melt-your-socks-off kiss that left him breathless and fuzzy-brained. "Brooke."

"Hmmm?"

She had her hot mouth on his throat, her equally hot hands running up and down his chest and abs, toying with his button fly. "How much did you have to drink?" he managed to ask, catching her wandering hands.

This didn't stop her lips, which were spreading hot, open-mouthed kisses along the rough scruff of his jaw and his neck. When she licked at the hollow of his throat, he nearly had an aneurysm. "*Bee.*"

She lifted her head, eyes at half-mast, mouth wet. "Two. Enough to be feeling nice and friendly toward you, but not enough for you to be worried."

"Meaning?"

"Meaning I'm consenting. Would you like it in writing?" she asked, tone pure smart-ass.

He let out a rough laugh. "I should."

"And how about you? Are *you* consenting?"

He reached out to pull her back down and kiss her again, but she held off, waiting on his answer.

He had to laugh. "Hell yes, I'm consenting. Open-endedly."

"That's not a word. And this is just a one-time thing," she said softly.

At the same words they used to say to each other all the time, their eyes met and held. It'd been bullshit then, and it was bullshit now, but he just smiled grimly. "Worried I'm going to fall for you?" he murmured.

She rocked against him. "Are you?"

He could hardly breathe for wanting her. "Never again."

"Honest to the end, huh?"

"Always," he said, tugging her face to his for another heart-stopping kiss before letting himself touch her everywhere he could reach, knowing he could've recognized her body by the feel of her alone. She was wedged between his chest and the steering wheel so they were nose to nose, belly to belly, her inner thighs hugged up to the outsides of his. Which lined up all their parts in a way that made thinking difficult. And then difficult became utterly impossible when she slid her hands beneath his shirt to touch him skin to skin, rocking her hips to his.

When he groaned, she popped open the buttons on his Levi's one at a time and wrapped her hands around his current favorite body part with a sexy little hum.

The blood in his brain veered south to where all the fun was, leaving his head spinning. "Not here," he managed to growl out. "I want you in my bed." He nipped her bottom lip. "I've spent a lot of nights dreaming of you there."

"I love your bed, but I'm not taking that risk."

"My bed's a risk?" he asked.

"Yes, because by the time we get there, one of us will remember the stick up one of our asses and change their mind."

He snorted. "If anyone in this truck has a stick up their ass, it's not me."

She tugged at his drenched shirt. *"Off."*

He decided not to argue with the hot chick sitting in his lap wanting him naked, and tugged his drenched shirt over his head. It hit the back seat with a wet *thunk,* and then he made sure hers did the same, grateful he'd parked at the far edge of the lot where the lights didn't reach. Her bra came loose in his fingers, and he sent that flying to join their shirts, filling his hands with her breasts. Her skin was chilled, and he worked hard at warming her up, pulling her in closer, encouraging her to rock against him.

She did, and bent low to press her mouth to the tat on his chest.

It was a good thing he was sitting down, because she made his legs weak. She was in the driver's seat—literally—and all he knew was that he needed this mindless, shockingly easy passion every bit as much as she seemed to. Every part of this, the feel of her beneath his hands, the scent of her, the little panting breaths she was making, her clear need for him . . . it all felt like a homecoming. His dead heart beat in his chest for her, making him feel things he'd thought were long gone. Which meant he was so much more messed up than he'd thought. He just hoped to God she couldn't read all that off him, and more so that he could control his feelings and move past them. But then her hands drew a slow line up his chest to encircle his neck, and she smiled at him, a smile that went all the way to her eyes.

No matter what she wanted him to believe, she wasn't giving off the vibes of a frenzied hookup. "Brooke—"

She kicked off her shoes and started to wriggle out of her shorts, her eyes hungry. Raw. She was baring herself to him, not just her body, and he lent his hands to the cause, stripping off her shorts. Bracing herself with her hands on his chest, she looked down at him, clearly taking pleasure from his body, which was more than gratifying because he certainly couldn't take his gaze off her. Nor his hands.

Apparently feeling the same, she slid her fingers into his hair, tightened her grip, and closed her teeth over his full lower lip, tugging lightly.

"Reenactment?" he asked, voice gruff with emotion as he reminded them both that their first time had been in his truck—not this one, but a real POS, missing the back windshield—and it'd been storming that night, too.

It'd been one of the best nights of his life.

"You remember," she murmured.

"I remember everything about you, Bee. About us."

"I'm not nearly as inebriated as we were that night."

"No." Caressing her soft skin, he leaned in and painted her in kisses while his fingers slid down her belly and beyond, absorbing her every passion-filled moan and sigh.

One night only, his ass. But just in case, he'd use his mouth and hands and body to make this count, make her remember what they'd once been to each other, if nothing else. She gasped when he nudged her barely there panties to the side. Her nails dug into his biceps as he brought her to the very edge and held her there. Watching her lose control was the most erotic thing he'd ever seen, and he drew out her pleasure, making sure she felt every sensation, every teasing stroke, every nibble, every kiss. And when she shuddered and cried out his name, he gripped her hips to keep her from sinking down on him and taking him deep.

"Now," she whispered, wriggling to get him in place. "Please, now."

"Brooke." Catching her, holding her still, he met her gaze. "I don't have a condom."

She stared at him, her eyes glittering with hunger and a need for him that humbled him to the core. "We don't need one," she whispered. "I'm clean, Garrett."

He kissed her softly. "So am I, but—"

"Remember? Pregnancy isn't a problem anymore."

Shit. He tried to cuddle her into him, but that wasn't what she wanted. Instead, she sank down on him, slowly, so damn slowly that it was sheer, beautiful torture, and then he could no longer think, at least not with his brain. Fisting his hands in her hair, he brought her mouth to his as they both began to move. Didn't take much to rev her up again, and hell, he was already there, and as she shuddered and cried out, he did the same, completely lost in her.

And fairly confident she was right there with him.

Brooke came awake to pain blooming throughout her entire body. Opening her eyes, she stared up at a startlingly blue sky and a helicopter rotor blade. She was on the ground, flat on her back, the only sounds the hiss of something from the downed helicopter and the innocuous song of insects humming in the otherwise silent day.

She jerked and . . . opened her eyes again?

Not in the jungle. Not on the ground where she'd been thrown from the crash.

Instead, she lay in Garrett's dark, soothingly cool bedroom, hugged up against his warm body while the crushing fear, dread, and horror lingered. She took a very careful, slow breath, hoping she hadn't woken him. *One breath, two breaths, three . . . four. One breath, two breaths, three . . . four.*

But the usual self-calming technique didn't work. She could still see herself lying on that mountain, covered in her own blood—

She slid out of bed, grabbed a shirt—his—and padded into the kitchen, followed by three curious cats.

She was standing at the sink sipping a glass of water when she felt him. He came up behind her and turned her, hugging her into him, his hand brushing her hair back from her face.

"I'm okay."

He gave her one of his patented long, steady looks and said nothing. Garrett was very good at silence.

She, however, was not. "Sometimes I have dreams."

"Because you've been hiking again? Climbing?"

She hadn't been climbing at all, but interesting that he assumed she had been. That she was brave enough. Because she wasn't. "Maybe," she murmured, but that wasn't true, either. She was pretty sure it was the fact that she was opening herself up to emotions again. The seven years of numbness hadn't been great, but the sparks of feeling after going so long without hurt like hell. She was way too vulnerable after lying so intimately wrapped around Garrett for the past few hours.

He just continued to hold her close, projecting warm, safe, calm vibes, and she began to relax. She hadn't really even noticed she was shivering until it began to slow and then subsided entirely.

"Hungry?" he asked.

"Yes."

She watched as he pulled stuff from the fridge and got out a pan. In no time at all, he produced two grilled cheese sandwiches. She stared, fascinated by the way he moved around the kitchen with the same calm efficiency he had when he was working. And it was all so effortless. How did he stay in such constant control? Was he really that good at compartmentalizing? And where did she sign up for a class?

"Admit it," she said. "Grilled cheese sandwiches are still the only thing in your arsenal."

"Hey, grilled cheese sandwiches are life. Sit," he instructed, cutting up the sandwiches and stacking them on a plate, adding a mountain of chips. All the while, she watched him. She couldn't help it. There was something incredibly sexy about a man wearing only a pair of jeans, making snacks in the kitchen at two in the morning after he'd made you writhe in pleasure for most of the night.

After they ate, he drew her back to his bed. She opened her mouth to say she needed to go, but he kissed her softly, gently, then tucked her into him, running his hands slowly up and down her back until she melted against him. He had a way of doing that, making her forget everything bad.

So yeah, okay, maybe she'd stay, just a little bit longer.

CHAPTER 12

All her other demons would just have to get in line.

"M ew."

Brooke sucked in some air, opened her eyes, and . . . drew a blank.

"*Mew, mew, mew!*"

Okay, she knew those grumpy voices.

"Give it a rest, ladies."

She knew that raspy voice, too, and it washed over her in the early-morning light. As did the realization that she'd spent the entire night with Garrett.

"I'll feed you all in a minute," he said, presumably to the cats.

Brooke sat up. At the movement, the cats glared at her. Ali McClaw and Chairwoman Miao were at their feet, Princess Jasmine on Garrett's chest, staking her claim.

Brooke apparently had done the same, because she was

snuggled up to his side, a leg thrown over him like *mine*. "Damn." Her voice was more than a little ragged around the edges as well. "It's morning?"

He came up on an elbow, dislodging the princess, who shifted to the end of the bed with a pissy expression. The man didn't have any such look. His face was pure sated, sexy male. The sheet had slipped low, exposing him to just below his hip bones, and she felt her mouth water.

"How did we get here?" she asked.

His expression changed. "I drove us home from the bar parking lot. You wanted to come in with me." He paused. "Please tell me you remember that."

Oh, she did. She'd led him out of the truck and into his house, where they'd spent the next few hours rediscovering their insatiable passion for each other. They'd done it on his kitchen counter, in his shower, and finally in his bed, all to their extremely mutual satisfaction. "I remember," she said, not exactly thrilled with having to admit it out loud. "I meant, how did we get here . . . *metaphorically*?"

Princess Jasmine hunkered down with a butt wriggle and then took a flying leap, destination: Garrett's lap. Catching her in midair, he tossed her gently over the side of the bed. But the other two cats held their positions like five-star generals, and he shook his head at them. "We've talked about this. The bed's off-limits."

"Wow," Brooke said to him. "Way to be tough." She waved a hand in their direction. "Shoo."

Neither of the cats budged, though they both narrowed their eyes. One growled low in her throat.

"Rude," she said, but she sort of got it. Garrett was theirs, and they didn't want to share. She could easily adopt the philosophy if she let herself. Instead, she slipped out of the bed and looked for her clothes. Her undies were MIA, so still wearing only his shirt, she bent for her shorts and apparently flashed him, because she heard a very male sound of approval.

"Commando," Garrett said approvingly. "I like it."

"Yes, well, you like pretty much everything, so . . ." She buttoned the shorts and then found her bra. Still wet. Her top wasn't much better, so she left them both where they were and kept Garrett's shirt on, hugging herself, hoping he wasn't going to make this into a big thing.

His eyes were heavy-lidded and heated as he crooked a finger at her. "Come back to bed."

Hell no. In the light of day, he'd be able to look deep into her eyes, and she wasn't sure she could continue to hide in plain sight now that they'd decimated each other so thoroughly.

"Nervous?" he asked.

More like turned on beyond belief. "I don't do nervous." She flashed a quick smile that she hoped he bought. "So . . . thanks for the ride last night. And . . ." She grimaced. "For, you know, what came after that."

"You mean you?" he asked with a tinge of amusement.

Rolling her eyes at the both of them, she headed to the door.

"Brooke—"

"No." Knowing what he was about to say, she shook her head. "We don't need to talk about it."

Garrett blew out a breath, like maybe he agreed with her, but here was the thing about Garrett and how the two of them differed at their very cores: If she wanted to not think about something, she did just that. She could ignore anything, even if it was right in front of her face, if she wanted to badly enough. But Garrett wasn't wired like her. If something bothered him, he got it out. And if that something required action, well, then he'd act. He was about doing the right thing, even if the right thing was also the hard thing. *Especially* if it was the hard thing.

He caught her at his bedroom door and pulled her around to look at him. He was still naked. Gloriously so, and apparently without a self-conscious bone in his body, although a certain "bone" did nudge her belly good morning. She sucked in a breath.

"Ignore that." He looked deep into her eyes.

"What?" she asked.

He shook his head. "I guess I'm just looking for some sort of sign that not acknowledging our past or what we were to each other—or where we're at now—bothers you or hurts you."

"And?"

"And . . ." He studied her, his eyes hooded. "I'm getting nothing. Not only is your head hard as rock, but so is your damn heart."

"And on that note," she said lightly while feeling anything but. "I've gotta go."

"I'll walk you."

"Not necessary. Seriously," she said when he pulled on a pair of jeans and looked around for his shirt before realizing she was in it. "I don't need you to walk me across the damn yard."

"So you'll let me give you an orgasm, but not walk you home?"

"Let's be honest. It was a whole bunch of orgasms." She paused and gave him a reluctant smile. "And they were very nice."

"They were a lot more than nice."

This was true. There was actually nothing nice about what he'd done to her. Erotic, yes, with moments of tenderness and affection and a whole lot of delicious, dirty, wicked intent.

"So what now?" he asked.

"I told you. I'm going next door."

"Interesting that you never call it 'home.'"

"You want the truth?" she asked.

"Always."

It was an uncomfortable reminder that there was plenty she hadn't been honest about, and he knew it. But she was tired, and that always left her feeling vulnerable, which meant her mouth spoke without permission from her brain. "I thought this would be a lot easier. I thought I'd come here, help Mindy, face you and my past, deal with it, and then go back to LA feeling like a new woman. I thought I'd get my old job back and prove to myself that I could conquer my fears." She shook her head. "But I still feel . . . lost. I don't know where home is anymore."

He stared at her for a beat and then gave a slow, understanding nod. "I get that."

Thanks to his rough childhood, she knew he did, and remembering that softened her. Going up on her tiptoes, she brushed a kiss on his sexily unshaven jaw. "I'll see you."

Sliding his hands to her hips, he turned his head and caught her mouth with his.

Instant desire—disturbing because she'd thought the long, sensually charged night they'd just shared would've been enough. But she was starting to worry she would never get enough.

A knock at his front door surprised them both. Brooke began to pull back, but Garrett tightened his hold. "Ignore it," he purred in the same wicked, should-be-illegal voice he'd used in the deep dark of the night.

The knock came again. "What if it's Mindy or the kids needing something?"

Expelling a deep breath, he headed out of the bedroom and down the hall. She followed, thinking that no man should look that good in a pair of dangerously low-slung Levi's and nothing else. "Uh . . . you might want to button those . . ."

He reached down to do just that, and if possible looked even more sexy as he opened the door. Since she'd stopped at the bottom of the stairs and out of sight, she couldn't see who it was, only Garrett's reaction. His broad shoulders froze for a beat and then, casual as you please, he leaned up against the doorjamb, hands sliding into his pockets, saying nothing.

"You probably weren't expecting me," a man said.

Garrett didn't budge. Still casual. Still calm. "I stopped expecting you before I knew the meaning of the word," he said.

Brooke stayed where she was, trapped between the social nicety of not wanting to intrude on something that was none of her business and her own damn insatiable curiosity.

"I know it's been a long time," the man said. "I also know you don't have any reason to believe me, but I've changed my life, turned it around." He paused, and when Garrett still didn't speak, he went on. "Been out of prison a year now. Asked around about you, and was told you were living here."

Holy shit. It was Garrett's dad. His mom had died when he was young. Gary, his dad, hadn't been around in years. At one point he'd been the town handyman, usually a drunk one. He'd been in and out of jail for petty theft, which was how Garrett had ended up in foster homes, and not always good ones, not until he landed in this house with Ann.

"Wow," Garrett said in an unimpressed voice. "A whole year this time."

Brooke still didn't move, but now for another reason entirely. Garrett hated the guy. No way was she going anywhere if there was a chance he'd need her. Though in what universe he'd ever need her, she had no idea.

"Yeah." His dad cleared his throat. "And I've realized some things. I'm only as big as my last mistake."

"Ah," Garrett said, his voice expressionless. "The power of AA in prison."

"Fifteen months sober," his dad said, sounding proud. "I'm looking to pick up some small jobs while I'm here, if you hear of anything."

Garrett didn't speak.

"Okay," his dad said into the awkward silence. "Well . . . here's my number. I was hoping we could try to get to know each other. Family is family, right?"

"You haven't wanted to be family in . . . well, ever," Garrett said. "You left when I was eight years old to do a bunch of stupid shit. *Eight,* Dad, and all on my own. You really expect me to want to get to know you now?"

"I was hoping. I mean, I don't expect forgiveness, or anything like that. Forgiveness is a gift, one that has to be freely given or it has no value."

"Yeah, and here's the thing," Garrett said. "I'm not interested. And I'd appreciate it if you didn't contact me again." He shut the door, turned, and saw Brooke at the bottom of the stairs, clearly eavesdropping.

"I'm sorry," she started. "I'm just—"

"Leaving, right?"

Right. It was night and day. Only a few minutes before he'd been completely open and relaxed. Now he was completely closed off to her, and hey, hadn't that been exactly what she wanted? But while she had her faults—*many* of them, actually— she thought maybe Garrett had a few surprising ones of his own, such as an obstinate streak a mile wide and, surprisingly, not a whole lot of capacity for forgiveness. Not that his dad deserved it. Nor did she, for that matter. "Do you want to talk about it?" she asked quietly.

He laughed, though it held no mirth. "Definitely not."

"Are you sure? It's a big deal, him showing up out of the blue after all this time. We could—"

"'We'?" he asked. "When have we ever been a 'we,' Brooke?"

A direct hit. She nearly staggered back from it, but instead forced herself to meet his gaze, knowing he was reeling. "I get it. You're upset at what just happened. But we could talk about it and—"

"There's nothing to talk about," he said. "And there's certainly no 'we.'"

Okay, so he'd just faced down his dad and been forcibly reminded of his abandonment.

And she'd done the same thing to him seven years ago.

If he wasn't going to forgive his father, he sure as hell wasn't going to forgive her. "Garrett—"

"Save it. This was a mistake." And with that, he moved past her, vanishing into the bathroom, leaving her with a clear understanding that *she* was the mistake. The lock clicking into place sounded like a cannon and carried a clear message—*stay out*. She was still standing there in the hallway when the shower went on. She exhaled slowly and told herself it didn't matter what he thought of her—none of it mattered. She was leaving soon anyway.

But she was lying to herself, because it *did* matter. Feeling more hurt than she thought possible, she made the walk across the yard, past the constantly improving—and ridiculously complicated—Slip 'N Slide.

Apparently, Linc and Garrett bought into the bigger-is-better mentality.

Men were dumb.

Still telling herself she didn't give a shit about anything, especially what Garrett thought of her, she got all the way to the guesthouse before realizing she'd left her keys at Garrett's. Perfect. Since she'd rather jump off a cliff than go back for them, she detoured to the big house, sneaking in the kitchen door wearing Garrett's shirt, her shorts, no shoes—which, like her keys, were still at Garrett's, where they could rot right along with him.

This early, the kitchen should've been empty. But of course

it wasn't. Mindy sat at the kitchen table sipping tea. She eyed Brooke's appearance. "Huh. I thought you didn't need a man."

"I don't," Brooke said. "But I could use a box of cookies and a nap."

Mindy snorted. "My walk of shame's usually going back for a shopping cart after figuring out I can't carry twenty-three items in my arms through the store."

Brooke sighed and headed for the teapot, because she was going to require caffeine. Copious amounts of it.

"Where were you? What were you doing?" Mindy gave Brooke another once-over. "Maybe the better question is, *who* were you doing?"

If she didn't recognize Garrett's shirt, no way was Brooke going to enlighten her. That was a can of worms best left shut. If she'd managed to keep her thing with Garrett to herself for all these years, she could sure as hell keep it up now. "It doesn't matter."

"Anyone I know?"

"Leave it alone, Min."

"Right." Her sister got up and refilled her mug, her posture projecting butt-hurt feelings. "I have to leave a lot of things alone when it comes to you, apparently. Like why you changed jobs. But hey, I get it, I'm not important enough in your life for you to confide in me anymore."

"I didn't mean it like that. I meant you have enough going on with you and Linc. You guys doing okay?"

Mindy shot her an *are you serious?* look. "You saw what he did."

"Look, I'm not exactly a fan of men right now, but I really do think he believed he was giving you what you wanted."

"By putting a huge load of more responsibility on my plate?"

"So he went about it wrong." Brooke shrugged. "His heart was in the right place. And it's Mom and Dad, Min. They probably sold the shop to him at a steal. If you're not into it, then sell it, make a mint, and sit on a pot of money."

"You think money is going to make me happy?"

"I think the only thing that's going to make you happy is you figuring out what you want."

Mindy looked stricken, then quickly turned her back on Brooke. "I thought you were on my side."

Brooke sighed. "It's not about sides. It's about liking where you're at in life. And I'm sure not going to judge anyone on that. I came here because you needed me. I wanted to help with the kids, and as it turns out . . ." She lifted her shoulders. "I like them. A whole lot."

Mindy turned back, her eyes bright. "Yeah?"

"Yeah. They're . . . amazing. You've done an amazing job with them. But, Min, you know I can't stay, right? Not even if you get me pretend jobs."

"The job is real. And they'd like to see you today to go over what they want."

She blew out a breath. "I feel like you're not hearing me."

"It's tailor-made for you, Brooke. You take pictures. Great ones. That's all they want."

The back door opened and in walked Garrett, wearing his typical work gear: boots, jeans, and a T-shirt advertising some tattoo shop in San Francisco called the Canvas Shop. His hair was still damp from a shower. He had his tool belt slung low around his hips, the leather creaking as he strode across the kitchen, looking sexy as hell, which pissed Brooke off.

His dark gaze met hers and memories crashed around in her head: him pressing her into the mattress, his hands fisted in her hair, his talented mouth on hers, their bodies moving fluidly, in sync . . .

Damn.

If any such memories from last night hounded *him,* he didn't give a single hint of it. He hadn't shaved, and there was a tension in his sexy, scruffy jaw belying the multiple orgasms they'd shared in the night.

"Hey," Mindy said, clueless to all of it. "Morning."

Garrett headed for the fridge.

"I keep meaning to ask you," Mindy said, apparently unbothered by his lack of verbiage. It wasn't like he was Chatty Cathy on the best of days. "How's Callie?"

At this, Garrett broke eye contact with Brooke to look at her sister. "What?"

"Remember I set you up on a date with Callie, my friend from the DMV in Paso Robles? You took her to coffee a few days ago after one of her shifts . . ." She trailed off at the look on Garrett's face. "Oh shit. Tell me you didn't forget to go."

Brooke had gone to school with Callie. She was a pretty, petite blond surfer who, at least in high school, couldn't have been sweeter or kinder.

Brooke decided she hated her.

Garrett grimaced.

"Are you *kidding me,*" Mindy said, whipping out her phone. "You are such an asshole."

Whether he'd forgotten about the date or just hadn't wanted to go, Brooke no longer hated Callie. She hated *herself* for fall-

ing for a man she'd told herself she no longer felt anything for.
A man who'd just told her she was a mistake.

Maddox came barreling into the room, naked, holding a
lightsaber and yelling "Arrrrrgggggg!" He took a flying leap at
Garrett, who easily snatched him in midair.

"Look what I caught," Garrett said. "A naked fish."

Maddox grinned and set his head on Garrett's shoulder.

Brooke's ovaries squeezed.

"Missed you, too, little man," Garrett said, and pressed his
jaw to Maddox's. After a cuddle, he set the heathen down. "Go
find some clothes and you can be my assistant today. Shoes
would be good, too."

Maddox went racing out of the room, barking in excitement.

Garrett, with a long, steady look at Brooke that quite clearly
conveyed what he thought of her, left as well.

Brooke let out a shuddery breath.

"What was that about?" Mindy asked.

"No idea." She set her cup in the sink. "Gotta go."

"Hey. The dish fairy's dead."

Brooke took her cup out of the sink and put it into the dishwasher.

"Where are you going?" Mindy asked.

"There's something I've got to do."

"Go sit at the top of the bluffs and take pictures?"

When Brooke gave her a look, Mindy shrugged. "Xena's
sister's daughter's boyfriend saw you up there looking a little
shaky. I worry."

Brooke ran the pads of her thumbs over her fingertips back
and forth. "You know I haven't been out in the wild on the job."

"Because of the helicopter crash."

Brooke nodded. "It changed me. I couldn't . . ." She shook her head. "I couldn't perform like I used to. And now adrenaline rushes give me panic attacks. I'm working on it, though."

Mindy's expression went earnest. "But don't you get it? That's why this photo job is perfect for you. It could be a step toward finding your old self again, right? Getting back into the action?"

"You don't know what you're talking about."

"Then tell me," Mindy dared her.

Brooke couldn't find her words, because suddenly she wasn't so sure of what she wanted, or what might make her happy.

Mindy, looking like she was following along, reading between the lines, went from earnest to worry. "Brooke—"

"No, it's fine. I'm fine," she said, because why get into it all now? She was leaving, and she intended to go back better off than she'd been when she left LA. Today she'd conquer the bluffs once and for all. Maybe tomorrow, she'd hit up the Playground, which was the locals' nickname for the rocky stretch of cliffs about ten miles north of Wildstone. Only the talented climbers ever dared go there. She'd taught herself to climb there as a kid, and had climbed it too many times to count. The very thought of going there now made her stomach hurt.

But she was tired of being afraid. If she climbed the Playground, she'd know she'd conquered that demon, at least.

All her other demons would just have to get in line.

CHAPTER 13

"Did you know there's fifty-five different kinds of
tampons? Regular, super, scented, unscented, with
applicator, without applicator . . . I mean, what
the hell do you do without an applicator?"

The next morning, Garrett went for a long run, hoping to
clear his head. It didn't happen. He'd just made his way
back to his driveway when Brooke stepped outside of Mindy's
house.

From across the two driveways they stared at each other.

He was all sweaty, but she looked fresh from a shower, damp
hair pulled into some complicated braid, wearing a tee with a
plaid flannel tied around her waist and little denim shorts—
emphasis on *little*.

He moved toward her, helplessly drawn. And maybe she felt
the same, as she met him halfway. They hadn't talked about

what had happened, and it was clear she didn't want to, because she put out a preemptive strike.

"I'm off to take a little time for myself before making Mindy happy and going to work on the county job," she said, gesturing to the camera hanging off her shoulder.

She was trying to make light of what was actually a big deal— her working outdoors again—and he nodded. "You okay?"

At the question, her polite smile vanished, replaced by a small but real one. "Yesterday, I shot Highway 1 and the coastline for this gig. Caught it at sunset with some fog hugging the water at the exact point where it was burning off. It wasn't exactly a hardship for the paycheck."

She wasn't motivated by money, never had been, and seeing that once constant spark for life in her eyes got to him, whether he liked it or not.

And for the record, he *didn't* like it.

"Today I'm working my way south," she said. "Plan to hit Morro Bay."

"The whole county could take you months."

She looked away at that. "I made it clear that I'll get the project outlined and started, but I can't be the one to finish it."

"You're leaving."

"Have to go by this weekend."

His chest had tightened, even as he knew her leaving sooner than later was the best thing for the both of them. "Have to, or want to?"

She shook her head and turned to go, but he caught her hand. Slowly he reeled her in, and then, because he'd clearly lost his mind, he covered her mouth with his. He had no idea what he thought he was doing other than riling them both up, which, mission accomplished . . .

At the touch of their mouths, desire and hunger had ignited, and it was a very long moment before they broke free and stared at each other.

She pointed at him. "What *is* that?"

"Insanity, clearly."

She snorted at the both of them and left.

Garrett thought about little else for the rest of the day, until now, as he washed off his tiling equipment outside one last time, since he'd just finished up Mindy and Linc's master bath. He was being watched by his three old biddies, who sat on the porch, tails swishing, eyes narrowing in disapproval every time a stray mist from the hose came within ten feet of them.

On the other side of the fence, his neighbor's horse kept snorting at him. She wanted attention. He looked up when he heard what sounded like an old, clunky truck pull up. In his gut he knew what he'd find when he turned to look, and yep, sure enough, it was his dad.

Terrific.

"*Mew*," said Chairwoman Miao, his watch cat. From the other side of the fence, Moose also whinnied a warning. Who needed a doorbell? Deciding to ignore his entire audience, Garrett continued to wash his tools.

He heard his dad get out of the truck, but he didn't step onto the property, instead staying at the end of the driveway. He didn't speak, and finally Garrett turned and looked at him. He could admit to being stunned at his dad's appearance. He was smaller than he remembered, and frail. His clothes were clean, but extremely worn. It was such a contrast to the big, tough guy from Garrett's past, where he'd always seemed larger than life.

"I didn't come to bother you," his dad said. He held up a jar of something. "I just want to leave you some beets. You seemed . . . tense, which gives you high blood pressure. Beets are really good for that, and also they help rejuvenate the liver."

"My liver's fine," Garrett said.

His dad nodded. "True. Only one of us was an alcoholic."

"One never stops being an alcoholic, Dad. Not for your job, not for your kid . . . not for anything."

"Also true." His dad set the jar of beets on Garrett's porch and moved back to his old Ford. It looked to be on its last legs, all beat to shit. Once upon a time, it might've been red, but now it was rust brown. In the front seat sat a huge black Labrador, his head hanging out the window enjoying the warm day, smiling around a tennis ball in his mouth.

The happy dog was such a contrast to the piece-of-shit truck and the shocking way his father had aged into a frail, haggard, hollowed-out old man that Garrett stopped what he was doing and came closer. "You've got a dog?"

"Snoop," his dad said proudly.

"Hey, Snoop." Garrett held out a hand to the dog, who happily dropped his ball to give Garrett a lick, his big tail going so fast it was a blur. "Thought you hated dogs," he said to his dad. "That's what you always told me."

His dad grimaced and rubbed a hand over his thinned-out gray hair. "The truth's that I couldn't take care of myself back then, much less you. No way could I have handled a dog. I'm sorry, son."

Garrett shook his head. "What are you really doing here? You need money?"

"No, nothing like that. I'm just here to—"

"Make amends. So you said."

His dad met Garrett's gaze. "I realize you have no reason to believe me, but I've changed."

"Save it," Garrett said. "I'm not interested. Feel free to go back to wherever you've been living since you got out, which I'm sure is better than Wildstone, where everyone remembers you as the town drunk."

"I was also a handyman, and a damned good one," his dad said, with a mildness that Garrett actually admired, because he was feeling anything but mild.

"Do you know what I remember most about my eighth birthday?" Garrett asked. "You picking me up after school, having come straight from the bar. On the way home, you drove off the road, through a front yard, and into someone's house. That one put you away for a year and was the first time I ended up in a foster home, and not a good one." Actually, it'd been the kind of place that nightmares and horror movies were made of, but he didn't want to think about it, much less discuss it.

His dad swallowed hard, but didn't break eye contact. "Shit, son. I'm so—"

"Sorry. Yeah, I know. You got out of prison at Christmastime. You realized you didn't have any money, so you decided to rob a liquor store that time. Later you told the judge it was a twofer: you thought you could get presents and booze at the same time. I didn't see you again after that, so I'm going to take

a hard pass on this family reunion you're looking for, thanks."
He turned to go back to cleaning his tools.

"I actually did see you again," his dad said.

Garrett looked back. His dad lifted a shoulder, his expression
dialed to regret and guilt and possibly shame. "When I got out,
I came to Wildstone. You were here, playing dodgeball with
some of the other kids. You were smiling. Happy." He paused.
"I'd never seen you look like that before. Seemed like you had
a real good thing you had going, you know? I didn't want to
blow that."

"Not even to say hi? Or make sure I really was okay?"

Shame crossed his dad's face. "Look, I was an asshole, all
right? We both know that you were far better off without me."

"So you thought me being raised by someone else was for
the best."

"Ann was a good woman."

"She was *amazing*," Garrett agreed. "She gave me my first
real home, my first unconditional love. She was my foundation.
She was everything a parent should be."

His dad winced, but still held eye contact and nodded—and
hell, that was actually something Garrett respected him for.
But it took a back seat to the piles of resentment built up inside
him, eating at him ever since his dad had knocked on his door
yesterday morning.

"Didn't you get my letter?" his dad asked. "Explaining why I
was leaving you here?"

"You mean the Dear John note? Yeah, I got it." And he'd
burned it. Ann had helped him work through some of his anger, and with time he'd learned to let it go. He'd done his best

to be a big brother to the other kids in the house, gotten close to the family next door—the Lemon sisters—and learned early on how to be a good caretaker. Growing up, he'd translated that into coaching and mentoring other kids like him, kids who otherwise might've slipped through the cracks and been lost. He'd stayed in Wildstone because he liked it here, because the place fulfilled him. He loved the wide-open spaces, the beauty of the hills and the ocean. A man could actually hear himself think here.

His dad didn't say anything more, and Garrett didn't look at him again. A few minutes later, he heard the truck start up with some coughing. The old man needed spark plugs.

Then there was nothing but his dad's dust in the air.

"Just like old times," he told the cats and horse, and went back to washing the tools. When he finished, he was suitably hot, tired, and also still pissed off. He needed a shower and sleep, but even more, he needed food. Since he hadn't been grocery shopping recently—a chore he hated more than cleaning cat litter, and he hated that pretty effing bad—there was nothing waiting for him inside. So he got into his truck.

He took the long way into town because he needed the brain rest. He passed a stretch of ranches and wineries, the lush land dotted with sprawling oak trees, cattle, and grapevines. There was also state land that was home to hiking trails and some hidden campgrounds. As he passed the trailhead and parking area, he took in the fact that there weren't many vehicles there yet. Not a surprise. When summer was in full swing, tourists would pour in, but it was early yet. This meant the few there stood out.

Specifically, a battered old Ford.

Shit. He made an illegal U-turn on the two-lane highway. A minute later, he parked at the trailhead and got out of his truck. He took the trail from the lot and came to the campgrounds where, sure enough, he found his dad standing near a campfire. He was with a few others, in the middle of handing one of them some money.

Clearly surprised to see Garrett, he fumbled. "Son, what are you doing here?"

"Was going to ask you the same thing."

"Oh." His dad pulled off his ball cap and scratched his head before putting the hat back on. "Just visiting some old friends."

Garrett really wanted to believe this, but he didn't. This campground was one of the few in the area that didn't charge overnight fees, making it a favorite spot for the homeless.

Snoop padded over, looking at Garrett with big, soulful brown eyes as he dropped his tennis ball at Garrett's feet, his tail sweeping the ground as it waved back and forth.

Squatting low, Garrett stroked his hand down the dog's back. "Hey, Snoop."

Snoop promptly melted into a puddle at Garrett's feet for a few pets. Garrett obliged, then picked up the ball and threw it.

Snoop happily chased after it, ears flopping, tail going a mile a minute.

"Now you've done it," his dad said. "He's going to want you to throw it until your arm falls off."

And sure enough, Snoop came back with the ball.

Garrett threw it again. "Are you living out here, Dad?"

"Nope. I'm good."

If only he could believe that, too. He threw the ball for a few more minutes and then turned to his dad. "I'm going to ask you again. Do you need money?"

"Absolutely not."

All right, then. With nothing else to say, Garrett got back into his truck and left.

Twenty minutes later, he was at the store. In the first aisle he ran into Callie, the woman Mindy had tried to set him up with. She looked over his cart, which held beer and eggs so far. "Okay, so you're clearly still single. Should I give you a second chance?"

At any other time, he'd have jumped on that. But he couldn't stop thinking about the night he'd spent with Brooke—*in* Brooke and *on* Brooke and . . . well, every which way with Brooke. Somehow, in spite of his efforts, she was worming her way in, knocking down his walls one by one, which was probably why he'd been such an asshole to her. Grimacing, he scrubbed a hand down his face, but no matter what he'd told her, he knew that for as long as she stuck around, there wouldn't be another woman for him.

With a regretful smile, Callie moved on.

He was still reeling from his epiphany when he ran into Linc in aisle five, pushing an overloaded cart with one arm and carrying Maddox, barking at high decibels, surfboard-style under the other. Linc still had a stethoscope around his neck, but his tie was loose and his hair was crazy. The mystery of this was solved when he shoved a hand through it as he reviewed what appeared to be a shopping list.

"Your kid's barking," Garrett said.

"I know." Linc set Maddox down. "He's got to go to the bathroom. We're almost done here. I think. Mindy's got tampons on the list. Did you know there's fifty-five different kinds of tampons? Regular, super, scented, unscented, with applicator, without applicator . . . I mean, what the hell do you do without an applicator?"

Garrett shrugged. "Hedge your bets and buy one of each."

Linc sighed.

"You figure out what to do about the smoothie shop yet? You keeping it or selling it?"

Linc slid him a look. "You really think I should sell? You don't think she's going to change her mind once she calms down? What if I sell and then she can't work there anymore?"

Maddox barked louder.

"Almost done here, buddy," Linc said, and turned to Garrett expectantly.

"Okay," Garrett said. "Let's put it this way. What I think is . . . you're screwed either way. The Lemon sisters don't really do calm."

Linc nodded grimly, then sighed. "Slip 'N Slide upgrade later?"

"Yeah, I drew up a new set of plans. The kids are gonna love the new course. It's Olympic quality."

They bumped fists and were about to go their separate ways when suddenly Maddox stopped barking. He'd shoved his pants to his ankles and was peeing into the bin of dog toys on the bottom shelf.

"Nice choice, kid," Garrett said, and went to move past Linc as if he'd never met the guy.

"Seriously?" Linc called after him.

Garrett ran one more errand and then he was on the road again. The sun was setting, but he had no trouble seeing that his dad's truck was still in the parking lot of the campground.

Yeah. He was definitely living there.

This time when he pulled into the parking lot, no one else was in sight. He got out of his truck and popped the hood on his dad's. He replaced the old spark plugs with the ones he'd bought at the auto parts store. Interestingly enough, though the truck was a piece of junk, it was clean. There was a single suitcase in the truck bed. In the back seat were a dog bed, a bag of dog food, a bag of tennis balls, and two dog bowls.

Snoop was living better than his owner.

There was a phone on the dash. A burner. With only a twinge of conscience, he violated his dad's privacy and opened the phone.

Garrett was the only contact in it.

With his gut in knots, he followed the scent of a campfire and found a small, raggedy-looking group of people seated on logs around it. In the background was a cluster of equally raggedy lean-tos and tents.

His dad looked up and paused. He rose with some difficulty, as if he was stiff and sore, prompting Garrett to start to reach out to steady him, but the stubborn old man shook his head. "I've got it. Everyone, this is my son, Garrett."

Some muttered a reply, but the most enthusiastic welcome came from Snoop, who bounded up and bumped his big head against Garrett's thigh in greeting.

"Let me get you some coffee," his dad said, leading Garrett

over to the leans-tos and tents, whose better days had been decades ago. His dad stopped in front of one, where there was a very small stack of firewood, a bag of dog food, and a beat-up old box. The contents were clean and very carefully organized: A loaf of bread. Some ketchup packets from a local drive-through. A box of no-brand dog biscuits. And a plate. Only one, along with a single fork, a knife, and a mug, which his dad reached for.

Garrett wanted to be hardened to this. His dad had left him, choosing alcohol over his own kid, when that kid had had nothing else in the world, no family, nothing. And yet he was having a hard time maintaining his anger and resentment. Still, he was going to give it the ol' college try. "You're living here, which means you lied to me. And why do you give away your money when you don't even have a pot to piss in?"

"I've got all I need."

"But—"

"I know what it looks like, Garrett, but I promise you, I'm good." Their eyes met. "I don't need more. I also don't deserve more."

Garrett rubbed the spot between his eyes, where a helluva headache was forming. "Everyone deserves more."

His dad was quiet a moment, looking off into the distance. "In prison, I met a social worker. He told me it's never too late to right your wrongs, and I need that to be true. I want to do right by you."

Dammit. Garrett really needed his dad to be that same selfish dick he remembered, so he could continue to soak in his own bad memories. But the only dick here was himself, because he wanted to walk away without looking back and not feel a thing. Unfortunately, he couldn't. "Dad, you can't stay out here. The nights are still too cold."

"The weather's about to change."

Garrett scrubbed a hand over his head, then stopped when he realized his dad had once again removed his baseball cap and was doing the exact same thing. He sighed. "Come home with me."

His dad looked as stunned as Garrett felt. "Oh. No. No, that's not necessary."

"Dad—"

"I'm happy here."

Garrett didn't have the brainpower to argue the point. He was so tired he felt his muscles quivering very slightly, and his eyes were practically crossed with the need to be closed for eight hours. With all he still had to do, he'd be lucky to get five.

"You look done in, son. Go home. I'm staying here."

"Suit yourself," he said, and for the first time since he was eight years old, he did something his dad asked. He walked away.

CHAPTER 14

"A Band-Aid will do it."

M indy stood in front of her bathroom sink, staring at herself in the mirror. She'd been doing YouTube yoga and daily sit-ups, which, for the record, she hated. She'd also given up wine and cookies.

A huge loss.

But she was now down three whole pounds. She'd been so proud of that, until she'd pulled on her favorite sexy lingerie. She'd wanted to remind Linc—who, by the way, didn't have any extra pounds on him, not a single damn one—what he was missing out on. He could give up carbs for one day and lose ten pounds. It was enough to make her hate him.

Except she loved him.

Ridiculously.

But she was also still furious with him. Not that any of it mattered, since he was sleeping on the couch.

She wanted that to change.

He startled her by poking his head into the bathroom, his gaze on the phone in his hand. She watched him via the mirror, holding her breath for his reaction, but he didn't look up. "Problem," he said. "Millie ran a little experiment on us. Apparently, she lost a tooth, put it under her pillow, and told no one for three days."

She gasped and whipped around. "Oh my God."

"Yeah, and obviously no money appeared under her pillow, so—" He finally looked up and caught sight of her and, with a husky groan, reached for her.

Seduction forgotten, she put a hand to his chest. "What did you tell her?"

"Who?"

"Your daughter!"

He fingered the spaghetti strap on her nightie, eyes hot. "What daughter?"

"Momma!" Millie said tearfully, appearing behind Linc. "Is the tooth fairy not real?"

"Oh, honey." Mindy dropped to her knees before her baby, her little girl, the one who was too young to not believe in the tooth fairy. "Listen, it's a busy time of year. Maybe she just got busy—"

"Tami at camp said that mommies and daddies are the tooth fairy. Is that true?"

Mindy looked at Linc. He dropped to his knees, too, and

turned Millie to face him. "Do you know why mommies and daddies pretend to be the tooth fairy?"

Millie, blinking her huge slay-me eyes, shook her head.

Linc kissed the tip of her nose. "Because they love their kids *so* much that they want them to have the joy of waking up the morning after they lose a tooth to find their prize. It's a tradition, and it makes parents as happy as it makes their kids."

Millie thought about that for a moment. "So giving me money makes you happy?"

Linc grinned. "Anyone ever tell you that you're too smart for your own good?"

"You, Daddy. All the time."

He gently tugged one of her pigtails. He was the only one allowed to touch her hair like that, and it made Mindy's heart squeeze hard.

"Do you think you can help us keep the secret for your brothers?" Linc asked. "For all the other holidays?"

A frown furrowed Millie's brow. "For all the other holidays . . . ?" Then her mouth dropped open. "Wait. So the Easter Bunny isn't real, either?" she wailed. "Or . . . *Santa Claus*?" Without waiting for an answer, she ran off sobbing to her room, which they knew because she slammed the door hard enough to rattle the windows.

"I've got this," Linc said, and went after Millie. When he came back ten minutes later, he shrugged. "She's okay. But I might've bribed her into being okay with the promise of a movie this weekend. With popcorn and soda."

"Why does everything keep going wrong?" Mindy asked.

"Okay, so that was my bad, and I feel shitty about the way it happened, but it's not the end of the world. She'd have found out sooner or later anyway, right?"

That it was true only made Mindy ache all the more. She'd lost her sister, and now she was losing her baby. And maybe her marriage. She closed her eyes. "I can't seem to find my happy, Linc. I know you're trying, but for the longest time it's just been me here with the kids, lonely as hell while you worked around the clock. I've got all this . . ."

"Resentment?" he asked softly.

She opened her eyes and bit her lower lip as she slowly nodded.

"I'm making changes, Min. I'm doing my best."

"I know."

"Do you?"

She gave him a nod, her gaze locked on his so he could see that she knew he was. "Yes, and you're not the only one trying to make changes. My happiness can't be based on you. It's gotta come from me. I'm working on that, too."

"Maybe I can help . . ." he murmured, reaching for her. Her heart took a little hopeful leap and she stepped into him, meeting him halfway. Their lips had almost touched when his phone buzzed.

She stilled.

And swore.

"Tell me it's not work," she said, fisting her hands in his shirt, her eyes on his mouth, which she wanted on her. "Tell me you're not on call."

He looked at his phone screen and grimaced.

"Seriously? You just got home. That means Ethan's on call, not you."

"He didn't answer his phone. One of our patients slipped and fell and broke his hip. I've got to meet the ambulance at the hospital."

A sigh escaped her and she gave him a little nudge that might have been more like a push. "Go."

"Min—"

"*Go.*" She gave a small smile at the look of genuine regret on his face. "It's okay, I get it. I do," she said, when he didn't look convinced. "It's what you do, it's who you are."

When he was gone, she stared at her pale reflection in the nightie that she'd hoped would fix things. But she was starting to realize the problem wasn't Linc at all—it was her.

THE NEXT MORNING, Mindy was sitting at the kitchen table sipping tea, staring at her binder. She was chilly, but the cold felt like it was coming from deep inside her, and she didn't know how to get warm.

Brooke staggered in the back door and headed right for the coffeepot. Given the untamed hair haloing her face and the camisole and matching teeny pajama boy shorts she was barely wearing, she was clearly right out of bed. She poured coffee into one of Linc's mugs that read WORLD'S BEST ~~FARTER~~ FATHER.

Mindy didn't want to be envious of her, but she was. In fact, she was green with it. Even wild, Brooke's hair was better—shinier, healthier—and her body . . . well, frankly, Mindy would kill for it. Lean, toned, yet curvy in all the right spots, without a spare ounce of fat. And when Brooke grabbed a chocolate chip croissant, made by one of Linc's patients, from a bag on the counter, Mindy hated her all the more.

"What?" Brooke asked.

"Nothing."

"Right. Steam's coming out of your ears for nothing." Brooke licked chocolate off her thumb.

Mindy felt her blood pressure rising. "You do realize you can't just parade around in your pj's like that. Linc's sleeping on the couch, and Garrett's in and out of this kitchen all the time, and you're practically buck-ass naked."

"Butt-ass naked," Brooke said.

"What?"

"The saying is 'butt-ass naked,' not 'buck-ass naked.'" Brooke looked down at herself. "And I'm more covered than I would be in a bathing suit. Or the tee and jean shorts I plan on wearing today. It's going to be hot as hell."

Mindy shut her binder. "You're missing my point."

Brooke reached for a second croissant. "Why is Linc still sleeping on the couch?"

Good question. She had no idea why he hadn't come to bed when he'd gotten home last night. She hadn't even heard him arrive. It made her cranky as hell. "Chocolate makes you break out," she heard herself say, only slightly gratified when Brooke hesitated with a bite halfway to her mouth. "And you used my expensive blender last night and didn't clean it."

"It's soaking," Brooke said. "I made myself margaritas."

"Also, you moved my boxes from the guesthouse. And left them outside."

"You mean the boxes that were stacked on the futon I'm sup- posed to sleep on?" Brooke asked. "Yes, I did move them. And they *had* to go outside—there was nowhere else to put them.

The place is the size of a postage stamp because—newsflash—it's not a guesthouse, it's a closet."

"We renovated it," Mindy said defensively, knowing her sister was right. "It's a guesthouse!"

Brooke shook her head. "You always do that."

"What?"

"Try to make everything in your life seem . . . bigger and better than it is."

Mindy felt her face heat. "Well, it's better than ignoring everything and anything that involves feeling something. You've stayed away from your family for seven years because . . ." Mindy tossed up her hands, shockingly close to tears. "Well, I'm not sure why. Maybe because we make you feel something."

"You do, and right now that something is irritation," Brooke said. "What's your problem this morning? Why don't you do us all a favor—take Linc to bed and get some happy, would you?"

That was just close enough to what Mindy actually wanted to do that it only made her feel worse. She wanted Linc to seduce her. Was that awful? He used to do it all the time.

Brooke sighed into the silence, put down her coffee—but not the croissant—and headed to the door.

"See?" Mindy said to her back. "You're doing it again, right now."

Brooke whirled back around. "What do you want from me? You needed my help with your kids, and I came through. You wanted me to stay, and I did. So please, tell me, what the hell is it that you want from me?"

It took Mindy a minute to speak, because she refused to cry. What did she want from her sister? She wanted what they'd once had. They'd drifted so far apart in the years since Brooke's accident. And Brooke had changed. She no longer wanted to hear Mindy's opinions—she no longer needed Mindy at all. "If I have to tell you what I want," Mindy finally said, "I don't want it."

"I can't guess, Min. Just say it."

"You know what? I don't want anything from you at all. Which makes sense, because we're grown-ups now, right? We don't need each other like we used to."

Brooke stilled for a beat. "Good to know," she finally said, and walked out.

"Great," Mindy said as the door slammed shut. And then burst into tears. She got one whole moment of self-pity before she heard the pitter patter of little feet approaching. She swiped at her face just as Millie appeared, wearing a cute sundress and a frown.

"What's wrong, baby?" Mindy asked.

"Everything!"

Mindy sighed. She'd definitely passed down the gene of talking in exclamation points.

"Daddy made us all brush our teeth. *Together!*"

And Millie hated sharing a sink. Or anything, really. Poor Princess Millie had been meant to be an only child. And royalty. "It's to save water," she reminded her daughter.

"I know, and the penguins are very important, but Momma, my brothers are *disgusting*." She walked to the sink to wash her hands, and Mindy stared at the back of her head. Someone had zip-tied her hair into a ponytail. "Millie, your hair . . ."

"Daddy did it. Said it was his morning to get us ready, and

I wasn't to go to you about it, even if I didn't like it. And remember how my sandal broke and you said I couldn't have new ones?"

"Yes," Mindy said, "because you broke it throwing it at Mason's head."

She nodded. "But this dress needs sandals, not sneakers, so . . . I asked Daddy for new sandals."

Mindy gave her a long look.

"Momma, I can't go to camp without shoes!" She stuck out her lower lip. "But Daddy said that he wouldn't buy me new ones, either, because you two are a team, so . . ." The girl thrust out one of her feet for inspection. She was wearing the sandals. The broken one had been fixed with Band-Aids. "He said a Band-Aid will do it."

Something in Mindy's chest tightened and warmed. "Maybe you'll think twice about throwing things at your brother's head."

Millie did an impressive eye roll and walked out. Probably to go find a new way to terrorize her siblings.

But Mindy did appreciate her baby's ability to solve her problem. Seemed she could learn a lesson or two from that, if only finding her happy was that simple.

THAT NIGHT, MINDY sat in her big bedroom all by herself. The kids were asleep, and Linc had been called for an emergency.

She knew that was out of his control, but she wouldn't want to come home to her, either. Turning on the kid monitors, she slipped out the back door. Back when she and Brooke had been young, they'd often have big blowups, and after, the one at fault would sneak into the other's bed late at night to apologize, and then they'd sleep together holding hands.

It'd been a whole lot of years, but Mindy was hoping the gesture would still mean something. The moon was nearly full, reflecting off the water of the pool, lighting her way to the guesthouse. She knocked softly, and when she got no response, she pressed her face to the window and peered in. She could see Brooke on the futon beneath a blanket, turned away from the door, watching a show streaming on her laptop.

Mindy let herself in, tripping over all the stuff. Her stuff. Linc's stuff. Kid stuff. Pool stuff. Brooke had tried to tell her this place wasn't a guesthouse of any sort, but she'd ignored it because she hadn't had the brainpower to devote to one more thing. She'd just shoved her sister in here with no thoughts to her comfort. Mindy had managed to make her feel unwelcome without even trying, in her own childhood home, no less.

Brooke didn't acknowledge her, not when she opened the door and not when she walked to the bed. "I'm sorry," Mindy said quietly. "I know I've been . . . difficult."

No reaction from Brooke, of course.

With a sigh, Mindy kicked off her shoes, set the child monitors on the coffee table, and got onto the futon. In the past, she'd read to Brooke long into the night because her sister had always wanted to know more about the world beyond Wildstone. Sometimes Mindy would change the characters' names to Mindy and Brooke Lemon, or she'd make up a Lemon Sisters Adventure. "I should've brought a book for old times' sake, yeah?"

Brooke maintained her silence.

Tough crowd. Exhausted, and worried she was never going to find her way back to her sister—or any other part of her life—Mindy settled in and closed her eyes. Which was when Brooke finally spoke. Her voice was quiet. Distant. "We're grown-ups now, Min. We don't need each other like we used to. Your words, remember?"

Mindy froze and felt her face heat, even though those *had* been her words. She just hadn't realized how harsh they were until she heard them hurtled back at her. Sliding out of the bed, she slunk back to her own, tiptoeing past Linc, who'd apparently gotten home and had fallen asleep on the couch. She went to her room, feeling even worse about her life than she'd felt that morning, which was saying something.

CHAPTER 15

"Don't look down, and whatever you do, don't let go."

Early the next morning, Brooke headed out with her camera and a huge to-go cup of tea in tow. She didn't mess around with her caffeine. She liked it hot and by the gallon. Halfway to her car, she stopped in surprise.

Garrett was leaning against the passenger door, casual as you please.

"What are you doing here?" she asked.

"I know you've been taking the early mornings to go hike or climb. Thought maybe I'd go with."

The morning part was true. She'd been going out on her own before helping Mindy with the kids or working on the photo gig. She'd been trying to reacquaint herself with . . . well, herself. "The point of going out alone is to be alone."

"Once upon a time we used to go together."

She rolled her eyes. "Yeah, well, we 'used to' do a whole lot of things." *Such as love each other . . .* She unlocked her car. "And you've got work."

"That's the perk of being my own boss. I set my hours."

To be honest, that was what she loved about the new photo gig, too. No set hours, and no one telling her what to do. "Trust me, you'll be bored. Because FYI, I walk. *Not* hike. *Not* climb."

Without responding, he took her hand and steered her to his truck.

"What's wrong with my car?" she asked.

"It's not a truck."

She rolled her eyes again. At this rate, if she kept it up, they'd roll right out of her head before she got back to LA.

He waited until they were both buckled in before he took off his sunglasses and turned to her.

"What?" she asked. "You just realized how dumb this is?"

"No. I just want to talk to you first."

"Oh boy." Nothing good ever came from a statement like that. "Look, we really don't need to talk about what happened. You made it clear what you think of me, and I get it, so—"

"You have no idea what I think. But I said something to you that I shouldn't have, and I can't let it stand."

She let out a breath. It was too early for emotions. She didn't have enough caffeine in her for it yet. "You're going to have to be more clear, since you said lots of things. Like . . . 'Oh yeah, babe, just like that,' and 'Brooke, you feel hot as f—'"

"I meant the next morning," he said, sliding her a look.

Right. "Well, as much fun as this talk would be, I'm going to take a hard pass . . ." She started to open the door, but he put a hand over hers.

"I said you were a mistake." He spoke quietly. "You're not. You never were."

Every muscle had clenched when he'd started this conversation, braced for something bad. So she felt unprepared for how his words went straight to her heart and squeezed so hard it took her a moment to speak. "It's okay if I am. I'd get it."

"You're not," he said with a quiet intensity that made her chest squeeze again.

Since he was still looking at her, seeming to be waiting for a response of some kind, she swallowed the lump in her throat and gave him a small but real smile and a nod. "Okay, thanks."

He nodded and matched her small smile, looking relieved. Realizing he didn't expect additional uncomfortable deep talk, or for her to spill her guts, her smile spread a little with a whole lot of relief. "So . . . we're okay?"

"As okay as we ever get," he said.

That, she could live with. "You don't need to come with, now that we're square."

"I know. But I'd like to, if that's okay with you."

Since she actually sort of wanted company, *his* company, she nodded and then had to ignore the way his smile made her get warm from the inside out.

They hit the road, and five minutes later, Garrett pulled into a convenience store. "A pit stop for snacks to take on the hike and climb."

"You mean walk," she said. "We're going on a *walk*."

"I've never known you to walk a day in your life. You've got two speeds, Brooke: full steam ahead and fast asleep."

She gave a rough laugh. "Yeah, well, as you might've noticed—things change." But not one to ever turn down food, she walked into the store and eyed the hot dogs rolling on the cooker at the checkout. It'd been years since she'd had a hot dog for breakfast. That streak ended today.

Garrett came up next to her, his arms loaded with a large assortment of chips, cookies, and other goodies. Dumping everything on the counter, he looked around for the still unseen clerk.

Brooke gestured to his stash. "You look like an unsupervised nine-year-old who was given a hundred bucks."

He grinned, and something low in her belly quivered. She eyed the Slim Jims in his pile and her senses were overtaken with memories, flashing her back to a climb they'd once taken up the rocky face of the Playground, where they'd watched the sunrise. It'd taken two hours to get to the top and she'd been starving. He'd pulled a Slim Jim from his pocket. She'd laughed at his idea of breakfast food, but she'd eaten her half, and then, at his insistence, his half as well. Then she'd nibbled his fingers and in turn he'd nibbled her mouth, and then they'd . . . well. She glanced up and met his gaze, which was hot and locked on hers.

She wasn't the only one remembering what had come next, how they'd pretty much leapt at each other. They'd been lucky no one had discovered them before they'd surfaced.

Garrett cleared his throat and looked around for the clerk. "Anyone home?"

"Right here." The elderly male voice sounded familiar to Brooke, but she couldn't quite place it. Not until the man came shuffling out from the back, straining to carry a crate of wine bottles that was clearly too heavy for him.

Garrett's dad.

"Hello, son," he said.

Brooke heard a *whoosh* of breath escape Garrett's lungs. But he recovered before she did, moving around the counter to take the heavy crate from his dad. "Where?" was all he said.

His dad pointed to a counter and Garrett set the case down. There was a horribly awkward beat of silence, and then his dad moved toward the cash register. "Anything else?" he asked, and looked at Brooke.

"Two hot dogs, please."

With a smile, he handed them to her and began to ring them up.

"What are you doing?" Garrett asked.

"Working."

"You know that's not what I mean."

His dad reached for a brown bag and slid their purchases into it, his hands shaking terribly.

Garrett reached out and took over. "I've got it," he said quietly.

"You replaced the spark plugs in my truck," his dad said. "Why?"

Brooke looked at Garrett in time to see him shrug. "Your truck needed them. It needs a lot of things."

The two men stared at each other awkwardly and then Garrett went back to tossing things into the bag.

Brooke felt her eyes sting at the look on Garrett's dad's face as Garrett did his job for him. Shame. Regret. She wanted to reach into her pocket and pull out all her money and hand it over so he didn't have to work like this, in a position that was clearly too physically demanding for him.

"Dad." Garrett pressed his thumbs to his eye sockets like they hurt before dropping his hands to his sides. "I've got a bunch of jobs I'm working on, and I'm shorthanded. I could use help."

"I don't need a pity job."

"Did I say anything about pity?"

The two men stared at each other some more. "I'll think about it," his dad said.

Garrett nodded and then turned to her. "Brooke."

She looked up and realized Garrett had their bag of goodies and was holding the door open for her. She smiled at his dad and walked out, aware of Garrett right on her tail. He opened the passenger door for her and waited until she'd climbed in and secured her seat belt before handing her their bag.

She set it at her feet as he walked around the front of the truck. She watched him scan the lot, clearly looking for something, and then fix on another truck parked close by. The windows were down and a smiling black Lab sat in the driver's seat. Garrett headed over there, and the dog's tail went crazy with excitement. Garrett gave him a one-armed hug and got a big wet kiss across his face for his efforts.

Brooke couldn't blame the dog—she had good reason to know that Garrett tasted delicious.

After a moment, he came back to the truck, slid behind the wheel, and pulled out of the lot. She waited, but he didn't speak as they headed west toward the ocean. She opened the bag and started doctoring up her hot dog with ketchup and mustard. She did the mustard with slow purpose, baiting him, because he hated mustard with the passion of a thousand suns and had always given her shit for using it.

He said nothing.

She repeated the routine with hot dog number two. Still nothing from Garrett, not even when she held out the last bite, slathered in mustard, and offered it to him. "Wow," she said. "You're taking this whole silent thing very seriously. You've really got nothing to say?"

"You smell like mustard."

She smiled.

He looked over at her and shook his head. Okay, so he wasn't feeling playful . . . And as for the intimidating intensity coming off him, the dark sunglasses were a nice touch. "Are we really just going to pretend that didn't happen?" she asked.

"Brooke."

That was it, just her name, uttered in a low warning tone that suggested he was considering pulling over to let her out. Before she could tell him to do just that, he'd turned off on the narrow dirt road, where if you knew the area, you could get to the good spots to climb, and an extremely little-known one in particular called the Playground.

Her heart started to pound. "Um."

He turned off the truck. "You don't want to talk about us, and I don't want to talk about my dad. You still up for this?"

"I assumed we were going to the bluffs," she said.

He pushed his sunglasses to the top of his head. "You used to say the bluffs were for tourists."

"When are you going to hear me—things change."

He paused, cocking his head to one side as he studied her. "Are you telling me you haven't been to the Playground at all?"

"That's what I'm telling you."

He arched a brow, and she sighed. "Look, I've wanted to. But if I've learned anything, it's that sometimes you've got to try a different route to get where you want to go."

"And where do you want to go?" he asked.

She tilted her head back and eyed the climb she hadn't made in years. "Up," she admitted.

He nodded and took in their view. "Do you trust me?"

She just looked at him.

A rough laugh escaped him. "Okay, so you don't."

"Actually, I do." She paused. "At least with my body—which I'm pretty sure I made clear several times the other night."

"But?"

"But my brain's a different beast."

He nodded. "Then let's just go for a walk."

"A walk. To the Playground," she said, heavy on disbelief.

"Yeah," he said. "Let's just go look at it."

So they got out of the truck. Again she tipped her head back and looked straight up the set of rocky cliffs that once upon a time she could've free climbed in her sleep. There were several options available. First there was what she'd always thought of as the safe way—only a 100-foot climb to a trail that you could use to walk the slow, long way around the back to the top. Second, there was a midlevel option on the far right, a 350-foot jaunt that caught the trail at the midway point. And third, there was the take-your-own-life-in-your-hands way to go, 750 vertical feet straight up.

"What are you thinking?" he asked.

"That I wish I hadn't eaten both hot dogs."

He snorted and she stepped closer to the rock, eyes locked on the easy route. She'd start there. And before she could give it too much thought, she reached for her first handholds.

Muscle memory was the most amazing thing, she discovered. Her body took over from her brain, and before she knew it, she was halfway up—which she knew because she made the mistake of looking down. "Oh shit," she whispered, freezing with fifty feet up or fifty feet down to go, a cool breeze brushing over her sweaty face.

"You're okay." Garrett was right behind her. As in *literally* behind her, practically on top of her, clearly in protective mode. "Breathe, Bee."

Right. She was holding her breath. She gulped in air as he climbed up next to her and came into her personal space bubble, letting go with one hand so he could wrap an arm around her. "Good. Do it again," he said, and watched her breathe for a beat before giving her a warm smile. "Remember the two tricks."

"Which are . . . ?"

"Don't look down, and whatever you do, don't let go."

With a breathless laugh, she turned her head and pressed her face into him, which, given their positions, meant into his armpit. He was warm but not sweaty, and he smelled . . . damn. Delicious. Basically the opposite of her. She was hot and clammy. And *very* sweaty. *One, two, three, four . . .*

"Look at me, Bee."

His voice was quiet, calm, and utterly authoritative, so much so that she lifted her head and met those mesmerizing light hazel eyes.

"You've got this."

He could have said, "I've got you," and that would've been sweet. But he'd said, "You've got this," meaning he *believed in her,* and somehow . . . somehow that converted her panic into confidence. With a nod, she looked up . . . and climbed the last fifty feet. Crawling shakily over the edge, she collapsed in a boneless heap. Not great for her ego, and neither was the way she was pulling in air like a beached fish. She hadn't even started up the trail to the top yet, but she found herself grinning at the sky anyway.

Garrett came over the edge with his usual animal grace. He didn't speak, just sat at her side, legs out in front of him, arms braced behind him, taking in the view. Letting her have her moment. She'd never felt more grateful to another human being in her entire life, and she felt tears sting her eyes. *No shame in that,* she told herself.

"There's no shame here at all," Garrett said quietly, making her realize she'd spoken out loud.

She drew in a deep breath. "My pulse is at stroke level," she said, pressing a hand to her pounding heart. "I'm considering throwing up. Fair warning."

He wrapped his hand around her wrist, and she realized he was checking her pulse.

"How bad is it?" she asked with an embarrassed laugh.

"Not bad considering you had two hot dogs, a gallon of tea, and a big adrenaline rush."

Rolling her eyes, she reached out and grabbed *his* wrist. His pulse was slow and steady, the bastard. "What would it take to get your heart rate as high as mine?"

He turned his head and slid her a look. "You in those white shorts from the other day."

That tugged a reluctant laugh from her, but she was actually feeling anything but amused. She was starting to realize how much more he'd anted up in this . . . whatever they were doing . . . so much more than she had. She'd kept things from the people who cared about her, and guilt was a heavy burden. Glancing over, she found Garrett looking out at the ocean, sprawled in all its glory for as far as the eye could see, which made it slightly easier to attempt to spill some hard-earned truth. Sitting up, she hugged her knees to her chest. "My feet haven't left the ground since the helicopter crash," she murmured.

He turned and looked at her, and if she'd thought her heart was beating fast before, that had nothing on what it was doing now, which was basically threatening to pound its way right out of her chest. She hadn't been the only one impacted by the crash. Not that he'd say so. Not that he'd let his emotions be more important than hers, and at the thought, at how much he'd given her without her even realizing it, she felt her eyes well. Swallowing hard, she forced herself to go on before she lost her nerve. "I haven't even flown—other than when I left the hospital in Peru to come back to the States, and they had to sedate me for that. It's not heights, necessarily. It's . . ." She grimaced. "This is going to sound really dumb . . . it's a fear of the adrenaline rush. It's . . . paralyzing."

"That's understandable. You nearly died. And several others

did," Garrett said, and paused for a long beat. "I got there just after your first surgery. You'd had some unexpected complications that demanded a second, more urgent surgery. I kissed you just before they rolled you away, do you remember?"

She nodded. It was the last thing she remembered before going under, the comfort of his solid, steady presence.

"It was so bad." He swallowed hard and shook his head. "The doctors weren't giving you great odds. I had no idea if I was going to get to see you again." His voice cracked, and so did her heart.

"And in some ways," he went on, "I didn't. I never saw that Brooke again."

She reached for him and he pulled her in, hugging her tight for a very long moment.

When she finally pulled back, her eyes were wet, and she thought his might have been, too. "Look at yourself now," he said firmly. "Not only are you still here, you're stronger than you've ever been. You're not just conquering your demons, Bee, you're stomping all over them."

"It seems like so long ago," she said quietly. "And yet sometimes it feels like it just happened. After, I couldn't do my job. I had to shift to behind the scenes, in a studio." She closed her eyes. "I still let it mess with me."

"Anyone would," he said quietly. "But you beat the fear today."

The thought brought a curve to her lips as he brushed his fingers along her jaw and into her hair. "The smile looks good on you." Their eyes met and held, and the moment extended as he slowly leaned in and brushed her mouth with his. She could feel his breath, warm on her face. She could feel the heat of his body, just barely touching hers, and she wrapped her hands around his wrists. "Thanks for today," she whispered.

In answer, he kissed her again. Drawn to his heat, his easy strength, the allure of his touch and what she knew it could do to her, she crawled into his lap. He pulled her in tight, his hands caressing and warming her now chilled limbs. Wanting to surrender to their crazy chemistry, she whispered his name and he pulled her down with him to the wild grass, his hands sliding up her thighs. He was deliciously heavy, and she was already forgetting that they weren't going to do this anymore and was a second away from tearing his clothes off when he pulled back.

His phone was ringing, which was a real blessing, because they were in public. Isolated, but still, anyone could have come upon them. Not that that would've stopped them in the old days.

Garrett answered his phone, and sitting as close to him as she was, she had no trouble hearing the person on the other end. It was an elderly female voice asking to speak to Garrett Montgomery.

"Speaking," he said.

"Garrett, this is your aunt, Rita Montgomery."

She felt the shock go through him at that.

"Hello?" the woman asked, sounding worried. "These new-fangled phones . . . Hello?"

"I'm here," Garrett said. "I just wasn't aware I had an aunt."

"Oh. Well, my goodness," the woman said. "I'm your father's older sister, Rita. He's never mentioned me then?"

"He's never mentioned much of anything at all," Garrett said. "How did you find me?"

"He pops in and out of my life as it suits him, the shithead.

He told me you were living in the house you grew up in. One of the men in my assisted living facility has a little hacking hobby. He got me your number."

"Interesting," Garrett said. "And illegal."

"I'm an old lady on a fixed income," she said dryly. "I'm not worried you're going to sue me."

"What *are* you worried about?"

"My idiot brother. There're some things you need to know."

"Such as?"

"Such as, he's got cancer. I'm sorry," she said more softly into Garrett's stunned silence. "But you needed to know."

Garrett's face was carefully blank, but Brooke could see the war of emotions in his dark gaze.

"He's on meds, and some of them can create dementia-like symptoms," his aunt said. "He should be staying with someone."

"Why isn't he staying with you?" Garrett asked.

"Are you hard of hearing, boy? He's an asshole and I don't want him." Then she disconnected.

Garrett pinched the bridge of his nose, like maybe he was getting a headache.

"You okay?" Brooke asked him.

"Yeah."

But of course he wasn't. "I'm so sorry, Garrett."

He shook his head. "Not your problem." Looking far more tense than he had when they'd come up here, he got to his feet. "Let's go."

They took the easy way down without speaking, and the silence continued until Garrett pulled over in front of Mindy and Linc's house. She turned to face him only to find that his expression read *Closed Off! Do Not Enter!* "At the risk of repeating myself," she said quietly, "do you want to talk about it?"

His smile was ironic and not super open. "I wonder how many times I've asked you that very question."

She nodded, belatedly realizing she'd almost forgotten that even though there were still feelings between them—and chemistry, buckets of chemistry—they weren't going to get a happily ever after. She probably needed to write that down somewhere until it sank in.

CHAPTER 16

"The apple and the tree and all that."

Since his day was already screwed up, Garrett did what he knew he needed to. He took himself and his gut ache back to the convenience store. He also had heartache, which he knew was from letting Brooke walk away. She wasn't good for him. She was leaving again soon, and she'd already destroyed him once.

But.

It was always the *but* that got him, and this was a big but.

He still loved her.

He was an idiot.

His dad's beat-up old truck was in the store lot. As before, Snoop stuck his big old head out in greeting, mouthing not one but two tennis balls, which he managed to huff out a hello around.

Garrett ruffled his fur and drew a deep breath. When he walked into the store, his dad looked up from where he was stocking cigarettes behind the counter and blinked. And then smiled so bright it actually hurt. "Son," he said, as if seeing Garrett again was the highlight of his day.

"What time do you get off?" Garrett asked. "We need to talk."

A young guy walked into the shop wearing low-slung board shorts in a loud Hawaiian print, flip-flops, and a beater tank top advertising a local brewery. He had long surfer hair and a lazy smile on his face. His name was Ace, and Garrett had gone to school with his older brother, who'd died of an overdose a decade ago. Ace had given up all drugs but weed—"It's a supplement, man"—and when his grandpa died and left him the store, he'd taken it over.

"Thanks for taking my shift for me," Ace said to Garrett's dad. "How did it go?"

"As you said it would—boring as hell."

Ace grinned. "Right on." He handed over some cash. "I know you're looking for something more permanent, and if anything comes up, I'll let you know."

Garrett's dad's smile dimmed just a little bit. "Sure. I understand."

They walked out of the store together, the two of them standing in the hot sun for a moment, taking in the day. Well, his dad was taking in the day. Garrett was arguing with himself. "Were you ever going to tell me that I've got an aunt?" he finally asked. "Or that you have cancer?"

His dad looked pained. "No."

"Jesus, Dad. Why the hell not?"

"Because my sister hates me—for good reasons, obviously—and you didn't need any help in that arena."

"And the cancer?"

His dad shrugged. "If alcoholism and fast living didn't kill me, I've got a hard time believing cancer will."

Garrett ran a hand over his face, and not for the first time caught his dad making the same gesture at the exact same time. They stared at each other.

His dad gave a very small smile. "The apple and the tree and all that."

"You need to come stay with me."

"That's a very kind offer," he said, without an ounce of sarcasm, which was more than Garrett could've managed. "But I can't put you out like that."

"The nights are still cold, Dad. You clearly need money, and watching you in that job, having to lift heavy stuff . . ." Garrett shook his head. "Just come stay for a few days until we figure something else out."

His dad looked away, his jaw muscles working as the famous Montgomery pride battled common sense, but he eventually gave a single nod. "Okay. Thanks. But just for a few days."

When Garrett pulled into his driveway a few minutes later, his dad's beat-up old truck followed. They got out and Garrett looked at Snoop. He hadn't thought this far ahead. "I've got Ann's cats. They hate dogs."

"Snoop can handle them," his dad said.

Sitting at his dad's feet, Snoop smiled around his tennis balls. He was game.

But Garrett shook his head. Snoop wasn't near tough enough

for this. "Let me go in first and try to corral them into the laundry room—"

"Son," his dad said. "Trust me."

Garrett gave him a look.

His dad nodded. "Okay, so you're not on the trust-me train, I get that." He put his hand on the porch railing and closed his eyes.

Garrett frowned and set a hand on his dad's arm. "What's wrong?"

"Nothing. Just tired."

"When did you eat last?"

His dad turned to Snoop. "Do you remember? It was breakfast, right? You had a leftover burger that the nice lady at the campsite gave us."

"I mean when was the last time *you* ate," Garrett said.

His dad shrugged, and Garrett shook his head. "I'll make us something right away." He opened the front door. "Be cool," he told the dog. "They're going to bitch at you, and I can't help that. I promised Ann they'd be safe until they die, but I'm pretty sure they're immortal."

The so-called welcoming committee was waiting. The three of them froze in unison when they caught sight of Snoop, sending him death glares.

Snoop stayed still, panting softly due to the heat, but— and Garrett would swear this on a stack of Bibles—*smiling* at the cats.

The old biddies slowly came forward to inspect poor Snoop. They circled him, sniffing at him like they smelled something rotten. To his credit, Snoop just sat quietly, accepting, bowing his head to each cat so she could sniff his face. Finally, the cats got bored, turned their attention to Garrett, and demanded food.

"Are you kidding me?" Garrett asked in disbelief. "Where's the dog hate?"

The ladies turned their expressions into mirrors of innocence.

His dad was walking through the place slowly, craning his neck to take it all in. "You've been renovating."

"No. I mean, yeah, but not lately."

"Why not?"

Garrett loved this old house, but it needed a lot of TLC, which he hadn't devoted to it in a long time. He had more jobs than he knew what to do with, but that wasn't what was holding him up. He figured what was the rush, when he wasn't close to filling it with a family of his own?

"I used to take you on my jobs with me sometimes," his dad said, running his hand along a ladder leaning against the foyer wall.

"I remember."

His dad looked up in surprise. "You do?"

"I remember you taking me to Caro's Café to fix some electrical problem in their kitchen. The owner, Carolyn, used to feed me. Once I dropped a plate and it broke. You told her you did it."

His dad shook his head. "Don't remember that. But what I do remember is Carolyn's cooking. She's passed now, I hear. Her daughters have taken over the café. Wonder if either of them cooks like their momma." He nudged the toe of his boot against a metal toolbox that had seen better days. "Well, would you look at that."

"It was Ann's," Garrett said. "She passed it down to me."

His dad had an odd look on his face.

"What?"

"Nothing."

"Dad, it's something. Speak your peace."

"Those are my tools, my toolbox. I gave them to her to give to you when you were ready for them."

So all this time he'd been using his dad's tools. He had no idea how to feel about that. Mad? Sad? Maybe a combination of both. There'd been a point in his life, several points, when in spite of Ann's love, he'd felt unwanted. Unworthy. And most definitely pissed off at the world. He had plenty of anger left over for his dad, and he wondered now, if he'd known the guy had come back, seen him happy, and chosen to let him stay and continue being happy . . . would that have changed anything?

They both turned at the sound of glass breaking.

Snoop's tail had swept a glass off the coffee table.

"Damn," his dad said. "Sorry, son." Moving forward, he dropped to his knees to reach for the glass shards. "Snoop's new at this whole inside thing."

"Don't." Garrett nudged his dad out of the way so he didn't cut himself. "I've got it. No worries," he said to the sheepish-looking dog. "It's okay." He looked at his dad. "I thought you've been out of prison for a year, and that you've had Snoop since shortly after that."

"That's right."

Garrett stared at him, taking in his dad's disheveled appearance and realizing the truth. His dad had been camping out, or living in his truck, this whole time. Maybe a combo of both. And so had Snoop. He rose with the broken glass and moved into the kitchen, not liking the ache in his chest as he tossed the glass into the trash. He opened his fridge to find them all food and saw the new six-pack of beer he'd just bought. He picked it up and shoved it into a cabinet, out of sight, so his dad wouldn't be tempted.

"What are you doing?"

He turned to face his dad, going for nonchalance. "Nothing."

His dad gave him a *get real* glance. "My vice was hard booze, not beer, but thanks for the vote of confidence."

Garrett blew out a breath and opened his mouth, but his dad shook his head.

"Don't bother. I get it. I'm not exactly working with a stellar track record here. But I'm not drinking again, son. Ever."

Garrett wasn't sure he bought that, but okay. He put the beer back and found his dad looking into the laundry room. "Do you need to do a load?"

"I go to the laundromat."

"You don't have to do that now." Garrett gestured to his washer and dryer, which was open, because that's how he did things. He managed to wash his clothes and get them into the dryer, but he rarely, if ever, remembered to retrieve and fold them. Instead, he lived out of the dryer. Today, like every day, a few items were hanging out of the machine from his morning search for fresh clothes. A pair of jeans, a T-shirt, and . . . a bra.

Brooke's, which she'd left here the night they'd slept together.

He nudged the clothes all the way into the dryer and shut the door.

"You're seeing someone," his dad said.

"No."

His dad raised a brow. "So you're one of them cross-dressers?"

"Okay, I'm seeing someone. Sort of. Maybe." Remembering how Brooke had left his truck a little while ago thanks to his own asshole behavior, he ran his hand over his face. "I don't know."

His dad smiled. "She's got you all twisted up. That's the very best kind of woman. What is she to you?"

His first instinct was to say "everything." She was *everything* to him. But in truth, that was a pipe dream, and an old one at that, so he just shook his head. "There aren't really words."

His dad nodded. "Yep, some women are like that."

Wasn't that the truth.

CHAPTER 17

"I came, I saw, and I forgot what I was doing."

Over the next few days, Brooke went through the motions. She took photos and made time early each morning to sneak out to the Playground. And if she had Garrett to thank for that, she hadn't yet mentioned it to him.

He'd been scarce. Okay, so she'd also done a bang-up job of avoiding him. Mindy, too, though her sister seemed to be avoiding her as well. And hey, if they didn't talk, they couldn't fight.

Denial, she was thy queen.

Her camera had once again become an extension of her, and it was currently the one good thing in her life. She took pics of the kids, her sister, Linc . . . even Garrett. She'd gotten pictures of his dad and Snoop, too, and as she did, a little voice inside her had said that if Garrett could forgive his father, he could certainly forgive her. But the truth was both simple and hard to take: She hadn't really forgiven *herself*.

Now it was late, and she was lying on the futon telling herself to get up and get ready for bed. She needed to get out of her clothes and brush her teeth, because she wouldn't be able to fall asleep without going through her nighttime routine. But for the first time in her life, her OCD left her alone as she stared at the ceiling, wondering what Garrett was doing and if he was thinking of her. She was certainly thinking of him. What would he say to a late-night visitor?

Her phone buzzed. It was Cole and Tommy, holding her hostage in a group text.

Tommy: You ever coming back or what?

Brooke: Of course I am.

Cole: Don't tease me.

Brooke: No, I mean it. And I want to talk to you when I get there.

Cole: Yes.

Brooke: But you don't even know what I want to talk about.

Cole: Yes to anything. I'm a desperate man.

Brooke: I want to go back out there, I want to be a principal photographer again.

Cole: Okay, yes to anything but that. That's a definite no. I'm not putting you out there where you could get hurt again.

Brooke: That's not a decision you get to make for me.

Cole: So come home and fight it out with me.

Brooke: I will. Soon. I'm not quite done here.

Tommy: It's about a guy, right? Why else would you be stalling? And don't forget to freak out when he wants more than a good time.

Brooke: That's ridiculous. I don't freak.

Tommy: No? Why do you think you're not wearing an engagement ring from Cole right now?

Brooke: Wait—Cole thinks about marrying me??????

Cole: USED TO. Note the past tense. Because falling for you is the equivalent of jumping without a parachute. No offense.

Tommy: He's not the right one for you anyway, sweetness. Just don't run from the one who is. Don't shut it down because you get scared.

Cole: You're reading Cosmo again, aren't you.

Tommy: So I like to be in touch with my feminine side, bite me.

Brooke: This convo is over. Good night.

She turned off her phone, even knowing Tommy was right. She shut things down when they got too personal. It usually happened somewhere around date three, at the inevitable "I'd like a family someday" dinner talk. That's when she made the decision for them both that it wouldn't work out. She knew this was because deep, *deep* down, she knew she didn't want to face talking about the option she'd lost in the helicopter accident, the option she hadn't even known she'd wanted.

Exhausted, she closed her eyes.

The thump, thump, thump *of the helicopter rotors spinning startled her, as did the sound of the pilot speaking with intense steadiness into his radio about making an emergency landing.*

Then she was in free fall.

She jerked awake with a silent scream on her lips, cold and clammy and utterly terrified. She was on her feet and out the door, her body taking control. She grabbed her keys with the intention of getting the hell out of Dodge, but she didn't go out front to her car.

It wasn't until she ran into Garrett's dark bedroom a minute later that she realized what she'd done.

Garrett sat straight up in bed. "What the—"

She dropped her keys and, without even counting her steps, launched herself at him. For a guy who'd clearly been dead to the world a second ago, he thankfully woke up fast, wrapping his arms around her, pulling her into his warm, hard body with a low, worried murmur, holding her tight. "Brooke, what is it?"

Unable to answer, she burrowed in closer.

GARRETT SHOOK OFF the last dregs of sleep and ran his hands over Brooke's body. No injuries that he could tell, at least no new ones. But she was alarmingly chilled—icy, even—and trembling like a leaf. "Bad dream?"

She nodded.

"It's okay now." He pressed his jaw to the top of her head. "You're okay, you're safe."

She didn't loosen her death grip on him, so he leaned back with her in his arms, pulling the covers up over them both. Again he stroked his hands over her to soothe and warm, until she slowly began to stop quivering and her body began to un-clench.

He thought maybe she'd actually fallen asleep on him when she finally took a slow, deep breath and lifted her head, her eyes luminous in the dark as they met his. "I knew better than to fall asleep without going through my nighttime routine. I knew something bad would happen."

"What happened?"

She squeezed her eyes shut. "Nothing. I'm sorry."

"For what? Bee, help me out here."

She choked out a laugh. "Everything. I'm sorry for everything."

"That covers a lot of ground."

She shrugged and bit her lower lip, and he gently pushed the hair back from her face, worried about the way she was breathing and the look in her eyes, worried because the last time she'd looked like this, she'd bailed for seven long years. "Talk to me, Bee."

She hesitated. "You've spent your life making good, smart choices. And I've spent mine doing the opposite of that."

"I'd never judge you on the decisions you've made."

"Except for the one where I walked away from Wildstone and my family. And you," she said.

Well, she had him there, and he winced.

"I really do regret how much I hurt you—"

"Don't," he said, closing his eyes. "You apologized and I heard you, and we've moved on."

"Not all the way," she said.

Their gazes met.

"You're still mad," she whispered.

"No. *No*," he said again, when she looked at him with doubt. "Not mad."

"Mistrusting, then."

There, she was right on. And he hated that it was true. Hated, too, that she could clearly read it in his expression, because she slid out of his bed. "I closed you out," she said, "and now you're returning the favor. And I understand. I do. I honestly had no idea how much it would suck, and I'm sorry for that, more than you'll ever know. And something else I now understand? This"—she gestured between them and then at the bed—"you knew this would be a bad idea, and you were right, because I'm having trouble separating the sex and the emotions that come with it." She gave him a small smile. "I should go. Night," she whispered, and walked out.

He leapt out of the bed to go after her and realized he wasn't wearing any clothes. The front door slammed while he was pulling on a pair of jeans. Forgoing anything else, he ran outside in time to see her running toward the Lemon property.

"Shit," he said, and started after her, but a scraping sound from behind him made him turn back.

His dad waved from the porch chair, Snoop at his side. He wore a T-shirt and boxers and nothing else.

"Yeah," his dad said with a sigh. "I came, I saw, and I forgot what I was doing. But mostly, it turns out that once you get in this chair, you're kinda stuck until someone a few decades younger who still has abdominals can pull you out."

Garrett strode over there and pulled him up. "Why didn't you say something? And where are your pants?"

"That's another funny story. Sort of." He grimaced. "I forgot 'em. I also forgot why I was coming outside in the first place, so don't bother asking me."

"Sorry to intrude."

They both turned at the sound of Brooke's voice. She was back, standing at the bottom of the porch steps, barefoot, hair wild around her face, eyes solemn, face pale. In her tiny jean shorts and tank top, she looked like jailbait.

"Brooke." With huge relief, Garrett took a step toward her, but she shook her head.

"Just forgot my keys." She moved past him and into the house, coming out not a minute later, keys in hand. Carefully not looking at Garrett, she turned to his dad. "We didn't get to formally meet. I'm Brooke Lemon."

His dad smiled at her. "And I'm Gary Montgomery, Garrett's dad, though not a particularly good one. As you can see, I forgot my pants. Sorry about that."

Brooke returned his smile. "I'm not a big fan of pants myself. And it's never too late to learn to be good at something, right?"

She was being effortlessly kind, handling his dad with more care and affection than Garrett had ever managed.

"Are you the one seeing my son?" his dad asked.

Garrett let out a breath. "Ignore him," he said, and took her hand. "We're not finished talking."

She raised a brow at his tone, which, okay, had definitely made that come out sounding like a demand, but it was more desperation than anything else.

"He don't seem to know much about women," his dad said to Brooke with a shake of his head. "But that might be my fault. I wasn't around to teach him anything."

Garrett shook his head. "Brooke. Can we talk? *Please?*"

"I'll just get out of your hair," his dad said, but then he sort of wobbled and sat back hard into the porch chair.

"Are you dizzy?" Brooke asked immediately, crouching at his dad's side, her hand on his wrist, checking his pulse. "Do you need medical attention?"

"No." His dad tried to wave her off. "I'm fine. I'm just getting too old for this shit."

Brooke nodded, but she didn't budge from his side, her eyes carefully assessing. "Every day I understand that phrase on an even deeper level than I ever have before. Is it too cold out here for you?" She glanced over her shoulder at Garrett with an accusing look, like this was all his fault.

And hell. It actually probably was.

"How long have you been out here?" she asked his dad.

"An hour or so. Garrett went to bed early, and I didn't want to bother him with the doorbell. Especially once I saw you rush inside."

Brooke very carefully didn't look at Garrett. "Sorry, I didn't see you."

"You were in a hurry."

"The bell doesn't work anyway," Garrett said.

"Sure it does. I fixed it yesterday."

Garrett didn't bother to sigh. "I told you not to worry about working on the house. You don't have to earn your keep here."

His dad's expression was dialed into stubborn, a look that Garrett was startled to realize he recognized all too well—from looking in the mirror.

"I think what your son means to say," Brooke said, "is *thank you* for fixing the doorbell."

"Manners don't run real strong in the Montgomery family," his dad said.

"Let's go," Garrett said to his dad. "I'll get you inside, and then . . ." He looked at Brooke. "I'll be right back."

He got his dad into bed, complete with extra blankets. But then he wanted a cookie. And then, like the children's book, a glass of warm milk to go with it. By the time Garrett got back outside, Brooke was long gone.

His phone vibrated with an incoming text. It was from his father from upstairs: *She needed a time-out. You're welcome.*

CHAPTER 18

"I'm prepared to do this slow and easy, or
hard and fast. Which is it going to be?"

Mindy lay in her great big huge bed with her cold feet,
missing her husband even though he stole her pillow
and hogged the blankets. She even missed his snoring.

He was late tonight.

He'd been really working at getting home earlier, taking over
the kids' bedtime regimen, and she'd loved watching him come
into his daddy-hood. But she'd been holding back with him,
a part of her just waiting for him to revert to his old habits,
even as she'd started softening toward the man she still loved
more than anything. What was holding her back? Fear. She was
afraid that if she gave in, she'd end up right back where she
started . . .

Alone and lonely.

Like she was right now . . .

Somehow she fell asleep in spite of herself and woke up to sunshine streaming into the bedroom. She looked at the clock and gasped. Ten thirty! She'd never slept so late in her life. She could hear the kids in the kitchen, and Linc's low calm voice.

He'd made her promises and he was keeping them.

Extra impressive since it was Saturday, and usually he traveled to a rural clinic to volunteer on weekends. She doubted he remembered they'd been invited to a birthday party for one of the neighborhood kids, at a small family-run winery only a few blocks away. If he'd remembered, she knew he'd have gone as far as he could to volunteer his services.

She padded down to the kitchen and stopped in shock. The kids were dressed. The place didn't look bombed. And Linc smiled at her in that way that had butterflies taking flight in her stomach. "We're party-ready."

She just stared at him.

"Do you want to stay home and enjoy the time to yourself?" he asked. "I've got this."

"Wow," she managed, and shook it off. "And no, I can't miss the party. It's at the Capriottis' winery. They'll have amazing food and mommy juice."

He flashed a small smile. "You mean wine?"

She smiled back. "Yes. And my plan was to take notes for Mason's birthday next month."

"You don't need to take notes. All we'll need is a hose. Garrett and I will have the Slip 'N Slide set up and we'll spray Mason and his buddies for as long as they want. Trust me, they'll have a great time. You'll get rave reviews."

And then, as she stood there in her pj's, crazy hair, and no makeup, he leaned in and brushed a kiss across her mouth. The pleasure curled her toes, but before she could so much as grab him and kiss him back, he pulled away and herded the kids toward the door.

"But . . . the party doesn't start for two hours," she said.

"We're going to Ethan's for a bit first," he said. "Cousin play-time. Take a few hours to yourself, Min."

That did sound good. She showered, dressed, and started baking for the shop, a chore that had never felt like a chore, but the house was too quiet. And . . . void of life.

What is wrong with me?

She quickly flipped through her binder to check her notes for the day and found herself staring at all the tabs, folders, and illustrations.

Huh. Clearly, Brooke and Millie weren't the only OCD Lemons around here. She shook her head, having trouble connecting with the crazy lady who'd created this binder. She had an entire section on things Linc was and was *not* allowed to do during his time between getting home from work and going to bed, including locking himself in the bathroom for an hour at a time. Granted, she didn't understand the appeal of sitting on the toilet and playing games on the phone, and also she could probably birth an entire baby in less time, but . . . who was she to judge his me-time?

She sighed. He'd been drowning every bit as much as she had, but he hadn't crumbled. Not once. He'd been steady as a rock.

She could admit she was jealous as hell of that.

Brooke staggered in the back door and as always headed straight for Mindy's expensive teas.

Mindy narrowed her eyes at her sister's cute short denim skirt. "Wait—is that my skirt?"

Brooke looked down at herself and shrugged. "Guess you know how it feels now, huh?"

"That skirt's my favorite."

"Is that why it was in a bag of clothes by the back door that Linc said was going to Goodwill?" Brooke wrapped her hands around a big mug and blew on the hot tea.

"It was not in that bag." Okay, that was a lie. The skirt was too tight on Mindy, but seeing it look adorable and also sexy on Brooke made her want her pre-baby bod back in a bad way. But more than that, she and Brooke had barely spoken all week. It was driving Mindy crazy. Her biggest fear was that Brooke would leave any day now, and they'd go back to barely ever seeing each other. "I wish you could talk to me," she said quietly.

"Now, there's a *really* bad idea."

"Why?" Mindy asked, mystified. "You used to talk to me all the time."

"Before you were judgy."

"I'm not judgy!"

Brooke held up her fingers an inch apart, the universal sign for *just a little*.

Mindy rolled her eyes. "I'm not."

"Remember that big summer bash Dad threw for you on your twenty-first birthday, the week after I graduated from high school?" Brooke asked.

"Yes."

"I slept with Garrett that night."

Mindy blinked. "You *what*?"

Brooke raised a brow.

Right. But her sister and her best friend . . . how had she not known? And why? In fact, there had been a time back then when she'd thought maybe Brooke and Garrett might end up together. She had to take a deep breath to try to slow her racing thoughts. "I'm not judging. But . . . please explain."

"You won't blow things out of proportion?"

Too late for that. "I'm just . . ." *Jealous. Jealous as hell.* "Um, curious on how Garrett, who was in *my* grade, who was in all of *my* classes, ended up in *your* bed."

"Well, technically not my *bed*," Brooke said. "We never did it here. The house was always too full. We did it at the bluffs, at the Playground, in his truck—"

"You slept with my best friend. He was mine, Brooke."

"No, actually, he wasn't. You had Linc. In fact, by the following year, you were preggers."

"I just can't believe you both kept it from me, that's all," Mindy said, and then stilled. "Wait. Are you two still . . ."

"At this moment? I can tell you with one hundred percent honesty that we are not," Brooke said tightly, and opened the fridge. She grabbed a peach and bit into it.

"You're supposed to wash fruit first," Mindy started, breaking off when Brooke just eyed her over the peach as she took another bite.

"Right." Mindy said with a sigh. "God forbid anyone try to tell you what to do. Or even to make a suggestion." She rose to check the oven, hating how pissy she felt. "Soon as these are done, I'm going upstairs to get ready for a birthday party for a little girl Millie goes to school with. The kids and Linc are meeting me there. Feel free to steal anything else of mine while I'm gone."

Thirty minutes later, she was dressed and still angry. It made no sense, but she felt left out, and embarrassed about that. And mad about all of it. She walked out of the house to her car and found Brooke leaning up against it. "What are you doing?"

"Going with," Brooke said.

"Why?"

"Do you want to be suspicious of my motives or grateful for the company?"

Mindy crossed her arms. "I'm going to stick with suspicious."

"Probably smart," Brooke said. "I'm going with because the Capriottis make excellent wine, and I could use some right now. It's five o'clock somewhere, right?"

And then suddenly there was a pang to go with the anger inside Mindy. She hated where she and Brooke were at, but had no idea how to break the barrier. She knew Brooke cared. Brooke had taken care of the kids, she'd had Mindy's back when it mattered. But Mindy wished . . . she wished they understood each other more. But for now, if a need for wine was all they had in common, she'd take it.

They made a run to McDonald's first because . . . well, hash browns and sausage biscuits were Mindy's very secret passion. Almost as good as orgasms, but since she could hardly remember those, maybe hash browns were even better. She pulled up to the pay window and a teenage kid stuck his head out. "Mindy, right?"

"Yes," Mindy said warily.

He thrust a bag at her. "A guy came through about half an hour ago and paid for your order. He said you were hot, and that you should have a nice day."

Mindy turned to look at Brooke in shock.

"Something you want to tell me?" Brooke asked.

"It's Linc. It's got to be."

Brooke gave her a long look.

"What?" Mindy asked defensively.

"That's some serious relationship goals right there, Min."

"Stop."

"No, you stop. You should marry that man. Oh wait, you already did."

"Yeah." Mindy found a smile. "I know he's amazing. I do. I just can't seem to . . ."

"Find your happy?" Brooke asked, humor gone, and in its place was genuine concern.

"Yeah," she admitted. "I'm having a lot of trouble with that."

"I get that. More than you know. And I also know it might be hard to hear, but a therapist could really help. Or maybe even meds. There's no shame in that, Min."

Mindy looked at her in surprise. "Sounds like you're speaking from experience."

"I saw a therapist and took anxiety meds for two years after the helicopter crash."

"Oh, Brooke," she murmured, her heart squeezing hard. "I wish—"

"No, it's okay. I needed to be alone. I needed to process. And

I did. I mean, I'm still the same Brooke, which means I'm often restless, and the OCD thing still flares up sometimes . . ."

Mindy bit her lower lip.

"Or a lot," Brooke said with a rueful smile. "But therapy helped me with the anxiety and also with finding some happy. I'm just saying, it's an option."

"I know. But I think I'm okay," Mindy said. "Really."

"Okay, good. Because it seems to me Linc's trying really hard, and I don't know much, but I do know it'll take both of you to make it happen."

"I know," Mindy said softly. "And we're working on it." And she'd work harder. If Brooke could come back from what she'd faced, Mindy could find her way back, too.

A few minutes later, they were at the gorgeous Capriotti winery. She'd just found Linc and the kids when she discovered a bigger problem than all her other ones: The theme of the party was clowns.

"Uh-oh," Brooke said.

"What?" Linc asked.

"Your wife's terrified of clowns."

It was true. Mindy had frozen to the spot. She'd been about to thank Linc for the McDonald's, but she couldn't breathe. There were clown balloons. Clown posters. Clown games . . .

Brooke turned to Linc. "Remember in high school when they hired a clown troupe for an assembly and she threw up on the lead clown's big red shoes?" She looked at Mindy. "You going to survive?"

"Who, me? Of course." Mindy forced an easy shrug, but she

was thinking meds would be great right about now. She managed a smile at Linc, who smiled back and then got pulled away by a parent they knew from school. She waited a beat, then turned to Brooke and hissed, "I'm totally not going to survive."

"Yes, you are," Brooke whispered back. "We're the Lemon sisters. We survive everything and keep on ticking. There are tons of people here. Surely we can find someone to gossip about and take your mind off the silly decorations. And hey, bonus, I only see one actual clown."

Carefully averting her gaze from said clown, Mindy eyed the crowd. "Everyone's skinny and beautiful."

"Yeah, so feel sorry for them because of all the Taco Tuesdays they've clearly missed."

Mindy choked out a half laugh, half sob. "God, I love you."

"Hey, look," Brooke said. "Brit's here." She pointed to their nanny, standing by an ice cream bar with a beautiful young woman about her age.

"Brit's a Capriotti," Mindy said, locking her gaze on their nanny and her girlfriend instead of the clown. They were holding hands and smiling, and when they both reached to lick their shared ice cream at the same time, they laughed and kissed. Mindy sighed in envy. Tonight. Tonight she'd get Linc back where he belonged, she vowed. In her damn arms.

"Inappropriate," a nearby mom said disapprovingly, eyes locked on Brittney and her girlfriend.

Mindy looked over at her in surprise. "What?"

"It's entirely inappropriate."

"Really?" Mindy asked. "Which part—the genuine young love, or that they're sharing what looks to be mint chocolate chip ice cream? Because let's be honest, mint in ice cream *is* entirely inappropriate. *And* disgusting."

"Bite your tongue, Min," Brooke said. "Mint ice cream is the bomb."

"My daughter's *four*," the woman said. "I'm not prepared to explain a gay couple to her."

"Sure." Mindy nodded. "Because you'd rather tell her about an immortal fat guy in a red suit who lives at the North Pole and travels around the world one night a year in a sleigh driven by flying reindeer than tell her about two people in love. Makes a lot of sense."

The woman rolled her eyes and walked off.

"Nicely done, Lemon," Brooke said, but Mindy let out a breath and shook her head.

"That was the room mother from Millie's class. I need wine, stat."

"On it," Brooke said, and walked off in search of wine.

The clown walked by Mindy and then stopped and did a double take. And then pantomimed something that Mindy didn't quite get because her heart was suddenly pounding in her ears. "Go on," she said, and gave a "shoo" gesture. "Nothing to see here."

The clown gave her a slow smile, a creepy-ass smile, and came a little closer.

"No, seriously. Back off."

The clown took another step toward her.

"Listen," Mindy said. "Don't mess with me, okay? Take one more step and you'll be sorry."

So of course the clown took one more step, just as Brooke

reappeared with Mindy's wine. "Hey, jackass," Brooke said, stepping in front of Mindy, blocking her from the clown. "Leave her the fuck alone."

The clown flipped Brooke off and then made an even cruder gesture toward Mindy.

"Are you kidding me?" Brooke asked, handing Mindy her wine. "You think just because you're behind the questionable protection of a stupid clown suit that you can just blindly come on to a woman? Stop being a big fat bag of dicks and back up out of our space."

The clown took a step into Brooke and chest-bumped her.

And Brooke punched him in his big red nose.

The clown fell backward on his ass, his nose fell off, and . . .

It was a woman, Mindy realized in shock. It was Michelle Avery, her high school mortal enemy. Michelle had been more popular than Mindy, prettier than her and smarter than her. And yet Michelle had made it her personal mission to make Mindy's life at school a personal hell. She'd stolen Mindy's iPod, she'd told teachers that Mindy had cheated off her, she'd tried to steal Linc on numerous occasions, and during their junior year, when Mindy and Linc had been on a break from each other, Michelle had kissed him.

Mindy hated her.

"You bitch!" Michelle screeched, and flew at Brooke, taking her by surprise.

They both hit the dirt, hard, Brooke on the bottom, appearing momentarily stunned by the clown sitting on her chest. "Get your fat ass off me!"

"Fat? How dare you!" Michelle screamed, and then they

were rolling, vying for top position. Michelle pulled Brooke's hair and swung a punch that only grazed Brooke's jaw because Brooke managed to get an elbow in Michelle's gut. But then Michelle pulled back her fist for another go, and from somewhere far away, Mindy heard, "Get the fuck off my sister, you bitch!"

It was *her*. Mindy was the one yelling, she realized, as she threw herself into the mix, trying to get between Michelle and Brooke to break things up. Instead, she took a punch meant for her sister, straight to her right eye. Stars burst in her head, and then it was lights-out.

She came to what could have been a year later, but turned out to have been only a few seconds. She was on the bottom now, drowning in a sea of bad polyester clown suit and what felt like cotton shoved down her throat.

Michelle's clown wig had come loose, and now Mindy was going to die down here, but then suddenly they were doused in icy-cold water.

Someone had turned the hose on them.

The dirt became mud, and as people waded in to separate them, some slipped and fell on top of the pile of limbs.

Mindy's life was flashing before her eyes when she was finally lifted to her feet by a stunned-looking Linc.

"Are you all right?" he asked.

She had no idea. She was bleeding from a few cuts, including one on her lip, but Brooke looked even worse, covered in mud, bleeding from a cut beneath her eye, holding her wrist funny, cradling it to her chest. Michelle was the dirtiest of all of them, dripping mud from every inch of her, but there was no blood on her that Mindy could see.

Linc took in the sight and his mouth tightened into a grim line. "Car," he said. "Now."

The kids stayed at the party with Brittney as he drove them to the hospital. No one spoke in the car, at least not until they arrived at the ER. Linc parked, and then Brooke suddenly started breathing funny. Her eyes dilated, her skin went pasty white. Every protective instinct came out in Mindy because she knew Brooke was having an anxiety attack, probably because the last time she'd been in the hospital, she'd nearly died. She reached out to hug her, but got a don't-you-dare-touch-me death glare.

Still worried, Mindy insisted on sharing a cubicle, so they ended up on twin cots, waiting to be treated while Linc was out front filling out paperwork.

In the silence, Mindy could hear Brooke still breathing too fast, and she struggled to sit up.

"What are you doing?" Brooke asked. "The nurse said to lie still and ice your eye until she can get a doctor. You never listen."

"Says the queen of breaking rules. And oh my God, you're also wearing my sandals. At my funeral, make sure to sit me up so I can see which of my clothes you've stolen to wear."

Brooke stared at her. "You've lost your collective shit."

"Yes! Now you're finally getting it." And since it hurt too much to stay seated, she lay back down.

"You know what really gets me?" Brooke asked a few minutes later.

"What?"

"That I only got three hits in. I needed to get that fourth hit in."

"Because you needed it to be an even number?"

"Because I really wanted to hit her again."

Mindy managed a laugh as the doctor came in. Nothing was broken except maybe her pride. Brooke's wrist was sprained, and she did need five stitches below her eye. After that was handled, the doctor left to write up a prescription for antibiotics for Brooke.

More awkward silence filled their cubicle. From the corner of her eye, Mindy could see Brooke doing a crossword puzzle on her phone, which she did only when she was deeply upset. Mindy argued with herself and then finally spoke. "I'm ready for my apology."

Without taking her gaze from her puzzle, Brooke gave her a suggestion. With her middle finger.

Mindy nodded. "Apology accepted." She paused. "You took a punch for me."

"Yeah. So?"

"So it cost you five stitches and a sprained wrist."

Brooke shrugged, like she'd have done more if she'd had to, and Mindy felt her throat close up tight. She sniffed, but the tide couldn't be stopped. A tear popped out.

Brooke looked up and stared at her. "What are you doing?"

"Nothing."

"You're crying."

"Am not!"

"Are too!" Brooke pointed at her. "Stop that. You know that's unfair. When you cry, you win, and it's not your turn to win, Min!"

"Then you should've cried first!" Mindy sobbed. "You stuck up for me."

"Well, duh. You're family."

Mindy cried harder.

Brooke sighed the sigh of a martyr. She stared up at the ceiling. Swung her foot. Sighed again. "Remember when we used to sneak out of the house to go to parties? Well, now I want to sneak out of parties to go home. That was a terrible party."

Mindy laughed and wiped her nose with her arm. "I'm sorry. I'm sorry I'm so self-absorbed and haven't taken good enough care of you. I'm going to do better. I just can't stop thinking about how you never told me about you and Garrett. I thought we were closer than that. I *want* to be closer than that."

"At the time, I guess I'd convinced myself there really wasn't much to tell."

"And now, with hindsight being twenty-twenty?"

Brooke waited a beat too long to say, "Same."

Mindy sat up. "You hesitated."

"Did not."

"You did. Come on, Brooke, lie to yourself if you have to, but not to me. If it were really nothing to you all those years ago, you'd have said so. Which means it was way more than nothing."

"Okay, fine." Brooke closed her eyes. "At the time, I guess I really did think it was a lot more than nothing. I thought it was . . ."

"What?"

"Everything," Brooke whispered. "I thought he was going to be my everything. And for what it's worth, I'm sorry. I didn't tell you back then because I knew you'd freak out. But you've kept things from me, too."

Brooke had had her heart broken and Mindy hadn't been

there for her, and it took her a moment to find her voice. "Like what?"

"Like how you no longer want the POP Smoothie Shop," Brooke said.

Mindy turned her head to look at her. "I had no idea that bothered you."

"It *doesn't* bother me, but it bothers *you*, so I'd have liked to have known about it."

Mindy felt . . . stunned. Brooke had wanted to be close, and what had she done? She'd let her vanish from her life without even a fight.

"And there's something else," Brooke said. "I was pregnant when the crash happened. I'd just found out."

Mindy gasped. "You were pregnant? With . . . Garrett?" At the truth in Brooke's eyes, a wave of anguish hit her. "Oh, Brooke, I'm so sorry. I hate that you couldn't trust me enough to tell me."

"It wasn't about trust," she said softly. "It was about being stupid enough to get pregnant in the first place, and being terrified about it. And then it was about losing the baby in the crash."

With a low sound of regret, Mindy began to struggle to get up.

"What are you doing?" Brooke asked. "What part of 'stay still' don't you understand?"

"Shit, I really need to do some damn sit-ups. I'm like a beached whale over here." She finally managed to get off her cot.

Brooke sighed loudly, but scooted over on her own and lifted up the hospital blanket.

It felt like a white flag, and Mindy was going to take it. She crawled into the bed with her sister and felt her heart swell. She didn't dare speak for fear of ruining the moment. So they sat in quiet. A nice quiet, for once. And then Brooke was back to her puzzle. "Hey," she said. "What's a seven-letter word for someone who's been a jerk?"

"Asshole?" Mindy asked.

Brooke touched her own nose and smiled.

And Mindy nearly choked on her own regrets. "I'm so sorry you didn't feel you could tell me."

"And I'm sorry I didn't tell. But, Min, I didn't talk to anyone about it except Garrett. And almost as soon as I told him, it was over. And . . ." She closed her eyes. "That's not all of it."

Mindy's heart tightened. "What? Tell me. Please tell me."

"I didn't just miscarry after the helicopter crash. During the surgery, things . . . happened."

"I know, Bee. You lost your spleen, some of your lower intestines, got an infection and almost died." Her eyes filled again. "We were all devastated for you. I wanted to crawl into your hospital bed and take care of you. I'm your big sister—I'm supposed to nurture you so hard that you get annoyed."

"Mission accomplished."

They both gave a watery laugh, but Brooke's faded. "I . . . can't get pregnant anymore."

Mindy stared at her, heart pounding at the reality of what her sister had gone through, *alone*. "What?"

"Please don't make me repeat it. But most of all, please don't cry anymore, you're probably already dehydrated. You break out when you're dehydrated. I don't want that on my head."

Mindy swallowed hard, not willing to let Brooke tease this away. "You can't have babies."

"No," Brooke whispered.

God. She couldn't imagine. "Do you want one of mine?"

Brooke choked out a low laugh. "Stop."

"No, I'm serious," Mindy said. "Take one. But not the good one. Not Millie."

And at that, the infallible Brooke Lemon burst into tears.

"No, oh, honey, no, I'm just kidding, you can totally have Millie," Mindy whispered frantically, and pulled Brooke into her arms, feeling her own heart break for her. "It's okay. We're okay."

Brooke sniffed and wiped her nose on Mindy's sleeve. "Are we?"

Mindy nodded. "Yes, even though if I was as OCD as you, I'd have to kill you for the snot." She sighed and hugged Brooke tight. "But we really are okay."

Brooke choked out a laugh and they hugged some more, and Mindy felt her heart begin to mend itself. She hoped Brooke's might do the same. They weren't perfect—they never had been. But they were sisters, blood, and they belonged together.

Suddenly, their curtain was yanked back, and Linc and Garrett stood there wearing mirroring expressions of stress and worry.

Linc strode straight to Mindy, cupped her face and tilted it up. "You okay?"

She nodded.

"Good." He dropped his hands and shoved them in his pockets.

"Now maybe you can explain to me what the hell you guys were doing brawling at a kids' birthday party."

"Hey, the clown was attacking her," Brooke said.

"You mean Michelle? Who Mindy's hated since elementary school?"

"She used to spit in my lunch!" Mindy said. Maybe yelled.

"Yes, because you"—he used finger quotes here—"'accidentally' stuck your gum in her hair."

Mindy stared into the sexy, wonderful face of the man she loved and adored beyond all imagination, but she didn't see love and adoration in return. Instead, she saw frustration. She bit her lower lip, then winced as she split it open again. "You're mad at me."

"I'm not mad. What I *am* is trying *very* hard. And you're not."

"Okay," she started. "That's not fair. I—"

"Stop." He grabbed some tissues from a box on the counter and carefully, with surprising gentleness, dabbed the blood dripping from her lip down her chin. "You're the one who's angry," he said softly.

"Hell yes, I'm angry!" she burst out. "My arch nemesis just went after my sister—"

"You're angry at *me*," he said. "And you're taking it out on everyone else." He scooped her up into his arms.

She gasped in shock. "What are you doing?"

"Taking over. I thought I could wait you out, out-patience you and let you come to me in your own time. But I'm tired of waiting, Min. I'm taking action."

She threw her arms around his neck and stared up into his

face. He'd never been as sexy to her as right in that moment. "What kind of action?" she asked breathlessly.

"Whatever it takes to get it through your thick skull that you're it for me, and that I love you. Now," he said fiercely, staring down at her, "I'm prepared to do this slow and easy, or hard and fast. Which is it going to be?"

She swallowed hard. "Linc?"

His expression relaxed. "Yeah, babe?"

She tightened her grip on him. "Can we do it both ways?"

Some of the serious sternness left his face, softening his gaze and mouth. "Any way you want. *All* the ways you want."

CHAPTER 19

By the time he was finished with her, she was a floppy rag doll, making contented purring noises.

B rooke watched Linc carry Mindy out of the ER cubicle. "I can't decide if I'm scared or happy for her," she murmured, quickly swiping at any lingering tears so Garrett couldn't see them. "And if you're here to talk, you should know I'm not in the mood."

Not speaking, he came close and tilted her face up to his to study her, his eyes filled with concern.

"I'm fine," she said.

"I will *pay* you to stop lying to me."

She sighed. "What does it matter, anyway, when you always know when I am? And how *is* it that you know? Because it's really irritating."

"Same way I know when you're not wearing a bra. God-given talent." He gave her a small smile. "Linc gave me a blow-by-blow of what happened at the party. How Michelle went after your sister and you went after her. Took her down, too, and she outweighs you by quite a bit."

"Don't tell her that. She'll kill you in your sleep."

"I'm proud as hell of you, Bee." His smile turned into a very male grin. "And a little turned on, too."

She shook her head, even as her tummy quivered in a very good way. "Men are dumb."

This made him laugh. "No doubt. You're both clear to leave, by the way." He scooped her up just as Linc had Mindy, and her body melted into his.

"Don't get any ideas," she said, wanting to put it out there so she didn't forget. She couldn't do this with him, knowing he was holding back as well as also holding on to old memories of when she'd shut him out. "I'm still mad."

"Makes two of us."

"So you're mad at you, too?" she asked in a smart-ass tone.

"Funny, but no. I'm mad at *you*."

He said this so calmly, it took a moment for the words to sink in. "Because of . . . last night?"

Not answering, he took her outside, where the day had gone to night without her. Managing to hold on to her and unlock his truck at the same time, he slid her in, all without jostling any of her aches and pains. And there were a lot of those, just beginning to make themselves known.

He angled in behind the steering wheel and started up the

engine. When he found her staring at him, he flashed that killer smile of his, and she felt an answering tug deep inside her. "Why are you smiling at me? You're mad, remember?"

"More like frustrated," he said. "You wear your past on your shoulder like a huge rock. It's hard to see beyond it."

"Well, then stop looking at it."

He gave her a long look.

Okay. So she was supposed to be a grown-up these days.

"You won't address it," he said. "You won't even look at it or acknowledge it, and yet it defines everything you do."

Wait. How was he turning this around on her? *Probably because it was her, this whole problem was her doing.* "Maybe I'm just a fiercely independent woman," she said. "You ever think of that?"

"Yes, and it's sexy as hell. But you're letting the past weigh you down, Bee."

"That's ridiculous," she said, even as her heart picked up the pace at the accuracy of his statement.

"If that was true," he said, "last night wouldn't have ended the way it did, with you running out on me. Again."

She stared out the window as the night deepened. The shadows of the rolling hills conjured up a sense of home and pride and longing, and damn, she loved this place. "I'm trying," she said softly. "But sometimes I just need a few minutes."

He nodded, accepting, and it wasn't an act. He was incredibly patient and unfailingly loyal. Always had been. "So tell me something," he said.

"What?" she asked warily.

"Why have you never told Mindy about us?"

Oh boy.

He took in her expression. "Am I your dirty secret, Brooke?"

"No, of course not." She paused. "Just today I told her about our past."

"But not our now."

She met his gaze. "No. But only because I'm never sure what the now is."

He gave a snort, but didn't say anything more about it. And when he got to their street, he didn't turn into Mindy's driveway. Instead, he pulled into his own.

"Is your dad still here?" she asked.

"Last night after you took off on me, he got restless. He left me a note that he had something to do and vanished with Snoop. A fucking note," he said in disgust.

And then there was what he didn't say. That once again he'd been left. How had she not connected the dots? She knew Garrett had abandonment issues, deep-seated ones, and he had every right to them. And she'd made them worse at every turn. Her heart actually hurt just thinking about it.

"I've been looking everywhere for him," Garrett said. "I left messages at the campgrounds, at the store . . . I even asked Mark Capriotti to keep an eye out for him."

"Mark Capriotti?" she asked in surprise.

"Besides being one of the owners of the winery where you just brawled with Michelle," he said dryly, "he's a local sheriff."

There was a grim tone to his voice that had her looking at him. "You think your dad's up to his old shenanigans," she said.

He shrugged. "Not sure what else I'm supposed to think."

Letting his dad move in had been a huge show of forgiveness

and strength on his part. But more than that, his clear worry and concern made her chest tighten at the man he'd become. "Maybe he meant what he said. That he simply had something to take care of. Or maybe . . . maybe he just needed a minute."

Garrett glanced over at her and then drove around the side yard to the back of his property and parked facing out to the valley below. He turned off the engine. "My dad and I . . ." He shook his head. "It's complicated. We're complicated. It's hard for me to think about it. I'd rather shove it deep away and forget it."

They were on the edge of something here, and she knew it. In spite of what they had done in bed—and in the shower, and on the counter, and up against a wall—they were also friends. Or so she hoped. "Trust me," she said. "Shoving things down deep isn't all it's cracked up to be."

He met her gaze. "For a long time, it was all I had. When I was a kid in the system, having visible emotions not only made me vulnerable, but it was actually dangerous."

She blew out a breath. It was hard to maintain any sort of distance from him at the best of times, but remembering and hearing what he'd been through in his childhood years was a sober reminder that life was too damn short to hold grudges. Scooting closer to him, she wrapped her arms around his neck.

With a rough male sound, he pulled her in and buried his face in her hair, reminding her that once upon a time, they'd been each other's safe haven. It seemed that maybe some things never changed. "I hate that you grew up the way you did," she whispered against his scruffy jaw.

He tightened his arms and brushed a kiss on her cheek. "I turned out okay."

She snorted. "Define okay."

A very small smile curved his mouth. "My point is that I don't need my dad around now," he said. "It's too late for us."

"I disagree," she said softly. "Maybe you need each other."

He went still, not moving, maybe not breathing, and she knew she had to be careful here. Garrett hated pity with a passion, and considered empathy and sympathy—at least when they were aimed at him—just as bad. "Have you thought that maybe he's really changed? Maybe he really does regret not being there for you and wants to try to right his wrongs. And I get that you don't need that, but it's possible he does."

"And it's also possible that you should listen to your own advice." And with that, he turned off the engine and exited the truck.

It was a warm but dark evening. Low-lying clouds hid the stars and whatever moon there might've been. Ahead of her, Garrett stood, hands in his pockets, staring out at the barely visible valley below. She stopped at his side and adopted his stance. They stood there like that through a few heartbeats before she spoke. "I agree," she said. "I should listen to my own advice. I came because I needed to clear the air with you and right some wrongs. But I stayed because I also needed to be here. Home. I needed to remember what I have here. And who."

He lost some of the tension in his shoulders at that, and his eyes warmed. But true to Garrett, he didn't rush her. Instead he said, "The ER doc suggested a warm bath to keep your undoubtedly sore muscles loose." He turned to the deck and hit the button to turn on the jets in the hot tub. "This'll help you more than a shower." He waited for her to make a move.

She had to admit, the bubbling water drew her like a moth

to a flame. Or like any warm-blooded female to Garrett. She stripped out of the scrubs the nurse had given her at the hospital. She stood there in her bra and panties and gestured at Garrett. "Well?"

"Well, what?"

"I'm not going to be the only one in my skivvies."

He toed off his boots and socks. He then tugged off his shirt and shoved down his jeans, kicking them away.

He was commando.

She took in his lean, hard body, lit only by the pale blue interior light of the hot tub, and felt her mouth water.

"You've got choices here," he said.

"Such as?"

"Such as, you put your clothes back on and go home to bed."

"Or?"

"Or you get in the hot tub and let me make you feel better."

"Without talking?" she asked hopefully.

"Definitely not without talking."

Walking next door was definitely the easier route, but the easy route had never really worked out for her. She started to climb into the hot tub, but Garrett stopped her, gesturing to her bra and panties.

"I'm not going to fight with you naked," she said.

"Who says we're going to fight?"

"Isn't that what we usually do?" She stared up into his dark eyes. There was something new to his expression now. Like he was testing her to see if she trusted him.

Did she?

Yeah, she decided. She did, and if that's what he needed to

see, she could absolutely give it to him. She unhooked her bra and let it hit the ground. Then she slid off her panties and tried to lift a leg to climb into the hot tub, stopping to gasp in pain. Shit, she *was* sore, big-time.

Garrett scooped her up and saved her, easily stepping into the water with her and slowly lowering them down into the bubbles. Because she was on his lap, held close to his body, she could attest to the fact he was telling her the truth—he was not in a fighting mood, but another mood entirely.

"You're in the driver's seat," he said quietly, and gave a little smile.

Turning so that her spine was to his chest, she leaned back on him, tilting her head against his shoulder and staring up into the night sky.

His arms came around her, and she sighed with pleasure.

"Comfortable?" he asked.

"Yes. Your siding needs to be treated."

"This place needs a lot of things."

"I could help you."

He seemed surprised.

"What?" she said. "I mean, granted, it's been a while, but you and I oil-stained the siding years ago, for Ann. So it's nothing we haven't done before."

"Well, if that's the rule today," he teased.

Heat flashed through her, but she shook it off with a laugh. "You have something to say," she guessed. "Lay it on me."

"All right." He didn't hesitate. "I've been thinking about what happened to you. And how you lied to me at the time about how badly you were hurt."

She'd been out of it when she'd been airlifted off the mountain after the helicopter accident. Things had been complicated by a foreign hospital and her being of legal age. When she'd become lucid just before her first surgery, she'd told the doctors she didn't want anyone to know the extent of her injuries. They'd obliged, not telling her family or Garrett a thing, which had enabled her to give them an abbreviated version of the truth. "I did," she said quietly.

"I want to know that you won't do anything like that ever again."

"I couldn't even if I wanted to," she said. "You're able to tell whenever I try."

He turned her so that she was straddling him, facing him. "I want you to stop trying. I want to be able to trust you with you."

His gaze held hers prisoner, searching, and she let out a long breath. "I'm getting there."

He cupped her face, letting a thumb gently glide just beneath her stitches. "Good."

"I've maybe even matured," she said, lighter now, allowing a teasing tone to come into her voice. "But not *mature* mature. I mean, I still have to say 'righty tighty, lefty loosey' to open stuff. And then there's the whole counting thing. Don't get me started."

Garrett smiled as his hands skimmed down her body. "I was really into the girl you were," he murmured. "You were such a feisty smart-ass who knew all my buttons and just how to push them. Every second with you was an adventure, a heart-thumping, adrenaline-rush adventure." Very gently, he slid his fingers into her hair. "I was addicted to you."

Since she was no longer that girl, nothing even close to that girl, maybe only a shell of that person, she started to tense.

"But the woman you've become . . ." he murmured.

She closed her eyes, not wanting to hear how she no longer measured up. "Don't—"

"You're smart instead of reckless. You think before you act or speak because you care about other people's feelings. You're still unpredictable as shit, but you're thoughtful, caring, warm . . . still a feisty smart-ass, though."

She could hear the smile in his voice.

"Love that part a lot," he murmured.

"An unpredictable, feisty smart-ass, huh?" she asked, unable to hide her own smile at his words and the meaning behind them. "I can't help but notice you said nothing about being sexy and mysterious."

"*Incredibly* sexy," he said. "And you're more of a mystery than you know." He pressed close, the heat of his body instantly enveloping her. "Brooke. Look at me."

She dragged her eyes open. His lashes were wet and spiky, his eyes almost black with intensity. "I've got something to say."

She licked her suddenly dry lips. "Garrett—"

"I'm still addicted to you," he said, and then kissed her, deep and hungry and powerful. The night, the moon, the stars all spun around her, and as it continued, she felt his warm hands brush her breasts. He raised his head and she arched her back, naked in the moonlight, begging without words for him to keep touching her, for him to find her irresistible, for him to want her, yearn for her, be unable to imagine his life without her, in spite of all her shortcomings and failings.

And where that thought came from, she had no idea.

He stood, easily boosting her in his arms, still kissing her as she wrapped her legs around him.

"Thought the warm water was healing," she managed.

"I've got something better." With both of them naked and dripping wet, he strode with her into his house, where they were met by three judging cats, eyes narrowed.

"Scram," Garrett said, heading straight up the stairs, still dripping water without a care.

"Wow. You stained the stair railings and wood trim in here. It looks great."

Garrett stopped walking and looked at her. "When you said 'wow,' I thought you were talking about my manly prowess."

"Your manly prowess is intact," she assured him. "But the railings and trim look amazing."

He took it in. "Son of a bitch. The guy can't mind his own damn business."

"I think you *are* his business," she said. "Are you telling me he stayed up all night doing this for you before he took off?"

His gaze slid to hers, and she bit her lower lip to keep a smile in. "You're wearing the same expression your cats are wearing," she said.

"Not *my* cats. Ann's cats."

"Uh-oh. Are you no longer in the mood?"

He shouldered opened his bedroom door and set her on his bed. Actually, it was more like tossed her on the bed. She bounced once and then he was on her, pinning her down to the mattress, letting her feel exactly what she did to him. "Okay," she practically purred, running her hands up his sleek, still damp back. His muscles bunched enticingly. "So you're still in the mood."

"With you, always," he said, rubbing his jaw to hers like a big cat. A big, feral cat. He lowered his head and pressed a kiss to the scar low on her belly, and her heart rolled over for him. Then he rose up and kissed her mouth.

It was a delicious, sensuous, erotic kiss with a lot of tongue, and heat exploded inside her, simultaneously rushing north to make her nipples happy and south to make the rest of her happy. When his mouth trailed along her throat, she just about lost consciousness. "Kiss me again," she demanded.

"Because you need it in twos?"

"Because I'm going to die if you don't kiss me again."

He flashed a grin, but before he could, there was a thump on his bedroom door.

"Ignore them," Garrett said.

"Them?" she squeaked, trying to sit up.

Garrett slid his hands around the backs of her thighs and tugged so that she fell flat on her back again. "The cats. They're jealous of you. I'm their man."

She laughed, but it backed up in her throat as his hands began performing his special brand of fire and magic, and then his mouth followed. He liked to kiss, a lot, and he especially liked to take his time about it, which always left her a panting, anticipatory, needy hot mess. *"Garrett."*

Sliding off the bed, he dropped to his knees between her legs. Eyes dark and heated and locked on hers, his hands skimmed the backs of her thighs, his gaze slowly traveled over the length of her body. "Pretty," he said roughly, and she felt a rush that was nearly an orgasm.

Then he put his mouth on her, and she was very glad there were only cats in the house, because she couldn't have kept quiet to save her own life.

By the time he was finished with her, she was a floppy rag doll, making contented purring noises. "I owe the cats for letting me share you," she said with a wide yawn, unable to keep her eyes open.

"Take as much of me as you want," he murmured. "I'm all yours."

She smiled as she drifted off, hoping against hope it might actually be true.

CHAPTER 20

"Skinny-dipping is off the table."

By the time Mindy and Linc left the hospital, picked up the kids, and got them fed, bathed, and into bed, Mindy was stick-a-fork-in-her done. She staggered into her bedroom and collapsed on the bed. Her hair flopped in her face. She was hot and sweaty and wearing her PMS shorts—which were really maternity shorts, but she'd die before admitting that.

She could hear Linc in the shower. She rolled across their big bed and caught sight of something on his nightstand. The Hawaii tickets, dated for next week. She'd actually completely forgotten about the trip he'd promised her, but the thought of having Linc to herself for days on end made her hope against hope that they really could get away, just the two of them. In one hotel room, with one bed and hopefully no couch . . .

When he came out of the bathroom wearing only a towel low on his hips, his hair still damp, her mouth watered.

He smiled at her sprawled on the bed. "Is that an invitation?"

She snorted and closed her eyes against the ache that the sight of him caused deep inside her. She'd tried seducing him with her favorite lingerie, but once again life had distracted him. Now here she was at her absolute worst, and he was being playful and sexy. "If it *was* an invite, would you notice?" she asked.

He set a knee on the bed, eyes dark and heated. "Oh yeah."

"You didn't notice the other night."

He crawled up the bed. "Babe, I *always* notice you."

She put a foot to his chest to halt his progress. "What was I wearing?"

"A hot-as-shit pale peach silky nightie that I wanted to take off with my teeth."

A happy shiver bolted through her, and she dropped her foot and closed her eyes. "So why didn't you?"

"Because I was busy traumatizing our daughter and stealing her childhood by letting her know that the tooth fairy and Santa Claus weren't real. Mindy . . ."

Something in his voice had her eyes flying open. He was giving her an odd look, like he was seeing something for the first time. "You really think I don't want you anymore?"

She shrugged. "I mean, I get it."

"Do you?" he murmured.

"Yes, of course!" She tossed up her hands. "I've had a bazillion babies. I'm not the young hot chick anymore. I've got stretch marks, and I'm cranky because I'm always on a stupid diet because stupid food goes right to my stupid ass now. And, um—" She broke off because he had slowly loosened his towel and tossed it on the floor. "Um . . ." She blinked. "I can't remember what I was saying."

Pulling her beneath him, he shot her a knowing grin. "You're right, you were the young hot chick. But you're even hotter now, with a real woman's body. I love it. I even love your crankiness. And I love you, Mindy."

He said it in the same unhesitating tone he reserved for all truths: The night is dark, rain is wet, and Linc loves Mindy.

"And when I told you I was going to fight for this, for us, I meant it." He ran his mouth along her jaw to her ear and gave it a light nip with his teeth. "Do you remember our first time?" he asked, voice husky, ignoring her attitude, clearly understanding that she wanted to be seduced, understanding that even that had become her responsibility in the marriage. He let his lips brush just behind her earlobe. It was her favorite spot to be teased, which he knew damn well. "Because I remember it. Kiss me, Min."

"I haven't brushed my teeth."

"I don't care."

She knew it was true because he was looking at her like she'd just hung the moon and the stars. For a whole lot of years, she'd felt that at any moment he might realize where he was, and with who, and leave her. But he never had. For whatever reason, Linc wanted her, and she decided she wasn't about to try to change his mind. But she did want to be clear about one thing. "Perfect Mindy is long gone," she said. "You know that, right?"

"I don't want Perfect Mindy," he said. "I want Trash Can Mindy."
She frowned. "Excuse me?"

"Do you remember our first kiss?"

"Yes," she said. "It was in fourth grade. You kissed me on the playground because Kenny Reddick dared you to. He'd been daring you since second grade, but it took you two years to get serious. I slugged you in the eye and got in trouble."

He grinned. "That wasn't a real kiss. I'm talking about our first *real* kiss."

She remembered that, too. They'd been in ninth grade, and by that point had been in a love-hate relationship for years: She could beat his ass in any track-and-field event, and he could explain biology and chemistry to her in a way she could understand. But nothing had ever happened between them.

He'd had a growth spurt that year, and suddenly their friendship had taken a turn, at least on her part. She'd started noticing things, like how he laughed, the way he looked at her, the fact that he smelled so good when all the other guys his age did not. And then there'd been his mouth. He had a great mouth. All her friends had already had their first kisses, and other firsts, too, and she'd had nothing.

She'd wanted him to kiss her, and when she'd told him so, he'd laughed. She might have killed him right then, but he'd leaned in and, still hugely amused, said that kissing her was *all* he'd thought about since elementary school.

That had taken a moment to set in. He hadn't been laughing at her, but at *himself*. And all that time he'd wanted to kiss her, too.

Naturally, that's when the bell had rung for homeroom. In

those days, school had ruined her life on a daily basis. But he'd been waiting for her after school, standing across the parking lot, leaning on a lamppost. She'd locked gazes with him and started walking his way, and then—

"Halfway to me, you walked into that trash can," he said.

Yep. That was exactly what had happened. She'd fallen over and into the trash can.

"*That's* the Mindy I want," he said. "The one who allowed herself to be human. I don't want a perfect person as my wife. I just want someone to be silly with, someone who loves being with me more than anything else."

"I do," she said. "That's why I freaked out about the shop. I want *more* time with you, not less. And with the shop in my name, I'd be as busy as . . . well, you."

He leaned in and kissed her softly, his hands going to her hips to hold her close. "I'm sorry, Mindy. Can we get past this?"

"I want to," she said earnestly, "but . . ."

"But you're still unsure," he said as if he understood. "You've got built-up resentment. I've been a bad boy." He rolled to his back, bring her along with him so that now she was straddling him. "Do you want to play reverse *Fifty Shades* on my ass? Would that help?"

This had her bursting out laughing, because one thing Linc wasn't—now or ever—was submissive. Smug bastard, smiling up at her. Confident. *Sexy.* "You know what?" she said. "Yes, I do. I want to tie you up."

"Yeah?" His voice was pure sex. "And then what?" His hands slid up and cupped her breasts, teasing them the way only he knew how. "Tell me. Tell me slowly and in great detail."

Across the yard, Brooke fell asleep in Garrett's arms and didn't move from that spot until a phone went off. She felt him reach past her for the cell on his nightstand. She lifted her head in a stupor and realized it was dawn. "What is it?" she asked. "Your dad?"

"No. A group text from Linc, sent to all of us. It says: *Everyone get your asses in the kitchen*."

"What the hell?"

When she and Garrett rushed into Linc and Mindy's kitchen a few minutes later, it was to find breakfast made and waiting.

"Okay," Brooke said, confused. "Did I die and go to heaven, or did you guys make up? Because Mindy hasn't cooked breakfast since she got back, and—"

"We made up!" Mindy said.

Brooke stared at her. There was most definitely a glow.

"Hold up," Linc said. He was wearing the same telltale glow as Mindy, but his head was cocked as he first studied Brooke, then Garrett.

Brooke instantly realized their mistake. In their rush to find out what was wrong, they'd run out of Garrett's house without a care. Meaning she was no doubt *also* wearing the "glow." She took a quick peek at Garrett, and yep. His hair was finger-tousled, by *her* fingers. His T-shirt was on inside out, and she realized she was wearing one of his shirts. "Oh, shit. We're screwed," she said beneath her breath.

"Yeah," Linc said, apparently possessing superhuman hearing. "You both definitely look . . . *screwed*."

Mindy took a good look and gasped. "Oh my God. You're . . . together again?"

That she'd asked this with such obvious joy and sincere hope made it a whole lot easier for Brooke to swallow that their secret was out.

The last secret.

At least, Brooke hoped to God it was the last secret.

Mindy gave up on getting an answer out of Brooke and turned to Garrett. "Yes?"

"Yes," he said. "But don't overreact—"

Mindy threw herself at him, hugging him tight. "I've been trying to find the perfect woman for you for so long and you were so annoying about it, not being helpful or interested. I had no idea why, but now I know. You were waiting for the right one, the only one." She snagged Brooke and dragged her into the hug as well. "Don't you dare hurt him," she said, and then eyed Garrett. "And don't you dare mess this up!"

Brooke managed to pull free. "So much for not overreacting. It was one night, Min. Don't get excited. So what did you drag us out of bed for?"

"To let you know that we got our shit together," Linc said. "Which calls for a celebration in the form of an overnight camping trip, like the good old days. I even managed to arrange foisting all the children off on friends tonight. Let's go get drunk, burn s'mores, dance to sappy country songs, and maybe Mindy'll even go skinny-dipping in the hidden falls with me."

"Ew," Brooke said, even though that was exactly what they'd done in the "old days."

"Sorry, but skinny-dipping is off the table," Mindy said. "My skinny-dipping days are over."

"But everything else sounds good, right?" Linc asked.

Mindy nodded.

"Perfect," he said. "I'll pack us up."

Mindy blinked at him. "Did you just trick me into going camping, where there's no electricity for my straightener or flush toilets?"

Linc shrugged unapologetically. "Negotiating is a skill." He looked at all of them. "Be here by three this afternoon, ready and packed."

"Two or four," Brooke said. "Not three."

"Two it is," Linc said easily.

"You're all batshit crazy," Garrett said.

"That's a yes, right?" Linc asked.

Garrett snatched a piece of perfectly crisped bacon, bit into it, and moaned. "If Mindy's going to cook."

"And you?" Linc asked Brooke.

Yeah, since she was just as crazy as the rest of them, if not more so, because suddenly she wanted much more than an overnight. "As long as there are s'mores."

CHAPTER 21

"Oh my God."

"Actually, it's Garrett. And *shh*."

The four of them hiked Robles Canyon. It was a steady but challenging trail that had Brooke's blood flowing and heart pumping in a good way. Before coming back to Wildstone, she hadn't challenged herself physically in a long time. Her body was loving it.

"I want s'mores," Mindy said, huffing and puffing. "I was going to resist, but I deserve them. I'm burning more calories than at spin class."

Several miles up, they came to a trail that led to an area few people knew about. There were three waterfalls feeding a small hidden lake. It was still chilly at night, and the area was deserted.

Happy about that, Brooke smiled. "We've got the place to ourselves."

"Because there're no toilets or hot showers," Mindy pointed out.

Linc leaned in and kissed his wife. "Our Hawaii getaway has both, I promise."

They built a fire, cooked hot dogs and s'mores, and drank liberally from the bottle of Jack that Linc had carried in.

By ten o'clock that night, Brooke was feeling no pain, and neither was anyone else. She watched from across the fire as Mindy and Linc slow danced, swaying in a loose embrace to a symphony of the nearby water and the crickets protesting the night. Even from a distance of twenty feet, she could see how much they loved each other. They kissed with surprising heat before Linc boosted Mindy up into his arms and carried her into their tent, his hands sliding up her thighs and disappearing under her sundress as they went.

Brooke sighed and turned away, her gaze locking in on Garrett.

He held out a hand.

She slipped hers into it and together they made their way to the water's edge, staring out at the small pool at the base of the first waterfall. The half-moon was partially obstructed by a few long, fingerlike clouds drifting over the night like a caress. The breeze carrying those clouds brushed Brooke's face.

"Are you thinking what I'm thinking?" he asked.

"Yes." She tore off her top and shorts, leaving her in the bathing suit she hadn't changed out of earlier. "Race you." And she took off around the edge of the lake, heading for the rocky ledge on the other side, where once upon a time they'd often raced to the top and jumped off in tandem into the water below.

She heard him right behind her. She was fast, but not fast enough. He'd stripped down to his board shorts and passed her with what looked like ease. She didn't sweat it. She knew she climbed faster than he did; she'd catch him on the rocks. And besides, the view from back here—watching that lean, toned body in motion, all those sleek muscles stretching and bunching—was making her more breathless than the run.

He beat her to the rocks, leaving her just beneath him as they began to climb, their puffing breaths making her laugh.

"Something funny?" he asked, spread-eagled on the rocks, head tilted up, searching for his next handhold.

"We're getting old."

"Bite your tongue, woman." And then he proceeded to beat her to the top.

"Dammit," she muttered, flopping over the ledge, lying there catching her breath. "I suck."

"Only if I'm very lucky."

She laughed, which backed up in her throat when he rolled to face her and tugged her into him. *He* wasn't laughing—he was looking down into her face with a softness he rarely showed the world and a heated affection that stole her breath.

"You don't even realize, do you?" he murmured.

"What?"

"You climbed up here without hesitation."

She stared at him, stunned.

He skimmed the pad of his thumb lightly over her lower lip, watching the movement. "I'm pretty sure it's because you were staring at my ass the whole time."

"Hey, it was my competitive spirit," she claimed. "I *really* wanted to beat you."

"*That*, I buy."

With a laugh, she wrapped her arms around his neck and tugged him over her. "But it might've been a little bit about your ass."

His hands slid down and cupped hers. "The feeling's entirely mutual."

"Yeah?"

"Yeah." He stared into her eyes. "Neither of us are big fans of talking about our feelings."

She laughed. "True. And . . . ? Because I definitely sense an 'and.'"

"And . . ." His smile faded from his mouth but remained in his eyes. "I like this."

She didn't pretend to not understand. "Me, too," she whispered, as a new emotion filled her. *Relief.* "So."

"So."

"Does this mean you're my boyfriend?" she asked.

He wriggled his eyebrows. "Depends."

She snorted. "On what?"

"Are you going to make me watch chick flicks? Are you going to steal my clothes? Make my lunches?"

She grinned at his teasing words, even as something quickened deep inside her. "Yes on the chick flicks. And I already steal your clothes. But it's a hard no on making your lunches."

"That part was just a test."

"For what?" she asked.

He stroked the hair back from her face. "To make sure you're really you. If you'd agreed to making my lunches, I'd have known you were an imposter."

He grinned down at her and then teased her lips with the

firm, full softness of his own, hijacking her thinking process. Was she just wishing it to be so, or was he actually making a promise of something more than just a few stolen moments of fire and magic? "To be honest," she said softly, "you're actually not my boyfriend."

He pulled back to look at her.

"Because boyfriends come and go."

"So do you." He'd said this lightly, so she knew he didn't mean to hurt her. And plus, it was the truth.

"I know," she said. "But you don't. Even when I'm gone for long stretches of time, even when I haven't been able to believe in myself, you do."

"And that makes me more than a boyfriend?" he asked.

She nodded, letting the sounds of the night speak for her as they stared into each other's eyes. Their bodies were touching from nose to toes, the throb of her racing pulse sounding in her ears, with Garrett's heart pumping calm and steady against her chest. "A lot more," she whispered.

His smile faded, replaced by something hot and intense and hungry. She reached for him and he met her halfway, kissing her with a hunger that had her skin coming alive with hot pleasure and her bones liquefying. With a moan for more, she wrapped herself around his hard, hot body, hoping, wishing, as she nuzzled his neck, that she didn't ever have to let go. She wanted to climb inside him, but barring that, she wanted this— needed this—and she rocked her hips to his. With a groan, he pulled back.

"Don't stop," she begged. "Oh my God."

"Actually, it's Garrett. And *shh*." He nudged her to her back, one big hand cradling the back of her head and the other adjusting her bikini to bare her to the night sky. "I used to think about what it would be like to get you like this." His hand began exploring. "Don't close your eyes."

"I think most people close their eyes before they pass out."

That made him laugh. "I've dreamed of this, Bee. You beneath the moonlight."

She already knew he was clever and diabolical with his hands and tongue, but she was still shocked when he put his mouth on her and she burst with shocking ease. She was still shuddering when she pushed him down to the rock and returned the favor, wanting to take him apart and put him back together as he just had her. Given his low oath, rough groan, and the way his fingers slid into her hair and fisted, she had done a decent job of it.

When they were both boneless and sated, Brooke let out a contented breath and stared up at the stars while the steady heartbeat of the only man she'd ever loved sounded beneath her ear.

After a few minutes, he tugged her into him and kissed her, slow and hot. "Again?" she whispered in disbelief.

"I can't get enough of you."

Ditto. And more terrifying than that, she was beginning to really think that maybe she could actually have this life, with him in it, and that they might really be able to make this work.

CHAPTER 22

"Don't listen to me. I'm barely caffeinated—"

A week later, Mindy woke up in bed next to her still sleeping husband and smiled. Tomorrow, she and Linc would leave on their better-late-than-never honeymoon trip to Hawaii. He'd reassured her that Ethan would come through to take over the practice for the week. Originally her mom and dad were going to come watch the kids, but Brittney had offered to watch them instead. Mindy knew she could've asked Brooke to do it, but her sister had already done so much for her.

Plus, Brooke had been packed to go back to LA for days now. But she hadn't left.

Mindy wasn't sure why, but she was afraid to ask and inadvertently set her leaving in motion. Either way, no matter how much she wanted to interfere, her sister would figure out her own life.

A life that looked like it would include Garrett. Mindy's heart felt so full about that, it was nearly bursting. "Need to get up and pack," she murmured to Linc.

"Babe, you've been packed for a week."

"There's packed, and there's *packed*. I need to add my new bathing suit."

Eyes still closed, Linc smiled. "I got us a private villa. You're not going to need a bathing suit."

Her body tightened in all her good places, and she started to roll over and jump him, but they were attacked by a munchkin with a soft giggle and Cheerio breath.

Mindy wrapped her arms around the sweet, warm body of her baby boy. "You're up early."

Maddox tossed his head back and barked as he wriggled on top of Linc, who groaned when a bony knee caught him in the groin. "Parenthood. Not for the weak," he grated out. Coming up on an elbow, he ruffled Maddox's wispy dark hair. "How about we let Mommy sleep in?" He rose from the bed and snatched Maddox up, hanging him off his back, much to the little boy's utter, screaming delight.

Mindy loved the sound, but her eyes were glued to her husband's bare back and the way his pajama bottoms hung low on his hips, showing off a world-class ass.

Mason came racing in. "Me, too, Daddy—me, too!"

Linc obliged, scooping him up as well, and then there were two squealing kids hanging off his back. In less than ten seconds, Millie had joined in, jumping up and down on the bed, impatiently waiting for her turn. Linc added her to the mix. The noise was horrendous. Over all of it, he grinned at Mindy, who felt her entire heart turn over and expose its tender underbelly for this man, whom she'd loved forever and never wanted to be without.

That was when his phone buzzed across his nightstand with an incoming text. Ignoring it in only the way a male could, he carried on with the kids. But when the phone went off for a second time in quick succession, Mindy glanced at it to make sure it wasn't an emergency.

It was a text from Ethan: *Hey, man, the divorce came through. Cookie wants to celebrate for a few days in Mexico to unwind. We bought last-minute flights. You don't mind, right?*

She must have made a sound, because Linc turned toward her and the smile died on his face. "What is it?"

"Millie, why don't you go to Daddy's desk and play office with your brothers?"

Playing "office" at Daddy's desk was one of Millie's very favorite things, and she looked thrilled.

Linc, not so much, since his office would look like a tornado had hit it when they were done, but he didn't say a word as the kids ran out with great enthusiasm. His gaze never left Mindy's as he came close. "What's wrong?"

She held out his phone. "Ethan left you a message."

Linc skimmed it and set the phone down without a word.

"Are you kidding me?" Mindy asked. "The divorce came through? I didn't even know he and Suzanne were getting one."

He let out a breath. "Suzanne bailed on him a few months ago and filed."

"So she finally grew a spine and kicked her Peter Pan husband out, and good riddance. What I don't understand is why you didn't tell me. And who's Cookie?"

"His new girlfriend."

"Oh my God," she gasped, staring at her husband in shock. "You're covering for him. Again. You've been doing it since he came along when you were four years old."

Linc's expression was stoic but steady. "You know he's had problems. Our mom—"

"Died when he was five," she finished for him. "And you were nine. You were just as vulnerable, Linc. Just as hurt. And yet you became a functioning adult, a doctor, for God's sake, who takes his responsibilities so seriously it's sometimes a detriment to yourself and your relationships."

"He's a doctor, too," Linc said quietly.

"Thanks to you." Mindy shook her head and backed away. "Listen, you're never going to see this my way, so—"

"You'd do anything for Brooke."

She stared at him, feeling tears fill her eyes. "Not fair. You know damn well I failed her. That I let her flounder after her accident because my own feelings were hurt. You'd never do that to Ethan."

Linc reached for her, but she held up a hand. "No. Listen, I get it, I get why you'd go to the ends of the earth for Ethan. I do. He's your brother. But he always comes first, ahead of us."

"I'll talk to him."

"This isn't on Ethan. Or even you. It's on me for not realizing where I stood in the lineup of your life. I'm not your number one. Or even your number two. It goes Ethan, then work, and *then* me and the kids. Sometimes I think you bought me the shop just to keep me too busy to miss you."

"Okay, I can see how you got there," he admitted. "But—"

"And not just about Ethan and the trip, or the shop," she said. "All my life, I've been a people-pleaser. My parents. You. The kids. Everyone. And in hindsight, I think that's why I cracked." She drew in a deep breath. "I love you, Linc, but I don't want to be anyone's number three."

"Mindy," he said, low and serious. "I heard you, believe me. Please, just give me a few minutes to fix this."

She let her eyes drift closed for a beat, because she had babies with this man. She had a life with this man whom she loved. And she did love him, so very, very much. He wouldn't be able to hurt her so badly if she didn't.

"Trust me?" he asked.

She wanted to, desperately. So she nodded, and leaving him to do whatever he was going to do, she went straight to the guesthouse.

Brooke wasn't there. Whirling, she strode across the yard to Garrett's house and knocked on the door.

He answered wearing a pair of jeans and nothing else. He had bedhead hair, no shirt, no socks, and a bite mark on his neck. "I need to talk to my sister," she said.

"She's not here."

She stared at him as the implications of the bite mark not being Brooke's ignited her temper.

Still raw from her fight with Linc, she stabbed a finger into Garrett's pec. "Tell me you're not sleeping around on my sister."

"No. Never," he said, catching her hand. "And ow." He narrowed his eyes at her. "She's with your kids. They just left for doughnuts because apparently you were very busy yelling at Linc. You didn't kill him, did you? Do you need help hiding his body?"

At that, she burst into tears.

Looking deeply pained, Garrett pulled her in for a hug. She clung for a moment, taking comfort in the embrace of one of her oldest friends before she leaned back and swiped at her eyes. "You'd help me hide his body?" she asked soggily.

"Yes."

"Would you help him hide mine?"

"Hell no. You'd come back from the dead just to haunt me for the rest of my life if I did that."

She rolled her eyes and then stared at him. "Are you one hundred percent serious about Brooke?"

"Yes," he said, without hesitation, and then paused, eyeing her like she was a locked-and-loaded rattlesnake. "You're not going to cry again, are you?"

"No." But she totally was. She looked around for a diversion. "I heard you've been looking for your dad."

Garrett shrugged. "I can't just leave him out there on the streets."

"That's where he was before he showed up."

"But I can't go back to the past, to before I knew he was sick. Life's annoying that way."

"Yeah." She huffed out a sigh.

He let out a low laugh. "Okay, let's hear it."

"Hear what?"

"Whatever Linc did."

"Do you have caffeine? This story requires caffeine."

They ended up in Garrett's kitchen, leaning against the counter, mainlining coffee as she told him.

Garrett didn't look surprised. "He feels responsible for Ethan," he said, "who, in spite of being a doctor, is also clueless, hapless, and incredibly needy. That drives Linc crazy. I hope you get that part of what he loves so much about you is that you're none of those things. You're smart, too, but you hold your own, and you've never been clueless, hapless, or needy a day in your life. He's lucky to have you, Min, and believe me, he knows it."

"I just don't want to be the last one he thinks about."

Garrett laughed. "Are you kidding? You're all he thinks about. He just knows that you've got what it takes to run the world you two have created so he can run his. You're everything to him. Let him prove it to you."

She took a deep breath and nodded. "I'll try." She paused. "You seem really happy. It looks good on you. Now that I know about your past with Brooke, what you were to each other, it makes so much sense, you and her. I just wish you could've told me."

Looking regretful, he shook his head. "I couldn't have explained it to myself back then, much less to someone who loved her as much as I did. And then when she was gone . . ." He shook his head. "It nearly killed me."

"Me, too," she said softly. "She said she needed space, and my parents and I made the mistake of giving it to her. We all reached out, but she wasn't great at responding or keeping in touch. I let myself get hurt by that instead of reading into it that maybe she needed me. I'm having a hard time forgiving myself for that."

Eyes shadowed with the memories, he nodded. "I was no better. I figured she'd moved on from me and her silence only proved it."

"I think she's going to let us in now. Do you think there's really a chance for you two?"

"Depends on who you're asking."

"You," she said. "I'm asking you."

"Then yes. But it's not up to me."

"I don't want her to get hurt."

"Neither do I."

"You love her," Mindy said softly, her heart squeezing in happiness for two of her favorite people.

"I do."

"Does she know you bought this place from Ann to someday fill it to the brim with your own family?"

At a sound behind them, they both turned and found Brooke standing in the doorway, covered in Mindy's children. Millie was on her back, piggyback-style, and Brooke had Maddox and Mason each under an arm. All three kids were holding on to a bag of what were presumably doughnuts, since there were chocolate and sprinkles all over their faces. They were each grinning from ear to ear.

Not Brooke, though. She was staring at Garrett. "I mean, it makes sense," she said, joining their conversation. "You'd make a great dad."

Mindy stood, heart in her throat at the look of utter devastation on her sister's face, who clearly knew she couldn't help

Garrett fulfill his dream. "I'm sorry, Brooke. Don't listen to me. I'm barely caffeinated—"

"Mindy," Garrett said quietly, eyes on Brooke. "I need you to give us a minute."

"Yes, but—" Oh God, this was bad. "Brooke, I shouldn't have opened my big mouth. Those were my words, not his, and—"

"It's okay," Brooke said. "Don't worry about it."

That was hard to do when Brooke was looking like Millie had the day Mindy and Linc had ruined Santa Claus for her. Feeling like she'd just set a train in motion that couldn't be stopped, Mindy opened her mouth, but Garrett put his hand on her arm. "I've got this. Take the kids home, okay?"

Mindy pulled Millie from Brooke's back, and then her two boys. When she leaned in to kiss Brooke's cheek, it was icy cold. "I'll be right next door if you need me," she said softly. "I'm so sorry." And then, though she didn't want to, she left.

CHAPTER 23

"I want your everything."

Garrett shut the door behind Mindy and turned to Brooke, whose eyes were hooded, expression completely closed off. She'd shut down, retreating inside herself, which was terrifying because the last time she'd done so, he hadn't seen her for seven years.

"Tell me you're not going to let an overheard conversation and a simple misunderstanding derail you. Or us," he said.

"There's no getting around the fact that it's still your dream to fill this place with kids," she said, turning away. "And no matter how much I love you, I can't give them to you."

All he heard were those three little words she'd never said to him before, and a wave of relief and exhilaration knocked into him. Pulling her around to face him, he dipped his knees to look into her eyes, his heart swelling in his chest. "You love me."

"Of course I love you!" she cried, flinging her hands up, which was better than how she'd been working her thumbs frantically over the tips of her fingers, back and forth, giving him a good idea of how upset she really was. As if there'd been any doubt.

"I've *always* loved you," she said. "But I can't love you enough to make up for the fact that I can't give you children."

Her first "I love you" had stopped his heart. The second "I love you," flung at him like a weapon, had nearly brought him to his knees. "So we adopt," he said with a calm he wasn't close to feeling. Calm had been replaced by equal parts hope and fear—hope that he could have this, her, and fear that she wouldn't let it happen. He reached for her hands to still her nervous fidgeting, not wanting her to be nervous or anxious at all. "Or we don't. We'll figure it out, Bee."

She closed her eyes and breathed for a moment, and he knew she was counting in her head, trying to self-soothe. "It's not that simple," she whispered.

"Have you been happy here? Yes or no?"

"Yes," she admitted. "I've loved being home again with my family. With you. It's been . . . everything. Everything I needed. But it was never going to be long-term. I mean, we haven't really even thought this through. You want different things than me. We're in different places."

He shook his head. "No. That's not it."

"Of course it is." She turned away from him, staring out the window. "What else could it be?"

Where did he start? "How about the fact that you've been packed to go for a week? You've just been waiting for an excuse to go and not look back. The only question is, will it be another seven years before you grace us with your presence again?"

Her spine had snapped straight as a pin and temper crackled out of her as she whipped back to face him. "Me leaving was *always* the plan." She poked a finger into his pec, hard. "You knew that. I told you, more than once." She stabbed him again. "I came here to try to make things right. I wanted to figure my shit out so I could go back and be me again. I know you don't understand, but for me it was about courage and bravery, facing my past and coming to terms with it."

He let out a mirthless laugh, because in spite of everything, his worst nightmare was about to come true. "You think you're being brave by running away from here? No. Fuck no, Brooke. The bravest thing you could do would be to at the very least keep Wildstone as your home base. You love your sister, you love her kids. And you love me. You ran away from that last time, and now you're going to do it again. And the worst part? I should have seen it coming." He shook his head. "You haven't changed at all, and apparently, neither have I."

She sucked in a breath and bowed her head a moment before meeting his gaze, her own eyes shimmering with rare tears. "I'm sorry. I've gotten too good at being alone."

"You were never alone, Brooke, never. You just chose to shut us out." This time *he* turned away, disgusted with the both of them. Her, for fooling him again, and himself, for knowing better and falling for her just as hard this time around anyway. "The real problem here is that you don't know what you want. Or maybe you do, but you're too scared to get it. You don't believe in this, in us." He took a step back. "Good to know that some things never change. I love you, too, Bee. You know that, or I hope you do. But I can't make you believe in me, in us. You have to do that yourself."

She turned to the door to leave, but then put her hand on the handle and paused. "I'm going back to LA in the morning," she said to the wood. "The old me would've just left, but I didn't want to do that to you again."

He let out a rough laugh, through lungs so tight that he couldn't draw in air. "Good luck. I hope you find what you're looking for."

There was a single heartbeat where she hesitated, and he felt hope grip him by the throat, but then she shook her head and was gone—this time, he was pretty sure, for good.

MUCH LATER, MINDY stood in her kitchen, sick with worry and anxiety. Her three babies were looking at her, so she put on a smile and opened her baking drawers, all three of them filled with things like measuring cups and spoons, wooden and plastic utensils, the works. Millie clapped her hands in delight. One of her favorite things to do was riffle through it all and put on pretend cooking shows, making her brothers be her captive audience.

Leaving them to it, Mindy headed for the cleaning supplies, because when life went to shit, she cleaned. When her vacuum shut off unexpectedly in the living room, she turned to find Linc standing there. He'd pulled the plug out of the wall.

"I don't want to fight with you," she said.

"On that, we're quite in agreement." Tossing the cord aside, he took her hand and led her to the couch. "I just want to talk."

"That's not exactly our strong suit." She was careful to not quite touch him, because he was wearing her favorite shirt of his, a gray UCSF Medical School T-shirt. It'd been worn to a buttery softness that clung to his broad shoulders. His cargo shorts had a bazillion pockets that she knew would be full of a huge assortment of things, but still always had room for him to take on the burden of whatever she didn't want to carry.

Dammit. She loved him so much.

Ignoring her clear personal space bubble, he pulled her in until they were thigh to thigh. He twisted to face her, his arm resting along the back of the couch, his body language telling her this was important to him, *she* was important to him, and she took a deep breath and let that wash over her.

"First things first," he said quietly, eyes on hers, his solemn. Intense. "I really did believe you wanted the shop. I've always hated that we never had enough money for it because of my student debt. I assumed you hated that, too, maybe even resented it."

"Linc—"

He put a finger to her lips. "You put your entire life on hold for me so I could go to medical school, which meant you working so we wouldn't starve. Then, just as we started to get it together, I got you pregnant. You never complained, never faltered, just kept us in the boat with life jackets on and steered the ship. You've put *all* of us, everyone you care about, ahead of yourself, and I wanted to return the favor. So I cashed in some investments and moved things around so you could have what I thought was your dream. I was wrong to do that without talking to you first." He ran a finger along her temple, over an earlobe, and smiled when she shivered. "We got an unexpected offer on the store," he said. "For more than I paid your parents for it. It's from Xena and her sister. They want their own franchise and apparently have for a while. It's your choice, of course, this time and for always. Whatever you want to do, I'm in."

She let out a careful breath. "Xena's perfect for it. I could go back to baking and selling her my stuff for the shop, assuming she wants it."

Linc's eyes warmed as he smiled. "Your stuff's amazing, I hope you know that. You can do whatever you want. You could take over the world if you set your mind to it. No one would know what hit them."

From the kitchen came a loud drumming sound that Mindy knew from experience was Mason sitting on the floor surrounded by upside-down pots and pans, beating them with her wooden spoons, headbanging like he was the drummer from an '80s rock band.

"Also"—Linc handed her the itinerary and tickets for Hawaii—"we're still going. Ethan and I had a serious talk."

"Ethan doesn't do serious."

"He does now."

She stared at the papers in her hand. "So . . . he's going to help handle the practice for the whole week? No emergencies?"

"It's not 'helping' when he owns half of it," he said. "But that's going to change, too. I told him I was cutting my hours back to something reasonable versus insane, because you and the kids didn't sign on for me running Dad's practice alone. I've missed too much precious time. I also told him if he didn't have time to devote to his half, we're selling. The hospital's been coming at us with offers for two years. It'd leave us as independent contractors and managers of the practice, but not owners, the biggest plus being that they'd add two additional MDs to the rotation. We'd all have reasonable shifts and time to work in the hospital and clinics if we want."

She stared up at him, afraid to hope. "Which is exactly what you've wanted to do."

He nodded, his expression endearingly earnest. "This works for us, right? It's what you want, too?"

The husky sincerity in his voice, coupled with his big, warm body pressed against hers and that finger tracing softly along her ear and down her throat, warmed her. "What I want," she murmured, "is for us to be on the same page."

His smile was sexy. "We're always on the same page. In bed . . ." He chuckled when she blushed. "Do you want to know when I first realized I'd fallen in love with you?"

"I thought it was Trash Can Mindy."

"No, that's when I first knew you were going to be mine. Junior year of high school, you came over to my family's house to watch a movie. You and my grandpa promptly fell asleep."

"Because you picked a *Star Wars* movie we'd seen a million times." She felt her face heat, remembering what had happened next. "I don't need to hear this story again, I already lived it—"

"And around halfway through, still dead asleep, you popcorn farted loud enough to wake the dead. *Pop, pop, pop.*" He grinned. "My grandpa fell out of his chair."

And the old man's dentures had gone skittering across the room. "Well, you fed me hot dogs. Hot dogs hurt my stomach!"

He was still smiling. "You jerked upright, horrified—which,

as a side note, you shouldn't have been. You should've been proud as hell because it was very impressive—"

"Please stop," she begged, covering her hot face.

"Remember what came next?"

Of course she did. He'd claimed the farts as his own, covering for her.

"I'm pretty sure that's when you fell in love with me, too," he said knowingly.

She sighed. "You laughed every time you looked at me for like three weeks."

"And you've been making me laugh ever since. I can't imagine my life without you in it, Min. You're all I've ever wanted. Hold on, I've got a surprise for you."

She eyed him warily. "I'm not going to pull your finger."

He grinned. "No, this is something much better."

"You've taken massage lessons?" she asked hopefully.

"No, but hold that thought." He vanished down the hall and came back with a three-ring binder that she'd never seen before.

"Open it," he said.

She began to flip through, and her pulse took a good, hard leap. "You redid the family schedule."

"I did."

He sounded cocky as all hell, and quite pleased with himself. She went back to eyeing what he'd done, and her heart melted. "You even color-coded it."

"Gave you purple," he said.

She met his gaze.

"Which is your favorite color, even though you tell everyone it's blue," he said.

He'd given himself half the work, along with giving the kids their own to-do charts. God, she loved this man. "You think you've got me all figured out," she managed through a thick throat.

"No." He sat next to her and pulled her into his lap. "And God knows, I might *never* have it all figured out. But I promise to always love you, to keep working on things, and to be a better partner to you. You deserve that, and I'll never stop giving you everything I've got. Please say you'll let me try to make you happy every day for the rest of your life." He kissed her softly. "I want this, Min. I want your early mornings, even the crabby ones. I want your fiery temper and the way you smile at me when I manage to calm you down, even when it's by accident. I want to share a bed with you, even when it's full of our crazy children. I want your everything."

Setting the binder aside, she straddled him and slid her fingers into his hair. "Even when I'm not all that lovable?"

"You're way too hard on yourself." He cupped her face. "You're *always* lovable. And tonight, when the kids are asleep, I'm going to prove it to you." Leaning in, he put his mouth to her ear and whispered exactly how he was going to do that, in great detail.

"Kids," she yelled, never taking her eyes off her sexy husband. "Early bedtime tonight!"

She wrapped her arms around him and held on tight, marveling that he was hers. All hers.

CHAPTER 24

"It's the orgasms."

Throat too tight to breathe, Brooke walked into the guest-house, trying to compartmentalize the different parts of her life that couldn't be reconciled. Trying to control her emotions.

But she couldn't control anything, much less herself. She was hurting, she was shaking, she was angry, and she knew, without a doubt, that whatever she did next was going to be incredibly stupid.

She didn't care.

Garrett was wrong. She wasn't running. She was simply going after what she wanted. Walking away from him was going to hurt, but she had to do it. She really did see herself taking on the world again. Maybe it wasn't for everyone, but it was her life. No kids, but hopefully a partner, if she met the right one.

You already met him.

She ignored this little voice in her head. She was a grown-up, and grown-ups couldn't always have everything they wanted. That was just a fact. She pulled out her phone.

Brooke: I'm coming back.

Cole: There is a God.

Brooke: If you missed me that much, I'll take a raise.

Cole: Funny. I was actually expecting a resignation letter. Even me, the hardheaded, coldhearted bastard I am, can tell when a person's found their place.

Brooke: Wildstone isn't my place.

Cole: Glad to hear it.

Brooke: I don't belong in Wildstone.

Cole: Music to my ears.

Brooke: I can't possibly end up here.

Cole: Shit. You're protesting too much. Quick, get in your car and come home right now before you realize it.

Brooke: You're as dramatic as Tommy. I'll be there in four
hours. And I want my old job back.

Her phone battery was low, and since she didn't have a car
charger or an extra battery, she plugged her phone into the wall
outlet and lay down to rest her eyes while it charged. "Just for a
few minutes," she told the room.

A few minutes later, she jerked awake. But it hadn't been only
a few minutes. It was six a.m., and she'd slept the rest of the
night away. Jumping to her feet, she staggered into the main
house, needing caffeine before hitting the road.

And maybe some sweet TLC from her three favorite little
people.

Her sister was looking over a pan of perfectly golden cinnamon rolls, calmly sipping tea and definitely looking like the
Mindy of old. Peaceful. Put together.

Serene.

Brooke stared at her.

"What?" Mindy asked.

"You look . . ." Brooke shook her head. "Really good."

"It's because we're leaving for Hawaii in two hours."

"Actually, it's the orgasms," Linc said as he came into the
room.

Mindy rolled her eyes, but she was smiling, too, glancing
over at Linc with the look of a well-loved woman.

Brooke drew a steady breath, happy for her sister, but filled
with a melancholy she couldn't have explained. "Well," she
said, trying for cheerful, "I'm out, too. Wanted to give you all a
hug good-bye first."

Mindy gasped. "No."

"And it's not your fault," Brooke said quickly, seeing the guilt on her sister's face. "So stop it. And don't cry."

Linc gave Brooke a hug. "You sure?" was all he asked, pulling back to see her face.

She nodded. "I want to get back to work."

"Uh-huh." Still holding on to her, he met her gaze. "As long as that's all it's about."

"What else would it be?"

Linc gave her a *get real* look.

Right. "I'm not running! Everyone needs to cut it out."

His expression said she wasn't fooling anyone, but Linc was a live-and-let-live kind of guy. He gave her one last squeeze, whispered, "You know where to find us when you need us," and stepped back.

Mindy was right there, hands on her hips, eyes now dialed to unhappy.

"I never planned on staying, Min." And that was the truth—at least in the very beginning. But somehow over the past couple of weeks with the kids, Mindy, Linc, her camera around her neck, *Garrett* . . . she'd started to realize she'd been feeling happier than she could remember feeling in years.

Mindy cupped Brooke's face. "I'm so sorry."

"Min, it's not your fault."

"I mean for what happened between us, you and me, to break us up from being sisters."

Brooke started to shake her head, but her sister gently squeezed to hold her in place. "Please let me say this. If you're going, I need to say it." Mindy drew in a deep breath. "I know you don't want to talk about what happened to you. I know you hate thinking about it. And that's a big part of why I never pushed you. You put limits on all of us, and I get it, I'm just a wife and a baker, and that you've done a lot of things I haven't. But I know you, Brooke. I love you, and I don't want you to throw away a chance at being happy just because you're scared and there's nobody you can talk to about it. I should've made you talk—*really* talk—to me before, about the crash, about Garrett. About everything."

"Come on," Brooke managed to say lightly through a very tight, burning throat. "You know me. No one can make me talk if I don't want to."

Mindy laughed a little, but then she shook her head. "See what I mean? You act like it's nothing, like you weren't broken, like everything's okay, even when it isn't. I should've pushed my way into your life, but I didn't because . . . well, frankly, because I was a bad sister. I let my hurt feelings get in the way. But I'm here now, and I want you to know that I see you and I'm here for you, whether you're happy or sad or hurt or pissed off, or just being plain stupid."

"Gee . . . thanks?"

"I wouldn't be back with Linc if it weren't for you," Mindy said seriously. "And I'd never forgive myself if I didn't say this—please at least tell Garrett how you really feel and give him a chance to tell you back. I've never seen two people who deserve happiness more. I know there's got to be a way to work this out—"

"There's not." Brooke forced a smile. "Believe me, we tried. Now give me a hug good-bye."

"No." Mindy shook her head. "You're not hugging me good-bye, because you're not leaving. It makes no sense. You're just afraid to put down roots, but you know what? You've never even given putting down roots a chance! And you know what else? My friend at the county offices said they were so excited about you and your work for them that they're wanting more. A lot more."

Brooke knew this—they'd contacted her as well.

"Are you really just going to walk away from the job?" Mindy asked.

"They knew I was temporary."

"Your entire life's temporary!"

Brooke took Mindy's hand and gently squeezed. "I've been in touch with them. They know I'm going. They've got all the work I've done up to this point."

"Oh my God, this is all so wrong! You belong here. With us." Mindy whirled to Linc. "Tell her."

"She's a big girl, babe. She makes her own decisions. We just back them."

Mindy huffed out a breath. "Well, if you're going to be reasonable." Her eyes filled with tears as she yanked Brooke in for a hard hug. A strangling hug.

"Too tight," Brooke gasped out dramatically. "Seriously, Min. Can't. Breathe." When Mindy didn't let go, Brooke sighed and squeezed her back. "Don't." She closed her eyes. "Please don't make this harder than it already is."

"But last time you left, you didn't come back for years!"

"I'll come back, Min, I promise," she heard herself say. "Besides, I love your kids."

"Really?"

Brooke's throat burned. "Of course I do. I love them like they're my own." And look at that, saying so didn't almost kill her like it would've a couple of weeks ago.

Mindy lifted her head, her drenched eyes meeting Brooke's, clearly understanding exactly how much this statement had cost her.

"We love you, too, Auntie Bee," Princess Millie said as she skipped into the room in a sunshine-yellow dress with a smiley-face emoji on the front and a kissy-face one on the back. Her tights were black and her high-top sneakers matched her dress. So did her beanie.

"Baby, you're going to melt at camp," Linc said. "It's going to be a hot one. Pick a different outfit."

"But Mommy didn't get me the one I *wanted* to wear. If she had, I'd be nice and cool."

"What did we say about manipulating and passive-aggressiveness?" Linc asked.

Millie huffed out a sigh. "That it's unbecoming." She looked at the tears on her mom's and Brooke's faces. "Did you tell Auntie Brooke about the tooth fairy and Santa Claus, too, Mommy?"

Just then Maddox and Mason tumbled into the room mid-sword fight, their weapons of choice being golf clubs.

Linc expertly disarmed his boys. "No murder or mayhem in the house," he said mildly. "Now give Auntie Bee kisses good-bye. She's going home, but she'll be back." He met Brooke's gaze. "She promised."

The kids all flew at her, and Brooke went to her knees to gather them in. Millie smelled like strawberries and rainbows.

The boys smelled like fresh-cut grass, the outdoors, and, in Maddox's case, like maybe he had to go to the bathroom very soon. She hugged them tight until they began to make the same dramatic noises she'd made when Mindy had hugged her too tight. God, she loved these little soul-suckers with all her heart. "I'll be back," she whispered, her throat raw.

"Will you bring ice cream?" Mason asked.

"Whatever you want," she managed.

"Promise?"

"Promise." Listen to her. Handing out promises left and right, and she knew with all her heart that she'd never break a single one of them.

CHAPTER 25

"Good to know the asshole trait flows down."

Garrett woke up with a huge weight on his chest. He lay there, eyes closed, knowing exactly what it was. While he knew he wasn't responsible for his mom dying young or his dad being in and out of jail and not available to parent, and then the string of foster homes . . . he *was* responsible for how he'd let it all affect him.

He knew he tended to skate through life. Oh, he enjoyed himself. He did. He loved renovating, so it'd never even felt like a job. He loved being outdoors and adventure seeking. He loved coaching and mentoring kids.

And all those things came easy to him.

The things that didn't come easy? He just didn't do. Like forging relationships that required any depth, at least outside of his tribe—Linc, Mindy, and, once upon a time, Brooke. And let's be honest: *They'd* chosen *him,* simply collecting him and claiming him with an ease he'd never seen before. He hadn't had to do a thing.

When his dad had showed up on his doorstep looking for forgiveness and a new start, it'd seemed insurmountably hard, so what had he done? He'd pulled his usual I-don't-need-anyone bullshit so that eventually his dad would walk away again. And he had.

That was on Garrett.

When Brooke had been skittish and nervous, even panicked, about coming back into his life, had he given her the patience and love that she'd needed? No. He'd concentrated on his own issues, and when things had started to get too deep and she'd gotten scared and turned tail and run, he'd let her go.

He hated what that said about him. Because of his fears and hang-ups, the best thing to ever happen to him had walked away.

For a second time.

He'd tried telling himself that his life had gone back to basics, that's all. His dad was gone, and that was normal. Brooke was gone, and that was normal, too. He was on his own again, not worrying about complicated relationships and how to make them all work. It was how he'd lived his entire life. It worked for him.

And if his chest ached with regrets and a sense of loneliness he hadn't expected, he told himself it would pass.

Everything passed, especially people.

That's what he'd always believed. But something had changed deep inside him. He was done with accepting these things without a fight.

It was time to go after what he wanted.

So, with that decided and all, why did he still feel like an elephant was sitting on his chest? He opened his eyes and figured it out. Not an elephant. Just three fat cats. He shifted and dumped them onto the mattress, and six narrowed eyes leveled him with varying degrees of scorn, annoyance, and temper. "Please feel free to sleep literally *anywhere* else," he said, and grabbed some clothes.

Brooke's car was gone, which sucked and made his stomach feel hollow. When his phone rang, he snatched at it, hoping it was her.

His luck wasn't that good. It was Mark Capriotti. "I just got in," Mark said. "And there's a note here from our overnight desk clerk. There was a sighting of your dad at the convenience store, but it's from yesterday, man."

"Better than nothing. And thanks." Garrett grabbed his keys and headed out. He knew his dad could be anywhere by now, but he'd start at the store.

"Seen my dad lately?" he asked Ace, who was behind the counter.

"You've asked me that just about every day for over a week now."

"Which isn't an answer," Garrett noted.

Ace blew out a breath and hesitated, looking guilty as hell.

Dammit. "Look, it's important. I wouldn't ask you to betray a confidence otherwise."

"Dude, I made a promise."

"He's sick," Garrett said. "Did he tell you that?"

From Ace's expression, it was clear he hadn't known. "He told me he refused to upend your life, not ever again."

Garrett absorbed the blow of that. "He didn't upend my life. I managed that all on my own. I owe him an apology and a real effort."

Ace looked at him for a long moment. "He's at the campground. In a gray tent he . . . appropriated."

"I've been there every damn day," Garrett said. "I haven't seen his truck."

"He sold it."

Fifteen minutes later, Garrett was at the campgrounds, heading up the trail. The weather had warmed, and there were at least twenty tents there now. He strode up to the only gray one in sight and stood at the zipped-up door, thinking this could go easy or hard. "Dad."

Nothing.

The hard way it was, then.

"Dad, there's no reason for you to stay out here," he said, staring at his boots. "I've got plenty of room for you and Snoop." He paused, knowing he needed to try harder. "I'd really like it if you came home."

Nothing.

Garrett pinched the bridge of his nose. "Listen, I was a dick, all right? You showed up after all those years, and I was nursing a grudge like a stupid little kid. I'm sorry I didn't try harder. I'm sorry I kept myself closed off to you. I'm sorry for a lot of things."

Still no movement from inside the tent.

He was batting 0 for 2 in the relationship department. "I don't want you to leave, Dad." There. He'd said it out loud. "I want you to live with me. I want to give us a shot at this dad-and-son thing." And he actually meant it.

There was a rustle from inside the tent and then a head appeared. A thirtysomething head, looking like he'd seen better times. "Dude. Wrong tent. But nice speech. I'd totally come home with you, man."

Garrett smiled grimly and moved through the small city of tents. He found another gray one, way in the back. "Anyone home?" he asked.

This time, the silence was loaded.

"Dad?"

The zipper slowly came undone, and Snoop stuck his head out to bark a greeting. His dad's head came next, his expression quiet and reflective.

"There you are," Garrett said with huge relief, and tried to remember his speech. But he was drawing a blank. "I made you an appointment with a doctor for this afternoon."

"I don't need a doctor. This was supposed to be about you, Garrett," his dad said quietly. "About how I treated you, how I failed you. About helping you make a home in that house you've been neglecting because . . . well, hell, I'm not sure why, but I bet a therapist would be happy to trace that back to something I did, too. I was here to make amends, Garrett. Not further screw you up. So, I'm moving on. I've got another job, and they really need me, so . . ." He started to retreat back into his tent.

Garrett was really getting tired of losing the people he cared about due to his own stubborn incompetence. *Sometimes you've got to try a different route to get where you want to go . . .* Brooke had taught him that. So he pulled out the big guns. "Dad, wait. Look at Snoop," he said. "He deserves a home, don't you think? He loves my house. Where else can he sniff kitty butts and eat

Tender Vittles right out of a sandbox?" He squatted low and hugged Snoop. "Forget about us, Dad, but think of Snoop. He needs this. Come home with me."

His dad looked at Snoop, who licked his face, then turned back to Garrett. "You're sure?"

"Positive."

His dad nodded and came out of his tent. "Then let's go."

"Your tent and stuff," Garrett said.

His dad looked back at it. "I'm going to leave it all here for someone in need. Unless I'll be needing it again . . . ?"

"No, you won't be needing it again," Garrett said firmly, and then the three of them headed down the trail.

A LITTLE BIT later, Garrett had his dad settled in and comfortable, and while he felt good about it, he wasn't done.

He had to get Brooke back, too.

There was delicious scent coming from the kitchen, and he followed it. Apparently epiphanies made one hungry because his stomach went off, reminding him he hadn't eaten in . . . he didn't know how long. He found his dad piling three plates with bacon and eggs.

"Where's the cutie?" his old man asked. "I made enough for everyone."

"She's gone."

His dad looked at him in surprise. "You screwed it up? What's wrong with you?"

"A lot, actually."

His dad pointed the spatula at him. "That girl's got a head

on her shoulders. She wouldn't have walked away without good cause. What the hell did you do?"

Garrett shook his head. "It's complicated."

"Of course it is, a woman's involved. But whatever bullshit you pulled, you can fix it with a sincere apology and a promise to do better."

"This isn't some simple misunderstanding, Dad. I accused her of being too chicken to go after what she really wanted. But it was me. I was the chickenshit who wasn't brave enough to fight for her."

"So you were stupid."

Garrett sighed. "Yeah."

His dad shook his head. "Good to know the asshole trait flows down."

"Gee, thanks, that's really helpful. I'm going after her, by the way."

"Yeah? What's taking you so long?"

"Clearly, I'm a dumbass."

His dad nodded and clapped a hand on his shoulder. "Don't worry. Knowing it is half the battle."

CHAPTER 26

"We're going to Disneyland!"

B rooke got to LA at midday, which meant she started her big return stuck in an LA traffic jam. She went straight to the studio and hit another major pet peeve—meetings that could've been handled with an email. Sitting in an office after being in Wildstone for weeks—hiking, taking pics again, enjoying the great outdoors—was sheer torture. She told herself she'd fix that by taking the job Cole had gotten her. There was a new show starting up in a few months. It would take her to South America for six months. Six months gone, without getting back to Wildstone to see the kids. Mindy and Linc.

Garrett . . .

If she closed her eyes, she could still see the look on his face when she'd walked away. Just remembering shriveled her heart more than a little. So the question was obvious. Why was she even here? Why had she run away instead of taking a stand for what she wanted, which was, at the very least, being part of her family again? She could've had that, a job, and some pretty amazing sex, but she'd had to blow it all up, and why?

It was exactly as Garrett had said: she was afraid. What she felt for him ran deeper and felt more real than she'd allowed in . . . well, ever, and she'd let the fear take over. The fear of not being enough—not for her family, not for Garrett.

Or was it because, as Mindy had accused, when shit had gotten real, way too real, she was simply afraid to put down roots, because if she did, it was like admitting her best days were behind her?

Both. It was both.

At the end of a long day in front of three huge computer screens, she leaned back in her chair and stared blindly up at the ceiling, running the pads of her thumbs over her fingers rhythmically. She didn't look over when she felt Cole drop into the chair beside her.

"I'm not taking that job," she said.

"The one you demanded I get you?"

"Yes." She turned to him. "I'm grateful to you. So grateful."

He sighed. "I don't want gratitude, Brooke."

"I know." She looked right at him. "But I can't give you what you want," she said softly.

He nodded and spoke just as quietly. "I know. You're going back."

"I'm going back," she agreed.

He looked pained.

"What?"

"Hearing you say it out loud . . ." He lifted a shoulder. "It makes it real. I mean, I already knew it. I knew it before you even came back. But it does make it easier to tell you something."

"What's that?"

He paused and held her gaze. "Garrett's here."

She jerked to her feet. *What?*

"Yeah. He's in the—"

That was all Cole got out before she tore out of the editing booth and plowed directly into Tommy.

"Whoa," he said, catching her. "Where's the fire?"

"I gotta go, Garrett's here."

Tommy nodded. "Yep. He's currently pacing the reception area. But—"

But *nothing.* She flew down the hall and into the open greeting area. There was a surprising crowd. Her sister. Princess Millie, Mason, and Maddox. Linc. Garrett's dad and Snoop, who gave a low *wuff* in greeting.

But she had eyes for only one person.

Garrett had turned at the sound of her footsteps. He stood there in jeans and his battered leather jacket over a Whiskey River T-shirt, along with a three-day beard and dark circles under his eyes.

He looked like the best thing she'd ever seen.

"Hi, Auntie Bee!" Millie yelled, and waved. "We're going to Disneyland tomorrow! And then the next day Mommy and Daddy are going to Hawaii. We don't get to go, but I get to get a princess dress at Disneyland! And—"

Linc took Millie's hand. "Baby, remember what we said in the car?"

"That I was to be quiet and let Garrett talk first. But, Daddy, he's not talking fast enough!"

"Hey, who wants a tour of the studio?" Tommy called out as he came up to Brooke's side. He gave her a wink. "Right this way, everyone!"

Linc leaned in to give Brooke a quick hug. "Don't kill her."

The "her" in question was clearly Mindy, who was right behind Linc.

Mindy rolled her eyes. "Well, excuse me for wanting to make sure this was done right," she said, and side-eyed Garrett.

Linc took her by the hand. "Okay, babe, come on."

Brooke's stomach was in knots and her heart was fluttering. She couldn't tear her gaze off Garrett as everyone followed Tommy and finally left them alone.

Since the two of them were chronic idiots, they stood in strained silence for a few beats, eyes locked. Normally she'd fight the urge to go to him, but she was tired of fighting. She'd been fighting herself, fighting the Brooke she was versus the Brooke she wanted to be, fighting her feelings for the amazing man standing in front of her. She must've finally moved, though, because suddenly she was in his arms, hers winding around his neck, her legs going around his waist.

With a rough sound of male pleasure, Garrett held her tight, lowered his head, and kissed her like it was the only thing keeping him alive.

"Hey, Brooke, Tommy's going to take us to—" Mindy again.

She broke off at the sight of them kissing, standing in the doorway where she'd poked her head back in.

Slowly Garrett let Brooke go and she put her feet back on the ground.

"No! Go back to kissing!" Mindy said quickly. "Ignore me!"

Brooke turned back to Garrett. They both started to talk at the same time, then stopped, laughed a little, and stared at each other again.

Garrett took her hand. "I'd like to be the gentleman here and let you go first, but I need you to know a few things."

Moved by the simple fact that he was even there, by just the sound of his voice, she couldn't really find words anyway, so she nodded.

"I let you leave Wildstone without saying some things that needed to be said." His voice was thick, husky, as if he was as moved by the sight of her as she was by him. "Since the helicopter crash, I've made a career of steering clear of real relationships. I've always needed to be the one to leave, before anyone else could leave me."

An involuntary sound of pain and regret escaped her, because after a life of being abandoned by those who loved him—including herself—of course he would have solved the problem in the only way he could. "Garrett, I'm so sorry—"

"Not why I told you that." He cupped her face. "Something changed for me the day you set foot back in Wildstone. Brooke, I want to be the guy who sticks through thick and thin. And I want that with you. I know you think I want a big family, but I want a *quality* family. I can go either way on kids. What I *can't* go either way on is having you in my life."

There was a sound in the doorway behind them, and Brooke turned to find Mindy still standing there, a hand to her heart, eyes shiny. "That's so beautiful," her sister whispered.

Linc appeared behind Mindy, mouthed *sorry* to Garrett and Brooke, and tugged her out of sight.

Garrett hadn't taken his gaze off Brooke. "I'm all in," he said. "Whatever you can give. You're it for me, Bee. You always have been. And I should've told you that before you left. My dad says being a dumbass runs in the family."

"You got him back."

"I did, and this time he's sticking."

She stared up at him, her throat tight. "I want to stick, too. I was coming back to you."

"Yeah?"

"Yeah."

A slow, warm smile curved his mouth. "So we were both prepared to fight for this."

"Very much," she said, needing him to know that. "Did you think you needed the whole town with you to convince me?"

"My dad and Snoop got into my truck and refused to let me leave without them. Then your nosy-ass sister—"

"Hey!" Mindy called out, making it clear she hadn't gone far.

"Want me to kill her?" Brooke asked.

Garrett just shook his head. "Not her fault. I should never have let you get away in the first place."

"Well, I *was* pretty determined to sabotage everything," Brooke told him with a smile.

He entangled their fingers and lifted her hand, pressing it briefly to his chest over his heart before brushing his lips to her palm. "I want to be with you, Bee. I know you believe your life doesn't really lend itself to relationships, but we've been in one since the day we met. I want to be with you wherever you are, here in LA or somewhere on the other side of the planet."

"But your entire life's in Wildstone."

"My life's with you."

She looked into his eyes and saw the truth. He'd seen the very worst of her—her demons, her fears—and he was still there. And she realized he'd done the same, let down his walls with her as well. He was her person, but even more amazing, he wanted her to be his person. "I want to go back to Wildstone," she said. "With you."

A collective gasp sounded but the doorway was empty. Brooke moved there and craned her neck around the corner. Everyone was stuffed together, unabashedly eavesdropping—and she did mean *everyone*: Garrett's dad, her sister and her entire family, all the occupants of the building, it seemed. "You need to get a life!" she said, and then laughed at herself. Apparently, they did have a life and *she* was a part of it, a big part, which made her feel . . . wow. Pretty damn lucky. Shaking her head at herself, she moved back to Garrett and slipped her arms around his neck. "I know it's only been a day, but I miss being outdoors. I miss my family. I miss you," she said softly, going on tiptoe to pepper his jaw with kisses. "I love you, Garrett."

"I know." He smiled. "But it's nice to hear you say it." He sank his fingers into her hair and met her gaze. "I love you, too, Brooke."

She grinned. "I know."

A laugh escaped his chest as everyone crowded back into the

room. Snoop reached them first and jumped up to join the embrace.

Mason hit them next and began climbing up Snoop to get to Garrett. Garrett scooped the kid up and bent again for Maddox. Brooke got Millie.

"Are you going to have kids?" Millie demanded to know.

Garrett smiled into Brooke's face. "Maybe we'll just share you and your brothers."

"You can have one of them!" Millie said. "Take both!"

"Millie," Mindy said.

Millie shrugged, like, *I tried, right?*

Then Mindy and Linc joined the group hug, and Garrett's dad, and Tommy. Cole had made himself scarce, and Brooke understood. "Thanks for being here," she told them all, her tribe, having to swallow past the threat of tears. "Thanks for coming for me."

"Always," Garrett said, his warm eyes and the way he held her, along with the huskiness in his voice, telling her how very much she meant to him.

"Always!" Mindy murmured as well, and Linc nodded.

"Always!" Millie mimicked.

"Always!" Mason yelled.

Maddox tipped his head back and howled.

"So it's unanimous," Garrett said. "To always, for forever and ever."

Brooke's breath caught. "For forever and ever."

EPILOGUE

Two years later

"I'm going to smother you with a pillow."

Summer had hit early and hard, leaving the patrons of Wildstone hot, sweaty, and grumpy as hell. It amused Brooke, because she could remember her years traipsing across the planet to places that had been hotter than hell with no air-conditioning, much less electricity. So she ignored all the bitching and told everyone to suck it up.

Except for Mindy. Whenever Mindy got uncomfortable, Brooke moved heaven and earth to help her. In fact, she stepped out the back door with a tray for her sister, carrying slices of her sweet lemon bread and a fresh pitcher of lemonade, the ice clinking gently against the glass.

"You're an angel." Mindy sighed from where she was stretched out on a lounge chair. "But I've got to pee."

"Again?" Brooke asked in disbelief. "It's been five minutes."

Mindy grimaced and waved a hand for help up, which Brooke gave because her sister was about a million years pregnant.

With Brooke and Garrett's baby.

When Mindy had first offered to be a surrogate for them a year after their wedding, Brooke had been stunned. But the idea was appealing because she had viable eggs—she just couldn't carry a baby.

But Mindy could. And she claimed that Brooke had helped her find her happy and she just wanted to give something back, something Brooke was missing.

It took a minute for Brooke to hoist Mindy out of the chair, and it was no easy feat. She didn't dare grunt with the effort, but Mindy managed a breathless laugh anyway. "I know, I'm the size of a house. Pass the sweet lemon bread. I'm starving."

Brooke eyed her sister's hugely swollen belly with no little amount of alarm. "Where are you going to put it?"

"Funny. Maybe I'm growing two babies in there, you ever think of that?"

Even knowing it wasn't true, Brooke felt herself pale. "That's just mean."

Mindy smirked and then stilled. "Uh-oh."

"Uh-oh, what?"

Water suddenly cascaded down the inside of Mindy's legs. Brooke looked down at it and then at Mindy. "*What's that?*"

"My water breaking." Mindy sighed dramatically. "Dammit!

Hey, hand me that sweet lemon bread before the guys find out I'm in labor and tell the doctor, because she won't let me eat until I push your baby out my vagina."

Brooke stared at her sister in horror. "You're in labor?"

"Yes." She smiled. "And you're in shock, otherwise you would have yelled at me for saying 'vagina.'"

"Stop talking and concentrate on my baby!" Brooke searched her pockets for her phone. "Don't panic, we've got a plan." Suddenly she was the one breathing like *she* was in labor. *One, two, three, four . . . One, two, three, four . . .* "Garrett's going to drive us. Linc will wait for Brittney to come watch the kids and then meet up with us at the hospital."

"Take your time, this baby's certainly going to," Mindy said, her mouth sounding full.

Brooke whipped back around and found her sister shoving sweet lemon bread into her mouth with alarming speed. She snatched the plate away. "The second my baby is out of you, I'm going to smother you with a pillow."

Mindy sighed. "You're not a lot of fun when you're having a baby." But then she gasped, grabbed Brooke in a death grasp, and doubled over. "Oh, shit. I always forget how much it hurts."

"Oh my God. Okay, you've got two choices. Stuff your face, or get to the hospital and get drugs."

"Hospital, please," Mindy said through clenched teeth. "Shit. Definitely yes to the drugs."

Brooke tipped her head back and yelled, *"Garretttttttt!"*

A few seconds later, her husband—she was never going to get tired of thinking that—rounded the corner of the house with a ready smile. "What's up?"

"Mindy's in labor!"

He turned to Mindy, slid his hands in her hair, and pressed his forehead to hers. "You okay?"

"I'd be better with some more sweet lemon bread," Mindy managed.

Garrett grinned and brushed a kiss on her cheek. "I'll make sure you get whatever you need." He turned to Brooke and tugged her into him so hard she had to throw her arms around his neck to stay upright. His smile was huge, his body humming with an energy she'd never felt from him before. "We've made it through our past," he said softly. "And now our future's here. You ready, babe?"

Her heart caught and swelled hard against her ribs.

"Always."

About the author

About the book

Read on

Insights,
Interviews
& More . . .

Meet Jill Shalvis

Susan Zweigle, ZR Studios.com

New York Times bestselling author JILL SHALVIS lives in a small town in the Sierras full of quirky characters. Any resemblance to the quirky characters in her books is . . . *mostly* coincidental. Look for Jill's bestselling, award-winning books wherever romances are sold, and visit her website for a complete book list and daily blog detailing her city-girl-living-in-the-mountains adventures. ◌

Author's Note

For a long time, I've had floating around in my head the story of two sisters, each deeply unsatisfied with where her life had taken her, so much so that they wanted to exchange lives with each other. That's not quite where I took *The Lemon Sisters,* but that was by accident, not design. Because when I started writing *that* story, I realized something.

Both Brooke and Mindy needed a wake-up call, needed to make some changes, but deep, deep down, they didn't covet what the other had. They coveted what *they* had.

But oh my goodness, it took a while to get there. I started the book with Mindy showing up at her sister's door a hot mess, which she basically dumped on Brooke. In real life, I don't have a sister, but if I did, I hope we would have the sort of relationship where I could do exactly that. But I did do that to a boyfriend once. And yes, I was as messed up as Mindy was.

When I was in my early twenties, I was in a car wreck, and my car got totaled. This was way before the days of Uber, and I lived in LA, so having no car was a big problem. My job was a going-nowhere position at barely minimum wage, and I was going to college at night. I was exhausted all ▶

3

Author's Note *(continued)*

the time and poor. I was eating a lot of ramen and peanut butter and apples. I lived in a two-hundred-square-foot studio apartment in Hollywood, and my rent got raised the same week my car was totaled.

I was a hot mess.

But with no sister to go dump my life on, I did the only thing I had available. I showed up at my relatively new boyfriend's apartment and completely lost it, sobbing and trying to talk at the same time. You know what I mean, right? When no one can understand a word you're saying, but you just keep going until you're doing that sort of hiccup-sobbing because you can no longer breathe? No? Just me?

My boyfriend put me on his couch and handed me a strawberry pie. I'll never forget that strawberry pie. I ate a third of it like I was a goldfish. I took a nap. I woke up and ate some real food (handed to me by the boyfriend) and watched TV and then napped some more.

When I got myself together, the boyfriend and his cousin had found me a cheap but decent car to buy. I upgraded my job. Found a better, safer apartment. All with some encouragement and help.

And a year from the day I'd shown up on that poor guy's doorstep, my life had turned itself around. So that old adage that things will get better? True. At least in my case, thankfully.

So it was fun going back to that time in my memories and having my characters sink as low as they could go in order to watch them work their way out of it. Brooke and Mindy took their own routes, of course, and there were a few steps forward and a few steps back, but they had each other to count on— even when they didn't know it.

I hope you enjoy their journey. I sure did. Oh, and what happened to that poor guy from my past? I married him. ☺

Best wishes,
Jill Shalvis ∾

Reading Group Guide

1. Would you ever swap lives with anyone in your family? Why or why not?

2. Would you rather be Brooke or Mindy?

3. Do you think Garrett should have forgiven Brooke for leaving him without telling him why?

4. What are some of the things in your past for which you'd like a do-over?

5. What are some of the ways that our childhoods affect our present/future?

6. Do you think Millie will have an easier time coping with her OCD traits with Brooke in her life?

7. Should Garrett's aunt have contacted him about his father's health, or should it have been Gary's choice?

8. Do you think the years apart have made make the sisters' relationship stronger?

9. Did Mindy overreact to Linc's purchase of the shop?

10. If the helicopter crash hadn't happened, do you think Brooke and Garrett would have stayed together, or would Brooke's wanderlust have eventually driven them apart? Or did they need the time apart after the crash to grow and appreciate each other? ∾

And now,
exclusive to this special Target edition,
read a bonus epilogue to the epilogue,
followed by an extended sneak peek
at Jill Shalvis's next book,

Wrapped Up in You

available everywhere September 2019!

BONUS EPILOGUE TO THE EPILOGUE

Five years later

Garrett climbed out of bed and Brooke admired the view as he rooted out a pair of jeans, pulled them up over the best ass she'd ever seen, and vanished from the bedroom. Since it was still oh dark thirty and she wasn't a crazy morning person like the rest of her people, her eyes drifted shut again.

She awoke some time later—it was light outside—when Snoop trotted his way into the room. He was carrying two tennis balls in his mouth and dropped them on the bed.

Morning presents.

With a sigh, she got out of bed and hugged him tight. "Let me guess. You want to play ball."

His tail started wagging faster.

"Soon. Come on." She made her way out of the room with the dog right on her heels. A minute later, she dropped into a dining room chair and groaned.

"Mornings still not your friend?" Garrett's dad asked, sounding amused where he stood at the range cooking breakfast.

She was pretty sure she managed a grunt.

Garrett eyed her over his iPad and then set it down to nudge a full mug of coffee toward her. It was preloaded with the perfect amount of cream and sugar. Still steaming. How he knew exactly when she'd stagger out of bed and come downstairs every morning, she would never know, but she was incredibly grateful, grabbing for it like she was a single breath away from dying of dehydration. She might have also made an unattractive cavewoman "gimme" sound. ▸

Bonus Epilogue to the Epilogue *(continued)*

He waited until she guzzled it down and the caffeine had begun to flow through her veins to laugh softly at her.

"Show-off," she finally muttered, and let out all her tension with a long sigh. "And God, I love you."

A smile played at the corners of his mouth. "You're welcome."

His smile tugged a helpless one from her. She loved that he knew her so well, that he understood she literally needed the caffeine kick before she was fit for human behaviors like conversing.

And he liked to converse with his wife.

His wife . . .

Yeah, that was never going to get old, she thought with a dopey smile, looking down at the diamond on her finger, wriggling it so it gleamed in the gray morning light.

"Careful, you're going to blind someone with that thing," Garrett's dad said, setting a plate in front of each of them. "I'm off. See you all tonight."

He still liked to spend his days at the campsite with his friends. Now that he'd gotten past chemo and was feeling better, he was enjoying life a whole lot more.

When they were alone in the kitchen, Garrett looked at Brooke. "You sleep okay?" he asked, knowing that for a whole lot of years, she hadn't been able to sleep at all, not without the dreams. Which had thankfully faded over the past few years.

With a nod, she gave him a laughing look. "And you know damn well that last night I was out like the living dead—once you finally let me go to sleep, that is."

His smile turned into a sexy, wolfish grin. "I didn't hear any complaining."

If anything, she'd been begging for more. "What time did Little Bee get up?"

"Five a.m. on the dot."

She groaned. Beatrice, their four-year-old daughter, was a lot of things. Precocious. Smart. Adorable . . . But one thing she was not was a sleeper. "Thanks for getting up with her."

He stood and pulled her from her chair. "You can pay me back later," he said, and gave her a heart-melting kiss.

"Me, too, Daddy—me, too!" Beatrice yelled as she came running into the kitchen, jumping up and down in glee.

Garrett scooped her up and kissed her on the tip of her little nose, making her squeal in delight. She'd inherited Brooke's wild and carefree hair, but other than that, Daddy and his "Little Bee" were the spitting image of each other, and looking at them never failed to warm Brooke's heart.

"You kiss Mommy different than you kiss me," Beatrice said, cupping Garrett's cheeks in her little hands.

"Very true," he said. "That's because we're married."

"Millie says you don't have to be married to kiss like that. She says a girl can kiss anyone she wants."

Millie was twelve going on thirty, and as far as Beatrice was concerned, the sun and the moon hung on everything her older, wiser cousin said.

"Not until she's old," Garrett said.

"How old?" Beatrice asked.

Garrett gave this some serious consideration. "*Old* old," he finally said.

"Is that why you and Mommy kiss each other like that, cuz you're *old* old?"

"Okay," Brooke said with a laugh, and pulled Beatrice from her daddy's arms and set her down. "It's Sunday, the day I promised we'd go on an adventure together, you and me, baby. What do you pick?"

"The bluffs!" Beatrice yelled in excitement. "I'm all ready!" Once again, she was bouncing up and down in excitement. "Snoop says he can't wait."

From where the dog was curled up on his bed in the corner, he thumped his tail in agreement.

Brooke looked outside. It was pouring.

"That's what they make raincoats for, Mommy!"

Brooke slipped into her rain boots by the back door and ▶

Bonus Epilogue to the Epilogue *(continued)*

turned to help Beatrice with hers, but Garrett was already crouched before their daughter, lending a hand. Rising to his full height, he handed Brooke her raincoat and grabbed his.

"You're coming with us?" she asked, surprised.

"You think I'm going to let my two favorite girls go adventuring without me?"

"I thought you wanted to finish working on the spare bedroom."

They had been slowly renovating in between fostering kids short-term. But they'd talked about doing long-term fosters and were working toward that goal.

"What I want for today," Garrett said, "is to be with my favorite girls in the rain." He kept his warm eyes on her. "You ready?"

Feeling suddenly emotional, she nodded and wrapped her arms around him. "Love you."

With a smile, he lowered his head, going in for another kiss, but Beatrice squeezed in between them. "Not again!"

With a laugh, they headed out. Garrett drove, and when they got to the beach, Beatrice was bouncing with uncontained joy. Since she objected to umbrellas, they all pulled on their hoods and walked up the bluffs in the rain, holding hands, Beatrice in the middle, shrieking with delight every time they lifted her up and swung her like a pendulum.

Since no one else was crazy enough to be out in the pouring rain, they had the bluffs to themselves. Brooke watched as Little Bee stomped through every puddle she came across on the way up, a huge smile on her face. At the top, she tilted her head back until her hood fell free. Closing her eyes, she tried to catch raindrops in her mouth until she lost her balance and staggered backward, crashing into her daddy.

Garrett picked her up and placed her on his shoulders, and she laughed some more because now she was even closer to the rain.

Her joy was utterly contagious.

"Put me down, Daddy, I need to chase the rain!"

Garrett obediently set her down. Then he slung an arm around Brooke as they watched their daughter chase the rain.

"I used to be afraid to dream that we'd ever get here," she whispered, so softly that it was barely audible, but he heard her.

Turning his head to her, he rubbed his jaw along hers. "I used to be afraid to dream we wouldn't." Cupping her face, his fingers sank in her wet hair as the rain danced over them. "You were all I ever wanted, Bee. Have to admit, for a while there, I wasn't sure it'd happen."

She went up on tiptoe and kissed him. "I'm a little slow on the uptake sometimes."

His smile was all in his eyes, his mouth serious. "Some things are worth waiting for." ❧

Coming Soon . . .
An Excerpt from

Wrapped Up in You

And now for a sneak peek at *Wrapped Up in You*, the
latest book in Jill Shalvis's *New York Times* bestselling
Heartbreaker Bay series, on sale everywhere September 2019.

CHAPTER 1

Dig Deep

S tay down."

No, she would not stay down. Mostly because Ivy Snow didn't know the meaning of the words. Not once in her hard-knock, scrappy life had she ever "stayed down." So she popped back up, using a spin and a roundhouse kick to level her opponent.

Her kickboxing partner and friend grinned from flat on her back. "That's gotta be worth at *least* a doughnut," Sadie said. "And you're buying."

"Can't," Ivy said, eyeing the time. "I've gotta get to work."

Sadie sat up and yawned. "I've got an hour, which means I'm going back to bed. And if I'm lucky, Caleb'll still be in it."

Caleb was Sadie's fiancé. Ignoring the little spurt of envy at the thought of having someone waiting in bed for her, Ivy hit the locker room to shower and change. Fifteen minutes later, she left the gym at her very least favorite time of the day, that being six a.m., suitably beaten up by her four-times-a-week kickboxing class.

She shivered. It was February in San Francisco, which meant it could be any weather at all. Today it was forty-five degrees, and she'd forgotten her jacket. She was on a budget, a tight one. But it wasn't worth freezing to death for a couple of bucks, so she decided to forgo walking and hopped on a bus rather than turn into a human popsicle.

A guy in a suit and sneakers and holding a huge energy drink took the seat next to her, giving her a not-so-discreet once-over. "Morning," he said. ▸

Yes, she'd just felt a little wistful about not having anyone waiting for her in her bed, but that was fantasy, and Ivy was nothing if not grounded in reality. Especially since she had a habit of going for Mr. Wrong, thanks to a pattern of being attracted to all things bad for her. For someone who prided herself on her sharply honed survival skills, she'd definitely failed herself in the man department. This was in good part thanks to a wanderlust lifestyle and a weakness for sexy grins that promised—and usually delivered—trouble.

But that was all behind her now. She'd promised herself. So she gave the guy a vague not-interested smile and turned away to look out the window. Rude? Maybe. But she was admittedly more than a bit calloused these days and—as every guy she'd ever let get too close had complained—a tough nut to crack. The words *cold* and *scary* had also been thrown around.

She didn't mind. She actually liked it, even as she realized the image went completely against her Disney princess–like moniker, "Ivy Snow." But hey, it wasn't like she'd named herself. Her mother had done that, reportedly on some good prescription meds at the time.

At her stop, she exited the bus and walked the last two blocks to work, getting a little happier with each step because one, exercise was over for the day, and two, she loved her job.

For as long as she could remember, her entire life had been temporary. She'd gone to fifteen different schools before getting her GED at age sixteen. As a result, she was a pro chameleon and excelled at temporary—temporary friends, temporary jobs, temporary life. It had suited her for a long time. Until it didn't.

She'd woken up one day about a year ago and had realized she'd changed. Moving around no longer suited her, and she was over living out of a backpack. So at the dubiously mature age of twenty-eight, she was now trying a new lane. She'd settled in the Cow Hollow District of San Francisco, running a thing called the Taco Truck and living in an apartment that had her name on the lease.

Roots. After a lifetime of running, being invisible, and just barely getting by, she was growing roots. She was going to get the life that until now had only existed for her on TV and in movies. Meaning friends and family, *real* family who'd stick with her through thick and thin. And maybe . . . maybe even someone to love.

It was unnerving that she was actively working toward the very things that had terrified her for most of her life, but she'd decided she would rather be scared shitless than live with regrets. So she'd learned to put a smile on her face, because everyone knew you had to fake it to make it, right?

The Taco Truck was parked in the alley behind the Pacific Pier building. She kept it there at night thanks to the fact that the owner of the building, Spence Baldwin, loved her food. On workdays, she pulled the truck out to the street at the entrance to the building's courtyard, always a gamble because her city permit hadn't yet come through.

She'd just moved the truck out of the alley and parked to set up for the day when her day's deliveries arrived. She received her preordered inventory and eyed the time. Six thirty. She opened at seven sharp, so she got started chopping ingredients, frying up meats, and arranging the makings for the day's menu. *Her* menu. She liked the work. Actually, she loved the work, and her boss wasn't bad, either. She smiled at that as she worked, because she was the boss. She owned the truck.

Okay, so she was making payments on it, but she was actually in the black. Everything about that thought improved her day on the spot. Today she wasn't going to worry about bills or permits. Or anything. She was going to enjoy herself, her food, and her new goals.

She turned around in her small but mighty space of seventy-five square feet. It was here where she worked her magic, making what she liked to think were the most delicious tacos in the Bay Area. It wasn't an easy job. She spent just as much time prepping and being a mechanic as she did being a chef. And then there ▶

was the ordering and buying of all the necessary supplies, not to mention the bookkeeping, which often kept her up late into the night.

Her work was never done, but she was good with that. Hell, she was great with that. After spending most of her life at the mercy of others, she thrived on being independent and having no one tell her what to do or when to do it.

She was still prepping when she heard voices outside. She handled breakfast and lunch on her own, and then her part-time helper, Jenny, came in the afternoons to handle the dinner crowd. For now, Ivy still had her CLOSED sign up, but the voices stopped right outside her truck. Men, at least two of them, possibly three. With a sigh, she opened the serving window and stuck her head out.

A trio of extremely hot guys dressed in running gear and looking hungry as hell glanced up from the menu board posted on the side of her truck. Ivy knew two of them, Caleb and Jake, both currently off the market, so she felt free to give them her flirtiest smile and shake her head. "Sorry, boys, not open for another twenty minutes."

Jake, who in spite of his wheelchair was one of the strongest, most stoic, badass men she knew, returned her flirty smile while upping it another factor, which she knew was just a ploy. He'd been dating someone for over a year now.

"But you make the best food in the city," he said sweetly, as if Ivy could be swayed by sweet. "And we've all gotta be at work by seven."

Caleb stood at his side. He was a friend and also a savior to Ivy, as he'd helped her navigate the purchase of her truck after dealing with the previous owner had become tricky. "I'm pretty sure you once said you owed me a favor," he said, also sweetly, and also always the negotiator.

Knowing the venture capitalist could talk anyone into just about anything, she laughed and gave in. "Fine. Figure out what you want, and make it quick. But then we're even, Caleb."

They weren't even. She owed him much more than an early breakfast, and they both knew it.

Having gotten his way as he always did, he smiled. "The usual for me."

"Me, too," Jake said.

Ivy nodded and turned her attention to the third man.

She'd never seen him before; she most certainly would have remembered. Like Caleb and Jake, he was in running gear that fit his leanly muscled bod—one that he held in a way that suggested military or cop. The always-on-alert, scared little kid she'd once been sent an automatic warning to her brain. *Danger, Will Robinson!*

But she was no longer helpless, she reminded herself. She no longer had to pretend to be tough and brave. She *was* tough and brave. So she kept her smile in place, forcing herself to relax. She had nothing to hide. Everything she did these days was on the up and up—she'd made sure of it.

And it wasn't exactly a hardship to look at him. His smile certainly was heart-stopping as he added his charm to both Caleb's and Jake's. And there *was* considerable charm. He had dark eyes and dark hair cut short, and in spite of his smile, when those eyes met hers, they gave nothing of his thoughts.

Yep, cop, she thought. *Too bad . . .*

ALL KEL O'DONNELL knew was that his body ached like a son of a bitch. Pushing it for a five-mile full-out run hadn't been the smartest of ideas after what he'd been through. But his more immediate problem was that if he didn't get food, and fast, his stomach was going to eat itself.

The woman in the taco truck turned to him for his order. "And you?" she asked, her voice slightly amused, as if life wasn't to be taken too seriously, especially while ordering tacos.

But he was taking this *very* seriously, as his hunger felt soul-deep. "What do you suggest?" he asked. ▶

19

An Excerpt from *Wrapped Up in You* (continued)

Her light green eyes slid to the menu written on the side of the truck, the menu she'd probably written herself.

Not one to waste words then. Something they had in common. "I mean, what's good?" he asked.

This caused twin groans from his cousin Caleb and their longtime friend Jake, which Kel ignored.

Not his server, though. She quirked a single brow, the small gesture making him feel more than he had in months. Certainly since his life had detonated several months ago, when he'd chased after a suspect and then been hit by the getaway car, getting himself punted a good fifteen feet into the air. No worries— the asphalt pavement had broken his fall, which was when he'd realized he'd been duped by a dirty cop. And not any dirty cop, but a longtime friend and also his partner, nearly costing him his career.

But hell, at least his life wasn't on the line this time, or his livelihood. It was just a pretty woman giving him some cute, sexy 'tude while waiting for him to choose between avocado and bacon tacos and spicy green eggs and ham tacos.

She glanced over at his running partners.

"You're going to have to excuse my dumbass cousin, Ivy," Caleb said. "Kel hasn't lived in San Francisco for a long time and doesn't know that you've got the best food truck in all of Cow Hollow. Hell, in the whole Bay Area."

"It's true," Jake said, and nudged Kel, and since Jake was in a wheelchair, Kel got the nudge right in the back of the knee and just about went down.

"Everything on the menu, and I do mean *everything*," Jake told him, "is gold. It'll all melt in your mouth and make you want to drop to your knees and beg Ivy here to marry you, trust me."

At this, Ivy sent Jake the sweetest smile Kel had ever seen. Then those compelling eyes were back on him, the sweet completely gone.

All right. So clearly he was rusty at this whole being human thing, but given the past six months of hell, this wasn't a surprise. He tried a slow, easy smile that had gotten him whatever he'd wanted in the past. "What do *you* like best?" he asked her.

Jake just grinned. "Aw, man, she's gonna eat you up and spit you out. I'm so happy."

Caleb just winced.

Ivy leaned out her serving window a little bit, bracing her weight on her elbows. She had hair the color of fire, a stunning pile of red held back by an elvish headband that left a few strands around her face, framing it. Her apron read I DON'T WANNA TACO 'BOUT IT. "What do I like best?" she echoed, a small smile playing on her lips.

"Yeah." Just looking at her, he could feel himself relax for the first time in . . . way too long. Something about her did that to him. Instant chemistry. He hadn't felt it often in his life, and it always ended up a train wreck, so why the hell he felt relaxed, he had no idea. But it had him flashing another smile. "How about you pick for me?"

A smile curved her mouth. "Fair warning—I like things hot."

"I *love* things hot," he said.

Caleb and Jake both shook their heads.

"I didn't think he was stupid," Jake murmured to Caleb.

"Shh. I don't want to miss him getting his ass handed to him."

Ivy just cocked her head at Kel. "Think you can handle the heat?" she asked.

"Oh yeah."

"Five minutes." And she shut the window on them.

Kel followed the guys to one of the two picnic tables at the entrance to the courtyard, where they sat to wait for their food.

Caleb looked at Kel and shook his head. "Man, as much as I enjoy seeing you get your ego squashed, I feel duty bound to warn you: Whatever's making you smile, it's never going to happen. Ivy's not the girl you have fun with and walk away from. And plus, she hates cops." ▶

"Agreed," Jake said. "You've got a better shot at stealing Sadie away from Caleb. And good luck with that. Your cousin's woman is batshit crazy over him, God knows why."

Caleb just smiled, apparently not feeling the need to defend his relationship.

Kel was happy for him. Very happy. Caleb hadn't given his heart away . . . ever. And for good reasons, which Kel had hated for him because he was a good guy. "About time you found someone who deserves you."

Caleb met his gaze. "I like having you here," he said quietly, kind enough to leave out the tone of recrimination. What he didn't add was that it'd been a long time, too long—which had been all Kel's fault. He'd spent the first ten years of his life here in the city, he and his sister and his parents. They'd lived next door to his aunt and her kids, including Caleb. Kel hadn't realized it at the time, but they'd all been poor as dirt, because his parents had always managed to make it seem like they'd had everything they'd needed.

Then his mom had destroyed the happy illusion with a single, shattering mistake, creating a huge rift none of them had recovered from. Two years later had come yet another blow. His dad had died, and Kel and his older sister, Remy, had gone to Idaho to be raised by their grandparents.

It'd sucked.

"You see Remy yet?" Caleb asked.

Kel's sister had moved back here to San Francisco after getting married last year. And no, he hadn't seen her yet. And yes, he was stalling.

"Your mom?" Caleb asked.

Kel slid him a look.

Caleb raised his hands. "Hey, just asking."

"Uh-huh. Do you ask all your employees such personal questions?"

"No, just my brother."

"I'm your *cousin*."

"You're my *brother*," Caleb said with meaning.

Kel sighed and looked over at Jake.

Jake shrugged. "He likes to adjust facts to suit him. But you knew that already."

Ivy came out of the truck with three baskets. She served Jake first, then Caleb, and finally Kel. She handed him his basket and stood there at his side, a tiny pixie of a woman in that sassy apron, elvish headband, and painted-on jeans, faded to a buttery softness with a few ragged holes that he somehow knew were authentic and not purchased that way. Her boots were serious and kickass, and because he was a very sick man, they turned him on.

Since she was clearly going nowhere until he tried her food, he took a bite of what looked like the most amazing breakfast taco he'd ever seen and . . . almost died. It was *very* spicy, but also the best thing he'd ever tasted.

Ivy smiled at him. "Still think you can handle the heat?"

Jake and Caleb were doubled over, laughing their asses off. "I'm not a cop," he managed to wheeze, holding her gaze while he took another bite. And another. Holy shit, yeah, he was going to eat her food the entire three weeks he was here. If he lived that long.

"He's a sheriff and ranch owner in Idaho," Caleb said helpfully. "So . . . *kind of* a cop."

"Also kind of a cowboy," Jake added.

Kel rolled his watering eyes. His grandparents had left him and Remy their ranch, which he oversaw, mostly by paying others to handle the day-to-day operations because his dad job was more like a 24/7 job. "I'm just a guy on vacay," he croaked out. The more accurate term would have been assigned/medical leave, but hell if he was going to share that, or the fact that his still healing broken ribs ached like a bitch, as did the deep bone bruising he'd suffered down the entire right side of his body from being pitched into the air by a moving vehicle.

Caleb snorted. "You don't do vacay. As evidenced by the fact that you agreed to work for me for the entire three weeks ▶

you're here. I needed him," he said to Ivy. "He's got serious skills.
He's going to manage security on several large projects, including
my most recently acquired building, the one being renovated
into condos." He looked at Kel. "Ivy's going to buy one with her
brother, who's an antiquities specialist. It's a great investment,"
he said like a proud parent, even though at thirty-two, he couldn't
have been more than five years older than Ivy.

"Actually, it might just be me investing," Ivy said. "Brandon
just got into that smokin' deal on the East Coast I was telling you
about."

"The auction house job."

"Yes, and it's going to keep him busy for a while, so . . ."
She shrugged. "I told him I'd go after this myself."

"That's too bad," Caleb said. "Was looking forward to meeting
him."

There'd been something to Ivy's tone that was off. Either she
was lying or stretching the truth—both things were automatic
alarms for Kel. But his eyes were still watering and his tongue
was numb, otherwise he might have joined the conversation.

Ivy reached out as if to take away his basket, but he held firm
to it and kept eating. He was starting to sweat, and he couldn't
feel his lips, but he also couldn't get enough.

"Okay, cowboy, it's your funeral," she said, and he couldn't tell
if she was impressed or horrified.

A few more people were milling around her truck now, and she
eyed her watch.

"They start lining up earlier every day," Caleb said.

"Hey, Ivy," one of the guys who was waiting called out.
"The fuzz! They're coming around the corner!"

"Crap!" Ivy ran toward her truck, yelling to the people
standing in line, "I'll be back in ten minutes. If you wait and save
my spot, I'll give you a discount!" And then she slapped
the window and door closed and roared off down the street.

Two minutes later a cop car drove by slowly, but kept going.

When it was gone, the group of people who'd been lining up all stepped into the empty parking spot Ivy had left.

Ten seconds later, a car came along and honked. The driver wanted the spot.

No one budged.

The window on the car rolled down and a hand emerged, flipping everyone the bird.

This didn't make anyone move, either, and finally the car drove off.

"What the hell?" Kel asked.

"She's not supposed to be on the street before seven," Jake said.

"I'm working on getting her a city permit," Caleb said. "They're extremely hard to get."

"But . . . those people are blocking the street. They could get a ticket."

"Thought you weren't a cop," Caleb said, looking amused.

Kel shook his head and went back to his tacos, and for a guy who believed in the law, when the incredible burst of flavors hit his tongue, he thought maybe he could understand the flagrant disregard of it in this one case. ▶

CHAPTER 2

Go Hard or Don't Go at All

That night, Ivy stayed up late paying the bills that couldn't wait any longer, setting aside the ones that could, playing around with her credit card, doing the monthly money dance between bank accounts. Just the insurance policies alone—general liability, business owner, commercial auto, self-employed health care—nearly killed her. But it was also an undeniable thrill to be legit.

For someone who'd grown up in dumpy trailers and motels across the South, living off her mom's cash tips from singing in lounges and crap bars, it was certainly surreal.

She even had a savings account, which made her smile every time she thought about it. Savings! She'd been in the city for just over a year now, living off next to nothing in order to put away every spare penny. She had eighteen grand, a fortune for her. But she was still two grand short for the down payment on a condo in Caleb's newly acquired and renovated building. The twenty thousand was only half the required down, but there was a first-time homebuyers program in play to ensure equality in housing, and the mortgage broker—Caleb—was going to match her down payment. The agreement was that she'd work off that debt by catering all of his business events, of which there were many. This was a good deal for both of them. Ivy didn't have to put up cash she didn't have, and Caleb was guaranteed her most excellent catering, if she said so herself.

For the first time in her life, she felt ridiculously proud of herself. She was so close to having it all together. She wanted that condo. *Needed* that condo. It would be 1,600 square feet of home, and it even came with a parking space for her truck.

Right now, the owner of the Pacific Pier building allowed her to park overnight in the alley, which was like having a golden ticket. But that was temporary, and playing Russian roulette with the parking police wasn't easy. Plus, she really wanted to have the truck more safely stowed at night, because she came from a world where your possessions could be taken away at any moment if you didn't clutch them tight to your chest. Having it so far from her apartment was a constant source of stress. Other than her slowly growing savings, the truck was all she had. And both were thanks to the business plan she'd painstakingly put together when she'd taken over the taco truck.

She'd come so far. Granted, she still had a long way to go, but pride filled her. And as usual, right on the heels of that was an odd sense of loneliness, because she didn't have anyone to show off to. Her mom was much more interested in her next gig than her children, so contact was extremely infrequent. As for Ivy's brother, he was sweet and charming and . . . utterly incorrigible. He was one of those guys who could use his powers for good or bad. He'd tried to choose good. It just hadn't worked out for him. It was always about the next get-rich-quick scheme. And unfortunately, along with those came trouble. She'd had to distance herself.

It'd hurt, because in spite of all his faults, Brandon was blood, and he cared about her in his own way. Which wasn't always the right way. Or any sort of legal way. The biggest problem they had was that she couldn't trust him to keep her safe or to put her first in a bad situation—which she only ever landed in when he was involved. Some of these memories were bad enough that they still haunted her.

So instead of wishing for her family to change, she'd gone west without a forwarding address and made her own connections. She'd made friends here and was happy. The only ▶

thing that kept her from enjoying her life fully was knowing she'd lied to everyone about her past.

But that was a problem for another day.

Leaning back in her kitchen chair, she looked around. Her apartment was a third-floor walk-up, and she used the word *apartment* loosely. The building had once upon a time been a single-family dwelling, and when the owners had renovated each of the floors into individual units back in the 1930s, they'd called the attic a "generous loft."

The 250 square feet hardly qualified for generous anything, but she had a roof that leaked only in big rainstorms, decent electricity—if she didn't run her toaster and her blow dryer at the same time—and could almost always get hot water for a good three to four whole minutes at a time.

But the best part of the deal was that the landlord, a sweet old lady named Evelyn, adored her and gave her a huge discount on the monthly rent—in exchange for leftovers from Ivy's truck every day.

Tonight that had been brisket tacos, and Evelyn had been thrilled. She'd talked Ivy into having a seat and joining her as she'd eaten, telling stories about her kids and her kids' kids . . . none of whom, at least that Ivy could tell, ever came and saw her.

Evelyn also always made Ivy tell her a story about herself as well, and tonight was no different. Evelyn had wanted to hear about Ivy's famed brother, so Ivy had drawn a deep breath and did what she did.

She told stories.

She was good at it; she'd been making up stories about her family since she was little, each different, each more exciting than the last, and all as far from the truth as she could possibly get. Because the truth wasn't a story; it was a nightmare. Mentally sifting through a long list of fantasies, Ivy told her landlord all about Brandon the artist, who was living in Paris at the moment, becoming famous for his incredible oil landscapes.

28

She left off the fact that he peddled stolen art instead of creating it, and it hadn't been Paris, France, but Paris, Texas.

Now, in the attic with her lights dimmed and the only sounds the creaking of the old bones of the building, Ivy shook her head and clicked on one of her open tabs to view her savings balance.

Still there, and she felt the smile curve her lips. A few more weeks and she'd be able to talk to Caleb about getting the paperwork started for the condo. Her condo. It was almost unreal to her, given how she'd grown up in a string of motels, each more roach infested than the last, because Brandon, ever the fun-loving, trouble-seeking stoner of their family, had burned down the one halfway nice trailer they'd had.

Ivy had left "home" at age sixteen to strike out on her own, couch surfing or living out of her car, working at whatever jobs she could get, mostly in bar kitchens, which was where she'd learned to cook. Cooking had given her purpose and, now, a job she loved.

With a smile, she changed venues, moving to her office desk, which was really her bed. She fluffed her pillows behind her and stretched out her legs. She considered going to sleep. It was late, midnight, and she had to be up at five a.m. for kickboxing class.

Ugh.

Well-known secret: Ivy hated kickboxing class. She hated the gym. She hated to work out at all, but she hated the way her clothes fit when she didn't do it even more. Still, she might've taken the extra hour to sleep if her exercise app didn't text her a notification each day with a picture of a guy working out, captioned: *This is Jack. Jack got up on time for his workout. Be more like Jack . . .*

Yes, her exercise app shamed her into getting up. And because she knew herself, she'd doubled down and bought a gym pass, knowing she was far too frugal not to go. So she'd go and get beat up and pay for the pleasure.

It was a part of her whole growing roots plan. When she'd first come to the city, she'd been oddly lonely and sad. She'd ▶

An Excerpt from *Wrapped Up in You* (continued)

gone to Google instead of a therapist she couldn't afford and had learned that exercise helped with depression. She still hated the gym. *Hated.* But she was a whole lot less sad.

So she tried to get to sleep, but couldn't. Something was niggling at her. Had she left something on in her truck? Had she left something plugged in? Had Jenny locked it up properly? She'd swear the answers to those questions were all yes, but . . . she couldn't shake the feeling.

There'd been many times in her life when her instincts were all she had, and they'd never failed her. The first time they'd kicked in, she'd been fourteen years old, Brandon sixteen. Since their mom worked nights, Brandon had been in charge. He'd had some new friends over to play darts in the yard—a hustle, of course. On a good night, Brandon could earn several hundred in cash.

But halfway through the evening, Ivy's instincts had kicked in, the hair on the back of her neck standing straight up. Not questioning it, she'd climbed out a back window of the trailer and huddled in the bushes, listening as some of the guys who'd become bored with losing money to Brandon had come inside to "have some fun with the hottie little sister."

Brandon had been furious when he'd found out and promised not to bring them around again. And he hadn't. But that didn't mean the trouble stopped. A year later, this time in a seedy motel in Florida, Brandon had been selling pot out of their single room, using the bathroom as his "office." He'd been open for business when Ivy had gotten the same hinky feeling, complete with the hair standing straight up on the back of her neck. Again, she'd sneaked out a window. She'd made it across the yard when the police had come, sirens screaming, into the lot and confiscated all of their possessions *and* Brandon.

Lesson learned. She never ignored her instincts now, never. Which meant she shut off her laptop, locked up, and headed down the stairs. It was only two miles to her truck. Normally, she'd just hoof it over there, because calling a Lyft was a luxury she'd given up for her saving account's sake. But no matter how badass she liked to think she was, she wasn't stupid. No way was she going to risk walking that far alone this late at night. Though it killed her, she opened her Lyft app.

Fifteen minutes later, she got out of the Lyft at the southeast corner of the building that housed O'Reilly's Pub. The place was packed and thriving. Music and laughter poured out of there as she walked by and stopped at the front of the alley to eye her truck.

All looked well. But unable to shake her weird feeling, she moved closer, and then she was running toward it, because the back door was cracked, the lock broken and dangling uselessly. ▶

CHAPTER 3

Leave It All in the Room

K el heard something—a female cry, maybe? It indicated fear, and he immediately ran in its direction, his eyes adjusting from the pub, where he'd been with Caleb.

They'd met up with a bunch of his cousin's friends for dinner and drinks, including Sadie, Caleb's lovely significant other. It'd been sort of a welcome-back-to-the-city thing, and although Kel had planned to lay low for the duration of his visit, being out tonight had been good. Caleb had toasted and roasted him with "Kel the Cowboy Does the City" jokes, cracking himself up.

None of it had bothered Kel—it'd all been in good fun—and sitting there surrounded by Caleb's tight-knit group of friends and the exciting energy of the city itself made his own not-great reality feel a million miles away.

He'd left San Francisco when he was twelve years old, and it hadn't been under the best of circumstances. He hadn't given it much playing time in his brain in the nearly two decades since, but being back had definitely opened the floodgates.

Suddenly, the pub had gotten too loud for him, and he'd left just after midnight, escaping to the courtyard attached to the pub. It was peaceful out here, and he took in the incredible architecture of the old building, the corbeled stone and exposed iron trusses, the large picture windows of the retail shops, the cobblestone beneath his feet, and the huge centerpiece fountain where idiots across the city came to toss a coin and wish for love.

And all of it was decorated for the holidays with garlands of evergreen entwined with twinkling white lights in every doorway and frame, along with a huge Christmas tree near the street entrance, making it look like a Christmas card. It'd rained earlier, so the cobblestone pavers were wet and shiny.

He'd stood there looking up at a sky that was vastly different from the one he had in Idaho, all the old memories stirred up and causing havoc in his head, the ones he'd thought he'd put to rest a long time ago.

That's when he'd heard the cry and then muttered cursing. He ran down the courtyard, passing the pet shop, the coffee shop, the tattoo place, the hundred-plus-year-old fountain in the middle, the wedding shop, the paint and wine place, the stationery store . . . and ended up at the alley opening to the street. There he turned in a slow circle, looking for . . . what, he had no idea.

He saw Ivy's taco truck. He'd noticed it earlier when he'd walked into the pub with Caleb. Now, catching movement in the alley, he stepped closer. The back door to the truck was open, and he could see the beam of a flashlight moving around inside.

Pulling his gun was automatic, and he stepped closer, catching a shadow of a figure inside. "Hands where I can see them," he called out.

The figure jerked, gasped, and then whirled around. In the ambient lighting, he immediately recognized her.

Ivy.

He slid his gun away. "You okay?"

"Hell, no, I'm not okay! Are you kidding me? You just gave me a freaking heart attack! What's wrong with you?" She had a hand to her heart. She'd startled hard, and for the beat before she'd recognized him, there'd been real fear in her eyes, something that had quickly turned into pissed off.

"What are you doing here?" she demanded.

"I was at the pub." He took in her appearance. Camo leggings, untied boots, huge black sweatshirt that threatened to swallow her whole and hit her at her knees. No makeup. Eyes stricken, mouth grim, her wild hair loose around her pale face. And he got the feeling whatever had brought her down here, it'd been ▶

without warning. "I'm going to ask you again," he said quietly. "Are you okay?"

She exhaled a long, shaky breath and then shook her head as she turned away from him. "Do you always carry a gun when you go out, Cowboy?"

"Yes."

"Always?"

"Yes."

"How about during the day?"

He gave her a look, wasted because she still had her back to him. "Still yes."

"How about when you're in bed with a woman?"

He knew what she was doing. Stalling. Also clearly trying to annoy him. But he'd been to hell and back, and on the return trip he'd learned how to shut himself off enough that he didn't get easily annoyed. "Do you always answer a question with another question?"

Again she shook her head. She moved to an industrial refrigerator and dropped to her knees in front of the low pullout freezer. When she went through the drawer, she made a sound of distress.

He was at her side in a second. "What is it?"

"Someone broke in. Took some money. Left my refrigerator and freezer door open, and it's been just long enough that nearly everything is ruined."

"Why did you have cash in here? And how much was taken?"

"It was petty cash, locked up in my cash drawer, and it was around a hundred bucks, which maybe doesn't seem like a lot to you, but to me it might as well be a grand."

Kel pulled out his phone. This got him a reaction.

She whipped around, eyes wide. "What are you doing?"

"Calling the cops."

The look on her face defied description. Incredulity and maybe instant wariness. "No, you're not."

Okay, definite wariness. Cops made her nervous. Interesting. "You have a problem with the police, Ivy?"

She tossed up her hands. "Why are you even here? *Go away.*"

He wasn't going to do that, for a bunch of reasons, the least being that she could be in danger. "Do you have something to hide?"

Ignoring him and his question, she pulled her phone from her pocket and sent a text. Then she went about turning on the lights. When a text came in, she read it, sighed, and slipped the phone away.

"Who was that?"

Ivy looked at him as if surprised he was still there. "My employee, Jenny. She closed up tonight like always and said everything was fine when she left, no problems."

She began methodically taking everything out of the fridge and freezer. When he tried to help, she "accidentally" elbowed him in the gut.

"Oops, sorry," she said, sounding anything but. "Stand back. Better yet, get out."

"Not going to happen."

She turned to him with hands on hips and blew a strand of hair from her face. "Why not?" she asked in exasperation.

"Because someone violated your personal space." He softened his voice. "And you seem shaken by that, as anyone would be. You shouldn't be alone."

"I'll call someone."

"Okay," he said, calling her bluff.

She stared at him and then rolled her eyes. "I can't, okay?"

"Why not?"

"It's too late."

"A friend won't care," he said. "Neither will a boyfriend." He hadn't meant to say that, but she was both the most infuriating and yet fascinating woman he'd ever met.

Her gaze shuddered and again she turned away. "Even if I ▶

called the police, they can't do much. It was just some light vandalism, and missing cash is impossible to trace."

He knew this to be true, frustrating as it was. "If you're not going to call anyone, I'm staying."

"Fine." She gathered up her red waves of hair and tamed it into submission with a hairband she'd had around her wrist. Then she slapped a pair of latex gloves against his chest and donned her own pair. "You can make yourself useful."

Kel called a 24/7 locksmith, who showed up and replaced the lock, while he and Ivy dumped what had to be hundreds of dollars' worth of food, since they couldn't be sure it was still safe to serve.

Kel paid the locksmith and in doing so pissed off Ivy. He hadn't meant to step on her pride, but he had the feeling she was already stretched thin, and the late-night cost of having the guy come out hadn't been cheap.

"I'm going to pay you back," Ivy said stiffly.

He hated that she was acting like an injured animal with her back up to the wall, so he did his best to give her lots of space. Not easy in the close quarters, but he deferred to her for what she wanted done and then quietly followed her example without pushing.

And he wanted to push. He wanted to know why she felt so . . . alone. Why she didn't trust anyone. But she wasn't exactly an open book, so he worked alongside her, meticulously scrubbing everything down.

"People rave about your food," he said.

She looked up, and he could tell the statement gave her pleasure, but she kept her cool. "Everyone loves a good taco."

"Do you do it all yourself?"

"I've got part-time help. Jenny's a grad student and helps serves the dinner crowd. But I do all the food stuff."

"You're a good cook." He cocked his head. "Or is the right word *chef*?"

She grimaced. "'Chef' seems a bit fancy for what I do."

"I've gone to upscale restaurants that don't come even close to what you manage to create inside this truck."

She bit her lower lip as if to hold back her smile, but those green eyes lit up. It was nice to see the spark back. He hated what the break-in had done to them, leaving them hollow and haunted.

"How did you learn to cook?" he asked.

"My earliest memories are of rifling through what was available to eat and making it seem better than it was," she said, and shrugged. Her head was down now; she was concentrating on scrubbing the counter as if her life depended on it. "I was four, maybe?" She shrugged again. "Turns out, I like to eat."

His chest had gone tight, and he had questions, so many questions, but he worked at keeping his mouth shut because he wanted her to keep talking.

"As I got older," she continued, "I realized I was good at it."

"Where did you grow up?" he asked, having detected a very slight, maybe southern accent in certain words.

"We moved around a lot, mostly the South, though. My first jobs were cooking in bars. Eventually I worked my way up to restaurants, honing my skills. But once a city rat, always a city rat. Staying in one place made me itchy and anxious. I liked being on the move, never settling down."

"You could work at any five-star restaurant in the city," Kel said.

She shook her head. "I'm not that good."

"Yes, you are."

Their gazes met and held. He'd have sworn the air shimmered and heated, but that was most likely either exhaustion or wishful thinking.

She looked away first. "I've always liked being able to move around when I want to. Running a food truck's the natural progression for me." She smiled. "Old habits die hard and all that."

She'd carefully left out any mention of family, and while he ▶

wanted to know so much more, he didn't want to spook her, either. "You've got a brother. Older? Younger?"

"Brandon's two years older." She was turned away from Kel now, still scrubbing. "He was fond of eating, too, so he was happy that one of us was willing to cook." She paused a moment. "He was the dessert king, though. We had quite the sweet tooth, and that was his job. Getting the sweets."

Her voice hadn't changed, but there was something off about her body language. It was defensive and didn't match her casual voice, and he realized it was the same way she'd acted when Caleb had mentioned her brother that morning. Wishing he could see her face, he asked, "What about your parents?"

She shrugged. "My dad was never around, and my mom worked nights singing in bar lounges and slept during the day."

"So you're self-taught," he said, and she laughed, although he wasn't sure it was with true mirth.

"Most definitely self-taught. How about you?" she asked, turning the tables on him. "Do you cook?"

"If I have to," he said, making her laugh again, which he enjoyed. "Not while I'm here, though. I'm staying with Caleb. His girlfriend, Sadie, has been cooking. My cousin's spoiled rotten and doesn't even know it."

"Oh, he knows it. Sadie's great."

"You know her?"

She nodded. "I was invited to the pub tonight, but I had work to do. You're here on vacation?" she asked, changing the subject. "And to work with Caleb?"

Not vacation. More like a leave of absence while his superiors pored over his last case, the one case in all the years he'd served in law enforcement to go bad. They'd decide his fate, which, for the record, he hated. "I've got two weeks off, and Caleb nagged me to come out here." His good humor faded some as he thought of that, of how, upon going back, his life could go one of two ways.

"To handle security on the new building," she said. "Because

Archer Hunt and his investigations and security company, who'd normally handle this, aren't available."

"You know a lot about Caleb."

"Everyone in this building are friends and coworkers. And most of them gossip like middle schoolers." She shook her head. "There aren't many secrets here."

"I'm getting that," Kel said. "I'm putting together security teams to manage and handle Caleb's new buildings. That and setting up the security systems, getting them in place to run smoothly after I'm gone. Caleb put some temporary contract workers in place to cover everything, but he needs someone in charge."

She met his gaze. "And you're good at being in charge."

A statement, not a question, and he was pretty sure it wasn't a compliment of any sort, so he did his best to look harmless and innocent.

With a snort, she went back to work.

Okay, so she wasn't easily fooled. And she was most definitely not a slacker. It was two hours before she was satisfied they'd cleaned and sterilized everything properly. Then she took out a small chalkboard, wiped it clean, and wrote: CLOSED FOR BREAKFAST, BUT WILL OPEN AT 11 FOR LUNCH. She hung it on the closed serving window.

"I'll need the morning to restock," she explained as they exited the trailer into the chilly night.

"And maybe to sleep," he said, noticing the time.

She shrugged, like sleep wasn't as important as her job.

He could understand that. He'd made his job more important than his life for years.

San Francisco never closed its eyes. Even at three in the morning, the city was hopping. Traffic flowing. People moving on the streets. With a bone-weary sigh, Ivy turned to the new lock on her truck. She struggled with it a moment, so he moved in close to help, once again making her jerk in surprise.

"Seriously," she snapped. "Stop sneaking up on me." ▶

Her fingers were freezing. He pulled his gloves from his jacket pocket and handed them to her.

"I'm not taking your gloves," she said, shoving her hands into her sweatshirt pocket.

"Not taking," he said. "Borrowing."

Her shoulders slowly lowered from where they'd been up at her ears. "Okay, thanks," she said, almost begrudgingly, making him laugh. "What?" she asked, eyes narrowed.

"You're as prickly as a porcupine."

She cocked her head. "Is that something you say on your ranch in Idaho?"

So she had been listening to their breakfast conversation earlier. Interesting. With another woman, he might've taken that as a sign of interest. With this woman, he had no idea. "It's something you say anywhere," he said. "Especially when it's true."

"I'm not a big people person," she admitted in a tone that said, *Sorry not sorry.* "People are often my biggest pet peeve." She looked at him as if he might say something about that.

"Hey," he said. "I get it."

"What's your biggest pet peeve?"

He thought about that. "I guess being lied to. Gets me every time."

She didn't say anything to this, and he eyed her taco truck. "And you're sure you don't want to call—"

"I'm sure."

"A friend might be good about now," he said. "I know Sadie, or any of the women in that very close-knit group, would want to be here for you."

"It's fine. I'm fine. Someone just needed cash and food and got sloppy. It's all cleaned up, no need to bother anyone about it."

He disagreed, but he knew enough about her already to know that pushing her into doing something she didn't want to do would only make her close off further. "Come on, you look done in. I'll walk you to your car."

She shook her head.

"You don't have a car," he said.

"I have a taco truck."

He smiled. "For which I'm incredibly grateful, since your food's amazing. How did you get here?"

"Lyft." She pulled out her phone, but he covered her hand with his. "I'll drive you."

She looked at him for a long beat, her hood up now, covering her gorgeous hair, her face not quite as pale, those eyes seeming to see right into him. Finally, she nodded, and he had no idea why he felt as if he'd just won the lottery. ▶

CHAPTER 4

Rise Up and Take the Challenge

Kel led Ivy to his truck, where he held open the door for her, waiting until she'd buckled up. When he walked around the front of the vehicle and slid behind the wheel a moment later, he felt the weight of her gaze. "Something on your mind?" he asked.

"Who taught you to be so polite?"

He laughed. He couldn't help it. His grandma would be laughing her ass off right now as well.

"Is something funny?" she asked a little stiffly. "And I take it back, by the way. You're not so polite after all."

"My grandparents practically had to beat manners into me," he said. "They'd be very amused to hear you say you think I'm polite."

"Your grandparents?" she asked. "Not your parents?"

"My dad died when I was twelve. My sister and I were sent to Idaho to be raised by our grandparents. They're both gone now."

Her smile faded. "I'm sorry. What about your mom?"

He concentrated on the road as he pulled into the street. "Where's your place?"

"The Tenderloin," she said, and gave him the address. "Are you not answering about your mom on purpose?"

"Yes."

She smiled at that, and he relaxed.

"I like it when you do that," he said.

"What?"

"Smile."

She rolled her eyes and looked out the window.

They didn't speak again, just drove through the city, lit within an inch of its life for the holidays, with festive garlands and twinkling lights on every block.

Then the neighborhood changed. The decorations vanished, as did pride of ownership, each street more run-down than the last.

Ivy had him stop at a very old, possibly falling off its axis Victorian that had seen better days—like five decades ago. It'd clearly been broken up into a few apartments, one per floor. He counted three floors and what was possibly an attic. He didn't like the street and layout, and he especially didn't like the bushes and shrubbery that were overgrown and too close to the house. The ground floor was a security nightmare. Someone could climb into any window virtually undetected. The top floor was just as bad, because there were gussets strengthening the angle of the structure that could easily be used to climb like a ladder up the corner of the place. "Tell me you don't live on the first or the top floor."

"I don't live on the first level."

He looked at her.

"But I do live on the top floor. It's the attic."

Shit.

Ivy unhooked her seat belt. "Thanks for the help." She turned to him and, in the soft ambient light, looked at him. Like really looked at him, as if maybe she were seeing him for the first time.

"How did you know anything was wrong?" he asked. "How did you know to show up at the truck?"

"Instincts," she said. "Just a feeling, I guess." She held his gaze. "And now the same question to you. How did you know anything was wrong?"

"I heard you cry out."

She cocked her head, eyeing him like he was a puzzle and she was missing some pieces. "Most people would've run the other way, but you ran toward what could've been a dangerous situation."

"I'm the law." ▶

An Excerpt from *Wrapped Up in You* (continued)

Something flickered in her gaze at that. She didn't like that he was a cop. "The law can be dirty," she said.

As he well knew, but he wasn't going there. Instead, he let a teasing tone come into his voice. "True. And I can be *very* dirty, but only when I'm off-duty, and only if you ask real nice."

She laughed out loud at that, the sound both soft and musical. "Okay, I'll give this to you—you're funny. And maybe also sexy as hell, but this isn't happening, Cowboy."

He'd take sexy as hell any day of the week. "We're just talking."

"Uh-huh," she said dryly. "But when men talk, they think they're flirting, and to them flirting leads to everything else, which is always a disappointment. And if I wanted to be disappointed, I'd just go inside and stream *The Bachelor*."

"How do you know I'd disappoint?"

"You're a man, aren't you?"

He slid her a look. "Coloring all of us with the same pen, then?"

She shrugged and slipped out of his truck. He got out, too, and there on the sidewalk, she put a hand to his chest. "You're not coming up until I invite you."

He liked the promise of "until," but he left it alone for now. "I'm not coming *in* unless you invite me," he clarified, extremely aware of the fact that even as they stood there, they were being watched by two homeless people sitting under a tree, a man smoking on the driveway next door, and two guys loitering at the corner. "But I *am* going to walk you to your door," he said firmly.

He waited for her response, keeping vigilant on their peripheral audience. Even twenty years ago, when he'd last been familiar with the city, this neighborhood was known for bad news, and he liked to be ready for the worst.

Ivy tilted her head as she studied him. "You're different."

"Now you're getting it." He took her hand. "Come on."

They passed the tree, under which were two women, each huddled beneath a pile of dirty blankets.

"Hey, girl," one of them said.

Ivy smiled. "Hey, Jasmine. Too cold to work?"

"My corner flooded, thanks to a broken hydrant."

"Sucks," Ivy said. "Hey, Martina. Bad week?"

Martina uncovered her head and nodded.

Ivy handed over something from inside her big purse. It was some food from her truck that hadn't spoiled but couldn't be served because she didn't know if it'd been handled.

"Thanks," Martina said. "Can Marietta still hang with you tomorrow afternoon?"

"Of course," Ivy said, and led Kel up the steps to the building.

"Who's Marietta?" he asked.

"Martina's daughter. Martina's bipolar and schizophrenic. She lives at home with her elderly mom and her fourteen-year-old daughter, but sometimes when she goes off her meds, she goes to the streets."

"Isn't her daughter old enough to stay alone?"

"Yeah, but I'd have killed for a safe place to stay when I was fourteen," she said. "Plus, she's having trouble with math, and it's my strong suit. Not to mention I've got heat and Netflix."

She unlocked the front door, which led to a hallway and a set of stairs. The hallway had fake, cheesy holly strung along the walls, held there by duct tape. There were lights, too, but they weren't working. At least someone had tried.

They began climbing, Kel eyeing Ivy with newfound respect. He was getting an idea of what her childhood had been like and why she wore an armor of toughness, but it seemed that shell of hers hid a tender heart.

The second-floor landing had even more holiday decorations, and he took a moment to admire the resourcefulness of someone who'd stacked Heineken beer cans—green and white—to make small Christmas trees.

"Why are you doing this?" Ivy asked as they kept climbing, sounding genuinely confused.

"Someone broke into your place of business. Maybe they hit your home, too." ▶

An Excerpt from *Wrapped Up in You* (continued)

"I told you, it was random. Someone just needing food and money."

"Probably," he agreed as they hit the next set of stairs.

She took off her hoodie and for a moment gave him a glorious view as he walked behind her on the steps. But then she tied the sweatshirt around her waist, once again covering a fantastic ass that had been perfectly showcased in her leggings. Now she wore only a tank top, and that was nice, too.

"I just want to make sure you get home safe. Is that so odd?"

She didn't answer.

Which was an answer in itself. In her world, it *was* odd.

They hit the third-floor landing. No holiday decorations here at all. The next set of stairs narrowed and steepened. At the top, there was a single door, and they had to stand very close together as Ivy unlocked it. Close enough that he caught the scent of her shampoo and noticed she had a tiny, dainty tattoo on the back of her right shoulder—THIS TOO SHALL PASS . . .

Ivy turned on a light. Kel poked his head in and took a quick glance around to make sure it was all clear. The open loft could be seen all in one glimpse. The steep pitch of the roof meant slanted walls, which limited much of her space, but open rafters allowed for a large fan to drop down and stir the air. The wood floors were scarred and scuffed and dotted with throw rugs. Furniture was sparse. A small couch and coffee table, a nook in the small kitchenette with a couple of barstools, and a four-poster bed in the far corner, covered with a thick quilt and what appeared to be at least a million pillows. All of it looked like it belonged in another time period.

She shrugged. "The price is right."

His gaze slid to hers. "I wasn't judging you."

"BS."

"Okay, so I was judging all the pillows. How do you sleep with that many?"

She laughed—that same sweet, infectious sound from earlier—

but didn't say anything, just shook her head. And remained firmly in her doorway, clearly blocking him from coming in any farther.

Yeah. Serious trust issues.

"Can I see your phone?" he asked.

She narrowed her eyes but fished it out of her pocket.

"Unlock it?"

"All right," she said, "but just so you're aware, that's *not* where I keep the nudes."

He smiled and thumbed his contact information into her phone.

"You really think I'm going to call you?" she asked, amused.

"If you have any more problems, I hope you will." He held out her phone. She reached for it, but he gripped it firmly for a second as their gazes met. "Ivy."

She stared at him, then lifted a shoulder. *Maybe,* the gesture said. Which was the best he was going to get.

Then, still maintaining eye contact, she took her phone, retreated a step, and slowly shut her door in his face.

He stared at the wood, thinking she was possibly the most fascinating and frustrating woman he'd ever met.

"Why are you still standing there?" came her voice from the other side of the door.

"I'm waiting for you to lock the door and slide your security chain," he said.

There was a beat of silence during which he imagined her pride—prickling at being told what to do—warring with her common sense. But then came the sound of the lock and the chain sliding into place.

"Night, Trouble," he said, and then he had no choice but to walk away. ▶

CHAPTER 5

Less Chitchatting, More Ass Kicking!

At five thirty in the morning, Ivy was flat on her back on the mats. With a groan, she rolled to her knees and got back up. She was in kickboxing class with her friends Tae, Abi, and Haley, and they were all lined up facing a row of punching bags.

Ivy's had punched back.

Sort of the theme of her life.

"Dig deep!" her instructor yelled.

"I'd like to go deep," Haley whispered on Ivy's left. Haley was an optometrist who worked on the second floor of the Pacific Pier building. "*Deep* back into my bed."

"Less chitchatting, ladies, and more ass kicking! If you never change, you'll never change!"

Ivy glanced at their personal trainer. Tina was dark skinned, dark eyed, and, thanks to sneakers with three-inch rubber-sole heels and black braids piled into a mountain on top of her head, also well over six feet tall. Tina's day job was running the coffee shop at the Pacific Pier building, and in the coffee shop she was all sweet, sexy sass.

In the gym, she was a tyrannical drill sergeant.

Ivy turned to Tae, who was Jake's sister, a mathematical wizard, and an insurance adjuster. "I thought she'd be as gentle here as she is at her coffee shop."

Tae laughed. "She's about as gentle as my brother. And they both learned it in the same place—the military."

"That's right, sweetcakes," Tina said. "Don't be fooled by this gorg hair and figure. Back when I was Tim and right out of the army, I was a middleweight champion."

"Wow." Haley looked impressed. "So you kick ass for real, not just for show."

"Nah." Tina smiled. "I like my face too much now. So class it is. But there's something immensely satisfying about kicking the shit out of a bag, isn't there?"

"*Yes,*" Ivy agreed. If there was one thing she liked about getting up early and having to exercise, it was the satisfaction of beating the shit out of a bag.

"Then let's get serious," Tina said. "Come on, ladies. This isn't elementary school, and you're not at recess. Look at Abi, she's brand spanking new here, and she's kicking your asses."

Everyone looked at Abi, who ran the wedding shop in the Pacific Pier building. She always looked perfectly together, but at the moment, she was drenched in sweat and breathing like she'd just run a 5K. But she waved cheerfully at everyone like she was having the time of her life.

Ivy sighed.

"You're on Tina Time, ladies," Tina barked. "So start moving." She had hands on hips, back to being the serious, tyrannical taskmaster.

And let's face it, Ivy needed a taskmaster.

"I want to see you go at it like you're eighteen again!" Tina yelled.

"I was stupid at eighteen," Ivy muttered.

"Hey," Tae said breathlessly. "If you can't look back on your younger self and say, 'Wow, I used to be stupid,' you're probably *still* stupid."

"More energy!" Tina yelled. "Again! One-two punch, jab, cross, and then a big front kick!"

Ivy repeated the routine to herself as she went through the motions, her limbs liquefying.

"We're targeting your shoulders, triceps, and core, as well as the quads and glutes," Tina said. "You ladies want nice asses, right? Go hard or don't go at all!"

"Going hard isn't always what it's cracked up to be," Tae ▶

An Excerpt from *Wrapped Up in You* (continued)

managed to gasp out, sagging against her bag, hugging it in order to stay upright. "I'm whupped."

"Leave it all in the room, ladies!"

Haley sighed. "I always do," she muttered. "Not that it's getting me anywhere."

"You gotta rise up and take the challenge! Don't hide!"

Ivy managed to keep up with the nonstop punching and kicking to the rhythmic beat, barely, but she was with Haley. She'd rather be back in bed.

When the torture—er, class—ended, they all crawled out of the gym, whimpering and sweating. Ivy hit the showers, dressed, and ran to catch the bus. Sagging back on her seat, she took a moment to close her eyes. She was exhausted from too little sleep, spending much of the few precious hours she'd had staring up at the rafters and the ancient fan that hung from them slowly whirling around and around.

Worrying. Stressing . . .

Yes, she played at being the tough girl on the block, but the truth—her truth—was that she was really a big, fat chicken. So the knowledge that someone had broken into her truck, the one she'd worked her fingers to the bone for, the one she'd bled for, heart and soul, killed her. It was *her* personal space, the first she'd ever had, and she felt incredibly proud of it.

And yet someone had helped themselves to it like it was nothing, destroying her door and a whole bunch of food and stealing her hard-earned cash.

And more . . .

She closed her eyes on that thought and shook her head, knowing it was far more than that. She'd played it off to Kel like it was no big deal, because she didn't need his help, didn't need *anyone's* help, but it *was* a big deal to her. From a lifetime of living where creaks in the night meant something bad, she'd always had a hard time falling asleep. Living in San Francisco the past year in one spot, the *same* spot, even with the rough neighborhood outside, she'd somehow started to believe she was safe.

But she was *never* safe, and she was far too alone. And last night had seriously shaken her sense of privacy and security and safety. Except . . .

She hadn't been alone.

Kel had stood there in the open truck door, gun drawn, eyes cool, calm, and sharp.

Shock had been Ivy's first emotion, and right on the heels of that had come a different emotion altogether. She still wasn't ready to put a name to it, but she did know one thing. With a panic attack looming and helpless rage making her shake, she'd felt backed into a corner, and she'd never been good at that. So of course, she'd reacted predictably, which meant she'd been cold and rude.

He hadn't deserved it. Not when he'd gone over and beyond, helping her clean up. The image of him at two in the morning, on his knees wearing pink latex gloves, helping her scrub the truck floor like it was the most important task in the world, brought a reluctant smile.

With a sigh, she got off the bus two stops early to hit the market, grabbing some fresh supplies to replace what she'd lost, along with some extras that she planned to use to apologize to Kel. Then she walked to her truck, shivering in the morning chill. She'd always thought California was the land of eternal warm sunshine, but whoever had coined that phrase had never been to San Francisco in December.

Inside her truck, she left the CLOSED FOR BREAKFAST sign in place and took a quick moment to access her banking app. She robbed her savings account to cover the unexpected costs of restocking for the week, then got to work.

Last night she and Kel had disinfected everything, but she was obsessive about the kitchen and needed to put her stamp on everything. So she filled her extra-deep sink with hot water and added some of the gentle cleanser she used to clean the expensive copper pots and pans, which cost more than her clothes and which she'd bought with no regrets. ▸

An Excerpt from *Wrapped Up in You* (continued)

When she'd finished, she put everything back in its place and cleaned and dried the sink. Then she pulled all her ingredients down from their various shelves. She'd organized everything perfectly and could find anything in seconds. She knew what she had at all times, which was how she'd been able to tell so quickly what had been taken last night.

And despite what she'd let Kel think, it hadn't been just food and petty cash.

Beneath the petty cash box had been another box, containing a few things that represented the only happy spots in an otherwise terrible childhood. A postcard of the Golden Gate Bridge framed by the California hills and the azure blue of the bay. She had no idea where she'd gotten it, but she'd had it for years and years, and it was a big part of why, when she'd decided to settle somewhere, she'd landed here. A picture of her mom onstage at a piano, singing with a melancholy look on her face that made Ivy ache, though she had no idea why. She'd rarely seen that soft side of her mom. The other pic she had was of Ivy and her aunt Cathy, her mother's sister, at a state fair. Ivy had been five, her hair rioting in wild red waves around her face. Her *smiling* face, because she'd been in Cathy's arms in front of a Ferris wheel. Cathy, the only true mother figure Ivy had ever had, died from cancer the year after the photo had been taken. Ivy didn't remember a whole lot of that time, but she could still remember Cathy always telling her:

Be smart.

Be brave.

Be vulnerable.

Her heart pinched at the memory. She'd hopefully done the smart and brave parts, but she'd actively done her best to never be vulnerable. She figured Cathy would understand.

There were also a few trinkets: a teeny-tiny notebook she'd used as a journal for a few years; a Beanie Babies bear dressed as a chef, given to her at her first cooking job by her boss, one of the few positive male role models she'd had up until that point. She'd been fifteen. Of course, he'd thought she was eighteen, but that was the story of her life. Pretending to be what she wasn't in order to get what she needed.

The last thing in the box had been a gold and diamond necklace, the one she'd taken with her when she'd run away from home. It'd been given to her by Aunt Cathy, who'd worn it every day of her life. About six months before her death, she'd carefully coiled it up and put it in Ivy's palm. "For when you need me," she'd said quietly.

It was years after her death before Ivy understood what her aunt had meant. The necklace turned out to hold not just sentimental value; it was worth several thousand dollars. Aunt Cathy had known that if Ivy ever needed money fast, she could sell it.

But the necklace she'd managed to keep safe all this time was gone.

And she hadn't told Kel. She didn't know why.

Okay, she did know why. Because there was only one person on the planet who'd known she had that necklace.

Her brother.

She had no idea what that meant. Had Brandon found her? And if he had . . . what did he want?

She got out the utensils and cooking implements she needed and then quickly started measuring and mixing dry ingredients for pancakes. She preheated a pan, added the wet ingredients into the dry, mixed everything, and then gently folded in fresh blueberries.

While the pancakes cooked, she put everything away meticulously and got out some eggs and thick slices of bacon. She preheated another pan, added the bacon, and flipped the pancakes. Cracking the eggs in a perfect break—so satisfying—she dropped them in next to the bacon. She slid the pancakes onto a plate and ladled out three more. Toast went down. Then she slid the eggs and bacon onto another plate. Turned the pancakes, buttered the bread, and quickly and efficiently ▶

cleaned up after herself before packing the food up, placing it in a special protective to-go bag, and slinging the strap over her shoulder.

She opened the back door and found several people standing there waiting, most of them her regulars. "I'm so sorry. I'm closed until eleven," she said, pointing to the sign.

"But you're making bacon," Sadie said. "I could smell it across the courtyard. I'd kill for bacon."

At Sadie's side, Haley and Tae both nodded.

"We earned bacon this morning at the gym," Tae said.

"I earned bacon in a much more satisfying way," Sadie said with a smile.

Sadie was possibly the only person Ivy had ever wanted to be her best friend. She'd never really had one, but she imagined that Sadie would be a perfect BFF. She was a tattoo artist at the Canvas Shop, the tattoo parlor on the other side of the courtyard, and was no-holds-barred tough in her own right. She was kind, but she was also a sarcastic smart-ass, which Ivy related to on a core level.

"I'm sorry," she told them. "But the truck was broken into last night and—"

They gasped in tandem, and Ivy shook her head, holding up a hand, which didn't stop them from all talking at once.

"Was anything taken?"

"Are you okay?"

"What can we do?"

"I'm fine, it's all fine," Ivy said, admittedly a little surprised and also warmed by their obvious concern. "They got some petty cash, but the fridge was left open and a bunch of the food spoiled. That's why I'm closed this morning."

Sadie reached out and took her hand. "I'm so sorry. You're really okay?"

"Yes. I wasn't here when it happened."

"That doesn't mean you can't be freaked out," Haley said, pushing her red-framed glasses farther up on her face, looking like the cutest little bookworm worrywart Ivy had ever seen. "I was robbed once, and even though it was my ex-girlfriend, it was still terrifying."

"Need some cleanup assistance?" Tae asked, always the efficient, calm one.

"I've got it handled, but thanks." The genuine outrage on their faces, along with the empathy, was new for Ivy, and she wasn't quite sure what to do with it all or how to respond. And they did seem to need a response. "Thank you," she tried again, relieved when they all nodded. "But it's really okay. Kel helped me clean up the mess."

The three women's necks swiveled sharply as they looked at each other and then back at Ivy.

"Kel?" Sadie asked. "Caleb's sexy cousin Kel?"

"He is sexy," Haley said. "I mean, men aren't my thing, but if they were . . ."

"He was walking across the courtyard yesterday," Sadie said, "and I saw a woman walk right into one of the lampposts when he smiled at her."

"What is it about a cowboy, I wonder," Tae mused.

"*Everything*," Sadie said, and everyone looked at Ivy expectantly.

"Hey, I'm off men," she said.

"Forever?" Haley asked. "And what about women?"

"For the foreseeable future, and yes, women, too," Ivy said. "And anyway, you deserve someone who isn't as colossally messed up as I am."

"Apparently, I'm attracted to messed up," Haley said morosely.

"It's not your fault girls are crazy," Sadie said.

Tae laughed. "Someone once gave me some good relationship advice," she said. "Make sure *you're* the crazy one."

"Ha," Haley said. "And done."

"Is that why you're not in a relationship?" Sadie asked Tae.

"I'm not in a relationship because both Liam and Chris Hemsworth are taken." ▶

They all smiled at the truth of that, but Ivy had sat next to Tae at the pub a few times. She knew Tae had recently come out of a really bad relationship, but in what way exactly, she wasn't sure. What she was sure of was that Tae was most definitely haunted by it.

And skittish.

Something Ivy understood at a core level, which made her incredibly sympathetic to what she suspected Tae was feeling about allowing anyone to get close ever again. Ivy wasn't opposed to an actual relationship instead of a quickie. In theory, anyway. But in reality, she didn't know the first thing about what a relationship might entail or demand from her. She suspected it might be things she couldn't provide, like pure honesty, transparency, and the like.

"I just haven't found what I'm looking for," Tae told Sadie.

"And what's that?"

"I don't know." Tae shrugged. "Maybe warm brown eyes, messy hair, a cute nose, and four paws." She smiled. "A golden retriever would be perfect."

They all laughed, and Ivy hitched the food pack higher on her shoulder. "I'm sorry about breakfast. I'll make it up to you guys at lunch, okay? But I've got to go."

"Don't forget tomorrow night's full moon midnight hike," Sadie said. "Elle sent out a group text yesterday to everyone."

Elle was the building manager, and she took her duties very seriously, organizing social events for the group that either lived or worked in the building. Ivy had gone to a few outings, but usually she begged off, feeling like the odd man out because everyone was so tight with one another and she was the new kid on the block.

Okay, not new exactly. She'd been here a year. And though Tae was Jake's sister, she'd only recently come back to town, which technically made her newer than Ivy. But Tae had a natural way with people, and she'd fit in seamlessly.

Ivy had never fit seamlessly into anything, including her own skin.

"Did you not get the text?" Haley asked Ivy.

She'd gotten the text, but she'd ignored it, thinking Elle probably automatically included everyone to be polite.

"Please come," Haley said. "You're usually too busy, but we'd so love to have you."

"I thought maybe the text was just for the core group of you."

"Of which you're a part," Sadie said, so easily that Ivy knew she meant it. "So say you'll be there."

Surprised and touched that it mattered whether she went, Ivy found herself nodding, even though she wasn't 100 percent sold on it. "I'll try."

IT WAS STILL early by the time she got to Caleb's newly renovated condo building in North Beach. She'd been here before a couple of times, walking through with Caleb, Sadie, and Keane Winters, the general contractor in charge of the project.

Ivy's condo wasn't a corner unit or the penthouse, or anything that stood out at all, and that was what she loved about it.

That and the fact that it would be all hers.

She walked through the underground parking garage to the security office and found Kel there with a few other people, standing around a table with a bunch of blueprints spread out before them.

Kel introduced her to the room: Keane, Carly and Roberto—both supervisors on Keane's renovation team—and Arlo and Stretch, who worked under Kel as building security.

Ivy smiled and made nice, but she couldn't concentrate on anything but Kel, feeling the weight of his gaze. Unable to resist, she turned to him and felt her pulse kick.

Ridiculous.

He was dressed, as always, in rugged and well-worn jeans, work boots, a T-shirt with an unbuttoned shirt over the top of ▶

An Excerpt from *Wrapped Up in You*
(continued)

it, and a ball cap worn backward. Casual clothes, but there was nothing casual about the lean, hard body hinted at beneath those clothes or, for that matter, the man himself.

And then there was how he moved with the careless grace of an athlete, his body suggesting it could handle just about anything thrown at it.

He smiled, and she felt a kick in the gut—a fact that told her two things. One, she was still stupid when it came to men. And two, he was going to be trouble for both her peace of mind and her heart.

Big trouble.